JULES VERNE

FOREWORD BY ISAAC ASIMOV

JULES

FOREWORD BY ISAAC ASIMOV

PLATT & MUNK
GREAT WRITERS
COLLECTION

VERNE

20,000 Leagues Under the Sea

⚓

*

Around the Moon

☉

*

PLATT & MUNK, *Publishers* • NEW YORK

Copyright © 1965. The Platt & Munk Co., Inc., New York, N.Y. 10010.
All rights reserved. Printed in the United States of America.

Library of Congress Catalog Card No. 65–15193.

CONTENTS

AROUND THE MOON

Father Jules

by Isaac Asimov

The name "Father Jules" has a special meaning for me. It conveys the respect, affection, gratitude and even envy that I feel, as a writer of modern science fiction, for the man who was so fortunate as to found a new type of literature that expresses so vividly the fantasies of our own age.

There has always been fantasy, of course. From time immemorial, bards, minstrels and tale-spinners have peopled the world with demons and fairies, angels and wizards, and with heroes stronger and more daring, and heroines more beautiful and good, than men and women could possibly be.

There were no rules to such fantasy, no bounds. Each dreamer wove his own storied tapestry, as rich and colorful as his imagination could envision or his words could create.

Then, in the nineteenth century, man was suddenly faced with a real-life fantasy that outstripped his wildest dreams— a telegraph that could carry a message faster than any giant in seven-league boots, a steamship that was swifter than Sindbad's magic ship, a smoke-belching iron horse, the locomotive, more fleet than the winged horse Pegasus, and countless other wonders of harnessed energy.

But this new fantasy had rules. While inventors applied the new findings of science to the uses of mankind, the scientists were laying out the boundaries of those applications. Energy must be conserved, they said; you can't get something out of nothing. In energy conversions, heat must take its toll—complete change of energy to work is impossible. Outer space is quite unlike the earth's atmosphere, and every planet, whether Mars, Venus or one yet undiscovered, has its own determinable size and gravity.

To accommodate these startling scientific facts an entire new type of fantasy was required. The world was waiting for a storyteller who would use his imagination to probe more deeply into the real-life fantasy engulfing the world; one who could look beyond the steamship and the locomotive to yet untried reaches of scientific exploration.

That new storyteller was Jules Verne, a Frenchman by birth, but a citizen of the world by instant and continuous readership. His first forecast of the direction of the future was *Five Weeks in a Balloon*, published in 1863.

The balloon was already invented, of course, but Verne went far beyond its current experimental use. From floating great distances in a balloon, his heroes went hurtling through space in a projectile shot out of a giant cannon. The story *Around the Moon*, included in this volume, describes such a flight.

Verne also penetrated deep into the mysterious world beneath the sea. In *20,000 Leagues Under the Sea*, one of Verne's most famous stories, Captain Nemo sails his submarine, the *Nautilus,* from the coral reefs of the Pacific to the polar cap.

Verne's heroes went around the world in eighty days; they traveled deep into the earth's crust; they explored the icy world of the polar regions; they hitch-hiked rides on comets.

There was no name for this kind of story in Verne's time, for the term "science fiction" was not to come into vogue until the 1930's. Verne's books were called "Extraordinary Voyages" and, indeed, they were the most extraordinary voyages that had ever been described up to his time.

I say this even though I know very well that Odysseus, Sindbad the Sailor and Lemuel Gulliver undertook some amazing voyages centuries before Verne. Their adventures, involving huge one-eyed giants, birds twenty times the size of elephants, and talking horses, are fantastic enough for anyone.

The older writers and storytellers, however, bound themselves to no such fast rules as those which Verne observed. For Verne made use of scientific phenomena, and explained events in accordance with the laws of science.

Verne was not always correct. For one thing, many facts unknown to the science of Verne's day have since been discovered. We can smile at Verne's apparent naïveté. Let us remember, however, that many facts will be uncovered in the future which will make our current theories and inventions seem obsolete and absurd.

Of course, even according to the science of his own day, Verne was occasionally wrong, for he was primarily a writer, not a scientist.

For instance, shooting a projectile out of a cannon at a velocity that will enable it to reach the moon would kill everyone on board in an instant, and this was understood a hundred and fifty years before Verne was born. Some of the details Verne offers and explains in the course of his space travel, are also a little wrong.

This, however, is not the important thing. What is important is that Verne recognized the necessity of being scientifically correct. He made a point of studying the scientific publications of his day, and tried to live up to the rules of the scientific game. Most of the time he *did,* and the amazing thing is that he could be so extraordinary *inside* those rules.

To be honest, Verne wasn't quite the first to write within scientific bounds. Edgar Allan Poe, a quarter of a century before Verne, had tried his hand at science fiction and had done well. However, Poe's Gothic tales of terror made a far greater impression on the public, and his few pioneer science fiction stories are almost forgotten.

Jules Verne's work, on the other hand, was instantly popular. Today, although Verne is "out of date," he is more popular than ever. We have submarines, now, far beyond anything Verne imagined, but the tale of Captain Nemo still absorbs us. We are on the point of traveling to the moon in vehicles far more sophisticated than the one in which the members of the Baltimore Gun Club were shot into space, but we still follow every moment of their voyage breathlessly.

And nowhere were Verne's writings more popular than in Russia and in the United States, the two nations which, half a century after Verne's death, were to poineer in taking space travel out of the realm of science fiction and into that of scientific fact.

Indeed, the popularity of Jules Verne in the two countries

met in my own family. My father was brought up in Russia and I (although I was born there) was brought up in the United States. When I began to write science fiction, my father asked me, "Have you ever read Zhool Vehrn?" (He pronounced the name French-fashion, for that was the only way he had ever heard it pronounced.)

I looked blank, so he explained, "He wrote about a man in a submarine and a group of men shot to the moon."

"Oh," I said excitedly (and when I'm excited, my Brooklyn accent shows), "you mean Joolz Voin."

But Vehrn or Voin, Russia or the United States, Jules Verne is the literary father of all modern science fiction.

West Newton, Mass.
January, 1965

20,000
LEAGUES
UNDER
THE
SEA

⚓

*

PART ONE

1. A Shifting Reef

THE YEAR 1866 was marked by a series of strange events revolving around a mysterious and puzzling phenomenon that is doubtless still vivid in the mind of the public. Particularly in the coastal communities—but even in the inland areas, peculiar but insistent rumors had spread, stirring up fear and apprehension. Seafaring people were understandably agitated—merchants, common sailors, captains of vessels, skippers and shipowners of both Europe and America—and naval officers and the various governments in all countries on the two continents were vitally concerned.

For some time past, vessels on the high seas had been encountering an enormous "thing," a long object, spindle-shaped, occasionally phosphorescent, and infinitely larger and swifter than any whale.

The facts that had accumulated about this apparition (entered in various logbooks) agreed with one another as to its shape, its untiring speed, its surprising power of locomotion, and the peculiar life with which it seemed endowed.

If it *was* some species of whale, it surpassed in size all those so far classified by scientists.

Taking an average of the various observations made at different times—rejecting the low estimate of a length of 200 feet as well as the exaggerated claim of a mile in width and three in length—one might fairly conclude that the phenomenon was considerably larger than any existing creature hitherto known to man.

That it existed was an undeniable fact; and, with that tendency which disposes the human mind in favor of the marvelous, we can understand the excitement produced in the entire world by this supernatural apparition.

On the 20th of July, 1866, the steamer *Governor Higginson,* of the Calcutta and Burnach Steam Navigation Company, had encountered a moving mass five miles off the east coast of Australia. Captain Baker thought at first that he had found an unknown sandbank; he was even preparing to determine its exact position, when two columns of water spouted out of the mysterious object and shot with a hissing noise a hundred and fifty feet into the air. Now, unless this was the intermittent eruption of a geyser, the *Governor Higginson* had to do with no less than an unknown aquatic mammal, which shot columns of water mixed with air and vapor from its blowholes.

Similar facts were observed on July 23 of the same year in the Pacific Ocean, by the *Columbus* of the West India and Pacific Steam Navigation Company. This extraordinary creature could therefore travel with surprising velocity; in an interval of three days, the *Governor Higginson* and the *Columbus* had observed it at points of the chart separated by a distance of more than 2,400 miles.

Fifteen days later and two thousand miles farther off, the *Helvetia,* of the Compagnie-Nationale, and the *Shannon,* of the Royal Mail Steamship Company, sailing to windward in that portion of the Atlantic lying between the United States and Europe, respectively signaled the monster to each other in 42° 15′ N. lat. and 60° 35′ W. long. In these simultaneous observations both ships reported the minimum length of the mammal as over 350 feet.

Now the largest whales, those which frequent those parts of the sea around the Aleutian, Kulammak, and Umgullich islands, have never exceeded 180 feet in length.

Everywhere the monster became the rage. It was sung about in cafes, ridiculed in the papers, and even presented on the stage. All kinds of stories were circulating about it. Caricatures of every gigantic and imaginary creature appeared in the papers, from the terrible white whale Moby Dick, to the immense kraken whose tentacles could entangle a 500-ton ship and drag it to the bottom.

About that time an unending controversy between those who believed and those who did not rocked the scholarly and scientific press. "The question of the monster" aroused everyone. Editors of scientific journals quarreled with believers in the supernatural, spilling seas of ink during this memorable campaign—and even some blood, for debates over the sea serpent frequently resulted in violent personal quarrels.

During the first months of 1867 the matter seemed forgotten, never to revive. Then new facts were brought before the public. Not only was it a scientific problem to be solved, but more than ever it had become a serious danger to be averted. The monster became a small island, a rock, a reef, but a reef that was vague, indefinite and of shifting proportions.

On the 5th of March, 1867, the *Moravian* of the Montreal Ocean Company, in 27° 30 ' lat. and 72° 15 ' long., struck on her starboard side a rock not marked in any chart for that area. With a favorable wind and her own 400 horsepower engines she had been making 13 knots when she struck. And had it not been for the superior strength of her hull she would have gone down with all 237 passengers she was bringing home from Canada.

The accident happened about five o'clock in the morning, just at daybreak. The officers on the quarter-deck hurried to the afterpart of the vessel. They studied the sea, and saw nothing but a strong eddy about three cables' length distant, as if the surface had been violently agitated. The bearings of the place were taken exactly, and the *Moravian* continued its route without apparent damage. Had it struck a submerged rock, or on an enormous wreck? They could not tell; but during subsequent repairs they discovered that part of her keel was broken off.

This fact, so grave in itself, might have been forgotten like many others, except for the fact that three weeks later, it was re-enacted under similar circumstances. But thanks to the ship involved, and the reputation of the owners, the circumstance became extensively circulated.

On April 13, 1867, in a calm sea with a favorable wind, the *Scotia* of the Cunard Company's line was in 15° 12 ' long. and 45° 37 ' lat. She was making 13.5 knots.

At seventeen minutes past four in the afternoon, while the passengers were having lunch in the great dining room, a slight shock was felt on the hull of the *Scotia,* on her quarter, a little aft of the port paddle.

The *Scotia* had not struck; she had *been* struck, and apparently by something sharp and penetrating rather than blunt. The shock had been so slight that no one would have been alarmed, had it not been for the shouts of the carpenter's watch. He rushed to the bridge, exclaiming, "We are sinking! we are sinking!"

At first the passengers were much frightened, but Captain Anderson hastened to reassure them. The danger could not be imminent. The *Scotia* divided into seven watertight compartments by strong partitions, could survive any leak. Captain Anderson went down immediately into the hold. He found that the sea was pouring into the fifth compartment; and the rapidity of the influx proved that the force of the water was considerable. Fortunately this compartment did not contain the boilers, or the fires would have been immediately extinguished. Captain Anderson ordered the engines stopped at once, and one of the men went down to determine the extent of the damage. Some minutes afterward they discovered a large hole, six feet in diameter, in the ship's bottom. Such a leak could not be stopped; and so the *Scotia* was obliged to continue her course with her paddles half submerged. She was then three hundred miles from Cape Clear, and after three days' delay, which caused great uneasiness in Liverpool, she docked at the company's berth.

The engineers who later inspected the *Scotia* in dry dock, could scarcely believe what they saw: at about seven feet below watermark was a rent in the exact shape of an isosceles triangle. The hole in the iron plate was so perfectly defined it could not have been more neatly done by a punch. It was clear, then, that the instrument producing the perforation was not of a common stamp; and after having been driven with prodigious strength, and piercing an iron plate one and three-eighths inches thick, had been withdrawn by a retrograde motion truly inexplicable.

This incident, and the subsequent conclusions resulted in exciting once more the torrent of public opinion. From this moment all unlucky casualties which could not be otherwise accounted for were put down to the monster. Such casualties, unfortunately, were considerable; for of three thousand ships whose loss was annually recorded at Lloyd's, the number of sailing vessels and steamships supposedly lost, from the absence of all news, amounted to not less than two hundred!

Now, it was the "monster" who, justly or unjustly, was accused of their disappearance, and for the increasing dangers of transatlantic travel. The public demanded peremptorily that the seas should at any price be relieved from this formidable cetacean.[1]

2. Pro and Con

AT THE period when these events took place I had just returned from a scientific expedition to the Badlands of Nebraska, in the United States. As Assistant Professor in the Museum of Natural History in Paris, I had been asked by the French Government to join that expedition. After six months in Nebraska, I arrived in New York toward the end of March, laden with a precious collection. My departure for France was set for the beginning of May. I was busy, meanwhile, in classifying my mineralogical, botanical and zoological riches, when the *Scotia* incident occurred.

[1] aquatic mammal

I was well informed on the subject which was the question of the day. How could I be otherwise? I had read and re-read all the American and European papers, but without being any nearer a conclusion. This mystery puzzled me. Unable to form an opinion, I jumped from one extreme to the other. That something strange had occurred could not be doubted, and the incredulous were invited to inspect the wound of the *Scotia.*

On my arrival at New York, the question was at its height. The hypothesis of the floating island and the unapproachable sandbank, supported by minds little competent to form a judgment, was abandoned. And, indeed, unless this "shoal" had a motor in its interior, how could it change its position with such astonishing rapidity?

From the same cause, the idea of an enormous floating wreck was given up.

There remained only two possible solutions of the problem, and these created two distinct parties: on one side, those who believed in a monster of colossal strength; on the other, those who were convinced it was a submarine vessel of enormous motive power.

But this last hypothesis, plausible as it was, could not stand against inquiries made in both Europe and America. That a private gentleman should have such a machine at his command was not likely. Where, then, and how could it have been built? And how could its construction have been kept secret? Certainly a government might possess such a destructive machine. And in these disastrous times when the ingenuity of man has multiplied the power of weapons of war, it was possible that without the knowledge of others, a state might try to build such a formidable engine.

But the hypothesis of a war machine collapsed before the

statements of the various governments. As public interest
was at stake, and transatlantic shipping suffered, their ve-
racity could not be doubted. Furthermore, how could the
construction of this submarine boat have escaped the public
eye? To keep it a secret would be very difficult, especially
for a state whose every act is persistently watched by powerful rivals.

After inquiries in England, France, Russia, Prussia,
Spain, Italy and America, even in Turkey, the hypothesis of
a submarine monitor was definitely rejected.

Upon my arrival in New York several persons did me the
honor of consulting me on the phenomenon in question. I
had published in France a work in quarto, in two volumes,
entitled, "Mysteries of the Great Submarine Grounds." This
book was highly thought of in the learned world, and
gained for me a special reputation in this rather obscure
branch of natural history. My advice was asked. As long as
I could deny the reality of the fact, I confined myself to a
decided negative. But soon finding myself driven into a
corner, I was obliged to explain myself categorically: "The
Honorable Pierre Aronnax, Professor in the Museum of
Paris," was called upon by the *New York Herald* to express
a definite opinion of some sort. I spoke for lack of will to
hold my tongue. I discussed the question in all its forms,
politically and scientifically, and I give here an extract from
a carefully-studied article which I published in the April
30th issue. It ran as follows:

> After examining one by one the different hypotheses, re-
> jecting all other suggestions, it becomes necessary to admit
> the existence of a marine animal of enormous power.
>
> The great depths of the ocean are entirely unknown to us.

Soundings cannot reach them. What passes in those remote depths—what beings live, or can live, twelve or fifteen miles beneath the surface of the waters—what is the organization of these animals, we can scarcely conjecture. However, the solution of the problem submitted to me may modify the form of the dilemma. Either we do know all the varieties of beings which people our planet, or we do not. If we do *not* know them all—if Nature has still secrets in ichthyology for us, nothing is more reasonable than to admit the existence of fishes, or cetaceans of other kinds, or even of new species, of an organization formed to inhabit the strata inaccessible to soundings, and which an accident of some sort, either fantastical or capricious, has brought at long intervals to the upper level of the ocean.

If, on the contrary, we *do* know all living kinds, we must necessarily seek for the animal in question amongst those marine beings already classed; and, in that case, I should be disposed to admit the existence of a gigantic narwhal.

The common narwhal, or unicorn of the sea, often attains a length of sixty feet. Increase its size fivefold or tenfold, give it strength proportionate to its size, lengthen its destructive weapons, and you obtain the animal required. It will have the proportions determined by the officers of the *Shannon,* the instrument required by the perforation of the *Scotia,* and the power necessary to pierce the hull of the steamer.

Indeed the narwhal is armed with a sort of ivory sword, a halberd, according to the expression of certain naturalists. The principal tusk has the hardness of steel. Some of these tusks have been found buried in the bodies of whales, which the unicorn always attacks with success. Others have been drawn out, not without trouble, from the bottoms of ships, which they have pierced through and through, as a gimlet pierces a barrel. The Museum of the Faculty of Medicine of

Paris possesses one of these defensive weapons, six feet, nine inches in length, and fifteen inches in diameter at the base.

Now suppose this weapon to be six times stronger, and the animal ten times more powerful; imagine it traveling at a speed of twenty miles an hour, and you obtain a shock capable of producing the recent catastrophes. Therefore, until further information is available, I maintain it to be a sea-unicorn of colossal dimensions, armed, not with a halberd, but with a real spur, as the armored frigates or the "rams" of war, which it equals in massiveness and motive power. Thus may this inexplicable phenomenon be explained, unless there be something over and above all that one has ever conjectured, seen, perceived or experienced—which is just within the bounds of possibility.

These last words were cowardly on my part; but, up to a certain point, I wished to shelter my dignity as professor, and not give too much cause for laughter to the Americans, who laugh well when they do laugh.

I reserved a way of escape for myself. In effect, however, I admitted the existence of the "monster." My article was warmly discussed, which procured it a high reputation. It rallied around it a certain number of partisans. The solution it proposed gave, at least, full liberty to the imagination. The human mind delights in grandiose conceptions of supernatural creatures. And the sea is precisely the best, the only medium through which these giants (compared with which terrestrial animals, such as elephants or rhinoceroses, are as nothing) can be produced or developed.

The seas support the largest of mammals, the whale; possibly they also conceal giant mollusks, or terrifying lobsters 300 feet long. Why not? In geological times, animals, reptiles and birds produced giant species. Could not the ocean's vast depths have harbored some titanic species of another age?

But I am getting carried away. I have dwelt long enough on these fantastic speculations, which have since become only too real for me.

However, at that time, the public had formed its opinion. Everyone believed that a supernatural monster, quite unlike a sea serpent, roamed the seas.

Many regarded it as a problem for science; others, more practical-minded, thought of ridding the ocean of this prodigious creature so that transatlantic travel would be safe again.

The industrial and commercial papers treated the question chiefly from this point of view. The *Shipping and Mercantile Gazette*, the *Lloyd's List*, the *Packet-Boat*, and the *Maritime and Colonial Review*, all insurance publications that threatened to raise their premium rates, were unanimous on this point. Public opinion had been pronounced. The United States was the first in the field; in New York they made preparations for an expedition destined to pursue this narwhal. A frigate of great speed, the *Abraham Lincoln*, was to be put in commission as soon as possible. The arsenals were opened to Commander Farragut for arming his frigate; but, as it always happens, the moment they decided to pursue the monster, it vanished. For two months no ship saw even an eddy. It seemed almost as if this sea-unicorn knew of the plot. It had been so much talked of, even through the Atlantic cable, that jesters pretended the creature had stopped a telegram in passage, and was making the most of the information it had obtained.

So when the frigate had been armed for a long campaign, and provided with formidable hunting gear, no one knew what course to pursue. Impatience grew. Then, on July 2 they learned that a steamer of the San Francisco line, en route from California to Shanghai, had seen the animal three weeks before in the north Pacific Ocean. The excitement created by this news was extreme. The ship was revictualed and well stocked with coal.

Three hours before the *Abraham Lincoln* left Brooklyn pier, I received a letter worded as follows:—

> To MR. ARONNAX, Professor in the Museum of Paris,
>   Fifth Avenue Hotel, New York.
>
>   SIR,—If you will consider joining the *Abraham Lincoln* in this expedition, the Government of the United States will take pleasure in having you represent France in the enterprise. Commander Farragut has a cabin at your disposal.
>
>   Very cordially yours,
>   J. B. HOBSON,
>   Secretary of the Navy

3. I Form My Resolution

THREE SECONDS before the arrival of J. B. Hobson's letter, I no more thought of pursuing the unicorn than of attempting the passage of the North Sea. Three seconds after reading the letter of the honorable Secretary of the Navy, I felt that my true vocation, the sole end of my life, was to chase this disturbing monster, and purge it from the world.

But I had just returned from a fatiguing journey. I was weary and longing for rest. I aspired to nothing more than again seeing my country, my friends, my little lodging by the Jardin des Plantes, and my precious collections. But nothing could keep me back! I forgot all—fatigue, friends, and collections—and accepted without hesitation the offer of the American Government.

"Besides," thought I, "all roads lead back to Europe (for my particular benefit), and I will not hurry me toward the coast of France. If this worthy animal will allow itself to be caught in European waters (for my particular benefit), I will not bring back less than two feet of his ivory halberd to the Museum of Natural History." But in the meanwhile I would seek this narwhal in the north Pacific, which was to return to France, by way of the Antipodes.

"Conseil," I called, in an impatient voice.

Conseil was my servant, a true, devoted Flemish boy, who had accompanied me in all my travels. I liked him, and he liked me. He was quiet by nature, regular from principle, zealous from habit, evincing little disturbance at the different surprises of life, very deft and apt at any service required of him; and despite his name, never giving advice— even when asked for it.

Conseil had followed me for the last ten years wherever science led. Never once did he complain of the length or fatigue of a journey, never make an objection to pack his portmanteau for whatever country it might be, or however far away, whether China or the Congo. Besides all this, he had good health which defied all sickness, and solid muscles but no nerves; good morals are understood. This boy was thirty years old, and his age to that of his master was as fifteen to twenty.

But Conseil had one fault; he was ceremonious to a degree, and would never speak to me but in the third person, which was sometimes provoking.

"Conseil," I said again, beginning with feverish hands to make preparations for my departure.

Certainly I was sure of this devoted boy. As a rule, I never asked him if it were convenient for him or not to follow me in my travels; but this time the expedition in question might be prolonged, and the enterprise might be hazardous in pursuit of an animal capable of sinking a frigate as easily as a nutshell. Here was matter for reflection, even to the most impassive man in the world. What would Conseil say?

"Conseil," I called a third time.

Conseil appeared.

"Did Monsieur call?" he said, entering.

"Yes, my boy; make preparations for me and yourself, too. We leave in two hours."

"As Monsieur pleases," replied Conseil quietly.

"Not an instant to lose; lock in my trunk all traveling utensils, coats, shirts, and stockings—without counting, as many as you can, and make haste."

"And Monsieur's collections?" observed Conseil.

"They will keep them at the hotel."

"We are not returning to Paris, then?" said Conseil.

"Oh! certainly," I answered evasively, "by making a curve."

"Will the curve please Monsieur?"

"Oh! it will be nothing; not quite so direct a road, that is all. We take our passage in the *Abraham Lincoln.*"

"As Monsieur thinks proper," coolly replied Conseil.

"You see, my friend, it has to do with the monster—the famous narwhal. We are going to purge it from the seas. A glorious mission, but a dangerous one! We cannot tell where we may go; these animals can be very capricious. But we will go wherever it shows itself; and we have a captain who doesn't know the meaning of fear."

"Wherever Monsieur goes, I'll go too," said Conseil.

"But consider carefully! I'm being quite frank with you. People don't always return from such expeditions!"

"As Monsieur wishes."

Our trunks were ready in fifteen minutes. Conseil had done everything with lightning speed, and I was sure nothing was missing, for he classified shirts and suits as carefully as he did birds and mammals.

Our luggage was transported to the deck of the frigate immediately. I hastened on board and asked for Commander Farragut. One of the sailors conducted me to the poop, where I found myself in the presence of a good-looking officer, who held out his hand to me.

"Mr. Pierre Aronnax?" said he.

"Himself," I replied. "Commander Farragut?"

"Welcome aboard, Professor; your cabin is ready."

I bowed, and leaving the commander in the midst of final preparations, I was conducted to my cabin.

The ship *Abraham Lincoln* had been well chosen and equipped for her new task. She was a frigate of great speed, fitted with high-pressure engines which admitted a pressure of seven atmospheres. Under this the *Abraham Lincoln* attained the mean speed of nearly 18.3 knots an hour—a considerable speed, but nevertheless insufficient to grapple with this gigantic cetacean.

The interior arrangements of the frigate corresponded to her nautical qualities. I was well satisfied with my cabin, which was in the afterpart, opening on the gun room.

"We shall be well off here," I said to Conseil.

"As well, by Monsieur's leave, as a hermit crab in the shell of a whelk," said Conseil.

I left Conseil to stow our trunks conveniently away and remounted the poop in order to survey the preparations for departure.

At that moment Commander Farragut was ordering the last moorings cast loose which held the *Abraham Lincoln* to the Brooklyn pier. So in a quarter of an hour, perhaps less, the frigate would have sailed without me. I should have missed this extraordinary, supernatural and incredible expedition, the recital of which may well meet with some suspicion.

But Commander Farragut would not lose a day nor an hour in scouring the seas in which the animal had been sighted. He sent for the engineer.

"Is the pressure up?" he asked.

"Yes, sir," replied the engineer.

"Full steam ahead," cried Commander Farragut.

4. Ned Land

CAPTAIN FARRAGUT was a good seaman, worthy of the frigate he commanded. His vessel and he were one. He was the soul of it. On the question of the monster there was no doubt in his mind, and he would not allow its existence to be disputed on board. He believed in it, as certain good women believe in the Leviathan—by faith, not by reason. The monster did exist and he had sworn to rid the seas of it. Either Captain Farragut would kill the narwhal, or the narwhal would kill the captain. There was no third course.

The officers on board shared the opinion of their chief. They were forever chatting, discussing, and calculating the various chances of a meeting, and all the time they scanned the vast surface of the ocean. More than one took up quarters voluntarily in the crosstrees, who would have cursed such a berth under any other circumstances. As long as the sun described its daily course, the rigging was crowded with impatient sailors, even though the *Abraham Lincoln* had not yet breasted the suspect waters of the Pacific. As to the ship's company, they desired nothing better than to meet the unicorn-fish, to harpoon it, hoist it on board, and dispatch it.

Besides, Captain Farragut had spoken of a certain sum of two thousand dollars, set apart for whoever should first sight the monster, were he cabin boy, common seaman or officer.

I leave you to imagine how eyes were strained on board the *Abraham Lincoln*.

For my own part I did not lag behind the others, and left my share of daily observations to no one. The frigate might have been called the *Argus,* for a hundred reasons. Only one among us, Conseil, seemed to protest, by his indifference, against the question which so interested us all, and did not share the general enthusiasm.

I have said that Captain Farragut had carefully provided his ship with every apparatus for catching the gigantic cetacean. No whaler had ever been better armed. We possessed every known engine, from the harpoon thrown by the hand to the barbed arrows of the blunderbuss, and the explosive balls of the duck gun. On the forecastle lay the very perfection of a breech-loading gun, very thick at the breech and very narrow in the bore, the model of which had been on display in the Exhibition that year. This precious weapon of American origin could shoot with ease a conical projectile of nine pounds to a mean distance of ten miles.

Thus the *Abraham Lincoln* wanted for no weapons of destruction; and, what was better still, she had on board Ned Land, the prince of harpooners.

Ned Land was a Canadian, with an uncommon quickness of hand, who had no equal in his dangerous occupation. Skill, coolness, audacity and cunning he possessed in a superior degree, and it must be a cunning whale to escape the stroke of his harpoon.

Ned Land was about forty years of age; he was a tall man, over six feet, powerfully built, grave and taciturn, and occasionally violent when contradicted. He attracted one's attention, especially for his bold and piercing eyes.

Who calls himself Canadian calls himself French; and, untalkative as Ned Land was, I must admit that he took a certain liking for me. My nationality drew him to me, no doubt. It was an opportunity for him to talk, and for me to hear, that old language of Rabelais which is still in use in some Canadian provinces. The harpooner's family was originally from Quebec, and was already a tribe of hardy fishermen when this town belonged to France.

Little by little Ned Land acquired a taste for chatting, and I loved to hear the recital of his adventures in the polar seas. He related his fishing, and his combats, with natural poetry of expression; his recital took the form of an epic poem, and I seemed to be listening to a Canadian Homer singing the *Iliad* of the regions of the North.

I am portraying this hardy companion as I really knew him. We are old friends now, united in that unchangeable friendship which is cemented amid extreme dangers.

Now, what was Ned Land's opinion upon the question of the marine monster? I must admit that he did not believe in it. He was the only one on board who did not share that universal conviction. He even avoided the subject, which I thought it my duty to press upon him.

One magnificent evening on July 30, three weeks after our departure, the frigate was abreast of Cape Blanc, thirty miles to leeward of the coast of Patagonia. We had crossed the Tropic of Capricorn, and the Straits of Magellan opened less than seven hundred miles to the south. Before eight days were over, the *Abraham Lincoln* would be ploughing the waters of the Pacific.

Seated on the poop, Ned Land and I were chatting of one thing and another as we looked at the mysterious sea, whose great depths had up to this time been inaccessible to the eye of man. I naturally led up the conversation to the giant unicorn, and examined the various chances of success or failure of the expedition. But as Ned Land had let me speak without saying much himself, I pressed him more closely.

"Ned," said I, "is it possible you are not convinced that the cetacean we are following exists? Have you particular reason for doubting?"

The harpooner looked at me fixedly for some moments before answering, struck his broad forehead with his hand (a habit of his), and said at last, "Perhaps I have, Mr. Aronnax."

"But Ned, you, a whaler by profession, familiar with all the great marine mammalia—*you* ought to be the last to doubt!"

"That is just it, Professor," replied Ned. "As a whaler I have followed many a cetacean, harpooned a great number, and killed several; but however strong or well-armed they have been, neither their tails nor their other fighting weapons would have been able even to scratch the iron plates of a steamer."

"But, Ned, they tell of ships which the teeth of the narwhal has pierced through and through."

"Wooden ships—that is possible," replied the Canadian; "but I have never seen it done; and until further proof, I deny that whales, other cetaceans or even a sea unicorn could ever produce the effect you describe."

"Well, Ned, I repeat it with a conviction resting on the logic of facts. I believe in the existence of a mammal powerfully organized, belonging to the branch of vertebrata, like the whales, or the dolphins, and furnished with a horn of defense of great penetrating power."

"Hum!" said the harpooner, shaking his head with the air of a man who would not be convinced.

"Notice one thing, my worthy Canadian," I resumed. "If such an animal is in existence, if it inhabits the depths of the ocean, if it frequents the strata lying miles below the surface of the water, it must necessarily possess an organization the strength of which would defy all comparison."

"And why this powerful organization?" demanded Ned.

"Because it requires incalculable strength to live in these strata and resist their pressure. Listen to me. Let us admit that the pressure of the atmosphere is represented by the weight of a column of water thirty-two feet high. In reality the column of water would be shorter, as we are speaking of sea water, the density of which is greater than that of fresh water. Very well, when you dive, Ned, as many times 32 feet of water as there are above you, so many times does your body bear a pressure equal to that of the atmosphere; that is to say, 15 pounds for each square inch of its surface. It follows, then, that at 320 feet this pressure equals that of 10 atmospheres, of 100 atmospheres at 3,200 feet, and of 1,000 atmospheres at 32,000 feet, that is, about six miles; which is equivalent to saying that if you could attain this depth in the ocean, each square three-eighths of an inch of the surface of your body would bear a pressure of 5,600 pounds. Ah! my brave Ned, do you know how many square inches you carry on the surface of your body?"

"I have no idea, Mr. Aronnax."

"About 6,500; and as in reality the atmospheric pressure is about 15 pounds to the square inch, your 6,500 square inches bear at this moment a pressure of 97,500 pounds."

"Without my perceiving it?"

"Without your perceiving it. And if you are not crushed by such a pressure, it is because the air penetrates the interior of your body with equal pressure. Hence perfect equilibrium between the interior and exterior pressures, which thus neutralize each other, and which allows you to bear it without inconvenience. But in the water it is another thing."

"Yes, I understand," replied Ned, becoming more attentive, "because the water surrounds me but does not penetrate."

"Precisely, Ned: so that at 32 feet beneath the surface of the sea you would undergo a pressure of 97,500 pounds; at 320 feet, ten times that pressure; at 3,200 feet, a hundred times that pressure; lastly, at 32,000 feet, a thousand times that pressure would be 97,500,000 pounds—that is to say, that you would be as flattened out as if you had been pulled from the plates of a hydraulic press!"

"The devil!" exclaimed Ned.

"Very well, my worthy harpooner, if some vertebrate, several hundred yards long, and large in proportion, can maintain itself in such depths—of those whose surface is represented by millions of square inches, that is by tens of millions of pounds, we must estimate the pressure they undergo. Consider, then, what must be the resistance of their bony structure and the strength of their organization to withstand such pressure!"

"Why!" exclaimed Ned Land, "they must be made of iron plates eight inches thick, like the armored frigates."

"As you say, Ned. And think what destruction such a mass would cause if hurled with the speed of an express train against the hull of a vessel."

"Yes—certainly—perhaps," replied the Canadian, shaken by these figures, but not yet willing to give in.

"Well, have I convinced you?"

"You have convinced me of one thing, sir, which is that, if such animals do exist at the bottom of the seas, they must necessarily be as strong as you say."

"But if they do not exist, you stubborn harpooner, how do you explain the accident to the *Scotia?*"

5. At a Venture

THE VOYAGE of the *Abraham Lincoln* was quite uneventful for some time. But there was one incident which revealed Ned Land's wonderful dexterity with the harpoon, and proved what confidence we might place in him.

On the 30th of June the frigate spoke some American

whalers, from whom we learned that they had seen nothing of the narwhal. But the captain of one of them, the *Monroe,* knowing that Ned Land was on board the *Abraham Lincoln,* begged for his assistance in taking a whale they had sighted. Commander Farragut was desirous of seeing the harpooner's skill in operation, and so gave him permission to go aboard the *Monroe.* And fate served our Canadian so well that, instead of one whale, he harpooned two with a double blow, striking one straight to the heart, and capturing the other after some minutes' pursuit.

Decidedly, if the monster ever met with Ned Land's harpoon, I would not bet in its favor.

Our frigate skirted the southeast coast of America, and on July 3rd we were at the mouth of the Straits of Magellan, off Cape Vierges. Commander Farragut would not attempt this tortuous passage, but set his course around Cape Horn.

The ship's crew agreed with him. It was possible that they might have met the narwhal in this narrow passage, although many of the sailors affirmed that the monster could not get through it, that "he was too big for that!"

About three in the afternoon on July 6, at fifteen miles to the south, the *Abraham Lincoln* rounded the solitary island, this lost rock at the extremity of the American continent to which some Dutch sailors gave the name of their native town, Cape Horn. The course was set toward the northwest, and the next day the frigate's propeller was at last beating the waters of the Pacific.

"Keep a sharp lookout!" the sailors called out.

And so we did, with both eyes and spyglasses—a little dazzled, it is true, by the prospect of the two thousand dollars which Commander Farragut had offered to the man who spied the monster first.

I myself, for whom money had no charms, was by no means the least attentive on board. I took but a few minutes for my meals and a few hours to sleep; and, indifferent to both rain and sun, I took up a stand on the poop-deck. Now leaning on the railing of the forecastle, now on the taffrail, I scanned eagerly the foam that whitened the sea as far as the eye could reach; and how often I shared the emotions of the crew, when some capricious whale raised its black back above the waves! The poop of the vessel was crowded in a moment. The cabins poured forth a torrent of sailors and officers, each with heaving chest and troubled eye watching the course of the cetacean. I looked and looked, till I was nearly blind, while Conseil, always phlegmatic, kept repeating in a calm voice:

"If Monsieur would not squint so much, he would see better!"

But vain excitement! Each time the *Abraham Lincoln* checked speed and made for the animal, it turned out to be a simple whale or common cachalot, which soon disappeared amid a storm of abuse.

The weather was good. The voyage was proceeding under the most favorable conditions. It was then the bad season in Australia—July of that zone corresponding to our January in Europe—but the sea was calm and clear, and easily scanned round a vast circumference.

On July 20 we cut across the Tropic of Capricorn at 105° long. and the 27th of the same month we crossed the equator on the 110th meridian. This passed, the frigate headed in a more decided westerly direction, and scoured the central waters of the Pacific. Commander Farragut thought, and with reason, that it was better to remain in deep water, and keep clear of continents or islands, which the beast itself seemed to shun, perhaps because there was not enough water for him. The frigate therefore passed at some distance from the Marquesas and Sandwich Islands, crossed the Tropic of Cancer, and made for the China seas.

We were in the theater of the last diversions of the monster; and to tell the truth, we no longer lived normally on board. The entire ship's crew were in a state of nervous excitement. They could not eat; they could not sleep. Twenty times a day, a mirage or an illusion fancied by some sailor seated on the taffrail, would cause violent anguish, and these emotional crises, twenty times repeated, kept us in a state of excitement so violent, a reaction was unavoidable.

And truly, reaction soon showed itself. For three months, during which every day seemed an age, the *Abraham Lincoln* furrowed the waters of the northern Pacific, chasing whales, deviating from her course, veering suddenly, stopping, putting on steam, and backing ever and anon at the risk of damaging her machinery. Not one point of the Japanese or American coasts was left unexplored.

The warmest partisans of the enterprise now became its chief detractors. Reaction mounted from the crew to the captain himself, and certainly, had it not been for resolute determination on the part of Captain Farragut, the frigate would have headed due south. This useless search could not last much longer. The good ship *Abraham Lincoln* had done her best. Never had a ship's crew shown more zeal or patience; its failure could not be blamed on them—there remained nothing but to return.

This opinion was presented to the commander. The sailors could not hide their discontent and the service suffered. I will not say there was a mutiny on board, but after a reasonable period of obstinacy, Captain Farragut (as Columbus did) asked for three days' patience. If in three days the monster did not appear, the man at the helm should give three turns of the wheel, and the *Abraham Lincoln* would make for European seas.

This promise was made on the 2nd of November. It had the effect of rallying the ship's crew. The ocean was scanned now with renewed interest. Each one wanted a last glance; eyes peered feverishly through spyglasses. It was a last grand challenge given to the giant narwhal, and he could scarcely fail to answer the summons and "appear."

Two days passed; we cruised with the steam at half pressure; a thousand schemes were tried to attract the attention and stimulate the apathy of the animal in case it was somewhere in those parts. Large quantities of bacon were trailed in the wake of the ship, to the great satisfaction (I must say) of the sharks. Small craft radiated in all directions around the *Abraham Lincoln* as she lay to, and did not leave a spot of the sea unexplored. But the night of the 4th of November arrived without the unveiling of this submarine mystery.

The next day, the 5th of November, at twelve the delay would (morally speaking) expire; after that time, Commander Farragut, faithful to his promise, was to turn the course to the southeast and abandon forever the northern regions of the Pacific.

The frigate was then in 31° 15′ N. lat. and 136° 42′ E. long. The coast of Japan still remained less than two hundred miles to leeward. Night was approaching. Eight bells had just struck. Thick clouds hid the new moon. The sea rolled gently under the stern of the vessel.

At that moment I was leaning forward on the starboard railing. Conseil, standing near me, was looking straight before him. The crew, perched in the ratlines, scanned the fading horizon. Officers with their night glasses scoured the growing darkness. At times the ocean sparkled under the rays of the moon as it darted between two clouds, then all trace of light was lost in the darkness.

I could see that Conseil was aware of the general influence. At least I thought so. Perhaps for the first time his nerves vibrated to a sentiment of curiosity.

"Come, Conseil," said I, "this is the last chance to pocket the two thousand dollars."

"May I be permitted to say, Monsieur," replied Conseil, "that I never reckoned on getting the prize; and, had the government of the Union offered a hundred thousand dollars, it would have been none the poorer."

"You are right, Conseil. It is a foolish affair after all, and one upon which we entered too lightly. What time lost, what useless emotions! We should have been back in France six months ago."

"In Monsieur's little room," replied Conseil, "and in your museum, sir, and I should have already classed all your fossils, sir. And the babiroussa would have been installed in its cage in the Jardin des Plantes, and have drawn all the curious people of the capital!"

"As you say, Conseil. I fancy we will run a fair chance of being laughed at for our pains."

"That's tolerably certain," replied Conseil, quietly; "I

think they will make fun of Monsieur. And, must I say
it?"

"Go on, my good friend."

"Well, Monsieur will only get his deserts."

"Indeed!"

"When one has the honor of being a savant as Monsieur
is, one should not expose one's self to—"

Conseil had not time to finish his compliment. In the
midst of general silence we heard the voice of Ned Land
shouting:

"Lookout, ahoy! the monster—on our weather beam!"

6. At Full Steam

At this cry the entire ship's crew rushed toward the harpooner—commander, officers, masters, sailors, cabin boys;
even the engineers and the stokers. The order to stop the
ship had been given, and the frigate now continued on her
own momentum.

The darkness was then profound, and however good the
Canadian's eyes were, I wondered how he had managed to
see, and what he had been able to see. My heart beat un-
bearably fast. But Ned Land was not mistaken, and soon
we all perceived the object he pointed to. At two cables'
length off the *Abraham Lincoln*'s starboard quarter, the sea
seemed to be illuminated from below. It was not a mere
phosphoric phenomenon. The monster was evidently submerged several fathoms below the surface, but threw out
that very intense but mysterious light mentioned in the reports of several captains. This magnificent irradiation must

have been produced by an agent of great *shining* power. The luminous part traced on the sea an immense oval, much elongated, whose center burned with white-hot intensity, and whose overpowering brilliance died out gradually.

"It is nothing more than a mass of phosphoric particles," cried one of the officers.

"No, sir, it is certainly not produced by sea organisms," I replied. "That brightness comes from some powerful electrical source. Besides, see, see! it moves; it is moving forward, backward; it is darting toward us!"

A general cry arose from the frigate.

"Silence!" said the captain. "Up helm; reverse the engines!"

Sailors and engineers rushed to their stations. The ship's direction was reversed, and the *Abraham Lincoln,* beating to port, described a semicircle.

"Right helm, go ahead," cried the captain.

These orders were executed, and the frigate moved rapidly from the burning light.

Or rather, she tried to sheer off, but the supernatural animal approached with a velocity double her own.

We gasped for breath. Stupefaction more than fear made us dumb and motionless. The animal gained on us, sporting with the waves. It made the round of the frigate, which was then making 14 knots, and enveloped it with its electric rings like luminous dust.

Then it moved off two or three miles, leaving a phosphorescent track, like those volumes of steam that the express trains leave behind. All at once, from the dark line of the horizon whither it had retired to regain its momentum, the monster rushed suddenly toward the *Abraham Lincoln*

with alarming rapidity, stopped suddenly about twenty feet
from the hull, and died out—not diving under the water,
for its brilliancy did not diminish gradually,—but suddenly,
and as if the source of this brilliant emanation were exhausted. Then it reappeared on the other side of the vessel,
as if it had turned and slid under the hull. At any moment
there might have been a fatal collision. Even so, I was
astonished at the frigate's maneuver. She fled and did not
attack.

On the captain's face, generally so impassive, was an
expression of complete astonishment.

"Mr. Aronnax," he said, "I do not know what formidable
being I am dealing with, and I will not imprudently risk the
safety of my ship in this darkness. Besides, how can we
attack this unknown thing, how defend ourselves from it?
Wait for daylight, and the scene will change."

"You have no further doubt, Captain, of the nature of
the animal?"

"No, sir; it is evidently a gigantic narwhal, of the nature
of an electric eel."

"Perhaps," I suggested, "one can only overcome it with a
torpedo."

"That may be," replied the captain. "And if it possesses
such dreadful power, it is the most terrible animal that ever
was created. That is why, sir, I must be on my guard."

The crew stood watch all night. No one thought of sleep.
The *Abraham Lincoln,* unable to reach any such velocity,
had slowed and cruised at half speed. As for the narwhal,
imitating the frigate, it let the waves rock it at will, and
seemed determined not to leave the scene. Toward midnight, however, it disappeared, or, to use a more appropri-

ate term, it "died out" like a large glowworm. Had it fled?
One could only fear, not hope. But at about one o'clock in
the morning we heard a deafening whistling, like water ex-
pelled under pressure.

The captain, Ned Land, and I were then on the poop,
anxiously peering through the profound darkness.

"Ned Land," asked the commander, "you have often
heard the roaring of whales?"

"Often, sir, but I've never sighted whales that brought me
in two thousand dollars. If I can only get within four
harpoons' length of it!"

"But to get near it," said the commander, "you will need
to have me put a whaleboat at your disposal."

"Certainly, sir."

"That will be trifling with the lives of my men."

"And mine, too," the harpooner said simply.

Around two in the morning, the burning light reappeared, no less intense, about five miles to windward of the
Abraham Lincoln. Notwithstanding the distance and the
noise of the wind and sea, one heard distinctly the swishing
of the animal's tail, and even its panting breath. It seemed
as though in breathing at the surface of the water, the
enormous narwhal sucked air into its lungs, just as steam is
sucked into the vast cylinders of a 2,000 horsepower engine.

"Hum!" I thought. "A whale with the strength of a
cavalry regiment is a formidable whale!"

We were on the *qui vive* till daylight, and prepared for
the combat. The implements for hunting the creature were
laid along the railings. The first mate loaded the blunder-
busses, which could shoot harpoons for a mile, and long

duck guns, with explosive bullets, which can mortally wound even the most powerful animals. Ned Land busied himself with sharpening his harpoon—a terrible weapon in his hands.

At six o'clock day began to break; and with the first glimmer of dawn, the electric light of the narwhal disappeared. At seven o'clock day was sufficiently advanced, but a thick sea fog obscured our view, and the best telescopes could not pierce it. That caused disappointment and anger.

I climbed the mizzenmast. Some officers were already perched on the mastheads. At eight o'clock the fog lay heavily on the waves, and its thick scrolls rose little by little. The horizon grew wider and clearer at the same time. Suddenly, just as on the day before, Ned Land's voice was heard:

"There it is, on the port quarter!"

Every eye was turned toward that point. There, a mile and a half from the frigate, a long blackish body emerged about three feet above the waves. Its tail churned violently, producing a considerable amount of foam. An immense track of dazzling whiteness marked the passage of the animal, and described a long curve.

As the frigate drew nearer, I examined the cetacean thoroughly.

The reports of the *Shannon* and the *Helvetia* had rather exaggerated its size, and I estimated its length at only 250 feet. As to its dimensions, I could only conjecture them to be admirably proportioned. While I watched this phenomenon, two jets of steam and water were ejected from its vents, and rose to the height of 120 feet; thus I ascertained its way of breathing. I concluded definitely that it belonged to the vertebrate branch, class mammalia.

The crew waited impatiently for their orders. The commander, after having observed the animal attentively, called the chief engineer.

"Sir," said the commander, "is the pressure up?"

"Yes, sir," answered the engineer.

"Well, stoke your fires and then full steam ahead."

Cheers greeted this order. The time for the struggle had arrived. Some moments later the two funnels of the frigate vomited torrents of black smoke, and the bridge quaked under the trembling of the boilers.

The *Abraham Lincoln,* pushed by her powerful propeller, went straight for the animal. The latter allowed her to come within half a cable's length; then, as if disdaining to dive, made a slight turn, and stood off a short distance.

This pursuit lasted nearly three-quarters of an hour, without the frigate gaining six feet on the cetacean. It was quite evident that at that rate we should never catch up with it.

"Well, Mr. Land," asked the captain, "do you advise me to put the boats out to sea?"

"No, sir," replied Ned Land; "because we won't take that beast easily."

"What shall we do then?"

"Put on more steam if you can, sir. With your leave, I mean to stand watch under the bowsprit, and, if we get within harpooning distance, I shall heave my harpoon."

"Good," said the captain. "Engineer, more pressure."

Ned Land went to his post. The fires were stoked to capacity, the propeller revolved forty-three times a minute, and steam poured from the valves. We heaved the log and calculated that the *Abraham Lincoln* was going at the rate of 18.5 knots.

But the accursed animal swam at the same speed.

For an hour the frigate kept up this pace, without gaining. It was humiliating for one of the swiftest ships in the American Navy. A stubborn anger seized the crew; the sailors abused the monster, who, as before, disdained to answer them; the captain was actually gnawing his beard.

The engineer was summoned again.

"You have a full head of steam?"

"Yes, sir," replied the engineer.

"Are the valves up to pressure?"

"Six and a half atmospheres."

"Get them up to ten."

The speed of the *Abraham Lincoln* increased. Her masts trembled and clouds of smoke choked the narrow funnels. They heaved the log a second time.

"Well?" asked the captain of the man at the wheel.

"It reads 19.3 knots, sir."

"More steam!"

The engineer obeyed. The manometer (pressure gauge) showed ten degrees. But the cetacean used up more fuel itself, no doubt, for without straining, it made 19.3 knots.

What a chase! I cannot describe the emotions I felt. Ned Land kept his post, harpoon in hand. Several times the animal let us get nearer. "We're gaining! we shall capture it!" cried the Canadian. But just as he was going to strike, the cetacean moved away with a rapidity that could not be estimated at less than thirty miles an hour. Even during our maximum speed, it mocked the frigate, going round and round it. A cry of fury broke from everyone!

At noon we were no nearer than we had been at eight in the morning.

The captain then decided to take more direct means.

"Ah," he said, "that animal goes quicker than the *Abraham Lincoln*. Very well! we will see whether it will escape our conical bullets. Send your men to the forecastle, sir."

The forecastle cannon was immediately loaded and fired. But the shot passed some feet above the cetacean, half a mile off.

"Another, more to the right," cried the commander, "and five dollars to whoever hits that infernal beast."

An old gunner with a gray beard—that I can see now—with steady eye and grave face, went up to the gun and took a long aim. There was a loud report, mingled with the cheers of the crew.

The bullet did its work; it hit the animal—and slid harmlessly off the rounded surface.

The chase began again, and the captain, leaning toward me, said:

"I will pursue that beast till my frigate bursts."

"Yes," I answered; "and you will be quite right to do it."

I wished the beast would exhaust itself, and not be insensible to fatigue like a steam engine. But it was of no use. Hours passed without its showing any signs of exhaustion.

However, it must be said in praise of the *Abraham Lincoln* that she struggled on indefatigably. She must have covered 300 miles on that unlucky day, November the 6th. But night came on, and obscured the rough ocean.

Now I thought our expedition was at an end, and that we should never again see the extraordinary animal. I was mistaken. At ten minutes to eleven in the evening the electric light reappeared three miles to windward of the frigate, as pure, as intense as during the preceding night.

The narwhal seemed motionless; perhaps, tired with its

day's work, it slept, letting itself float with the undulation of the waves. Now was a chance of which the captain resolved to take advantage.

He gave his orders. The *Abraham Lincoln* kept up half steam, then coasted silently in order not to alert its adversary. Frequently whales are found to be so sound asleep that they can be successfully attacked, and Ned Land had harpooned more than one in this way. The Canadian took up his post again under the bowsprit.

The frigate stopped about two cables' length from the animal. No one breathed; a deep silence reigned on the bridge. We were not a hundred feet from the burning focus, the light of which increased and dazzled our eyes.

At this moment, leaning on the forecastle bulwark, I saw below me Ned Land grappling the martingale in one hand, brandishing his terrible harpoon in the other, scarcely twenty feet from the motionless animal. Suddenly his arm straightened, and the harpoon was thrown. I heard the sonorous stroke of the weapon, which seemed to have struck a hard body. The electric light went out suddenly, and two enormous waterspouts broke over the bridge of the frigate, rushing like a torrent from stem to stern, overthrowing men and breaking the lashings of the spars. A fearful shock followed, and I was thrown over the rail into the sea without having time to stop myself.

7. An Unknown Species of Whale

THIS UNEXPECTED fall so stunned me that I have no clear recollection of my sensations at the time. I was at first drawn down to a depth of about twenty feet. I am a good swimmer (though without pretending to rival Byron or Poe, who were masters of the art), and in that plunge I did not lose my presence of mind. Two vigorous strokes brought me to the surface of the water. My first thought was to look for the frigate. Had the crew seen me disappear? Had the *Abraham Lincoln* veered around? Would the captain put out a boat? Might I hope to be saved?

The darkness was intense. I caught a glimpse of a black mass disappearing in the east, its beacon lights dying out in the distance. It was the frigate! I was lost.

"Help, help!" I shouted, swimming toward the *Abraham Lincoln* in desperation.

My clothes encumbered me; they seemed glued to my body, and paralyzed my movements.

I was sinking! I was suffocating!

"Help!"

This was my last cry. My mouth filled with water; I struggled against being drawn down the abyss. Suddenly my clothes were seized by a strong hand, and I felt myself quickly drawn up to the surface of the sea; and I heard, yes, I heard these words pronounced in my ear:

"If Monsieur would be so good as to lean on my shoulder, Monsieur would swim with much greater ease."

I seized my faithful Conseil's arm.

"Is it you?" I said. "Really you?"

"Myself," answered Conseil; "and awaiting Monsieur's orders."

"That shock threw you as well as me into the sea?"

"No; but being in Monsieur's service, I followed him."

The worthy fellow thought that was quite natural!

"And the frigate?" I asked.

"The frigate?" replied Conseil, turning on his back. "I think Monsieur had better not count too much on her."

"You think so?"

"At the time I threw myself into the sea, I heard the men at the wheel say, 'The propeller and rudder are broken.' "

"Broken?"

"Yes, broken by the monster's teeth. It is the only injury the *Abraham Lincoln* has sustained. But it is a bad lookout for us—she no longer answers her helm."

"Then we are lost!"

"Perhaps so," calmly answered Conseil. "However, we have still several hours before us, and one can do a good deal in some hours."

Conseil's imperturbable coolness set me up again. I swam more vigorously; but cramped by my clothes which stuck to me like a leaden weight, I had great difficulty in bearing up. Conseil saw this.

"Will Monsieur allow me to slit them?" he asked. And, slipping an open knife under my clothes, he ripped them up from top to bottom very rapidly. Then he cleverly slipped them off me while I swam for both of us.

Then I did the same for Conseil, and we continued to swim near to each other.

Nevertheless, our situation was really as bad as before. Perhaps our disappearance had not been noticed; and if it had been, the frigate could not tack without a helm. Conseil argued on this supposition, and laid his plans accordingly. This quiet boy was perfectly self-possessed. We then decided that, as our only chance of safety was being picked up by the *Abraham Lincoln's* boats, we ought to try to wait for them as long as possible. I resolved then to conserve our joint strength so that both should not be exhausted at the same time. This is how we managed it: one of us would lie on his back, quite still, with arms crossed and legs stretched out, while the other would swim and push him on ahead. This towing business did not last more than ten minutes at a time; and relieving each other thus, we could swim on for some hours, perhaps till daybreak. Poor chance, but hope is so firmly rooted in the heart of man! Moreover, there were two of us. Indeed I declare, though it may seem improbable, if I sought to destroy all hope—if I wished to despair, I could not.

The collision of the frigate with the cetacean had occurred about eleven o'clock in the evening before. I reckoned then we should have eight hours to swim before sunrise, quite possible if we relieved each other. The sea, very calm, was in our favor. Sometimes I tried to pierce the intense darkness that was only dispelled by the phosphorescence caused by our movements. I watched the luminous waves that broke over my hand.

Near one in the morning I was overcome with fatigue. My limbs stiffened in violent cramp. Conseil was obliged to keep me up, and our preservation devolved on him alone. I heard the poor boy pant; his breathing became short and hurried. I felt that he could not keep up much longer.

"Leave me! Leave me!" I said to him.

"Leave Monsieur? Never!" he replied. "I would drown first."

Just then the moon appeared through a cloud that the wind was driving to the east. The surface of the sea glittered with its rays. This kindly light reanimated us. My head felt better again. I looked to the horizon and saw the frigate!

She was five miles from us, a hardly discernible dark mass. But no boats!

I would have cried out. But what good would it have done at such a distance? My swollen lips could utter no sounds. Conseil could still shout, and I heard him repeat at intervals, "Help! Help!"

We suspended our movements for an instant; we listened. It seemed to me as if a cry answered the cry from Conseil. "Did you hear?" I murmured.

"Yes! Yes!"

And Conseil gave one more despairing cry.

This time there was no mistake! A human voice responded to ours! Was it the voice of another unfortunate creature, abandoned in the middle of the ocean, some other victim of the shock sustained by the vessel? Or, rather, was it a boat from the frigate that was hailing us in the darkness?

Conseil made a last effort, and, leaning on my shoulder while I struck out in a desperate effort, he raised himself half out of the water, then fell back exhausted.

"What did you see?"

"I saw—" he murmured; "I saw—but do not talk—reserve all your strength!"

What had he seen? Then, I know not why, the thought of the monster came into my head for the first time. But that voice! The time is past for Jonahs to take refuge in whales' bellies! However, Conseil was towing me again. He raised his head sometimes, looked before us, and uttered a cry of recognition, and was answered by a voice that came nearer and nearer. I scarcely heard it. My strength was exhausted; my fingers stiffened; I could cling with my hand no longer; my mouth, convulsively opening, filled with salt water. Cold crept over me. I raised my head for the last time, then I sank.

At this moment a hard body struck me. I clung to it. Then I felt that I was being drawn up, that I was brought to the surface of the water, that my chest had collapsed—I fainted.

It is certain that I soon came to, thanks to the vigorous rubbings that I received. I half opened my eyes.

"Conseil!" I murmured.

"Does Monsieur call me?" asked Conseil.

Just then, by the waning light of the moon which was sinking down to the horizon, I saw a face which was not Conseil's and which I immediately recognized.

"Ned!" I cried.

"The same, sir, who is seeking his prize!" replied the Canadian.

"Were you thrown into the sea by the shock to the frigate?"

"Yes, Professor; but more fortunate than you, I was able to find a footing almost directly upon a floating island."

"An island?"

"Or, more correctly speaking, on our gigantic narwhal."

"Explain yourself, Ned!"

"Only I soon found out why my harpoon had not entered its skin and was blunted."

"Why, Ned, why?"

"Because, Professor, that beast is made of sheet iron."

The Canadian's last words produced a sudden revolution in my brain. I wriggled myself quickly to the top of the being, or object, half out of the water, which served us for a refuge. I kicked it. It was evidently a hard, impenetrable body, and not the soft substance that forms the bodies of

the great marine mammalia. If this hard body were a bony
covering, like that of the antediluvian animals, I should be
free to class this monster among amphibious reptiles, such
as tortoises or alligators.

But, no! the blackish back that supported me was
smooth, polished, without scales. The blow produced a
metallic sound; and, incredible though it may be, it seemed,
I might say, as if it was made of riveted plates.

There was no doubt about it! This monster, this natural
phenomenon that had puzzled the learned world, and overthrown and misled the imagination of seamen of both
hemispheres, it must be owned, was a still more astonishing
phenomenon, inasmuch as it was simply human construction.

We had no time to lose, however. We were lying upon
the back of a sort of submarine boat, which appeared, as far
as I could judge, to be a huge fish of steel. Ned Land's mind
was made up on this point. Conseil and I could only agree
with him.

Just then a bubbling began at the back of this strange
thing, which evidently moved by propeller, and it began to
move. We had just time to seize hold of the upper part,
which rose about seven feet out of the water. Happily its
speed was not great.

"As long as it sails horizontally," muttered Ned Land, "I
do not mind; but if it takes a fancy to dive, I would not give
two straws for my life."

The Canadian echoed my own fears. We must communicate immediately with the beings, whatever they were, shut
up inside the machine. I searched all over the outside for an
opening; but the lines of the iron rivets, solidly driven into
the joints of the iron plates, were clear and uniform. Be-

sides, the moon disappeared then, and left us in total darkness.

At last this long night passed. My indistinct remembrance prevents my describing all the impressions it made. I
can only recall one circumstance. During a sudden calm, I
fancied I heard vague sounds, a sort of fugitive harmony
produced by words of command. What was, then, the mystery of this submarine craft, of which the whole world
vainly sought an explanation? What kind of beings existed
in this strange boat? What mechanical agent caused its
prodigious speed?

Daybreak appeared. The morning mists surrounded us,
but they soon cleared off. I was about to examine the top-
side of the hull, which formed a kind of horizontal platform, when I felt it gradually sinking.

"Oh! confound it!" cried Ned Land, kicking the resound-
ing plate. "Open, you inhospitable rascals!"

Happily then, the sinking movement ceased. Suddenly we
heard a noise, like iron plates pushed violently aside, from
the interior of the boat. One iron plate was removed and a
man appeared, uttered an odd cry, and disappeared immediately.

Some moments afterward eight strong men, with masked
faces, appeared noiselessly, and drew us down into their
formidable machine.

8. Mobilis in Mobili

THIS FORCIBLE abduction, so roughly carried out, was accomplished with lightning rapidity. I trembled with apprehension. With whom were we dealing? No doubt some new

breed of pirates, roaming the sea in their own fashion. Hardly had the narrow panel closed on me when I was enveloped in darkness. My eyes, dazzled from the daylight, could distinguish nothing. My naked feet clung to the rungs of an iron ladder. Ned Land and Conseil, held firmly in the men's grasp, followed me. At the bottom of the ladder a door opened, and shut after us immediately with a bang.

We were alone. Where, I could not say, hardly imagine. All was black, and such a dense black that, after some minutes, my eyes had not been able to discern even the faintest glimmer.

Meanwhile, Ned Land, furious at these proceedings, gave free vent to his indignation.

"Confound it!" he cried, "these people match the north islanders for hospitality! They may even be cannibals. I shouldn't be surprised at it, but I swear they will not eat me without a struggle."

"Calm yourself, friend Ned, calm yourself," replied Conseil quietly. "Do not cry out before you are hurt. We are not quite done for yet."

"Not quite," sharply replied the Canadian, "but pretty near, at all events. Things look black. Happily, I still have my bowie knife, and I can always see well enough to use it. The first of these pirates who lays a hand on me——"

"Do not excite yourself, Ned," I said to the harpooner, "and do not compromise us by useless violence. Who knows that they will not listen to us? Let us rather try to find out where we are."

I groped about. In five steps I came to an iron wall made of plates bolted together. Then, turning back, I struck against a wooden table near which were ranged several stools. The boards of this prison were concealed under a thick mat, which deadened the noise of the feet. The bare walls revealed no trace of window or door. Conseil, going around the reverse way, met me, and we went back to the middle of the cabin, which measured about 10 by 20 feet. As to its height, Ned Land, in spite of his own great height, could not measure it.

Half an hour had already passed without our situation being bettered, when the dense darkness suddenly gave way to extreme light. Our prison was suddenly lighted; that is to say, it became luminous, and so bright I could not bear it at first. In its whiteness and intensity I recognized that electric light which played around the submarine boat like a magnificent phosphorescence. After shutting my eyes involuntarily, I opened them, and saw that this luminosity came from a half globe, unpolished, in the roof of the cabin.

"At last we can see," cried Ned Land, who, knife in hand, stood on the defensive.

"Yes," said I; "but we are still in the dark about ourselves."

"Monsieur must have patience," said the imperturbable Conseil.

The sudden lighting of the cabin enabled me to examine it minutely. It contained only a table and five stools. The invisible door might be hermetically sealed. Not a sound could be heard. All seemed dead in the interior of this boat. Did it move, did it float on the surface of the ocean or dive into its depths? I could not guess.

There was a noise of bolts, the door opened, and two men appeared.

One was short, very muscular, broad-shouldered, with

robust limbs, strong head, an abundance of black hair, thick mustache, a quick penetrating look, and the vivacity which characterizes the people of southern France.

The second stranger merits a more detailed description. I noted his characteristic qualities directly: self-confidence—because his head was well set on his shoulders, and his black eyes looked around with cold assurance; calmness—for his skin, rather pale, showed his coolness of blood; energy—evinced by the rapid contraction of his lofty brows; and courage—because his deep breathing denoted great power of lungs.

Whether this person was thirty-five or fifty years of age I could not say. He was tall, had a large forehead, straight nose, a clearly cut mouth, beautiful teeth, with fine tapered hands, indicative of a highly nervous temperament. This man was certainly the most admirable specimen I had ever met. One particular feature was his eyes, rather far from each other, and which could take in nearly a quarter of the horizon at once.

This faculty—I verified it later—gave him a range of vision far superior to Ned Land's. When this stranger fixed upon an object, his eyebrows met, his large eyelids closed to contract the range of his vision, and he looked as if he then magnified the objects lessened by distance, as if he pierced those sheets of water so opaque to our eyes and read the very depths of the sea.

The two strangers, in caps of sea-otter fur and sea boots of sealskin, were dressed in clothes which allowed free movement of the limbs. The taller of the two, evidently the chief on board, examined us minutely without saying a word; then, turning to his companion, talked with him in an unknown tongue. It was a sonorous, harmonious and flexible dialect; the vowels suggesting many languages.

The other replied by a shake of his head and two or three incomprehensible words. Then he seemed to question me by a look.

I replied in good French that I did not know his language; but he seemed not to understand me, and my situation became more embarrassing.

"If Monsieur were to tell our story," said Conseil, "perhaps these gentlemen may understand some words."

I began to tell our adventures, articulating each syllable clearly, and without omitting one single detail. I announced our names and rank, introducing in person Professor Aronnax, his servant Conseil, and Master Ned Land, the harpooner.

The man with the soft, calm eyes listened to me quietly, even politely, and with extreme attention; but nothing in his countenance indicated that he had understood my story. When I finished, he said not a word.

There remained one resource, to speak English. Perhaps they would know this almost universal language. I knew it—as well as the German language—well enough to read it fluently, but not to speak it correctly. But, anyhow, we must make ourselves understood.

"Go on in your turn," I said to the harpooner; "speak your best Anglo-Saxon, and try to do better than I."

Ned did not beg off, and recommenced our story.

To his great disgust, the harpooner could not make himself more intelligible than I had. Our visitors did not stir. They evidently understood neither English nor French.

Very much embarrassed after having vainly exhausted

our resources of communication I did not know what to do when Conseil said:

"If Monsieur will permit me, I will relate it in German."

But in spite of the elegant terms and good accent of the narrator, the German language had no success. At last, nonplussed, I tried to remember my first lessons and narrate our adventures in Latin, but with no better success. This last attempt being of no avail, the two strangers exchanged some words in their unknown language and retired.

The door shut.

"It is an infamous shame," cried Ned Land, who broke out for the twentieth time. "We speak to those rogues in French, English, German, and Latin, and not one of them has the politeness to answer!"

"Calm yourself," I said to the impetuous Ned; "anger will do us no good."

"But, don't you see, Professor," replied our irascible companion, "that we shall die of hunger in this iron cage?"

"Bah!" said Conseil philosophically; "we can hold out for some time yet."

"My friends," I said, "we must not despair. We have been worse off. Do me the favor to wait a little before forming an opinion upon the commander and crew of this boat."

"My opinion is formed," replied Ned Land sharply. "They are rascals."

"Possibly, but from what country?"

"From the land of rogues!"

"My brave Ned, that country is not clearly indicated on the map of the world; but I admit that the nationality of the two strangers is hard to determine. Neither English, French nor German, that is quite certain. However, I am inclined to think that the commander and his companion were born in the warm latitudes. There is southern blood in them. But I cannot decide by their appearance whether they are Spaniards, Turks, Arabians, or Indians. As to their language, it is quite incomprehensible."

"There is the disadvantage of not knowing all languages," said Conseil, "or the disadvantage of not having one universal language."

As he said these words, the door opened. A steward entered. He brought us clothes, coats and trousers, made of a stuff I did not know. I hastened to dress myself, and my companions followed my example. During that time the steward—dumb, perhaps deaf—had arranged the table and laid three plates.

"This is something like!" said Conseil.

"Bah!" said the angry harpooner, "what do you suppose they eat here? Tortoise liver, filleted shark, and beefsteaks from sea dogs."

"We shall see," said Conseil.

The dishes, of bell metal, were placed on the table, and we took our places. Undoubtedly we were dealing with civilized people, and, had it not been for the electric light which flooded us, I could have fancied I was in the dining room of the Adelphi Hotel at Liverpool, or at the Grand Hotel in Paris. I must say, however, that there was neither bread nor wine. The water was fresh and clear, but it was water and did not suit Ned Land's taste. Among the dishes which were brought to us I recognized several fish, delicately dressed; but some, although excellent, I could not place, nor tell whether they belonged to the animal or vegetable kingdoms. As to the dinner service, it was elegant and in perfect taste. Each utensil—spoon, fork, knife, plate—had a letter engraved on it, with a motto above it, of which this is an exact facsimile:

Mobilis in Mobili

The letter N was no doubt the initial of the name of the enigmatical person who commanded at the bottom of the seas.

Ned and Conseil made no comments. They devoured the food, and I did likewise. I was, besides, reassured as to our fate; it was evident that our hosts would not let us die of want.

However, everything has an end, even the hunger of people who have not eaten for fifteen hours. Our appetites satisfied, we felt overcome with exhaustion.

My two companions stretched themselves on the cabin carpet and were soon sound asleep. For my own part, too many thoughts crowded my brain, too many insoluble questions pressed upon me, too many fancies kept my eyes half open. Where were we? What strange power carried us on? I felt—or rather fancied I felt—the machine sinking down to the lowest beds of the sea. Dreadful nightmares beset me; I saw in these mysterious depths a world of unknown animals among which this submarine boat seemed to be of the same kind, living, moving, and formidable as they. Then my brain grew calmer, my imagination wandered into vague unconsciousness, and I soon fell into a deep sleep.

9. Ned Land's Temper

How LONG we slept I do not know, but our sleep must have lasted long, for it rested us completely from our fatigues. I woke first. My companions had not moved, and were still stretched in their corner.

Hardly roused from my somewhat hard couch, I felt my brain freed, my mind clear. I then began an attentive examination of our cell. Nothing was changed inside. The prison was still a prison—the prisoners, prisoners. However, the steward during our sleep had cleared the table. I breathed with difficulty. The heavy air seemed to oppress my lungs. Although the cell was large, we had evidently consumed a great part of its oxygen. Indeed, each man consumes in one hour the oxygen contained in more than 176 pints of air, and this air, charged with a nearly equal quantity of carbonic acid, becomes unbreathable.

The atmosphere of our prison, and no doubt that of the entire submarine boat, needed renewing. That gave rise to a question in my mind. How would the commander of this floating dwelling place proceed? Would he obtain air by chemical means, in getting by heat the oxygen contained in chlorate of potash, and in absorbing carbonic acid by caustic potash? Or—a more convenient, economical and consequently more probable alternative—would he rise to the surface of the water like a whale, and so renew for twenty-four hours the atmospheric provision?

In fact, I was already obliged to increase my respirations to eke out of this cell the little oxygen it contained, when suddenly I was refreshed by a current of pure air, an invigorating sea breeze, charged with iodine. I opened my mouth wide, and saturated my lungs.

At the same time I felt the boat rolling. The iron-plated monster had evidently just risen to the surface of the ocean to breathe, after the fashion of whales. I found out from that the mode of ventilating the boat.

When I had inhaled this air freely, I sought the conduit pipe, which conveyed to us the beneficial whiff, and I was not long in finding it. Above the door was a ventilator through which volumes of fresh air renewed the impoverished atmosphere.

I was making my observations when Ned and Conseil awoke almost at the same time, under the influence of this reviving air. They rubbed their eyes, stretched themselves, and were on their feet in an instant.

"Did Monsieur sleep well?" asked Conseil, with his usual politeness.

"Very well, my brave boy. And you, Mr. Land?"

"Soundly, Professor. But, I don't know if I am right or not, there seems to be a sea breeze!"

A seaman could not be mistaken, and I told the Canadian all that had passed during his sleep.

"Good!" he said. "That accounts for those roarings we heard when the supposed narwhal sighted the *Abraham Lincoln*."

"Quite so, Master Land; it was taking air."

"Only, Mr. Aronnax, I have no idea what o'clock it is, unless it is dinnertime."

"Dinnertime! My good fellow! Say rather breakfast-time, for we certainly have begun another day."

"So," said Conseil, "we have slept twenty-four hours?"

"That is my opinion."

"I will not contradict you," replied Ned Land. "But dinner or breakfast, the steward will be welcome."

"Master Land, we must conform to the rules on board, and possibly our appetites are ahead of the dinner hour."

"That is just like you, friend Conseil," said Ned impatiently. "You are never out of temper, always calm; you would return thanks before grace, and die of hunger rather than complain!"

But the time was getting on, and we were fearfully hungry, and this time the steward did not appear. It was rather too long to leave us, if they really had good intentions. Ned Land, tormented by the cravings of hunger, grew still angrier, and notwithstanding his promise, I dreaded an explosion when one of the crew appeared.

For two hours more Ned Land's temper increased; he cried, he shouted, but in vain. The walls were deaf. There was no sound to be heard in the boat; all was still as death. It did not move, for I should have felt the trembling motion of the hull under the influence of the propeller. Plunged in the depths of the waters, it belonged no longer to earth; this silence was dreadful.

I felt terrified, Conseil was calm, Ned Land roared.

Just then we heard steps outside. The locks were turned, the door opened, and the steward appeared.

Before I could stop him, the Canadian had thrown the man down and held him by the throat. The steward was choking under the grip of his powerful hand.

Conseil was already trying to unclasp the harpooner's hand from his half-suffocated victim, and I was going to fly

to the rescue, when suddenly I was nailed to the spot by
hearing these words in French:

"Be quiet, Master Land; and you, Professor, will you be
so good as to listen to me?"

10. The Man of the Seas

IT WAS the commander of the vessel who thus spoke.

At these words Ned Land rose suddenly. The steward,
nearly strangled, tottered out on a sign from his master. But
such was the power of the commander on board that not a
gesture betrayed the resentment which this man must have
felt toward the Canadian. Conseil interested in spite of himself, I stupefied, awaited in silence the result of this scene.

The commander, leaning against the corner of a table
with his arms folded, scanned us with profound attention.
Did he hesitate to speak? Did he regret the words which he
had just spoken in French? One might almost think so.

After some moments of silence, which not one of us
dreamed of breaking, "Gentlemen," said he, in a calm and
penetrating voice, "I speak French, English, German, and
Latin equally well. I could, therefore, have answered you at
our first interview, but I wished to know you first, then to
reflect. The story told by each one, entirely agreeing in the
main points, convinced me of your identity. I know now
that chance has brought before me Mr. Pierre Aronnax,
Professor of Natural History at the Museum of Paris, entrusted with a scientific mission abroad, Conseil, his servant, and Ned Land, of Canadian origin, harpooner on

board the frigate *Abraham Lincoln* of the navy of the United States of America."

I bowed assent. It was not a question that the commander put to me. Therefore there was no answer to be made. This man expressed himself with perfect ease, without any accent. His sentences were well turned, his words clear, and his fluency of speech remarkable. Yet, I did not recognize in him a fellow countryman.

He continued the conversation in these terms:

"You have doubtless thought, sir, that I have delayed long in paying you this second visit. The reason is that, after determining your identity I wished to weigh maturely what part to act toward you. I have hesitated much. Most annoying circumstances have brought you into the presence of a man who has broken all the ties of humanity. You have come to trouble my existence."

"Unintentionally!" I said.

"Unintentionally?" replied the stranger, raising his voice a little. "Was it unintentionally that the *Abraham Lincoln* pursued me all over the seas? Was it unintentionally that you took passage in this frigate? Was it unintentionally that your cannon balls rebounded off the plating of my vessel? Was it unintentionally that Mr. Ned Land struck me with his harpoon?"

To these recriminations I had a very natural answer to make, and I made it.

"Sir," I said, "no doubt you are ignorant of the discussions which have taken place concerning you in America and Europe. You do not know that various collisions with your submarine machine have excited public feeling in two continents. I omit the theories without number proposed to

explain that of which you alone possess the secret. But you
must understand that, in pursuing you over the high seas of
the Pacific, the crew of the *Abraham Lincoln* believed they
were chasing some powerful sea monster of which it was
necessary to rid the ocean at any price."

A half smile curled the lips of the commander; then, in a
calmer tone:

"Mr. Aronnax," he replied, "dare you affirm that your
frigate would not as soon have pursued and cannonaded a
submarine boat as a monster?"

This question embarrassed me, for certainly Captain
Farragut might not have hesitated. He might have thought
it his duty to destroy a contrivance of this kind, as he would
a gigantic narwhal.

"You understand then, sir," continued the stranger, "that
I have the right to treat you as enemies?"

I answered nothing, purposely. For what good would it
be to discuss such a proposition, when force could destroy
the best arguments?

"I have hesitated some time," continued the commander;
"nothing obliged me to show you hospitality. If I chose to
separate myself from you, I should have no interest in seeing you again; I could place you upon the deck of this
vessel which has served you as a refuge, I could sink beneath the waters, and forget that you had ever existed.
Would not that be my right?"

"It might be the right of a savage," I answered, "but not
that of a civilized man."

"Professor," replied the commander quickly, "I am not
what you call a civilized man! I have done with society
entirely, for reasons which I alone have the right of appre-

ciating. I do not, therefore, obey its laws, and I desire you never to allude to them before me again!"

This was said plainly. A flash of anger and disdain kindled in the eyes of the Unknown, and I had a glimpse of a terrible past in the life of this man. Not only had he put himself beyond the pale of human laws, but he had made himself independent of them, free in the strictest acceptation of the word, quite beyond their reach! Who, then, would dare to pursue him at the bottom of the sea, when, on its surface, he defied all attempts made against him?

What vessel could resist the shock of his submarine *Monitor?* What armor, however thick, could withstand the blows of his spur? No man could demand from him an account of his actions; God, if he believed in one—his conscience, if he had one—were the sole judges to whom he was answerable.

These reflections crossed my mind rapidly, while the stranger was silent, absorbed, and as if wrapped up in himself. I regarded him with mingled fear and interest.

After rather a long silence the commander resumed the conversation.

"I have hesitated," he said, "but I have thought that my interest might be reconciled with that pity to which every human being has a right. You will remain on board my vessel, since fate has cast you here. You will be free; and, in exchange for this liberty, I shall impose only one single condition. Your word of honor to submit to it will suffice."

"Speak, sir," I answered. "I suppose this condition is one which a man of honor may accept?"

"Yes, sir; it is this: it is possible that certain events, unforeseen, may oblige me to consign you to your cabins for some hours or some days, as the case may be. As I desire never to use violence, I expect from you, more than all the others, a passive obedience. In thus acting I take all the responsibility: I acquit you entirely, for I make it an impossibility for you to see what ought not to be seen. Do you accept this condition?"

Then things took place on board which, to say the least, were singular, and which ought not to be seen by people who were not placed beyond the pale of social laws. Among the surprises which the future was preparing for me, this might not be the least.

"We accept," I answered; "only I will ask your permission, sir, to address one question to you—one only."

"Speak, sir."

"You said that we should be free on board."

"Entirely."

"I ask you, then, what you mean by this liberty?"

"Just the liberty to go, to come, to see, to observe even, all that passes here—save under rare circumstances—the liberty, in short, which we enjoy ourselves, my companions and I."

It was evident that we did not understand one another.

"Pardon me, sir," I resumed, "but this liberty is only what every prisoner has of pacing his prison. It cannot suffice us."

"It must suffice you, however."

"What! we must renounce forever seeing our country, our friends, our relations again?"

"Yes, sir. But to renounce that unendurable worldly yoke which men believe to be liberty is not perhaps so painful as you think."

"Well," exclaimed Ned Land, "never will I give my word of honor not to try to escape."

"I did not ask you for your word of honor, Master Land," answered the commander coldly.

"Sir," I replied, beginning to get angry in spite of myself, "you abuse your situation toward us; it is cruelty."

"No, sir, it is clemency. You are my prisoners of war. I keep you, when I could, by a word, plunge you into the depths of the ocean. You attacked me. You came to surprise a secret which no man in the world must penetrate—the secret of my whole existence. And you think that I am going to send you back to that world which must know me no more? Never! In retaining you, it is not you whom I guard—it is myself."

These words indicated a resolution taken on the part of the commander against which no arguments would prevail.

"So, sir," I rejoined, "you give us simply the choice between life and death?"

"Simply."

"My friends," I said, "to a question thus put there is nothing to answer. But no word of honor binds us to the master of this vessel."

"None, sir," answered the Unknown.

Then, in a gentler tone, he continued:

"Now, permit me to finish what I have to say to you. I know you, Mr. Aronnax. You and your companions will not, perhaps, have so much to complain of in the chance which has bound you to my fate. You will find among the books which are my favorite study the work which you have published on 'the depths of the sea.' I have often read it. You have carried out your work as far as terrestrial science permitted you. But you do not know all—you have not seen all. Let me tell you then, Professor, that you will not regret the time passed on board my vessel. You are going to visit the land of marvels."

These words of the commander had a great effect upon me. I cannot deny it. My weak point was touched; and I forgot, for a moment, that the contemplation of these sublime subjects was not worth the loss of liberty. Besides, I trusted to the future to decide this grave question. So I contented myself with saying:

"By what name ought I to address you?"

"Sir," replied the commander, "I am nothing to you but Captain Nemo; and you and your companions are nothing to me but the passengers of the *Nautilus*."

Captain Nemo called. A steward appeared. The captain gave him his orders in that strange language which I did not understand. Then, turning to the Canadian and Conseil:

"A repast awaits you in your cabin," he said. "Be so good as to follow this man.

"And now, Mr. Aronnax, our breakfast is ready. Permit me to lead the way."

"I am at your service, Captain."

I followed Captain Nemo; and as soon as I had passed through the door I found myself in a kind of passage lighted by electricity similar to the waist of a ship. After we had proceeded a dozen yards a second door opened before me.

I then entered a dining room, decorated and furnished in severe taste. High oaken sideboards, inlaid with ebony, stood at the two extremities of the room, and upon their shelves glittered china, porcelain, and glass of inestimable value. The plate on the table sparkled in the rays which the luminous ceiling shed around, while the light was tempered and softened by exquisite paintings.

In the center of the room was a table richly laid out. Captain Nemo indicated the place I was to occupy.

The breakfast consisted of a certain number of dishes the contents of which were furnished by the sea alone; and I was ignorant of the nature and mode of preparation of some of them. I acknowledged that they were good, but they had a peculiar flavor, which I easily became accustomed to. These different aliments appeared to me to be rich in phosphorus, and I thought they must have a marine origin.

Captain Nemo looked at me. I asked him no questions, but he guessed my thoughts, and answered of his own accord the questions which I was burning to address to him.

"The greater part of these dishes are unknown to you," he said to me. "However, you may partake of them without fear. They are wholesome and nourishing. For a long time I have renounced the food of the earth, and I am never ill now. My crew, who are healthy, are fed on the same food."

"So," I said, "all these eatables are from the sea?"

"Yes, Professor, the sea supplies all my wants. Sometimes I cast my nets in tow, and I draw them in ready to break. Sometimes I hunt in the midst of this element, which appears to be inaccessible to man, and quarry the game which dwells in my submarine forests. My flocks, like those of Neptune's old shepherds, graze fearlessly in the immense prairies of the ocean. I have a vast property there, which I cultivate myself, and which is always sown by the hand of the Creator of all things."

"I can understand perfectly, sir, that your nets furnish

excellent fish for your table; I can understand also that you hunt aquatic game in your submarine forests; but I cannot understand at all how a particle of meat, no matter how small, can figure in your bill of fare."

"This which you believe to be meat, Professor, is nothing else than filet of turtle. Here are also some dolphins' livers, which you take to be ragout of pork. My cook is a clever fellow, who excels in dressing these various products of the ocean. Taste all these dishes. Here is a preserve of sea cucumber, which a Malay would declare to be unrivaled in the world; here is cream furnished by the cetacea, and sugar from a lichen of the North Sea; and, lastly, permit me to offer you some preserve of anemones, which is equal to that of the most delicious fruits."

I tasted, more from curiosity than as a connoisseur, while Captain Nemo enchanted me with his extraordinary stories. "You like the sea, Captain?"

"Yes; I love it! The sea is everything. It covers seven-tenths of the terrestrial globe. Its breath is pure and healthy. It is an immense desert where man is never lonely, for he feels life stirring on all sides. The sea is only the embodiment of a supernatural and wonderful existence. It is nothing but love and emotion; it is the 'living infinite,' as one of your poets has said. In fact, Professor, Nature manifests herself in it by her three kingdoms—mineral, vegetable, and animal. The sea is the vast reservoir of Nature. The world began with the sea, so to speak; and who knows if it will not end with it? In it is supreme tranquillity. The sea does not belong to despots. Upon its surface men can still exercise unjust laws, fight, tear one another to pieces, and be overwhelmed with earthly horrors. But at thirty feet below its level their reign ceases, their influence is quenched, and their power disappears. Ah! sir, live—live in the bosom of the waters! There only is independence! There I recognize no masters! There I am free!"

Captain Nemo suddenly became silent in the midst of this enthusiasm by which he was quite carried away. For a few moments he paced up and down, much agitated. Then he became more calm, regained his accustomed coldness of expression, and turning toward me said: "Now, Professor, if you wish to go over the *Nautilus,* I am at your service."

Captain Nemo rose. I followed him. A double door, contrived at the back of the dining room, opened, and I entered a room equal in dimensions to that which I had just quitted.

It was a library. High pieces of furniture, of black violet ebony inlaid with brass, supported upon their wide shelves a great number of books uniformly bound. They followed the shape of the room, terminating at the lower part in huge divans covered with brown leather, which were curved, to afford the greatest comfort. Light movable desks, made to slide in and out at will, allowed one to rest one's book while reading. In the center stood an immense table covered with pamphlets, among which were some newspapers, already of old date. The electric light flooded everything; it was shed from four unpolished globes half sunk in the volutes of the ceiling. I looked with real admiration at this room, so ingeniously fitted up, and I could scarcely believe my eyes.

"Captain Nemo," I said to my host, who had just thrown himself on one of the divans, "this is a library which would do honor to more than one of the continental palaces, and I am absolutely astounded when I consider that it can follow you to the bottom of the seas."

"Where could one find greater solitude or silence, Professor?" replied Captain Nemo. "Did your library in the museum afford you such perfect quiet?"

"No, sir; and I must confess that it is a very poor one compared to yours. You must have six or seven thousand volumes here."

"Twelve thousand, Mr. Aronnax. These are the only ties which bind me to the earth. But I had done with the world on the day when my *Nautilus* plunged for the first time beneath the waters. That day I bought my last volumes, my last pamphlets, my last papers, and from that time I wish to think that men no longer think or write. These books, Professor, are at your service. You may use them freely."

I thanked Captain Nemo, and went up to the shelves of the library. Works on science, morals, and literature abounded in every language; but I did not see one single work on political economy; that subject appeared to be strictly proscribed. Strange to say, all these books were irregularly arranged, in whatever language they were written; and this medley proved that the captain of the *Nautilus* must have read indiscriminately the books which he took up by chance.

"Sir," I said to the captain, "I thank you for having placed this library at my disposal. It contains treasures of science, and I shall profit by them."

"This room is not only a library," said Captain Nemo, "it is also a smoking room."

"A smoking room!" I cried. "Then one may smoke on board?"

"Certainly."

"Then, sir, I am forced to believe that you have kept up communication with Havana."

"No," answered the captain. "Accept this cigar, Mr. Aronnax; and, though it does not come from Havana, you will be pleased with it, if you are a connoisseur."

I took the cigar which was offered me; its shape recalled the London brands but seemed to be made of golden leaf. I lighted it at a little brazier, which was supported upon an elegant bronze stem, and drew the first whiffs with the delight of a smoker who has not smoked for two days.

"It is excellent, but it is not tobacco."

"No!" answered the captain, "this tobacco comes neither from Havana nor from the East. It is a kind of seaweed, rich in nicotine, with which the sea provides me, but somewhat sparingly."

At that moment Captain Nemo opened a door which stood opposite to that by which I had entered the library, and I passed into an immense room, splendidly lighted.

It was a vast chamber, 30 feet long, 18 wide, and 15 high. A luminous ceiling, decorated with light arabesques, shed a soft, clear light over all the marvels accumulated in this museum. For it was in fact a museum, in which an intelligent and prodigal hand had gathered all the treasures of nature and art, with the artistic confusion which distinguishes a painter's studio.

Thirty first-rate pictures, uniformly framed, separated by bright drapery, ornamented the walls, which were hung with tapestry of severe design. I saw works of great value, the greater part of which I had admired in the special collections of Europe, and in the exhibitions of paintings.

Some admirable statues in marble and bronze, after the finest antique models, stood upon pedestals in the corners of this magnificent museum. Amazement, as the captain of the *Nautilus* had predicted, had already overcome me.

"Professor," said this strange man, "you must excuse the unceremonious way in which I receive you, and the disorder of this room."

"Sir," I answered, "without seeking to know who you are, I recognize in you an artist."

"An amateur, nothing more, sir. Formerly I loved to collect these beautiful works created by the hand of man. I sought them greedily, and ferreted them out indefatigably, and I have been able to bring together some objects of great value. These are my last souvenirs of that world which is dead to me. In my eyes, your modern artists are already old; they have two or three thousand years of existence; I confound them in my own mind. Masters have no age."

Under elegant glass cases, fixed by copper rivets, were classed and labeled the most precious productions of the sea which had ever been presented to the eye of a naturalist. My delight as a professor may be conceived.

Apart, in separate compartments, were spread out chaplets of pearls of the greatest beauty, which reflected the electric light in little sparks of fire; pink pearls, torn from the pinna marina of the Red Sea; green pearls, yellow, blue, and black pearls, the curious productions of the divers molluscs of every ocean, and certain mussels of the northern seas; lastly, several specimens of inestimable value. Some of these pearls were larger than a pigeon's egg, and were worth millions.

Therefore, to estimate the value of this collection was simply impossible. Captain Nemo must have expended millions in the acquirement of these various specimens, and I was thinking what source he could have drawn from, to have been able thus to gratify his fancy for collecting, when I was interrupted by these words:

"You are examining my shells, Professor? Unquestionably they must be interesting to a naturalist; but for me they have a far greater charm, for I have collected them all with my own hand, and there is not a sea on the face of the globe which has escaped my researches."

"I can understand, Captain, the delight of wandering about in the midst of such riches. You are one of those who have collected their treasures themselves. No museum in Europe possesses such a collection of the produce of the ocean. But if I exhaust all my admiration upon it I shall have none left for the vessel which carries it. I do not wish to pry into your secrets, but I must confess that this *Nautilus,* with the motive power which is confined in it, the contrivances which enable it to work, the powerful agent which propels it, all excite my curiosity to the highest pitch. I see on the walls of this room instruments of whose use I am ignorant."

"You will find these same instruments in my own room, Professor, where I shall have much pleasure in explaining their use to you. But first come and inspect the cabin which is set apart for your own use. You must see how you will be accommodated on board the *Nautilus.*"

I followed Captain Nemo through one of the doors opening from each panel of the great lounge. He conducted me toward the bow, and there I found not a cabin, but an elegant room with a bed, dressing table and several other pieces of excellent furniture.

I could only thank my host.

"Your room adjoins mine," said he, opening a door, "and mine opens into the lounge that we have just quitted."

I entered the captain's cabin: it had a severe, almost a monkish aspect. A small iron bedstead, a table, some toilet articles; the whole lighted by a skylight. No comforts, the strictest necessities only.

Captain Nemo pointed to a seat.

"Be so good as to sit down," he said. I seated myself, and he began to talk.

11. All by Electricity

Sir," said Captain Nemo, showing me the instruments hanging on the walls of his room, "here are the contrivances required for the navigation of the *Nautilus*. Here, as in the lounge, I have them always under my eyes, and they indicate my position and exact direction in the middle of the ocean. Some are known to you, such as the thermometer, which gives the internal temperature of the *Nautilus;* the barometer, which indicates the weight of the air and foretells the changes of the weather; the hygrometer, which marks the dryness of the atmosphere; the storm glass, the contents of which, by decomposing, announce the approach of tempests; the compass, which guides my course; the sextant, which shows the latitude by the altitude of the sun; chronometers, by which I calculate the longitude; and glasses for day and night, which I use to examine the points of the horizon when the *Nautilus* rises to the surface of the waves."

"These are the usual nautical instruments," I replied,

"and I know their use. But these others, no doubt, suit the particular requirements of the *Nautilus*. This dial with movable needle is a manometer, is it not?"

"It is actually a manometer. But by communication with the water, whose external pressure it indicates, it gives our depth at the same time."

"And these other instruments, the use of which I cannot guess?"

"Professor, I ought to give you some explanations. Will you be kind enough to listen to me?"

He was silent for a few moments, then he said:

"There is a powerful agent, obedient, rapid, easy, which conforms to every use, and reigns supreme on board my vessel. Everything is done by means of it. It lights, warms it, and is the soul of my mechanical apparatus. This agent is electricity."

"Electricity?" I cried in surprise.

"Yes, sir."

"Nevertheless, Captain, your ship possesses an extreme rapidity of movement which does not suggest electrical power. So far the dynamic force of electricity has been utilized to produce only a small amount of energy."

"Professor," said Captain Nemo, "my method of producing electricity is not the usual one employed. You know what sea water is composed of. A thousand grams contain 96.5 per cent water and about 2.66 per cent sodium chloride; then, in a smaller quantity, chlorides of magnesium and potassium, magnesium bromide, magnesium sulphate, and sulphate and carbonate of lime. You see, then, that sodium chloride forms a large part of it. So it is this sodium that I extract from the sea water, and use as my basic ingredient. I owe all to the ocean; it produces electricity and electricity gives heat, light, motion, and, in a word, life to the *Nautilus*."

"But not the air you breathe?"

"Oh! I could manufacture the air necessary for my consumption, but it is useless, because I go up to the surface of the water when I please. However, if electricity does not furnish me with air to breathe, it works at least the powerful pumps that are stored in spacious reservoirs, and which enable me to prolong at need, and as long as I will, my stay in the depths of the sea. It gives a uniform and unintermittent light, which the sun does not. Now look at this clock; it is electrical, and goes with a regularity that defies the best chronometers. I have divided it into twenty-four hours, like the Italian clocks, because for me there is neither night nor day, sun nor moon, but only that factitious light that I take with me to the bottom of the sea. You see that it is now just ten o'clock in the morning."

"Exactly."

"Another application of electricity. This dial hanging in front of us indicates the speed of the *Nautilus*. An electric thread connects it with the propeller, and the needle indicates the real speed. We are now cruising at a uniform speed of 15 knots."

"It is marvelous! And I see, Captain, you were right to make use of this agent that takes the place of wind, water, and steam."

"We have not finished, Mr. Aronnax," said Captain Nemo, rising. "If you will allow me, we will examine the stern of the *Nautilus*."

I was now familiar with the anterior part of this submarine boat. Here is the exact division, starting from the ship's prow: the dining room, 15 feet, separated from the library by a watertight partition; the library, 15 feet long; the huge lounge, 30 feet, separated by a second watertight partition from the captain's room, 15 feet in length; mine, 7½ feet; and, lastly, a reservoir of air, 22½ feet, that extended to the bows. Total length, 105 feet. The partitions had doors that were shut hermetically by means of a rubber seal, and they insured the safety of the *Nautilus* in case of a leak.

I followed Captain Nemo through the waist, to the center of the vessel. There, a sort of well opened between the two partitions. An iron ladder, fastened with an iron hook to the partition, led to the upper end. I asked the captain what the ladder was used for.

"It leads to a small boat, a pinnace," he said.

"What! Do you have a pinnace?" I exclaimed in surprise.

"Of course; an excellent vessel, light and insubmersible, that serves either as a fishing or as a pleasure boat."

"But then, when you wish to embark, you are obliged to come to the surface of the water?"

"Not at all. This boat is attached to the upper part of the hull of the *Nautilus,* and is stored in a cavity made for it. It is decked, quite watertight, and held together by solid bolts. This ladder leads to a manhole made in the hull of the *Nautilus* that corresponds with a similar hole made in the side of the boat. By this double opening I get into the pinnace. The crew shuts the opening in the *Nautilus;* I shut the other by means of screw pressure. I undo the bolts and the pinnace goes up to the surface of the sea with lightning rapidity. I then open the panel of the bridge, carefully shut till then; I mast my boat, hoist my sail, take my oars and I'm off."

"But how do you get back on board?"

"I do not come back, Mr. Aronnax; the *Nautilus* comes to me."

"By your orders?"

"By my orders. An electric thread connects us. I telegraph to it, and that is enough."

"Really," I said, astonished at these marvels, "nothing could be more ingenious."

After having passed by the cage of the staircase that led to the platform I saw a cabin about six feet long in which Conseil and Ned Land, enchanted with their repast, were eating avidly. Beyond them a door opened into a 10-foot kitchen situated between the large storerooms. There electricity, better than gas itself, did all the cooking. Electric wires, connected to platinum sponges under the stoves, produced a regular heat that was evenly distributed. Electricity also heated a distilling apparatus which, by evaporation, furnished excellent drinking water. Near this kitchen was a bathroom that furnished hot and cold water.

Beyond the kitchen were the crew's quarters, 16 feet in length. But the door was shut and I could not see its arrangement, which might have given me an idea of the number of men employed on board the *Nautilus*.

At the bottom was a fourth partition that separated this area from the engine room. A door opened and I found myself in the compartment where Captain Nemo—certainly an engineer of a very high order—had arranged his machinery of locomotion. This engine room, well-lighted, was at least 65 feet in length. It was divided into two parts: the first contained the materials for producing electricity, and the second the machinery that connected it with the propeller. I examined it all with great interest, for I was eager to understand the workings of the *Nautilus*.

"You see," said the captain, "I use Bunsen's contrivances, not Ruhmkorff's. Those would not have been powerful enough. Bunsen's are fewer in number, but strong and large, which experience proves to be the best. The electricity produced passes forward, where it works, by electromagnets of great size, on a system of levers and cog-wheels that transmit the movement to the propeller shaft. This propeller, the diameter of which is nineteen feet, and the thread twenty-three feet, performs about twenty revolutions in a second."

"And you get then?"

"A speed of 50 knots."

"I have seen the *Nautilus* maneuver before the *Abraham Lincoln,* and I have a good idea of its speed. But I am also considering where it goes. It must be maneuverable to the right, to the left, above, below. How do you get to great depths, where there is an increasing resistance rated by hundreds of atmospheres? How do you return to the surface of the ocean? And how do you maintain yourselves at the optimum depth? Am I asking too much?"

"Not at all, Professor," replied the captain, with some hesitation, "since you may never leave this submarine boat. Come into the lounge; it is our usual study, and there you will learn all you want to know about the *Nautilus.*"

12. Some Figures

A MOMENT afterward we were seated on a divan in the lounge, smoking. The captain showed me a sketch that gave the plan, section and elevation of the *Nautilus*. Then he began his description in these words:

"Here, Mr. Aronnax, are the several dimensions of the boat you are in. It is an elongated cylinder with conical ends. It is very like a cigar in shape, a shape already adopted in London in several constructions of the same sort. The length of this cylinder, from stem to stern, is exactly 230 feet, and its maximum breadth is 26 feet. It is not built quite like your long-voyage steamers, but its lines are sufficiently long and its curves prolonged enough, to allow the water to slide off easily and oppose no obstacle to its passage. These two dimensions enable you to obtain the approximate cubic area of the *Nautilus*. Its volume measures about 100,000 cubic feet, taking into account its elliptical shape; that is to say, when completely immersed it displaces that amount of water, or weighs about 3,100 tons.

"When I made the plans for this submarine vessel I meant that nine-tenths should be submerged: consequently it ought only to displace nine-tenths of its bulk; that is to say, only to weigh that number of tons. I could not, therefore, exceed that weight in constructing it on the aforesaid dimensions.

"The *Nautilus* is composed of two hulls, one inside, the other outside, joined by T-shaped irons, which render it very strong. Indeed, owing to this cellular arrangement it resists like a block, as if it were solid. Its sides cannot yield;

it coheres spontaneously and not by the tightness of its rivets; and its perfect union of the materials enables it to defy the roughest seas.

"These two hulls are composed of steel plates whose density is from seven- to eight-tenths that of water. The first is not less than two inches and a half thick and weighs 394 tons. The second envelope, the keel, 20 inches high and 10 thick, weighs only 62 tons. The engine, the ballast, the various mechanical accessories and apparatus appendages, the partitions and bulkheads, supplies, books, furnishings, crew, etc., are figured at a total of approximately 2,434 tons. Do you follow all this?"

"I do."

"Then, when the *Nautilus* is afloat under these circumstances, one-tenth is out of the water. Now, if I have made reservoirs of a size equal to this tenth, or capable of holding 310 tons, and if I fill them with water, the boat, weighing then 3,100 tons, will be completey immersed. That is just what happens, Professor. These reservoirs are in the lower part of the *Nautilus*. I turn on taps and they fill, and the vessel sinks from the surface."

"Well, Captain, but now we come to the real difficulty. I can understand your rising to the surface; but, diving below the surface, does not your submarine contrivance encounter a pressure, and consequently undergo an upward thrust of one atmosphere for every 30 feet of water, just about 15 pounds per square inch?"

"Just so, sir."

"Then, unless you quite fill the *Nautilus,* I do not see how you can draw it down to those depths."

"Professor, you must not confound statics with dynamics

or you will be exposed to grave errors. There is very little labor spent in attaining the lower regions of the ocean, for all bodies have a tendency to sink. When I wanted to find out the necessary increase of weight required to sink the *Nautilus,* I had only to calculate the reduction of volume that sea water acquires according to the depth."

"That is evident."

"Now, if water is not absolutely incompressible, it is at least capable of very slight compression. Indeed, after the most recent calculations this reduction is only .000436 of an atmosphere for each 30 feet of depth. If we want to sink 3,000 feet, I keep in mind the reduction of bulk under a pressure equal to that of a column of water of 1,000 feet. The calculation is easily verified. Now, I have supplementary reservoirs capable of holding a hundred tons. Therefore I can sink to a considerable depth. When I wish to rise to the level of the sea, I only let off the water, and empty all the reservoirs if I want the *Nautilus* to emerge from the tenth part of her total capacity."

I had nothing to object to these reasonings.

"I admit your calculations, Captain," I replied; "I should be wrong to dispute them since daily experience confirms them; but I foresee a real difficulty in the way."

"What, sir?"

"When you are about 1,000 feet deep, the walls of the *Nautilus* bear a pressure of 100 atmospheres. If, then, just now you were to empty the supplementary reservoirs, to lighten the vessel, and to go up to the surface, the pumps must overcome the pressure of 100 atmospheres, which is 1,500 pounds per square inch. From that a power ——"

"That electricity alone can give," said the captain hastily. "I repeat, sir, that the dynamic power of my engines is almost infinite. The pumps of the *Nautilus* have an enormous power, as you must have observed when their jets of water burst like a torrent upon the *Abraham Lincoln*. Besides, I use subsidiary reservoirs only to attain a mean depth of 750 to 1,000 fathoms, and that with a view of managing my machines. Also, when I have a mind to visit the depths of the ocean five or six miles below the surface, I make use of slower but not less infallible means."

"What are they, Captain?"

"That involves my telling you how the *Nautilus* is worked."

"I am impatient to learn."

"To steer this boat to starboard or port, to turn, in a word, following a horizontal plan, I use an ordinary rudder fixed on the back of the stern-post, and with one wheel and some tackle to steer by. But I can also make the *Nautilus* rise and sink, and sink and rise in a vertical movement by means of two inclined planes or side fins, fastened to the sides of the vessel, opposite the center of flotation. These fins move in every direction and are worked by powerful levers from the interior. If the fins are kept parallel with the boat, it moves horizontally. If slanted, the *Nautilus,* according to their inclination, and by propeller power, either sinks diagonally or rises diagonally as it suits me. If I wish to rise faster, I ship the propeller, and the pressure of the water causes the *Nautilus* to rise vertically like a balloon filled with hydrogen."

"Bravo, Captain! But how can the steersman follow the route under the water?"

"The steersman is in a glazed box that is raised above the hull of the *Nautilus* and furnished with lenses."

"Are these lenses capable of resisting such pressure?"

"Perfectly. Glass, which breaks at a blow is, nevertheless, capable of offering considerable resistance. During some experiments of fishing by electric light in 1864 in the northern seas, we saw plates less than a third of an inch thick resist a pressure of 16 atmospheres. Now, the glass that I use is not less than 30 times thicker."

"Granted. But, after all, in order to see, the light must exceed the darkness, and in the midst of the darkness in the water, how can you see?"

"Behind the steersman's cage is a powerful electric reflector, the rays from which light up the sea for half a mile in front."

"Ah! bravo, bravo, Captain! Now I can account for this phosphorescence in the supposed narwhal that puzzled us so. I now ask you if the collision of the *Nautilus* and of the *Scotia,* that has made such a stir, was the result of a chance encounter?"

"Quite accidental, sir. I was sailing only one fathom below the surface of the water when the shock came. It had no fatal result."

"No, sir. But now, about your encounter with the *Abraham Lincoln?*"

"Professor, I am sorry, it was one of the best vessels in the American Navy; but it attacked me and I was bound to defend myself. I contented myself, however, with putting the frigate out of combat; she will not have any difficulty in getting repaired at the next port."

"Ah, Commander, your *Nautilus* is certainly a marvelous boat."

"Yes, Professor; and I love it as if it were part of myself.

If danger threatens one of your vessels on the ocean, the first impression is the feeling of an abyss above and below. On the *Nautilus* men's hearts never fail them. No defects to be afraid of, for the double shell is as firm as iron; no rigging to attend to; no sails for the wind to carry away; no boilers to burst; no fire to fear, for the vessel is made of iron, not of wood; no coal to run short, for electricity is the only mechanical agent; no collision to fear, for it navigates alone in deep water; no tempest to brave, for when it dives below the water it reaches absolute tranquillity. This, sir, is the perfection of vessels! And if it is true that the engineer has more confidence in the vessel than the builder, and the builder than the captain himself, you understand the trust I repose in my *Nautilus;* for I am at once captain, builder, and engineer."

"But how could you construct this wonderful *Nautilus* in secret?"

"Each separate portion, Mr. Aronnax, was brought from different parts of the globe."

"But these parts had to be put together and arranged?"

"Professor, I had set up my workshops upon a desert island in the ocean. There my workmen, that is to say, the brave men that I instructed and educated, and myself have put together our *Nautilus*. Then, when the work was finished, fire destroyed all trace of our proceedings on this island that I could have jumped over if I had liked."

"Then the cost of this vessel is great?"

"Mr. Aronnax, an iron vessel costs $225 per ton. Now the *Nautilus* weighed 3,100. It came therefore to $697,500, with $400,000 more for fitting it up—over $1,500,000 including the works of art and the collections it contains."

"One last question, Captain Nemo."

"Ask it, Professor."

"You are rich?"

"Immensely rich, sir; and I could, without missing it, pay the national debt of France."

I stared at the singular person who spoke thus. Was he playing upon my credulity? Only the future could tell.

13. The Black River

THAT PORTION of the earth's surface which is covered by water is estimated at upward of 94,000,000 acres. This fluid mass comprises 2,250,000,000 cubic miles, which would form a spherical body, the weight of which would be three quintillion tons. To comprehend the meaning of these figures, it is necessary to observe that a quintillion is to a billion as a billion is to unity; in other words, there are as many billions in a quintillion as there are units in a billion. This mass of fluid is equal to about the quantity of water which would be discharged by all the rivers of the earth in 40,000 years.

During the geological epochs the ocean originally prevailed everywhere. Then by degrees, in the Silurian period, mountains appeared, islands emerged, then disappeared in partial deluges, reappeared, became settled, formed continents, till at length the earth became set geographically as we see in the present day. The solid had wrested from the liquid over 37,657,000 square miles.

The shape of continents allows us to divide the waters into five great portions: the Arctic, the Antarctic, the Indian, the Atlantic, and the Pacific Oceans.

The Pacific Ocean extends from north to south between the two polar circles, and from east to west between Asia and America, over an extent of 145 degrees longitude. It is the quietest of seas; its currents are broad and slow; it has medium tides and abundant rain. Such was the ocean that my fate destined me first to travel over under these strange conditions.

"Sir," said Captain Nemo, "we will, if you please, take our bearings and fix the starting point of this voyage. It is 11:45 A.M. I will go up again to the surface."

The captain pressed an electric clock three times. The pumps began to drive the water from the tanks; the needle of the manometer marked by a different pressure the ascent of the *Nautilus,* then it stopped.

"We have surfaced," said the captain.

I went to the central staircase which opened onto the platform, climbed the iron steps, and found myself on the upper part of the *Nautilus.*

The platform was only three feet out of water. Both ends of the *Nautilus* were spindle shaped like a cigar. I noticed that its iron plates, slightly overlapping, resembled the shell which sheathes the bodies of our large terrestrial reptiles. It explained to me how natural it was, in spite of all glasses, that this boat should have been taken for a marine animal.

Toward the middle of the platform the longboat, half buried in the hull of the vessel, formed a slight excrescence. Fore and aft rose two cages of medium height with inclined sides and partly enclosed by thick lenticular glasses: one for the steersman who directed the *Nautilus,* the other containing a brilliant lantern.

The sea was beautiful, the sky pure. We could scarcely feel the broad undulations of the ocean. A light breeze from

the east rippled the surface of the waters. The horizon, free
from fog, made observation easy. Nothing was in sight. Not
an island. A vast, watery desert.

Captain Nemo, by the help of his sextant, took the altitude of the sun, to determine our latitude. He waited for
some moments till the disc touched the horizon. While taking observations not a muscle moved; the instrument might
have been held by a hand of marble.

"Twelve o'clock, sir," he said. "When you like ———"

I cast a last look upon the sea and descended to the
lounge.

"And now, sir, I leave you to your studies," added the
captain; "our course is ENE, our depth is twenty-six fathoms. Here are maps on a large scale by which you may
follow it. The lounge is at your disposal, and, with your
permission, I will retire." Captain Nemo bowed, and I remained alone, lost in thoughts all bearing on the commander of the *Nautilus*.

For a whole hour I was deep in these reflections, seeking
to pierce this mystery so interesting to me. Then my eyes
fell upon the vast planisphere spread upon the table, and I
placed my finger on the very spot where the given latitude
and longitude crossed.

The sea has its large rivers like the continents. They are
special currents known by their temperature and their
color. The most remarkable of these is known by the name
of the Gulf Stream. Science has determined there are five
principal currents: one in the north Atlantic, a second in
the south, a third in the north Pacific, a fourth in the south,
and a fifth in the southern Indian Ocean. It is even probable
that a sixth current existed at one time or another in the

northern Indian Ocean, when the Caspian and Aral Seas formed but one vast sheet of water.

At our point indicated on the planisphere one of these currents was rolling, the Kuro-Scivo of the Japanese, or the Black River. Leaving the Gulf of Bengal, where it is warmed by the perpendicular rays of a tropical sun, this current crosses the Straits of Malacca along the coast of Asia, turns into the north Pacific to the Aleutian Islands, carrying with it trunks of camphor trees and other similar debris, and tingeing the waves of the ocean with the pure indigo of its warm water. It was this current that the *Nautilus* was to follow. I followed it on the planisphere, saw it lose itself in the vastness of the Pacific, and felt myself drawn with it, when Ned Land and Conseil appeared at the door of the lounge.

My two brave companions were thunderstruck at the wonders spread before them.

"Where are we, where are we?" exclaimed the Canadian. "In the museum at Quebec?"

"My friends," I answered, making a sign for them to enter, "you are not in Canada, but on board the *Nautilus,* 150 feet below the level of the sea."

"Mr. Aronnax," said Ned Land, "can you tell me how many men there are on board? Ten, twenty, fifty, a hundred?"

"I cannot answer you, Mr. Land; it is better to abandon for a time all idea of seizing the *Nautilus* or escaping from it. This ship is a masterpiece of modern ingenuity and I should be sorry not to have seen it. Many people would accept the situation forced upon us, if only to move among such wonders. So be quiet, let us observe and see what passes around us."

"See!" exclaimed the harpooner. "But we can see nothing in this iron prison! We are walking—we are sailing—blindly."

Ned Land had scarcely pronounced these words when all was suddenly darkness. The luminous ceiling was gone, so rapidly that my eyes burned.

We remained without stirring, not knowing what surprise awaited us, whether agreeable or disagreeable. A sliding noise was heard: one would have said that panels were working at the sides of the *Nautilus*.

"It is the end of the end!" said Ned Land.

Suddenly light broke at each side of the lounge through two oblong openings. The liquid mass appeared vividly lit up by an electric gleam. Two crystal plates separated us from the sea. At first I trembled at the thought that this frail partition might break, but strong bands of copper bound them, giving an almost infinite power of resistance.

The sea was distinctly visible for a mile all around the *Nautilus*. What a spectacle! What pen can describe it? Who could paint the effects of the light through those transparent sheets of water, and the softness of the successive gradations from the lower to the superior strata of the ocean?

We know the transparency of the sea and that its clarity is far beyond that of rock water. The mineral and organic substances which it holds in suspension heighten its transparency. In certain parts of the ocean, at the Antilles, for example, a bed of sand can be seen with surprising clearness under nearly 75 fathoms of water. The solar rays seem to penetrate to a depth of 150 fathoms. But in this middle depth traveled over by the *Nautilus,* the electric brightness was produced even in the bosom of the sea. It was not luminous water, but liquid light.

On each side a window opened into this unexplored abyss. The obscurity of the lounge showed to advantage the brightness outside, and we looked out as if this pure crystal had been the glass of an immense aquarium.

"You wished to see, friend Ned; well, you see now."

"Curious! Curious!" muttered the Canadian, who, forgetting his ill-temper, seemed to submit to some irresistible attraction. "One would come farther than this to admire such a sight!"

"Ah!" thought I to myself, "I understand the life of our captain. He has made a world apart for himself in which he treasures all his greatest wonders."

For two whole hours an aquatic army escorted the *Nautilus*. During their games, while they rivaled each other in beauty, brightness and velocity, I distinguished the green labre; the banded mullet marked by a double line of black; the round-tailed goby, white with violet spots on the back; the Japanese scombrus, a beautiful mackerel of these seas, with a blue body and silvery head; the brilliant azurors, whose name alone defies description; some banded spares, with variegated fins of blue and yellow; the woodcocks of the seas, some specimens of which are three feet long; Japanese salamanders; spider lampreys, serpents six feet long, with eyes small and lively, and huge mouths bristling with teeth; and many other species.

Our imagination was at a peak; interjections followed quickly on each other. Ned named the fish and Conseil classed them. I was in ecstasies with the vivacity of their movements and the beauty of their forms. Never had it been given to me to surprise these animals, alive and at liberty, in their natural element. I will not mention all the varieties which passed before my dazzled eyes, the entire collection

of the seas of China and Japan. These fish were more
numerous than the birds of the air, attracted, no doubt, by
the brilliant focus of the electric light.

Suddenly the light came on again in the lounge; the iron
panels closed and the enchanting vision disappeared. But
for a long time I dreamed on, till my eyes fell on the instruments hanging on the partition. The compass still
showed the course to be ENE, the manometer indicated a
pressure of five atmospheres, equivalent to a depth of 25
fathoms, and the electric log gave a speed of 15 knots. I
expected Captain Nemo, but he did not appear. The clock
marked the hour of five.

Ned Land and Conseil returned to their cabin, and I
retired to my chamber. My dinner was ready. It was composed of turtle soup made of the most delicate hawksbills,
of a surmullet served with puff paste (the liver of which,
prepared by itself, was most delicious), and filets of the
emperor holocanthus, whose savor seemed to me superior
even to salmon.

I passed the evening reading, writing and thinking. Then
sleep overpowered me, and I stretched myself on my couch
of zostera, and slept profoundly, while the *Nautilus* glided
rapidly through the current of the Black River.

14. A Note of Invitation

THE NEXT day, November 9, I awoke after a long sleep of
12 hours. Conseil came, according to custom, to know
"how I passed the night," and to offer his services. He had
left his friend the Canadian sleeping like a man who had

never done anything else all his life. I let the worthy fellow chatter as he pleased, without caring to answer him. I was preoccupied by the absence of the captain during our sitting of the day before, and hoping to see him today.

As soon as I was dressed I went into the lounge. It was deserted. I plunged into the study of the shell treasures hidden behind the glasses.

The whole day passed without my being honored by a visit from Captain Nemo. The panels of the lounge did not open. Perhaps they did not wish us to tire of these beautiful things.

The course of the *Nautilus* was ENE, her speed 12 knots, the depth below the surface between 25 and 30 fathoms.

The next day, the 10th of November, the same desertion, the same solitude. I did not see one of the ship's crew. Ned and Conseil spent the greater part of the day with me. They were astonished at the puzzling absence of the captain. Was this singular man ill? Had he altered his intentions with regard to us?

After all, as Conseil said, we enjoyed perfect liberty; we were delicately and abundantly fed. Our host kept to his terms of the treaty. We could not complain, and indeed the singularity of our fate reserved such wonderful compensation for us that we had no just complaint.

That day I commenced the journal of these adventures which has enabled me to relate them with more scrupulous exactitude and minute detail.

The 11th of November, early in the morning. The fresh air spreading over the interior of the *Nautilus* told me that we had come to the surface of the ocean to renew our

supply of oxygen. I directed my steps to the central staircase, and mounted the platform.

It was six o'clock. The weather was cloudy, the sea gray
but calm, scarcely a billow. Would Captain Nemo, whom I
hoped to meet, be there? I saw no one but the steersman in
his glass cage. Seated upon the projection formed by the
hull of the pinnace, I inhaled the salt breeze with delight.

By degrees the fog disappeared under the action of the
sun's rays, the sun rose from behind the eastern and horizon, the sea flamed under it. The scattered clouds showed
lively tints of beautiful colors, and numerous "mare's tails,"
which betokened wind for that day. But what was wind to
this *Nautilus,* which tempests could not disturb!

I was admiring this joyous rising of the sun, so gay, and
so life-giving, when I heard steps approaching the platform.
I was prepared to salute Captain Nemo, but it was his second, whom I had already seen on the captain's first visit,
who appeared. He advanced on the platform, not seeming
to see me. With his powerful glass to his eye, he scanned
every point of the horizon with great attention. Then he
approached the panel and pronounced a sentence in exactly
these terms. I have remembered the phrase, for every morning it was repeated under exactly the same conditions. It
was thus worded:

"Nautron respoc lorni virch."

What it meant I could not say.

After these words the second went below. I thought that
the *Nautilus* would now submerge, so I returned to my
chamber.

Five days sped thus, without any change in our situation.
Every morning I mounted the platform. The same phrase

was pronounced by the same individual. But Captain Nemo did not appear.

I had made up my mind that I should never see him again, when on the 16th of November, on returning to my room with Ned and Conseil, I found on my table a note addressed to me. I opened it impatiently. It was written in a bold clear hand, the characters rather pointed, recalling the German type. The note was worded as follows:

To Professor Aronnax,
     On board the *Nautilus*.

                                        November 16, 1867.

Captain Nemo invites Professor Aronnax to a hunting party, which will take place tomorrow morning in the forests of the Island of Crespo. He hopes that nothing will prevent the professor from being present, and will with pleasure see him joined by his companions.

                              Captain Nemo,
                         Commander of the *Nautilus*.

"A hunt!" exclaimed Ned.

"And in the forests of the Island of Crespo!" added Conseil.

"Oh! then the gentleman is going on terra firma?" replied Ned Land.

"That seems to me to be clearly indicated," said I, reading the letter once more.

"Well, we must accept," said the Canadian. "But once more on dry ground, we shall know what to do. Indeed, I shall not be sorry to eat a piece of fresh venison."

Without seeking to reconcile Captain Nemo's manifest

aversion to islands and continents, and his invitation to
hunt in a forest, I contented myself with replying:

"Let us first see where the Island of Crespo is."

I consulted the planisphere, and in 32° 40′ N. lat. and
157° 50′ W. long., I found a small island, recognized in
1801 by Captain Crespo, and marked in the ancient Spanish maps as Rocca de la Plata, the meaning of which is The
Silver Rock. We were then about 1,800 miles from our
starting point, and the course of the *Nautilus,* a little
changed, was bringing it back toward the southeast.

I showed this little rock, lost in the midst of the North
Pacific, to my companions.

"If Captain Nemo does sometimes go on dry ground," I
said, "he at least chooses desert islands."

Ned Land shrugged his shoulders without speaking, and
he and Conseil left me.

After supper, which was served by the steward, mute and
impassive, I went to bed.

On awakening the next morning, I felt that the *Nautilus*
was perfectly still. I dressed quickly and entered the lounge.

Captain Nemo was there, waiting for me. He rose,
bowed, and asked me if it was convenient for me to accompany him. As he made no allusion to his absence during
the past eight days I did not mention it, and simply answered that my companions and myself were ready to follow him.

We entered the dining room, where breakfast was served.

"Mr. Aronnax," said the captain, "pray share my breakfast without ceremony; we will chat as we eat. For though I
promised you a walk in the forest, I do not undertake to
find hotels there. So breakfast as a man who will most likely
not have his dinner till very late."

I did honor to the repast. It was composed of several kinds of fish, and slices of sea cucumber, and different sorts of seaweed. Our drink consisted of pure water, to which the captain added some drops of a fermented liquor extracted by the Kamchatkian method from a seaweed called *Rhodomenia palmata*. At first, Captain Nemo ate without saying a word. Then he began:

"Sir, when I proposed to you to hunt in my submarine forest of Crespo you evidently thought me mad. Sir, you should never judge lightly of any man."

"But, Captain, believe me——"

"Be kind enough to listen and you will then see whether you have any cause to accuse me of folly and contradiction."

"I listen."

"You know as well as I do, Professor, that man can live under water, providing he carries with him a sufficient supply of air. In submarine operations the workman, clad in an impervious dress, with his head in a metal helmet, receives air from above by means of forcing pumps and regulators."

"That is a diving apparatus," said I.

"Just so, but under these conditions the man is not at liberty; he is attached to the pump which sends him air through a rubber tube, and if we were obliged to be thus held to the *Nautilus,* we could not go far."

"And the means of getting free?" I asked.

"It is to use the Rouquayrol apparatus, invented by two of your own countrymen, which I have brought to perfection for my own use, and which will allow you to risk yourself under these new physiological conditions without any organ whatever suffering. It consists of a reservoir of thick iron plates in which I store the air under a pressure of 50 atmospheres. This reservoir is fixed on the back by means of braces, like a soldier's knapsack. Its upper part forms a box in which the air is kept by means of a bellows, and therefore cannot escape unless at its normal tension. In the Rouquay-rol apparatus such as we use, two rubber pipes leave this box and join a sort of tent which holds the nose and mouth; one is to introduce fresh air, the other to let out the foul, and the tongue closes one or the other according to the wants of the respirator. But I, in encountering great pressures at the bottom of the sea, was obliged to shut my head, like that of a diver, in a ball of copper; and it is to this ball of copper that the two pipes, the inspirator and the expira-tor, open."

"Perfectly, Captain Nemo; but the air that you carry with you must soon be used; when it contains only 15 per cent oxygen it is no longer fit to breathe."

"Right! But I told you, Mr. Aronnax, that the pumps of the *Nautilus* allow me to store the air under considerable pressure, and on those conditions the reservoir of the ap-paratus can furnish air for nine or ten hours."

"I have no further objections to make," I answered. "I will only ask you one thing, Captain—how can you light your road at the bottom of the sea?"

"With the Ruhmkorff apparatus, Mr. Aronnax; one is carried on the back, the other is fastened to the waist. It is composed of a Bunsen battery which I do not work with bichromate of potash, but with sodium. A wire is intro-duced which collects the electricity produced and directs it toward a particularly-made lantern. In this lantern is a spiral glass which contains a small quantity of carbonic gas. When the apparatus is at work this gas becomes luminous, giving out a white and continuous light. Thus provided, I can breathe and I can see."

"Captain Nemo, to all my objections you make such crushing answers that I dare no longer doubt. But if I am forced to admire the Rouquayrol and Ruhmkorff inventions, I must be allowed some reservations with regard to the gun I am to carry."

"But it is not a gun for powder," answered the captain.

"Then it is an air gun."

"Doubtless! How would you have me manufacture gunpowder on board without either saltpeter, sulphur, or charcoal?"

"Besides," I added, "to fire under water in a medium 855 times denser than the air we must conquer very considerable resistance."

"That would be no difficulty. There exist guns, according to Fulton, perfected in England by Philip Coles and Burley, in France by Furcy, and in Italy by Landi, which are furnished with a peculiar system of closing out water, which can fire under these conditions. But I repeat, having no powder, I use air under great pressure, which the pumps of the *Nautilus* furnish abundantly."

"But this air must be rapidly used?"

"Well, have I not my Rouquayrol reservoir, which can furnish it at need? A tap is all that is required. Besides, Mr. Aronnax, you must see yourself that, during our submarine hunt we can spend but little air and but few balls."

"But it seems to me that in this twilight, and in the midst of this fluid, which is very dense compared with the atmosphere, shots could not go far, nor easily prove mortal."

"Sir, on the contrary, with this gun every blow is mortal;

and, however lightly the animal is touched, it falls as if struck by a thunderbolt."

"Why?"

"Because the balls sent by this gun are not ordinary balls, but little cases of glass. These glass cases are covered with a case of steel and weighted with a pellet of lead; they are real Leyden bottles into which the electricity is forced to a very high tension. With the slightest shock they are discharged, and the animal, however strong it may be, falls dead. I must tell you that these cases are size number four, and that the charge for an ordinary gun would be ten."

"I will argue no longer," I replied, rising from the table. "I have nothing left me but to take my gun. At all events, I will go where you go."

Captain Nemo then led me aft; and in passing before Ned's and Conseil's cabin I called my two companions, who followed promptly. We then came to a cell near the machinery room, where we dressed for our undersea explorations.

15. A Walk on the Bottom of the Sea

This cell was, to speak correctly, the arsenal and wardrobe of the *Nautilus*. A dozen diving suits hung from the partition awaiting our use.

Ned Land, on seeing them, showed evident repugnance to dress himself in one.

"But, my worthy Ned, the forests of the Island of Crespo are nothing but submarine forests."

"Good!" said the disappointed harpooner, who saw his

dreams of fresh meat fade away. "And you, Mr. Aronnax, are you going to dress yourself in those clothes?"

"There is no alternative, Master Ned."

"As you please, sir," replied the harpooner, shrugging his shoulders; "but, as for me, unless I am forced, I will never get into one."

"No one will force you, Master Ned," said Captain Nemo.

"Is Conseil going to risk it?" asked Ned.

"I follow Monsieur wherever he goes," replied Conseil.

At the captain's call two of the ship's crew came to help us dress in these heavy and impervious clothes made of rubber without seams and constructed expressly to resist considerable pressure. One would have thought it a suit of armor, both supple and resisting. This suit formed trousers and waistcoat. The trousers were finished off with thick boots weighted with heavy leaden soles. The texture of the waistcoat was held together by bands of copper, which crossed the chest, protecting it from the great pressure of the water, and leaving the lungs free to act; the sleeves ended in gloves, which in no way restrained the movement of the hands. There was a vast difference noticeable between these consummate outfits and the old cork breastplates, jackets and other contrivances so highly favored in previous decades.

Captain Nemo and one of his companions (a sort of Hercules, who must have possessed great strength), Conseil and myself were soon enveloped in the clothes. There remained only the matter of enclosing our heads in metal helmets. But before proceeding to this operation, I asked the captain's permission to examine the guns.

One of the *Nautilus* men gave me a simple gun, the butt end of which, made of steel and hollow in the center, was rather large. It served as a reservoir for compressed air which a valve, worked by a spring, allowed to escape into a metal tube. A box of projectiles in a groove in the thickness of the butt end contained about 20 of these electric balls, which, by means of a spring, were forced into the barrel of the gun. As soon as one shot was fired, another was ready.

"Captain Nemo," I said, "this arm is perfect, and easily handled: I only ask to be allowed to try it. But how do we reach the bottom of the sea?"

"At this moment, Professor, the *Nautilus* is resting at five fathoms, and we have nothing to do but to start."

"But how shall we get off?"

"You shall see."

Captain Nemo thrust his head into the helmet, Conseil and I did the same, not without hearing an ironical "Good sport!" from the Canadian. The upper part of our uniform terminated in a copper collar upon which was screwed the metal helmet. Three holes, protected by thick glass, allowed us to see in all directions by simply turning our heads. As soon as it was in position, the Rouquayrol apparatus on our backs began to act; and I found that I could breathe with ease.

With the Ruhmkorff lamp hanging from my belt and the gun in my hand, I was ready to set out. But to tell the truth, imprisoned in these heavy garments and glued to the deck by my leaden soles, it was impossible for me to take a step.

But this state of things was provided for. I felt myself being pushed into a little room near the wardrobe room. My companions followed, towed along in the same way. I heard a watertight door, furnished with stopper plates, close upon us, and we were in profound darkness.

After some minutes a loud hissing was heard. I felt the cold mount from my feet to my chest. Evidently from some part of the vessel they had, by means of a tap, given entrance to the water, which was invading us, and with which the room was soon filled. A second door cut in the side of the *Nautilus* then opened. We saw a faint light. In another instant our feet trod the bottom of the sea.

And now, how can I retrace the impression left upon me by that walk under the waters? Words are impotent to relate such wonders! Captain Nemo walked in front, his companion followed some steps behind. Conseil and I remained near each other, as if an exchange of words had been possible through our metallic cases. I no longer felt the weight of my clothing, nor of my shoes, my reservoir of air, or my thick helmet, in the midst of which my head rattled like an almond in its shell.

The light, which lit the soil 30 feet below the surface of the ocean, astonished me by its power. The solar rays shone through the watery mass easily and dissipated all color, and I clearly distinguished objects at a distance of 150 yards. Beyond that the tints darkened into fine gradations of ultramarine and faded into vague obscurity. Truly this water which surrounded me was but another air denser than the terrestrial atmosphere, but almost as transparent. Above me was the calm surface of the sea.

We were walking on fine, even sand, not wrinkled, as on a flat shore, which retains the impression of the billows. This dazzling carpet, really a reflector, repelled the rays of the sun with wonderful intensity, which accounted for the

vibration that penetrated every atom of liquid. Shall I be
believed when I say that, at the depth of 30 feet I could see
as well as in broad daylight?

For a quarter of an hour I trod on this sand sown with
the impalpable dust of shells. The hull of the *Nautilus,* resembling a long shoal, disappeared by degrees; but its lantern, when darkness should overtake us in the waters,
would help to guide us on board.

Soon forms of objects outlined in the distance were discernible. I recognized magnificent rocks, hung with a tapestry of zoophytes of the most beautiful kind.

It was then ten in the morning; the rays of the sun struck
the surface of the waves at an oblique angle, and in their
light, decomposed by refraction as through a prism, flowers,
rocks, plants, shells and polypi were edged by rainbow
colors. It was marvelous, a feast for the eyes, this complication of colored tints, a perfect kaleidoscope of green, yellow, orange, violet, indigo and blue; in a word, the whole
palette of an enthusiastic colorist! I wanted to communicate
to Conseil my lively sensations, and rival him in expressions
of admiration. For aught I knew Captain Nemo and his
companion might be able to exchange thoughts by means of
signs previously agreed upon. So, for want of better, I
talked to myself; I declaimed in the copper box which covered my head, thereby expending more air in vain words
than was perhaps wise.

Various kinds of isis, clusters of pure tuft coral, prickly
fungi, and anemones formed a brilliant garden of flowers,
decked with their collarettes of blue tentacles, sea stars
studding the sandy bottom. It was a real grief to me to crush
under my feet the brilliant specimens of molluscs which

strewed the ground by thousands, of hammerheads, do-
naciae (veritable bounding shells), of staircases, and red
helmet shells, angel wings, and many others produced by
this inexhaustible ocean. But we were bound to walk, so we
went on, while above our heads waved medusae whose um-
brellas of opal or rose pink, escalloped with a band of blue,
sheltered us from the rays of the sun and fiery pelagiae,
which, in the darkness, would have strewn our path with
phosphorescent light.

All these wonders I saw in the space of a quarter of a
mile, scarcely stopping, and following Captain Nemo, who
beckoned me on by signs. Soon the nature of the soil
changed; to the sandy plain succeeded an extent of slimy
mud which the Americans call "ooze," composed of equal
parts of siliceous and calcareous shells. We then traveled
over a plain of seaweed of wild and luxuriant vegetation.
This sward was of close texture, and soft to the feet, and
rivaled the softest carpet woven by the hand of man. But
while verdure was spread at our feet, it did not abandon our
heads. A light network of marine plants, of that inexhaustible family of seaweed of which more than two thousand
kinds are known, grew on the surface of the water. I noticed that the green plants were nearer the top of the sea,
while the red were at a greater depth, leaving to the black
or brown the care of forming gardens and parterres in the
remote beds of the ocean.

We had been away from the *Nautilus* about an hour and
a half. It was near noon; I knew by the sun's rays, which
were no longer refracted, and the magical colors disappeared by degrees. We walked with a regular step. As the
bottom sloped downward the light took a uniform tint. We

were at a depth of 327 feet, under a pressure of six atmospheres.

At this depth I could still see the rays of the sun, though feebly; their intense brilliancy had been succeeded by a reddish twilight, somewhere between day and night, but we could still see well enough; it was not necessary to resort to the Ruhmkorff apparatus as yet. At this moment Captain Nemo stopped; he waited till I joined him, and then pointed to an obscure mass, looming in the shadow, at a short distance.

"It is the forest of the Island of Crespo," I thought; and I was not mistaken.

16. A Submarine Forest

We had at last arrived on the borders of this forest, doubtless one of the finest of Captain Nemo's immense domains. He looked upon it as his own, and considered he had the same right over it that the first men had in the first days of the world. And, indeed, who would have disputed with him the possession of this submarine property? What other hardier pioneer would come, hatchet in hand, to cut down the dark copses?

This forest was composed of large tree plants; and the moment we penetrated under its vast arcades, I was struck by the singular position of their branches—a position I had not yet observed.

Not an herb which carpeted the ground, not a branch which clothed the trees, was either broken or bent, nor did they extend horizontally; all stretched up to the surface of the ocean. Not a filament, not a ribbon, however thin they might be, but kept as straight as a rod of iron. The fuci and lianas grew in rigid perpendicular lines, due to the density of the element which had produced them. Motionless yet, when bent to one side by the hand, they directly resumed their former position. Truly it was the region of perpendicularity!

I soon accustomed myself to this fantastic position, as well as to the comparative darkness which surrounded us. The soil of the forest seemed covered with sharp blocks, difficult to avoid. The submarine flora struck me as being very perfect, and richer even than it would have been in the arctic or tropical zones, where these productions are not so plentiful. But for some minutes I involuntarily confounded the genera, taking animals for plants; and who would not have been mistaken? The fauna and the flora are too closely allied in this submarine world.

These plants are self-propagated, and the principle of their existence is in the water, which upholds and nourishes them. The greater number, instead of leaves, shoot forth blades of capricious shapes comprised within a scale of colors pink, carmine, green, olive, fawn, and brown.

"Curious anomaly, fantastic world!" one naturalist has said, "in which the animal kingdom blossoms and the vegetable does not!"

In about an hour Captain Nemo gave the signal to halt. I, for my part, was not sorry, and we stretched ourselves under an arbor of alariae, the long, thin blades of which stood up like arrows.

This short rest seemed delicious to me; there was nothing wanting but the charm of conversation; but, impossible to

speak, impossible to answer, I only put my great copper
head to Conseil's. I saw the worthy fellow's eyes glistening
with delight, and, to show his satisfaction, he shook himself
in his breastplate of air in the most comical way in the
world.

After four hours of this walking I was surprised not to
find myself dreadfully hungry. How to account for this state
of the stomach I could not tell. But instead I felt an insurmountable desire to sleep, which happens to all divers. And
my eyes soon closed behind the thick glasses, and I fell into
a heavy slumber, which the movement alone had prevented
before. Captain Nemo and his robust companion, stretched
in the clear crystal, set us the example.

How long I remained buried in this drowsiness I cannot
judge, but, when I awoke, the sun seemed sinking toward
the horizon. Captain Nemo had already risen, and I was
beginning to stretch my limbs, when an unexpected apparition brought me briskly to my feet.

A few steps off a monstrous sea spider, about thirty-eight
inches high, was watching me with squinting eyes, ready to
spring upon me. Though my diver's suit was thick enough
to defend me, I could not help shuddering with horror.
Conseil and the sailor of the *Nautilus* awoke at this moment. Captain Nemo pointed out the hideous crustacean,
which a blow from the butt end of the gun knocked over,
and I saw the horrible claws of the monster writhe in terrible convulsions. This incident reminded me that other
animals more to be feared might haunt these obscure
depths, against whose attacks my diving suit would not protect me. I had never thought of it before, but I now resolved
to be on my guard. Indeed, I thought that this halt would

mark the termination of our walk; but I was mistaken, for, instead of returning to the *Nautilus,* Captain Nemo continued his bold excursion. The ground was still on the incline, its declivity seemed to be getting greater, and to be leading us to greater depths. It must have been about three o'clock when we reached a narrow valley, between high perpendicular walls, situated about seventy-five fathoms deep. Thanks to the perfection of our apparatus, we were 45 fathoms below the limit which nature seems to have imposed on man in his submarine excursions.

I say 75 fathoms, though I had no instrument by which to judge the distance. But I knew that even in the clearest waters the solar rays could not penetrate farther. And accordingly the darkness deepened. At ten paces not an object was visible. I was groping my way, when I suddenly saw a brilliant white light. Captain Nemo had just put his electric apparatus into use; his companion did the same, and Conseil and I followed their example. By turning a screw I established a communication between the wire and the spiral glass, and the sea, lit by our four lanterns, was illuminated for a circle of 36 yards.

As we walked I thought the light of our Ruhmkorff apparatus could not fail to draw some inhabitants from their dark couches. But if they did approach us, they at least kept at a respectful distance from the hunters. Several times I saw Captain Nemo stop, put his gun to his shoulder, and after some moments drop it and walk on. At last, after about four hours, this marvelous excursion came to an end. A wall of superb rocks, in an imposing mass, rose before us, a heap of gigantic blocks, an enormous, steep granite shore, forming dark grottos, but which presented no practicable slope; it was the prop of the Island of Crespo. It was the earth! Captain Nemo stopped suddenly. A gesture of his brought us all to a halt; and, however desirous I might be to scale the wall, I was obliged to stop. Here ended Captain Nemo's domains. And he would not go beyond them.

The return began. Captain Nemo had returned to the head of his little band, directing their course without hesitation. I thought we were not following the same road to return to the *Nautilus*. The new road was very steep, and consequently very painful. We approached the surface of the sea rapidly. But this return to the upper strata was not so sudden as to cause relief from the pressure too rapidly which might have produced a serious physical disorder such as internal lesions, so fatal to divers. Very soon light reappeared and grew, and, the sun being low on the horizon, the refraction edged the different objects with a spectral ring. At 31½ feet deep we walked amid a shoal of little fishes of all kinds, more numerous than the birds of the air and also more agile; but no aquatic game worthy of a shot had as yet met our gaze. At that moment I saw the captain shoulder his gun quickly and follow a moving object into the shrubs. He fired; I heard a slight hissing, and a creature fell stunned at some distance from us. It was a magnificent sea otter, an enhydrus, the only exclusively marine quadruped. This otter was five feet long, and must have been very valuable. Its skin, chestnut-brown above and silvery underneath, would have made one of those beautiful furs so sought after in the Russian and Chinese markets: the fineness and the luster of its coat would certainly fetch $400. I admired this curious mammal, with its rounded head ornamented with short ears, its round eyes, and white whiskers like those of a cat, with webbed feet and nails, and tufted tail. This precious animal, hunted and tracked by fishermen and now very rare, has fortunately taken refuge in the northern parts of the Pacific, or its race would soon have become extinct.

Captain Nemo's companion took the beast, threw it over his shoulder, and we continued our journey. For one hour a plain of sand lay stretched before us. Sometimes it rose to within two yards and some inches of the surface of the water. I then saw our image clearly reflected, drawn inversely, and above us appeared an identical group reflecting our movements and our actions; in a word, like us in every point, except that they walked with their heads downward and their feet in the air.

I noticed what was apparently the passage of thick clouds forming and vanishing rapidly; but on reflection I understood that these seeming clouds were due to breaking waves overhead. I could even see the fleecy foam which their broken tops multiplied on the water, and the shadows of large birds passing above our heads, whose rapid flight I could discern on the surface of the sea.

On this occasion I was witness to one of the finest gunshots which ever thrilled a hunter. A large bird of a great wingspread hovered, clearly visible, above us. Captain Nemo's companion shouldered his gun and fired when it was only a few feet above the waves. The creature fell stunned, and the force of its fall brought it within the reach of the dexterous hunter's grasp. It was an albatross of the finest kind.

Our march had not been interrupted by this incident. For two hours we followed these sandy plains, then fields of algae very disagreeable to cross. Candidly, I was exhausted when I saw a glimmer of light, which, for a half mile, broke the darkness of the waters. It was the lantern of the *Nautilus*. In less than 20 minutes we would be on board, and I would be able to breathe with ease, for the air my reservoir supplied was now very deficient in oxygen. But I did not reckon on an accidental meeting which delayed our arrival for some time.

I had remained some steps behind, when I presently saw Captain Nemo coming hurriedly toward me. With his strong hand he bent me to the ground, his companion doing the same to Conseil. At first I knew not what to make of this sudden attack, but I was soon reassured by seeing the captain lie down beside me and remain immovable.

I was stretched on the ground, just under the shelter of a bush of algae, when, raising my head, I saw some enormous mass, casting phosphorescent gleams, pass blusteringly by.

My blood froze in my veins as I recognized two formidable sharks which threatened us—a couple of tintoreas, terrible creatures, with enormous tails and dull glassy stares, the phosphorescent matter ejected from holes around the muzzles. Monstrous brutes, which would crush a whole man in their iron jaws. I did not know whether Conseil stopped to classify them; for my part, I noticed their silver bellies and their huge mouths bristling with teeth from the very unscientific point of view of a possible victim.

Happily the voracious creatures do not see well. They passed without seeing us, brushing us with their brownish fins, and we escaped by a miracle from a danger certainly greater than meeting a tiger full face in the forest. Half an hour later, guided by the electric light, we reached the *Nautilus*. The outside door had been left open, and Captain Nemo closed it as soon as we had entered the first cell. He then pressed a knob. I heard the pumps working in the midst of the vessel, I felt the water sinking from around me, and in a few moments the cell was entirely empty. The inside door then opened and we entered the vestry.

There our diving suits were removed, not without some trouble, and, fairly worn out from want of food and oxygen, I returned to my room, in great wonder at this surprising excursion at the bottom of the sea.

17. Four Thousand Leagues under the Pacific

THE NEXT morning, the 18th of November, I had quite recovered from my fatigues of the day before and went up onto the platform, just as the second lieutenant was uttering his daily phrase.

I was admiring the magnificent aspect of the ocean when Captain Nemo appeared. He did not seem to be aware of my presence, and began a series of astronomical observations. Then, when he had finished, he went and leaned on the cage of the watch light, and gazed abstractedly on the ocean. In the meantime, a number of the sailors of the *Nautilus,* all strong and healthy men, had come up on the platform. They came to draw up the nets that had been laid all night. These sailors were evidently of different nations, although the European type was visible in all of them. I recognized some unmistakable Irishmen, Frenchmen, some Slavs, and a Greek, or a Candiote. They were civil, but among themselves they used that odd language, the origin of which I could not guess, nor could I question them.

The nets were hauled in. They were the large "chaluts,"

like those used on the Normandy coast, great pockets kept open by the waves and a chain fixed in the smaller meshes. These pockets, drawn by iron poles, swept through the water and gathered everything in their way. That day they brought up curious specimens from those productive coasts.

I reckoned that the haul had brought in more than nine hundredweight of fish. It was a fine haul, but not to be wondered at; the nets are let down for several hours, and enclose in their meshes an infinite variety. We had no lack of excellent food, and the rapidity of the *Nautilus* and the attraction of the electric light could always be counted on to renew our supply. These products of the sea were immediately lowered through the panel to the steward's room, some to be eaten fresh, others pickled.

The fishing ended, the provision of air renewed, I thought that the *Nautilus* would continue its submarine excursion. I was preparing to return to my room, when, without further preamble, the captain turned to me, saying:

"Professor, is not this ocean gifted with real life? It has its tempers and its gentle moods. Yesterday it slept as we did, and now it has awakened after a quiet night. Look!" he continued, "it wakes under the caresses of the sun. It is going to renew its diurnal existence. It is an interesting study to watch the play of its organization. It has a pulse, arteries, spasms; and I agree with the learned Maury, who discovered in it a circulation as real as the circulation of blood in animals.

"Yes, the ocean has indeed circulation, and to promote it the Creator has caused things to multiply in it—caloric, salt, and animalculae."

When Captain Nemo spoke thus he seemed altogether changed, and aroused an extraordinary emotion in me.

"Also," he added, "true existence is there; and I can imagine the foundations of nautical towns, clusters of submarine houses which, like the *Nautilus,* would ascend every morning to breathe at the surface of the water—free towns, independent cities. Yet who knows whether some despot——"

Captain Nemo finished his sentence with a violent gesture. Then, addressing me as if to chase away some sorrowful thought:

"Mr. Aronnax," he asked, "do you know the depth of the ocean?"

"I only know, Captain, what the principal soundings have taught us."

"Could you tell me, so that I can suit them to my purpose?"

"Here are some," I replied, "that I remember. If I am not mistaken, a depth of 24,000 feet has been found in the north Atlantic, and 7,500 feet in the Mediterranean. The most remarkable soundings have been made in the south Atlantic, near the thirty-fifth parallel, and they gave 36,000 feet, 42,000 feet, and 45,000 feet. It is reckoned that if the bottom of the sea were leveled, its mean depth would be about one and three-quarters leagues."

"Well, Professor," replied the captain, "we shall show you better than that, I hope. As to the mean depth of this part of the Pacific, I tell you it is only 12,000 feet."

Having said this, Captain Nemo went toward the panel, and disappeared down the ladder. I followed him and went into the big lounge. The propeller was immediately put in motion, and the log showed we were traveling at 20 knots.

During the days and weeks that passed Captain Nemo was very sparing of his visits. I seldom saw him. The lieutenant pricked the ship's course regularly on the chart, so I could always tell exactly the route of the *Nautilus*.

Nearly every day, for some time, the panels of the lounge were opened, and we were never tired of penetrating the mysteries of the submarine world.

The general direction of the *Nautilus* was southeast, and it cruised at between 300 and 450 feet. One day, however, I did not know why, it touched the bed of the sea. The thermometer indicated a temperature of 39.6° Fahrenheit, a temperature that at this depth seemed common to all latitudes.

At three o'clock in the morning of the 26th of November the *Nautilus* crossed the Tropic of Cancer at 172° long. On the 27th we sighted the Sandwich Islands where Cook had died on February 14, 1779. By this time we had traveled 4,860 leagues from our starting point. In the morning, when I went up to the platform, I spotted Hawaii, two miles to windward. I could clearly see its cultivated slopes, and the several mountain chains running parallel to the coast, and the volcanoes overtopped by Mauna Kea, which rises 13,796 feet above sea level. Besides other things, the nets brought up several flabellaria and graceful polyps peculiar to that part of the ocean. The direction of the *Nautilus* was still to the southeast. It crossed the equator December 1, in 142° long.; and on the 4th of the same month, after a rapid crossing without incident, we sighted the Marquesas. I saw, three miles off, Martin Point in Nukuhiva, the largest of the group that belongs to France. I saw only the woody mountains against the horizon because Captain Nemo did not wish to get close. There the nets brought up beautiful specimens of fish—some with azure fins and tails like gold, the flesh of which is unrivaled, some almost without scales and of exquisite flavor; others with bony jaws and yellow-tinged gills, as good as bonitos—all fish that would help to fill our larder. After leaving these charming islands protected by the French flag, the *Nautilus* sailed over about a 2,000-mile area, from the 4th to the 11th of December.

On the day of December 11 I was busy reading in the lounge. Ned Land and Conseil were watching the luminous water through the half-open panels. The *Nautilus* was immovable. While its reservoirs were filled, it stayed at a depth of 3,000 feet, a relatively uninhabited region of the ocean where large fish were seldom seen.

I was reading a charming book by Jean Macé, *Servants of the Stomach,* and gaining some valuable pointers, when Conseil interrupted me.

"Will Monsieur come here a moment?" he said in a curious voice.

"What is the matter, Conseil?"

"I want Monsieur to look."

I went over and leaned on my elbows before the panes to watch.

In a full electric light an enormous black mass, quite immovable, was suspended in the midst of the waters. I watched it attentively, seeking to find out the nature of this gigantic cetacean. But a sudden thought crossed my mind. "A vessel!" I said, half aloud.

"Yes," replied the Canadian, "a disabled ship that has sunk perpendicularly."

Ned Land was right: we were close to a vessel whose

tattered shrouds still hung from their chains. The keel seemed to be in good order, and had been wrecked at most some few hours. Three stumps of masts, broken off about two feet above the bridge, showed that the vessel had had to sacrifice her masts. But, lying on her side, she had filled, and she was heeling to port. This skeleton of what she had once been was a sad spectacle as she lay lost under the waves, but sadder still was the sight of the bridge where some corpses, bound with ropes, were still lying. I counted five—four men, one of whom was standing at the helm, and a woman standing by the poop holding an infant in her arms. She was quite young. I could distinguish her features, which the water had not decomposed, by the brilliant light from the *Nautilus*. In one despairing effort she had raised her infant above her head—poor little thing!—whose arms encircled its mother's neck. The attitude of the four sailors was frightful, distorted as they were by their convulsive movements, while making a last effort to free themselves from the cords that bound them to the vessel. The steersman alone, calm, with a grave, clear face, his gray hair glued to his forehead and his hand clutching the wheel of the helm, seemed even then to be guiding the three broken masts through the depths of the ocean.

What a scene! We were dumb; our hearts beat fast before this shipwreck, taken as it were from life and photographed in its last moments. And I saw already, coming toward it with hungry eyes, enormous sharks, attracted by the human flesh.

However, the *Nautilus*, turning, went around the submerged vessel, and in one instant I read the name on the stern: *Florida, Sunderland*.

18. Vanikoro

THIS TERRIBLE spectacle was the forerunner of the series of maritime catastrophes that the *Nautilus* was destined to meet in its route. As long as it went through more frequented waters, we often saw the hulls of shipwrecked vessels that were rotting in the depths, and deeper down cannons, bullets, anchors, chains and a thousand other iron materials eaten up by rust. On December 11 we sighted the Tuamotu Archipelago, the old "dangerous group" Bougainville had called them, that extend over an area of 1,200 miles east-southeast to west-northwest, from Ducie Island to Lazareff. These islands together make up an area of 920 square miles and include 60 groups of islands, among them Gambier, administered by France. They are coral formations, raised slowly but continuously, created by the daily work of polyps. This new island will eventually be joined to the neighboring groups. Then a fifth continent will stretch from New Zealand and New Caledonia, and from thence to the Marquesas.

One day, when I was suggesting this theory to Captain Nemo, he replied coldly:

"The earth does not need new continents, but new men."

On December 15 we passed to the east the bewitching group of the Societies and graceful Tahiti, queen of the Pacific. I saw in the morning, some miles to the windward, the elevated summits of the island. These waters furnished our table with excellent fish, mackerel, bonitos, and some varieties of a sea serpent.

On the 25th of December the *Nautilus* sailed among the

New Hebrides, discovered by Quiros in 1606, explored by
Bougainville in 1768, and named by Cook in 1773. This
group is composed principally of nine large islands forming
a band 360 miles long, from NNS to SSW, between 15° and
2° S. lat., and 164° and 168° long. We passed near to
Auru Island that at noon looked like a mass of green
woods, surmounted by a peak of great height.

It was Christmas Day and Ned Land seemed unhappy
over the absence of any Christmas celebration. I had not
seen Captain Nemo for a week. Then, on the morning of
the 27th he came into the lounge, acting as though he had
seen me only five minutes before. I was busily tracing the
route of the *Nautilus* on the planisphere. The captain came
up to me, put his finger at one spot on the chart, and said
this single word: "Vanikoro."

The effect was magical! It was the name of the islands on
which La Pérouse's ships had been lost! I rose suddenly.

"The *Nautilus* has brought us to Vanikoro?" I asked.

"Yes, Professor," said the captain.

"And I can visit the celebrated islands where the *Boussole* and the *Astrolabe* struck?"

"If you like, Professor."

"When will we reach these islands?"

"We are there now."

Followed by Captain Nemo, I went up to the platform
and greedily scanned the horizon.

To the northeast two volcanic islands emerged of un-
equal size, surrounded by a coral reef that measured forty
miles in circumference. We were close to Vanikoro, really
the one to which Dumont d'Urville gave the name of Isle de
la Recherche, and exactly facing the little harbor of Vanou,

situated in 16° 4′ S. lat., and 164° 32′ E. long. The earth seemed covered with verdure from the shore to the summits in the interior that were crowned by Mount Kapogo, over 2,000 feet high. The *Nautilus,* having passed the outer belt of rocks by a narrow strait, found itself among breakers where the sea was from 30 to 40 fathoms deep. Under the verdant shade of some mangroves I perceived some savages, who appeared greatly surprised at our approach. In the long black body, moving between wind and water, did they not see some formidable cetacean that they regarded with suspicion?

Just then Captain Nemo asked me what I knew about the wreck of La Pérouse.

"Only what everyone knows, Captain," I replied.

"And could you tell me what everyone knows about it?" he inquired ironically.

"Easily."

I related to him all that the last works of Dumont d'Urville had made known—works from which the following is a brief account.

La Pérouse and his second, Captain de Langle, were sent by Louis XVI, in 1785, on a voyage of circumnavigation. They embarked in the corvettes the *Boussole* and the *Astrolabe,* neither of which was again heard of. In 1791 the French Government, justly uneasy as to the fate of these two sloops, manned two large merchantmen, the *Recherche* and the *Esperance,* which left Brest the 28th of September under the command of Bruni d'Entrecasteaux.

Two months after they learned from Bowen, commander of the *Albemarle,* that the debris of shipwrecked vessels had been seen on the coasts of New Georgia. But D'Entrecas-

teaux, ignoring this communication—rather uncertain, besides—directed his course toward the Admiralty Islands,
mentioned in a report of Captain Hunter's as being the
place where La Pérouse was wrecked.

They sought in vain. The *Esperance* and the *Recherche*
passed before Vanikoro without stopping there, and, in
fact, this voyage was most disastrous, as it cost D'Entrecasteaux his life as well as those of two lieutenants and
several crewmen.

Captain Dillon, a shrewd old Pacific sailor, was the first
to find unmistakable traces of the wrecks. On the 15th of
May, 1824, his vessel, the *St. Patrick,* passed close to Tikopia, one of the New Hebrides. There a native came
alongside in a canoe, sold him the handle of a sword in
silver that bore the print of characters engraved on the hilt.
The native pretended that six years before, during a stay at
Vanikoro, he had seen two Europeans who belonged to
some vessels that had run aground on the reefs some years
ago.

Dillon guessed that he meant La Pérouse, whose disappearance had troubled the whole world. He tried to get on
to Vanikoro, where, according to the native, he would find
numerous debris of the wreck, but winds and tides prevented him.

Dillon returned to Calcutta. There he interested the
Asiatic Society and the Indian Company in his discovery. A
vessel, to which was given the name of *Recherche,* was put
at his disposal, and he set out, the 23rd of January, 1827,
accompanied by a French agent.

The *Recherche,* after touching at several points in the
Pacific, cast anchor before Vanikoro, the 7th of July, 1827,

in that same harbor of Vanou where the *Nautilus* was at this time.

There she collected numerous relics of the wreck—iron utensils, anchors, pulley strops, swivel guns, an 18-pound shot, fragments of astronomical instruments, a piece of crownwork, and a bronze clock bearing this inscription— *"Bazin m'a fait,"* the mark of the foundry of the arsenal at Brest about 1785. There could be no further doubt.

Dillon, having made all inquiries, stayed in the unlucky place till October. Then he quitted Vanikoro and directed his course toward New Zealand. He put into Calcutta on April 7, 1828 and returned to France, where he was warmly welcomed by Charles X.

But at the same time, without knowing Dillon's movements, Dumont d'Urville had already set out to find the scene of the wreck. And they had learned from a whaler that some medals and a cross of St. Louis had been found in the hands of some savages of Louisiade and New Caledonia. Dumont d'Urville, commander of the *Astrolabe,* had then sailed, and two months after Dillon had left Vanikoro he put into Hobart Town. There he learned the results of Dillon's inquiries, and found that a certain James Hobbs, second lieutenant of the *Union* of Calcutta, after landing on an island situated 8° 18′ S. lat., and 156° 30′ E. long., had seen some iron bars and red stuffs used by the natives of these parts. Dumont d'Urville, much perplexed, and not knowing how to credit the reports of unreliable journals, decided to follow Dillon's track.

On February 10, 1828, the *Astrolabe* appeared off Tikopia and took on as guide and interpreter a deserter found on the island, made her way to Vanikoro, sighted it on the

12th, lay among the reefs until the 14th, and not until the 20th did she cast anchor within the barrier in the harbor of Vanou.

On the 23rd several officers went around the island and brought back some unimportant trifles. The natives, adopting a system of denials and evasions, refused to take them to the unlucky place. This ambiguous conduct led them to believe that the natives had ill-treated the castaways, and indeed they seemed to fear that Dumont d'Urville had come to avenge La Pérouse and his unfortunate crew.

However, on the 26th, appeased by some presents and understanding that they had no reprisals to fear, they led M. Jacquireot to the scene of the wreck.

There, in three or four fathoms of water, between the reefs of Pacou and Vanou, lay anchors, cannons and pigs of lead and iron, embedded in the limy concretions. The large boat and the whaler belonging to the *Astrolabe* were sent to this place and, not without some difficulty, their crews hauled up an anchor weighing 1,800 pounds, a brass gun, some iron pigs and two copper swivel guns.

Dumont d'Urville, questioning the natives, learned, too, that La Pérouse, after losing both his vessels on the reefs of this island, had constructed a smaller boat, only to be lost a second time. Where, no one knew.

But the French Government, fearing that Dumont d'Urville was not acquainted with Dillon's movements, had sent the sloop *Bayonnaise,* commanded by Legoarant de Tromelin, and which had been stationed on the west coast of America, to Vanikoro. The *Bayonnaise* cast her anchor before Vanikoro some months after the departure of the *Astrolabe,* but found no new document; but stated that the savages had respected the monument to La Pérouse. That is the substance of what I told Captain Nemo.

"So," he said, "no one knows now where the third vessel perished that was constructed by the castaways on the island of Vanikoro?"

"No one knows."

Captain Nemo said nothing, but signed to me to follow him into the large lounge. The *Nautilus* sank several yards below the waves, and the panels were opened.

I hastened to the aperture, and under the crustations of coral, covered with fungi, I recognized certain debris that the drags had not been able to tear up—iron stirrups, anchors, cannons, bullets, capstan fittings, the stem of a ship, all objects clearly proving the wreck of some vessel, and now carpeted with living flowers. While I was looking on this desolate scene, Captain Nemo said in a sad voice:

"Commander La Pérouse set out the 7th of December, 1785, with his vessels the *Boussole* and the *Astrolabe*. He first cast anchor at Botany Bay, visited the Friendly Islands and New Caledonia, then directed his course toward Santa Cruz, and put into Nomuka, one of the Ha'apai group. Then his vessels struck on the unknown reefs of Vanikoro. The *Boussole*, which went first, ran aground on the southerly coast. The *Astrolabe* went to her help, and ran aground, too. The first vessel was destroyed almost immediately. The second, stranded under the wind, resisted some days. The natives made the castaways welcome. They installed themselves in the island, and constructed a smaller boat from the debris of the two large ones. Some sailors stayed willingly at Vanikoro; the others, weak and ill, set out with La Pérouse. They directed their course toward the

Solomon Islands, and there perished with everything, on the
westerly coast of the chief island of the group, between
Cape Deception and Cape Satisfaction!"

"How do you know that?"

"By this, that I found on the spot of the last shipwreck."
Captain Nemo showed me a tin box stamped with the
French arms, and corroded by the salt water. He opened it,
and I saw a bundle of papers, yellow but still readable.

They were the instructions of the naval minister to Commander La Pérouse, annotated in the margin in Louis
XVI's handwriting.

"Ah! it is a fine death for a sailor!" said Captain Nemo at
last. "A coral tomb makes a quiet grave; and I trust that I
and my comrades will find no other."

19. Torres Strait

DURING THE night of the 27th or 28th of December the
Nautilus left the shores of Vanikoro with great speed. Her
course was southwesterly, and in three days she had traveled over the 750 leagues that separated it from La Pérouse's group and the southeast point of Papua.

Early on January 1, Conseil joined me on the platform.

"Will Monsieur permit me to wish him a happy New
Year?"

"Why, Conseil, exactly as if I were at Paris in my study
at the Jardin des Plantes! Well, I accept your good wishes,
and thank you for them. Only, I will ask you what you
mean by a 'happy New Year' in our situation. Do you mean
the year that will bring us to the end of our imprisonment,

or the year that sees us continue this strange voyage?"

"Really, I do not know how to answer, Monsieur. We are sure to see curious things, and for the last two months we have not had time to be bored. The last marvel is always the most astonishing; and, if we continue this progression I do not know how it will end. It is my opinion that we shall never again see the like. I think then, with no offense to Monsieur, that a happy year would be one in which we could see everything."

On January 2 we had traveled 11,340 miles, or 5,250 French leagues, since our starting point in the Sea of Japan. Before the ship's prow stretched the dangerous shores of the Coral Sea, off the northeast coast of Australia. Our boat lay along some miles from the redoubtable bank on which Cook's vessel was almost lost, the 10th of June, 1770. Cook's ship struck a rock but did not sink. The piece of coral was broken off by the shock, and fixed itself in the vessel's keel.

I wished to visit the reef, 360 leagues long, against which the sea, always rough, broke with great violence, and with a noise like thunder. But just then the *Nautilus* sank down to a great depth, and I could see nothing of the high coral walls. I had to content myself with the different specimens of fish brought up by the nets. I remarked among others some germons, a species of mackerel as large as a tunny, with bluish sides and striped with transverse bands, that disappear as the animal matures. These fish followed us in shoals, and furnished us with very delicate food. We took also a large number of giltheads, about one and a half inches long, tasting like dorys; and flying fire fish like submarine swallows, which, in dark nights, light alternately the air and water with their phosphorescent light.

Two days after crossing the Coral Sea, on January 4, we sighted the Papuan coasts. On this occasion, Captain Nemo informed me of his intention to get into the Indian Ocean by the Strait of Torres. His communication ended there.

The Torres Strait is nearly 34 leagues wide, but it is obstructed by an innumerable quantity of islands, islets, breakers, and rocks that make its navigation almost impossible, so that Captain Nemo took all precautions. The *Nautilus,* floating betwixt wind and water, went at a moderate pace. Her propeller, like a whale's tail, beat the waves slowly.

Profiting by this, my two companions and I went up to the deserted platform. Before us was the steersman's cage, and I expected that Captain Nemo was there directing the course of the *Nautilus.* I had before me the excellent charts of the Strait of Torres, and I consulted them attentively. Around the *Nautilus* the sea dashed furiously. The course of the waves, that went from southeast to northwest at the rate of two and a half miles, broke on the coral that showed itself here and there.

"This is a bad sea!" remarked Ned Land.

"Detestable indeed, and one that does not suit a boat like the *Nautilus.*"

"The captain must be very sure of his route, for I see there pieces of coral that would do for its keel if it only touched them slightly."

Indeed the situation was dangerous, but the *Nautilus* seemed to slide like magic off these rocks. The boat did not follow the routes of the *Astrolabe* and the *Zélée* exactly, for they proved fatal to Dumont d'Urville. It bore more northward, coasted the Islands of Murray, and came back to the southwest toward Cumberland Passage. I thought the *Nautilus* would pass it by, when, turning northwest, we passed a number of little-known islands and islets near the Island Sound and Canal Mauvais.

I wondered if Captain Nemo, foolishly imprudent, would steer his vessel into that pass where Dumont d'Urville's two corvettes touched, when, swerving again and cutting straight through to the west, he steered for the Island of Gilboa.

It was then three in the afternoon. The high tide began to recede. The *Nautilus* approached the island with its remarkable border of screw pines. He stood off at about two miles distant. Suddenly a shock threw me off balance. The *Nautilus* had just touched a rock, and lay immovable, slightly to port.

When I arose, I perceived Captain Nemo and his lieutenant on the platform. They were studying the position of the vessel and exchanging words in their incomprehensible dialect.

The *Nautilus* was situated thus: Two miles off the starboard side was Gilboa, stretching from north to west like an immense arm. Toward the south and east we saw coral reefs exposed by the ebb. We had run aground at high tide—it looked bad for the *Nautilus*. Fortunately, the vessel had not suffered, for her keel was solidly joined. But if she could neither glide off nor move she ran the risk of being forever fastened to these rocks, and then Captain Nemo's submarine vessel would be done for.

I was reflecting thus when the captain, cool and calm, always master of himself, approached me.

"An accident?" I asked.

"No, an incident."

"But an incident that will oblige you perhaps to become an inhabitant of this land from which you flee?"

Captain Nemo looked at me curiously and made a negative gesture, as much as to say that nothing would force him to set foot on terra firma again. Then he said:

"Besides, Mr. Aronnax, the *Nautilus* is not lost; it will yet carry you into the midst of the ocean's marvels. Our voyage is only begun, and I do not wish to be deprived so soon of the honor of your company."

"However, Captain Nemo," I replied, without noticing the ironical turn of his phrase, "the *Nautilus* ran aground in open sea. Now, the tides are not strong in the Pacific; and, if you cannot lighten the *Nautilus* I do not see how it will be refloated."

"The tides are not strong in the Pacific: you are right there, Professor. But in Torres Strait there is a difference of 4½ feet between the level of high and low seas. Today is the 4th of January, and in five days the moon will be full. Now, I shall be very much astonished if that satellite does not raise these masses of water sufficiently to render me a service I shall be indebted to her for."

Having said this, Captain Nemo, followed by his lieutenant, redescended to the interior of the *Nautilus*. As to the vessel, it was immovable, as if the coralline polyps had already walled it up with their indestructible cement.

"Well, sir?" said Ned Land, who came up to me after the captain had departed.

"Well, friend Ned, we will wait patiently for the tide on the 9th, for it appears that the moon is to put us afloat."

"Really?"

"Really."

"And this captain is not going to do anything since the tide will suffice," said Conseil simply.

The Canadian looked at Conseil, then shrugged his shoulders.

"Sir, you may believe me when I tell you that this piece of iron will navigate neither on nor under the sea again; it is only fit to be sold for its weight. I think, therefore, that the time has come to part company with Captain Nemo."

"Friend Ned, I do not despair of this stout *Nautilus* as you do; and in four days we shall know whether we can count on these Pacific tides. Regarding the other matter, flight might be possible if we were in sight of the English or French coast; on the Papuan shores it is another thing. But there will be time enough for that if the *Nautilus* does not refloat."

"But do they know, at least, how to be sensible? There is an island. On that island there are trees; under those trees, terrestrial animals, bearers of cutlets and roast beef to which I would willingly give a trial."

"In this, friend Ned is right," said Conseil, "and I agree with him. Could not Monsieur obtain permission from his friend Captain Nemo to put us on land, if only so we don't forget how to walk on solid ground?"

"I can ask him, but he will refuse."

"Will Monsieur risk it?" asked Conseil. "Then we shall know the extent of the captain's amiability."

To my great surprise, Captain Nemo gave me the permission I asked for, and he gave it very agreeably without even exacting from me a promise to return to the vessel. But flight across New Guinea might be very perilous, and, in any case, I should not have counseled Ned Land to attempt it. Better to be a prisoner on board the *Nautilus* than to fall into the hands of the natives.

At eight o'clock, armed with guns and hatchets, we got off the *Nautilus*. The sea was fairly calm; a slight breeze blew on land. Conseil and I rowing, we sped along quickly, and Ned steered in the straight passage that the breakers left between them. The boat was well handled and moved rapidly.

Ned Land could not restrain his joy. He was like a prisoner who has escaped from prison and forgets that he will have to re-enter it.

"Meat! We are going to eat some meat—and what meat!" he exclaimed. "Real game!"

"I do not say that fish is not good; we must not abuse it. But a piece of fresh venison grilled on live coals will agreeably vary our ordinary fare."

"Glutton!" said Conseil. "He makes my mouth water."

"It remains to be seen," I said, "if these forests are full of game, or if the game is not such as will hunt the hunter himself."

"Well said, Mr. Aronnax," replied the Canadian, whose teeth seemed sharpened like the edge of a hatchet. "But I will eat tiger—loin of tiger—if there is no other quadruped on this island."

"Friend Ned is uneasy about it," said Conseil.

"Whatever it may be," continued Ned Land, "the first animal I see with four paws without feathers, or with two paws without feathers, will be greeted by my shot."

"Well, now! Master Land's imprudences are beginning again."

"Never fear, Mr. Aronnax," replied the Canadian. "I do

not need more than 25 minutes to find you the sort of dish I have in mind."

At 8:30 A.M. the boat from the *Nautilus* ran softly aground on a heavy sand after having happily passed the coral reef that surrounds the Island of Gilboa.

20. A Few Days On Land

I WAS much moved at touching land again. Ned Land stamped on the soil as if to take possession of it. Yet it was only two months before that we had become, according to Captain Nemo, "passengers on board the *Nautilus*," in reality, its prisoners.

In a few minutes we were within musket shot of the coast. The view of the island was observed by a beautiful curtain of forests. Enormous trees, the trunks of some reaching a height of 200 feet, were tied to each other by garlands of bindweed, natural hammocks rocked by a light breeze. There were mimosas, figs, hibiscus and palm trees mingled together in profusion; and under the shelter of their verdant vault grew orchids, leguminous plants and ferns.

But without noticing all these beautiful specimens of Papuan flora, the Canadian abandoned the agreeable for the useful. He discovered a coconut palm, shook down some of the fruit, broke it, and we drank the milk and ate the nut with a satisfaction that protested against the ordinary food on the *Nautilus*.

"Excellent!" said Ned Land.

"Exquisite!" replied Conseil.

"And I do not think," said the Canadian, "that he would

object to our introducing a cargo of coconuts on board ship."

"I do not think he would, but he would not taste them."

"So much the worse for him," said Conseil.

"And so much the better for us," replied Ned Land. "There will be more for us."

"One word only, Master Land," I said to the harpooner, who was beginning to ravage another coconut tree. "Coconuts are good things, but before filling the canoe with them it would be wise to reconnoiter and see if the island does not produce some substance more useful. Fresh vegetables would be welcome on board the *Nautilus*."

"Monsieur is right," replied Conseil; "and I propose to reserve three places in our vessel, one for fruits, another for vegetables, and a third for the venison, of which I have not yet seen the smallest specimen."

"Conseil, we must not give up," said the Canadian.

"Let us proceed," I returned, "but cautiously. Although the island seems uninhabited, it might contain some individuals with peculiar tastes in game."

"Ho! ho!" said Ned Land, moving his jaws significantly.

"Well, Ned!" said Conseil.

"My word!" returned the Canadian. "I'm beginning to understand the charms of cannibalism."

"Ned! Ned! what are you saying? You, a man-eater? I won't feel safe with you any more, especially as I share your cabin. I might perhaps wake up one day to find myself half devoured."

"Friend Conseil, I like you, but not enough to eat you unnecessarily."

"I would not trust you," replied Conseil. "But enough. We must absolutely bring down some game to satisfy this

cannibal, or else one of these fine mornings Monsieur will
have only half a servant to serve him."

While we were talking thus, we moved deeper into the
somber arches of the forest, and for two hours we scruti-
nized it in all directions.

Chance rewarded our search for eatable vegetables, and
one of the most useful products of the tropical zones furnished us with precious food that we missed on board. I
mean the breadfruit tree, which is very abundant on the
Island of Gilboa; I remarked chiefly the seedless variety,
known in Malaya as *rima*.

Ned Land knew these fruits well. He had already eaten
many during his numerous voyages, and he knew how to
prepare the fruit. Moreover, the sight of them excited him,
and he could contain himself no longer.

"Mr. Aronnax," he said, "I shall die if I do not taste a
little of this breadfruit pie."

"Taste it, friend Ned—taste it as you want. We are here
to make experiments—make them."

"It won't take long," said the Canadian.

With a lens, he lighted a fire of dead wood that crackled
joyously. During this time Conseil and I chose the best
samples of the breadfruit. Some were not yet ripe, and their
thick skin covered a white but rather fibrous pulp. Others,
the greater number yellow and gelatinous, waited only to be
picked.

Conseil brought a dozen to Ned Land, who placed them
on a bed of hot coals after cutting them in thick slices, all
the while repeating:

"You will see, Professor, how good this bread is. More so
when one has been deprived of it so long. It is not even

bread," added he, "but a delicate pastry. You have never eaten it?"

"No, Ned."

"Very well, prepare yourself for a succulent treat. If you do not ask for more I am no longer the king of harpooners."

After some minutes parts of the fruits were completely roasted. The inside looked like white pastry, its flavor like that of an artichoke.

I must confess that this bread was excellent and I ate with great relish.

"What time is it now?" asked the Canadian.

"Two o'clock at least," replied Conseil.

"How time flies on firm ground!" Ned Land sighed.

"Let us be off," replied Conseil.

We returned through the forest and added to our collection by raiding some cabbage palms for little beans that I recognized as the *abrou* of the Malays; also yams of a superior quality. We were loaded down when we reached the boat.

At last, at five o'clock in the evening, loaded with our riches, we quitted the shore, and half an hour later we hailed the *Nautilus*. No one appeared on our arrival. The enormous iron-plated cylinder seemed deserted. Once the provisions were on board I went to my room, and after supper slept soundly.

The next day, the 6th of January brought no change to the vessel. Not a sound inside, not a sign of life. The pinnace rested by the ship in the same place we had left it. We resolved to return to the island. Ned Land hoped to be more fortunate in hunting than on the day before, and wished to visit another part of the forest.

At dawn we set off. The boat, carried on by the waves that flowed to shore, reached the island in a few minutes.

We landed, and thinking it was better to let the Canadian lead, we followed Ned Land, whose long limbs threatened to out-distance us. He wound up the coast toward the west; then fording some torrents, he gained the high plain that was bordered with admirable forests. We saw some king-fishers along the watercourses, but they would not let us get near. Their circumspection proved to me that these birds knew what to expect from our species, and I concluded that, if the island was not inhabited, at least human beings occasionally frequented it.

After crossing a rather large prairie we arrived at the skirts of a little wood that was enlivened by the songs and flight of a large number of birds.

"There are only birds," said Conseil.

"But they are eatable," replied the harpooner.

"I do not agree with you, friend Ned, for I see only parrots there."

"Friend Conseil," said Ned gravely, "the parrot is like pheasant to those who have nothing else."

"And," I added, "this bird, suitably prepared, is well worth the knife and fork."

Indeed, under the thick foliage of this wood a world of parrots were flying from branch to branch, only needing a careful education to speak the human language. For the moment they were chattering with parrots of all colors. Grave cockatoos seemed to meditate upon some philosophical problem, while brilliant red lories passed like a piece of bunting carried by the breeze; there were papuans in the finest azure colors, and in all a variety of winged things most charming to behold, but few were edible.

A bird peculiar to these lands, which has never passed beyond the Arrow and Papuan islands, was not to be seen, however. But fortune reserved it for me before long.

After passing through a moderately thick copse, we found a plain obstructed with bushes. I saw then those magnificent birds, the disposition of whose long feathers obliges them to fly against the wind. Their undulating flight, graceful aerial curves and the shading of their colors attracted and charmed one. I had no trouble in recognizing them.

"Birds of paradise!" I exclaimed.

The Malays, who carry on a great trade in these birds with the Chinese, have several means that we could not employ for taking them. Sometimes they put snares on the tops of high trees that the birds of paradise prefer to frequent. Sometimes they catch them with a viscous birdlime that paralyzes their movements. They even go so far as to poison the fountains that the birds generally drink from. But we were obliged to fire at them during flight, which gave us little chance to bring them down; indeed, we vainly exhausted half our ammunition.

About eleven o'clock in the morning we came to the first range of mountains that form the center of the island. We had killed nothing so far. Hunger drove us on. The hunters had relied on the products of the chase, and they were wrong. Happily Conseil, to his great surprise, made a double shot and secured breakfast. He brought down a white pigeon and a wood pigeon, which, cleverly plucked and suspended from a skewer, was roasted before a fire of dead wood. While these interesting birds were cooking, Ned prepared the breadfruit. Then the wood pigeons were devoured to the bones, and declared excellent. The nutmeg, with which they are in the habit of stuffing their crops, flavors their flesh and renders it delicious eating.

"What do you want now, Ned?"

"Some four-footed game, Mr. Aronnax. All these pigeons are only side dishes and trifles; and until I have killed an animal with cutlets I shall not be content."

"Nor I, Ned, if I do not catch a bird of paradise."

"Let us continue hunting," replied Conseil. "Let us go toward the sea. We have come to the first slopes of the mountains, and I think we had better return to the forest area."

That was sensible advice, and we followed it. After walking for an hour we reached a forest of sago trees. Some inoffensive serpents glided away from us. The birds of paradise fled at our approach, and truly I despaired of getting near one when Conseil, who was walking in front, suddenly bent down, uttered a triumphant cry, and came back to me bringing a magnificent specimen.

"Ah! bravo, Conseil!"

"Monsieur is very kind."

"No, my boy, that was excellent, catching a living bird with just your hands."

"If Monsieur will examine it, he will see that I do not merit such praise."

"Why, Conseil?"

"Because this bird is as drunk as a quail."

"Drunk!"

"Yes, sir; drunk with the nutmegs that it devoured under the nutmeg tree under which I found it. See, friend Ned, see the monstrous effects of intemperance!"

"By Jove!" exclaimed the Canadian, "I've had no gin for two months and you reproach me!"

However, I examined the curious bird. Conseil was right. The bird, drunk with the juice, was quite powerless. It could not fly; it could hardly walk.

This bird belonged to the most beautiful of the eight species that are found in Papua and in the neighboring islands. It was the large emerald bird, the rarest kind. Three feet in length, its head was comparatively small; its eyes, placed near the opening of the beak, were also small. But the shades of color were beautiful—a yellow beak, brown feet and claws, nut-colored wings with purple tips, pale yellow at the back of the neck and head, and emerald color at the throat, chestnut on the breast and belly. Two horned, downy feathers rose from the base of the tail. These long light feathers of admirable fineness completed this marvelous bird that the natives have poetically named the "bird of the sun."

But if my wishes were satisfied by the possession of the bird of paradise, the Canadian's were not. Happily, about two o'clock, Ned Land brought down a magnificent hog from the brood of those the natives call *bari-outang*. Ned Land was very proud of his shot. The hog, hit by the electric ball, fell stone dead. The Canadian skinned and cleaned it properly, after having taken half-a-dozen cutlets destined to furnish us with a grilled repast in the evening. Then the hunt was resumed, marked still more by Ned and Conseil's exploits.

Indeed, the two friends, beating the bushes, roused a herd of small kangaroos that fled and bounded away, but not so rapidly that the electric capsule did not stop their course.

"Ah, Professor!" cried Ned Land, who was carried away by the delights of the chase, "what excellent game for a stew! What a supply for the *Nautilus!* Two! three! five down! And to think that we shall eat that flesh while the idiots on board shall not have a crumb!"

I think that, in the excess of his joy, the Canadian might have killed them all. But he contented himself with a single dozen of these interesting marsupials. These animals were quite small. They were a species of those "kangaroo rabbits" that live habitually in the hollows of trees and whose speed is extreme; but they are moderately fat and furnish, at least, estimable food. We were very satisfied with the results of the hunt. Happy Ned proposed to return to this enchanting island the next day, for he wished to depopulate it of all the edible quadrupeds. But he had reckoned without his host.

At six o'clock in the evening we were again on the shore; our boat was moored to the usual place. The *Nautilus,* like a long rock, emerged from the waves two miles from the beach. Ned Land got started immediately on the important dinner business. He understood cooking very well. The *barioutang,* grilled on the coals, soon scented the air with a delicious odor.

Indeed, the dinner was excellent. Two wood pigeons completed this extraordinary menu. The sago pasty, the artocarpus bread, some mangoes, half-a-dozen pineapples, and the liquor fermented from some coconuts, overjoyed us. I'm inclined to think that my worthy companions were a bit befuddled.

"Suppose we don't return to the *Nautilus* this evening," said Conseil.

"Suppose we never return?" added Ned Land.

Just then a stone fell at our feet and cut short the harpooner's proposition.

21. Captain Nemo's Thunderbolt

WE LOOKED to the edge of the forest, my hand arrested on its way to my mouth, Ned Land's concluding its mission.

"Stones do not fall from the sky," remarked Conseil, "or they would merit the name aerolites."

A second stone, carefully aimed, made a savory pigeon's leg fall from Conseil's hand and gave still more weight to his observation. We all three arose, shouldered our guns, and made ready to reply to any attack.

"Are they apes?" cried Ned Land.

"Very nearly—they are savages."

"To the boat!" I said, hurrying to the sea.

It was indeed necessary to beat a retreat, for about twenty natives armed with bows and slings appeared on the skirts of a copse that masked the horizon to the right, hardly a hundred steps from us.

Our boat was moored about sixty feet from us. The savages approached us, not running, but making hostile demonstrations. Stones and arrows fell thickly.

Ned Land did not wish to leave his provisions; and in spite of his imminent danger he carried his pig on one side and kangaroos on the other. He went tolerably fast, however. In two minutes we were at the boat. To load it with our provisions and arms, to push it out to sea and ship the oars, was the work of an instant. We had not gone two cable lengths when a hundred savages, howling and gesticulating, entered the water up to their waists. I watched to see if their appearance would attract some men from the *Nautilus* onto the platform. But no. The vessel, lying off, was absolutely deserted.

Twenty minutes later we were on board. The panels were open. After making the boat fast, we entered the interior of the *Nautilus*.

I descended to the lounge, and heard music. Captain Nemo was bending over an organ, plunged in a musical ecstasy.

"Captain!"

He did not hear me.

"Captain!" I said, touching his hand.

He shuddered, and turning around said, "Ah! it is you, Professor? Well, did you have a good hunt? Have you botanized successfully?"

"Yes, Captain, but we have unfortunately brought a troop of bipeds whose vicinity troubles me."

"What bipeds?"

"Savages."

"Savages!" he echoed ironically. "So you are astonished, Professor, at having set foot on a strange land and finding savages? Savages! Where are they not? Besides, are they worse than others, these whom you call savages?"

"But, Captain——"

"How many have you counted?"

"A hundred at least."

"Mr. Aronnax," replied Captain Nemo, placing his fingers on the organ stops, "if all the natives of Papua were assembled on this shore the *Nautilus* would have nothing to fear from their attacks."

The captain's fingers were then running over the keys of the instrument, and I remarked that he touched only the black keys, which gave his melodies an essentially Scots character. Soon he had forgotten my presence, and had plunged into a reverie that I did not disturb. I went up again to the platform. Night had already fallen, for in this low latitude the sun sets rapidly and without twilight. I could only see the island indistinctly; but the numerous fires lighted on the beach showed that the natives did not think of leaving it. I was alone for several hours, sometimes thinking of the natives—but without any dread of them, for the imperturbable confidence of the captain was catching— sometimes forgetting them to admire the splendors of the night in the tropics. My remembrances went to France in the train of those zodiacal stars that would shine in some hours' time. The moon beamed in the midst of the constellations of the zenith.

The night slipped away without any mischance. The islanders were frightened, no doubt, at the sight of a monster aground in the bay. The panels were open, and would have offered an easy access to the interior of the *Nautilus*.

At six o'clock in the morning of January 8 I went up on the platform. The dawn was breaking. The island soon showed itself through the dissipating fogs, first the shore, then the summits.

The natives were there, more numerous than on the day before—five or six hundred perhaps—some of them, profiting by the low water, had come onto the coral, at less than two cable lengths from the *Nautilus*. I distinguished them easily; they were true Papuans, with athletic figures, men of good race, large high foreheads, large but not broad and flat, and white teeth. From the lobes of their ears, cut and distended, hung chaplets of bones. Most of these savages were naked. Among them I remarked some women, dressed from the hips to knees in a crinoline of herbs sustained by a vegetable waistband. Some chiefs had ornamented their necks with crescents and collars of glass beads, red and white. Nearly all were armed with bows, arrows and shields, and carried on their shoulders a sort of net containing those round stones which they cast from their slings with great skill. One of these chiefs, rather near to the *Nautilus*, examined it attentively. He was, perhaps, of high rank, for he was draped in a mat of banana leaves notched around the edges, and set off with brilliant colors.

I could easily have knocked down this native, who was quite near, but I thought it better to wait for a hostile demonstration. Between Europeans and savages it is proper for the Europeans to parry sharply, not to attack.

During low water the natives roamed about near the *Nautilus,* but were not troublesome; I heard them frequently repeat the word "Assai," and by their gestures I understood that they invited me to go on land, an invitation that I declined.

So on that day the little boat did not take us hunting, to the great displeasure of Master Land, who could not complete his provisions.

This adroit Canadian employed his time in preparing the viands and meat that he had brought off the island. As for the savages, they returned to the shore about eleven o'clock in the morning, as soon as the coral tops began to disappear under the rising tide; but I saw their numbers had increased considerably on the shore. Probably they came from the neighboring islands, or very likely from Papua. However, I had not seen a single native canoe. Having nothing better to do, I thought of dragging these beautiful limpid waters, under which I saw a profusion of shells, zoophytes, and marine plants. Moreover, it was the last day that the *Nautilus* would be in these parts, if it floated in open sea the next day, according to Captain Nemo's promise.

I therefore called Conseil, who brought me a little light drag very like those for the oyster fishery. Now to work! For two hours we fished unceasingly, but without bringing up any rarities. The drag was filled with midas ears, harps, melames, and particularly the most beautiful hammers I have ever seen. We also brought up some sea slugs, pearl oysters, and a dozen little turtles that were reserved for the pantry on board.

But just when I expected it least, I put my hand on a wonder, I might say a natural deformity, very rarely met with. Conseil was just dragging, and his net came up filled with divers ordinary shells, when, all at once, he saw me plunge my arm quickly into the net, draw out a shell, and heard me utter a cry.

"What is the matter, sir?" he asked in surprise. "Has Monsieur been bitten?"

"No, my boy, but I would willingly have given a finger for my discovery."

"What discovery?"

"This shell," I said, holding up the object of my triumph.

"It is simply an olive porphry."

"Yes, Conseil; but, instead of being rolled from right to left, this olive turns from left to right."

"Is it possible?"

"Yes, my boy; it is a left shell."

Shells are all right-handed, with rare exceptions; and when by chance their spiral is left, amateurs are ready to pay their weight in gold.

Conseil and I were absorbed in the contemplation of our treasure, and I was promising myself to enrich the museum with it, when a stone unfortunately thrown by a native struck against, and broke, the precious object in Conseil's hand. I uttered a cry of despair! Conseil took up his gun and aimed at a savage who was poising his sling at ten yards from him. I would have stopped him, but his blow took effect and broke the bracelet of amulets which encircled the arm of the savage.

"Conseil!" cried I. "Conseil!"

"Well, sir! do you not see that the cannibal has commenced the attack?"

"A shell is not worth the life of a man," I said.

"Ah! the scoundrel!" cried Conseil; "I would rather he had broken my shoulder!"

Conseil was in earnest, but I was not of his opinion. However, the situation had changed some minutes before, and we had not perceived. A score of canoes surrounded the *Nautilus*. These canoes, scooped out of the trunks of trees, long, narrow, well adapted for speed, were balanced by means of long bamboo poles which floated on the water. They were managed by skillful, half-naked paddlers, and I watched their advance with some uneasiness. It was evident that these Papuans had already had dealings with

the Europeans and knew their ships. But this long iron
cylinder anchored in the bay, without masts or chimneys,
what could they think of it? Nothing good, for at first they
kept at a respectful distance. However, seeing it motionless,
by degrees they took courage and sought to familiarize
themselves with it. Now this familiarity was precisely what
was necessary to avoid. Our arms, which were noiseless,
could only produce a moderate effect on the savages who
have little respect for aught but blustering things. The
thunderbolt without the reverberations of thunder would
frighten man but little, although the danger lies in the lightning, not in the noise.

At this moment the canoes approached the *Nautilus,* and
a shower of arrows alighted on it.

I went down to the lounge, but found no one there. I
ventured to knock at the door that opened into the captain's
room. "Come in," was the answer.

I entered, and found Captain Nemo deep in algebraical
calculations of x and other quantities.

"I am disturbing you," I said, for courtesy's sake.

"That is true, M. Aronnax," replied the captain; "but I
think you have serious reasons for wishing to see me?"

"Very grave ones: the natives are surrounding us in their
canoes, and in a few minutes we shall certainly be attacked
by many hundreds of savages."

"Ah!" said Captain Nemo quietly, "they are come with
their canoes?"

"Yes, sir."

"Well, sir, we must close the hatches."

"Exactly, and I came to say to you——"

"Nothing can be more simple," said Captain Nemo. And,

pressing an electric button, he transmitted an order to the ship's crew.

"It is all done, sir," said he, after some moments. "The pinnace is ready and the hatches are closed. You do not fear, I imagine, that these gentlemen could stave in walls on which the balls of your frigate have had no effect?"

"No, Captain, but a danger still exists."

"What is that, sir?"

"It is that tomorrow, at about this hour, we must open the hatches to renew the air of the *Nautilus*. Now, if, at this moment, the Papuans should occupy the platform, I do not see how you could prevent them from entering."

"Then, sir, do you suppose they will board us?"

"I am certain of it."

"Well, sir, let them come. I see no reason for hindering them. After all, these Papuans are poor creatures, and I am unwilling that my visit to the island should cost the life of a single one of these wretches."

Upon that I was going away, but Captain Nemo detained me, and asked me to sit down by him. He questioned me with interest about our excursions on shore, and our hunting; and seemed not to understand the craving for meat that possessed the Canadian. Then the conversation turned on various subjects, and without being more communicative, Captain Nemo showed himself more amiable.

Among other things, we happened to speak of the situation of the *Nautilus*, run aground in exactly the same spot in this strait where Dumont d'Urville was nearly lost. Apropos of this:

"This D'Urville was one of your great sailors," said the captain to me, "one of your most intelligent navigators. He was the Captain Cook of you Frenchmen. Unfortunate man of science, after having braved the icebergs of the South Pole, the coral reefs of Oceania, the cannibals of the Pacific, to perish miserably in a railway train! If this energetic man could have reflected during the last moments of his life, what would have been uppermost in his last thoughts, do you suppose?"

So speaking, Captain Nemo seemed moved, and his emotion gave me a better opinion of him. Then, chart in hand, we reviewed the travels of the French navigator, his voyages of circumnavigation, his double detention at the South Pole, which led to the discovery of Adelaide and Louis Philippe, and fixing the hydrographical bearings of the principal islands of Oceania.

"That which your D'Urville has done on the surface of the seas," said Captain Nemo, "that have I done under them, and more easily, more completely than he. The *Astrolabe* and the *Zélée,* incessantly tossed about by the hurricane, could not compare to the *Nautilus,* quiet repository of labor that it is, truly motionless in the midst of the waters.

"Tomorrow," added the captain, rising, "tomorrow, at 2:40 P.M. the *Nautilus* shall float, and sail undamaged through the Strait of Torres."

Having pronounced these words curtly, Captain Nemo bowed to dismiss me and I went back to my room.

There I found Conseil, who wished to know the result of my interview with the captain.

"My boy," I said, "when I feigned to believe that his *Nautilus* was threatened by the natives of Papua, the captain answered me very sarcastically. I have but one thing to say to you: have confidence in him, and sleep in peace."

"Has Monsieur no need of my services?"

"No, my friend. What is Ned Land doing at this moment?"

"If Monsieur will excuse me," answered Conseil, "friend Ned is busy making a kangaroo pie which will be a marvel."

I remained alone and went to bed, but slept indifferently. I heard the noise of the savages who stamped on the platform, uttering deafening cries. The night passed thus, without disturbing the ordinary repose of the crew. The presence of these cannibals affected them no more than the soldiers of a masked battery care for the ants that crawl over their fortification.

At six in the morning I arose. The hatches had not been opened. The inner air was not renewed, but the reservoirs, filled ready for any emergency, were now resorted to and discharged several cubic feet of oxygen into the exhausted atmosphere of the *Nautilus*.

I worked in my room till noon without having seen Captain Nemo even for an instant. On board no preparations for departure were visible.

I waited a while longer, then went into the big lounge. The clock marked half-past two. In ten minutes it would be high tide: and if Captain Nemo had not made a rash promise, the *Nautilus* would be immediately afloat. If not, many months would pass ere she could leave her bed of coral.

However, some warning vibrations began to be felt in the vessel. I heard the keel grating against the rough calcareous bottom of the coral reef.

At 2:35 P.M. Captain Nemo appeared in the lounge.

"We are going to start," said he.

"Ah!" I replied.

"I have given the order to open the hatches."

"And the Papuans?"

"The Papuans?" answered Captain Nemo, slightly shrugging his shoulders.

"Will they not come inside the *Nautilus?*"

"How?"

"Only by leaping over the hatches you have opened."

"Mr. Aronnax," quietly answered Captain Nemo, "they will not enter the hatches of the *Nautilus* in that way, even if they were open."

I looked at the captain.

"You do not understand?" said he.

"Hardly."

"Well, come and you will see."

I directed my steps toward the central staircase. There Ned Land and Conseil were slyly watching some of the ship's crew who were opening the hatches, while cries of rage and fearful vociferations resounded outside.

The port lids were pulled down outside. Twenty horrible faces appeared. But the first native who placed his hand on the stair rail, struck from behind by some invisible force, I know not what, fled, uttering the most fearful cries and making the wildest contortions.

Ten of his companions followed him. They met with the same fate.

Conseil was in ecstasy. Ned Land, carried away by his violent instincts, rushed onto the staircase. But the moment he seized the rail with both hands, he, in his turn, was overthrown.

"I am struck by a thunderbolt," he cried with an oath.

This explained all. It was no rail, but a metallic cable charged with electricity from the deck communicating with the platform. Whoever touched it felt a powerful shock—

and this shock could have been mortal if Captain Nemo had discharged into the conductor the whole force of the current. It might truly be said that between his assailants and himself he had stretched a network of electricity which none could safely pass.

Meanwhile Papuans, paralyzed with terror, had beaten a retreat. As for us, half laughing, we consoled and rubbed the unfortunate Ned Land who swore like one possessed.

But at this moment the *Nautilus,* raised by the last waves of the tide, quitted its coral bed exactly at the fortieth minute fixed by the captain. Its propeller swept the waters slowly and majestically. Its speed gradually increased, and sailing on the surface of the ocean, the *Nautilus* quitted safe and sound the dangerous passes of the Strait of Torres.

22. "Aegri, Somnia"

THE FOLLOWING day, January 10, the *Nautilus* continued its course between two seas, but with such remarkable speed that I could not estimate it at less than 35 knots. The rapidity of its propeller was such that I could neither follow nor count its revolutions. When I reflected that this marvelous electric agent, after having afforded motion, heat, and light to the *Nautilus,* still protected it from outward attack, and transformed it into an ark of safety which no profane hand might touch without being thunderstruck, my admiration was unbounded, and from the structure it extended to the engineer who had called it into existence.

Our course was directed to the west, and on the 11th of January we doubled Cape Wessel, situated in 135° long.

and 10° N. lat., which forms the east point of the Gulf of Carpentaria. The reefs were still numerous, but more equalized, and marked on the chart with extreme precision. The *Nautilus* easily avoided the breakers of Money to port and the Victoria reefs to starboard, placed at 130° long. and on the 10th parallel, which we strictly followed.

On the 13th of January Captain Nemo arrived in the Sea of Timor, and recognized the island of that name in 122° long.

From this point the direction of the *Nautilus* inclined toward the southwest. Its prow was set for the Indian Ocean. Where would the fancy of Captain Nemo carry us next? Would he return to the coast of Asia or would he approach again the shores of Europe? Improbable conjectures both, to a man who fled from inhabited continents. Then would he go south? Was he going to round the Cape of Good Hope, then Cape Horn, and finally go to the Antarctic? Would he come back at last to the Pacific where his *Nautilus* could sail free and independently? Time would show.

After having skirted the sands of Cartier, of Hibernia, Seringapatam, and Scott, last efforts of the solid against the liquid element, on the 14th of January we lost sight of land altogether. The speed of the *Nautilus* was considerably abated as with irregular course it sometimes swam in the bosom of the waters, sometimes floated on their surface.

During this period of the voyage Captain Nemo made some interesting experiments on the varied temperature of the sea, in different beds. Ordinarily these observations are made by means of rather complicated instruments and with somewhat doubtful results, by means of thermometrical sounding leads, the glasses often breaking under the pressure of the water, or an apparatus grounded on the variations of the resistance of metals to the electric currents. Results so obtained cannot be correctly calculated. Captain Nemo, on the other hand, went himself to test the temperature in the depths of the sea, and his thermometer, placed in communication with the different sheets of water, gave him the required degree immediately and accurately.

It was thus that, either by overloading its reservoirs or by descending obliquely by means of its fins, the *Nautilus* successively attained the depth of nine, twelve, fifteen, twenty-one, twenty-seven, thirty thousand feet, and the definite result of this experience was that the sea preserved an average temperature of 40° Fahrenheit, at a depth of 5,000 fathoms under all latitudes.

On the 16th of January the *Nautilus* rested motionless only a few feet beneath the surface of the waves. Its electric equipment and propeller were motionless, and the vessel drifted at the mercy of the currents. I supposed that the crew was occupied with interior repairs.

My companions and I then witnessed a curious spectacle. The hatches of the lounge were open, and as the beacon light of the *Nautilus* was not in action, a dim obscurity reigned in the water. I observed the sea under these conditions, the largest fish appearing no more than scarcely defined shadows, when the *Nautilus* was suddenly bathed in bright light. I thought at first that the beacon had been lighted and was casting its electric radiance into the liquid mass. I was mistaken, and after a rapid survey perceived the answer.

The *Nautilus* floated in the midst of a phosphorescent

bed which, in this obscurity, became quite dazzling. It was produced by myriads of luminois animalcula whose brilliancy was increased as they glided over the metallic hull of the vessel. I was surprised by lightning flashes among these luminous waters, as though they were streams of molten lead from an ardent furnace, or metallic masses brought to a white heat. By force of contrast, certain portions of light appeared to cast a shade in the midst of the general ignition, from which all shade seemed banished. No; this was not the calm irradiation of our ordinary lightning. There was unusual life and vigor: this was truly living light!

In reality, it was an infinite agglomeration of colored infusoria, of veritable globules of jelly provided with a threadlike tentacle, and of which as many as 25,000 have been counted in less than two cubic half inches of water.

For several hours the *Nautilus* floated in these brilliant waves, and our admiration increased as we watched the marine monsters disporting themselves like salamanders. I saw there, in the midst of this fire that burns not, the swift and elegant porpoise (the indefatigable clown of the ocean), and some swordfish ten feet long, those prophetic heralds of the hurricane whose formidable sword would now and then strike the glass of the lounge. Then appeared the smaller fish, the balista, the leaping mackerel, wolf thorntails, and a hundred others which striped the luminous atmosphere as they swam. This dazzling spectacle was enchanting! Perhaps some atmospheric condition increased the intensity of this phenomenon. Perhaps some storm agitated the surface of the waves. But at this depth of several feet the *Nautilus* was unmoved by its fury and reposed peacefully in still water.

So we progressed, incessantly charmed by some new marvel. The days passed rapidly away and I took no account of them. Ned, according to habit, tried to vary the diet on board. Like snails we were fixed to our shell, and I declare it is easy to lead a snail's life.

This life seemed easy and natural and we thought no longer of the life we led on land; but something happened to recall us to the strangeness of our situation.

On the 18th of January the *Nautilus* was in 105° long. and 15° S. lat. The weather was threatening, the sea rough and rolling. There was a strong east wind. The barometer, which had been going down for some days, foreboded a coming storm. I went up onto the platform just as the second lieutenant was taking the measure of the horary angles, and waited, according to habit, till the daily phrase was said. But on this day it was exchanged for another phrase not less incomprehensible. Almost directly I saw Captain Nemo appear with a glass, looking toward the horizon.

For some minutes he was immovable, without taking his eye off the point of observation. Then he lowered his glass and exchanged a few words with his lieutenant. The latter seemed to be a victim of some emotion that he tried in vain to repress. Captain Nemo, having more command over himself, was cool. He seemed, too, to be making some objections to which the lieutenant replied by formal assurances. At least I concluded so by the difference of their tones and gestures. For myself, I had looked carefully in the direction indicated without seeing anything. The sky and water were lost in the clear line of the horizon.

However, Captain Nemo walked from one end of the

platform to the other, without looking at me, perhaps without seeing me. His step was firm but less regular than usual. He stopped sometimes, crossed his arms and observed the sea. What could he be looking for on that immense expanse?

The *Nautilus* was then some hundreds of miles from the nearest coast.

The lieutenant had taken up the glass and examined the horizon steadfastly, going and coming, stamping his foot and showing more nervous agitation than his superior officer. This mystery must necessarily be solved before long; and upon an order from Captain Nemo the engine increased its power, making the propeller turn with great rapidity.

Just then the lieutenant drew the captain's attention again. The latter stopped walking and directed his glass toward the place indicated. He looked long. I felt very much puzzled and descended to the lounge where I took out an excellent telescope that I generally used. Then leaning on the cage of the watch light that jutted out from the front of the platform, I set myself to look over all the line of the sky and sea.

But my eye was no sooner applied to the glass than it was quickly snatched out of my hands.

I turned around. Captain Nemo was before me, but I did not know him. His face was transfigured. His eyes flashed sullenly; his teeth were set; his stiff body, clenched fists, and head shrunk between his shoulders betrayed the violent agitation that pervaded his whole frame. He did not move. My glass had fallen from his hands and rolled at his feet.

Had I unwittingly provoked this fit of anger? Did this

incomprehensible person imagine that I had discovered some forbidden secret? No; I was not the object of this hatred for he was not looking at me; his eye was steadily fixed upon the impenetrable point of the horizon. At last Captain Nemo recovered himself. His agitation subsided. He addressed some words in a foreign language to his lieutenant, then turned to me. "Mr. Aronnax," he said, in rather an imperious tone, "I require you to keep one of the conditions that bind you to me."

"What is it, Captain?"

"You must be confined, with your companions, until I think fit to release you."

"You are the master," I replied, looking steadily at him. "But may I ask you one question?"

"None, sir."

There was no resisting this imperious command. It would have been useless. I went down to the cabin occupied by Ned Land and Conseil, and told them the captain's determination. You may judge how this communication was received by the Canadian.

But there was no time for altercation. Four of the crew waited at the door and conducted us to that cell where we had passed our first night on board the *Nautilus*.

Ned Land would have remonstrated, but the door was shut upon him.

"Will Monsieur tell me what this means?" asked Conseil.

I told my companions what had passed. They were as much astonished as I, and equally at a loss to account for it.

Meanwhile, I was absorbed in my own reflections and could think of nothing but the strange fear depicted in the captain's countenance. I was utterly at a loss to account for it when my cogitations were disturbed by these words from Ned Land:

"Hallo, breakfast is ready."

And indeed the table was laid. Evidently Captain Nemo had given this order at the same time that he had hastened the speed of the *Nautilus*.

"Will Monsieur permit me to make a recommendation?" asked Conseil.

"Yes, my boy."

"Well, it is that Monsieur take breakfast. It is prudent, for we do not know what may happen."

"You are right, Conseil."

"Unfortunately," said Ned Land, "they have only given us the ship's fare."

"Friend Ned," asked Conseil, "what would you have said if the breakfast had been entirely forgotten?"

This argument cut short the harpooner's recriminations. We sat down to table. The meal was eaten in silence.

Just then the luminous globe that lighted the cell went out and left us in total darkness. Ned Land was soon asleep, and what astonished me was that Conseil went off into a heavy slumber. I was thinking what could have caused his irresistible drowsiness, when I felt my brain becoming stupefied. In spite of my efforts to keep my eyes open they would close. A painful suspicion seized me. Evidently soporific substances had been mixed with the food we had just taken. Imprisonment was not enough to conceal Captain Nemo's projects from us; sleep was also necessary. I then heard the panels shut. The undulations of the sea, which caused a slight rolling motion, ceased. Had the *Nautilus* quitted the surface of the ocean? Had it gone back to the motionless bed of the sea? I tried to resist sleep. It was impossible. My breathing grew weak. I felt a mortal cold freeze my stiffened and half-paralyzed limbs. My eyelids fell like leaden caps over my eyes; I could not raise them. A morbid sleep, full of hallucinations, bereft me of my being. Then the visions disappeared and left me in complete insensibility.

23. The Coral Kingdom

THE NEXT day I awoke with my head singularly clear. To my great surprise, I was in my own room. My companions, no doubt, had been reinstated in their cabin without having perceived it any more than I. Of what had passed during the night they were as ignorant as I was, and to penetrate this mystery I could count only on a chance revelation.

I then thought of quitting my room. Was I free again, or still a prisoner? Quite free. I opened the door, went to the half deck, climbed the central stairs. The panels, shut the evening before, were open. I went onto the platform.

Ned Land and Conseil waited there for me. I questioned them; they knew nothing. Lost in a heavy sleep in which they had been totally unconscious, they had also been astonished at finding themselves in their cabin.

As for the *Nautilus,* it seemed as quiet and mysterious as ever. It floated on the surface of the waves at a moderate pace. Nothing seemed changed on board.

The second lieutenant then came onto the platform and gave the usual order below.

As for Captain Nemo, he did not appear.

Of the people on board, I saw only the impassive steward, who served me with his usual dumb regularity.

About two o'clock I was in the lounge, busied in arranging my notes, when the captain opened the door and appeared. I bowed. He made a slight inclination in return
without speaking. I resumed my work, hoping that he
would perhaps give me some explanation of the events of
the preceding night. He made none. I looked at him. He
seemed fatigued; his heavy eyes had not been refreshed by
sleep; his face looked very sorrowful. He walked to and fro,
sat down and got up again, took a chance book, put it
down, consulted his instruments without taking his habitual
notes, and seemed restless and uneasy. At last he came up
to me, and said:

"Are you a doctor, Mr. Aronnax?"

I so little expected such a question that I stared some
time at him without answering.

"Are you a doctor?" he repeated. "Several of your colleagues have studied medicine."

"Well," I said, "I am a doctor and resident surgeon to the
hospital. I practiced several years before entering the museum."

"Very well, sir."

My answer had evidently satisfied the captain. But, not
knowing what he would say next, I waited for other questions, reserving my answers according to circumstances.

"Mr. Aronnax, will you consent to prescribe for one of
my men?" he asked.

"Is he ill?"

"Yes."

"I am ready to follow you."

"Come, then."

I own that my heart beat fast, I don't know why. I saw a certain connection between the illness of one of the crew and the events of the day before, and this mystery interested me at least as much as the sick man.

Captain Nemo led me to the poop of the *Nautilus,* and into a cabin situated near the sailors' quarters.

There on a bed lay a man about forty years of age, with a resolute expression of countenance, a true type of an Anglo-Saxon.

I leaned over him. He was not only ill; he was wounded. His head, swathed in bandages covered with blood, rested on a pillow. I undid the bandages and the wounded man looked at me with his large eyes and gave no sign of pain as I did it. It was a horrible wound. The skull, shattered by some deadly weapon, had exposed the brain, which was much injured. Clots of blood had formed in the bruised and broken mass, in color like the dregs of wine.

There were both contusion and suffusion of the brain. His breathing was slow, and some spasmodic movements of the muscles agitated his face. I felt his pulse. It was intermittent. The extremities of the body were growing cold already, and I saw death must inevitably ensue. After dressing the unfortunate man's wounds, I readjusted the bandages on his head, and turned to Captain Nemo.

"What caused this wound?" I asked.

"What does it matter?" he replied evasively. "A shock broke off one of the levers of the engine, and struck him. But your opinion as to his state?"

I hesitated before giving it.

"You may speak," said the captain. "This man does not understand French."

I gave a last look at the wounded man.

"He will be dead within two hours or less."

"Can nothing save him?"

"Nothing."

Captain Nemo's hand contracted, and some tears glistened in his eyes, which I thought incapable of shedding any.

For some moments I still watched the dying man, whose life ebbed slowly. His pallor increased under the electric light over his deathbed. I looked at his intelligent forehead furrowed with premature wrinkles, produced probably by misfortune and sorrow. I tried to learn the secret of his life from the last words that escaped his lips.

"You can go now, Mr. Aronnax," said the captain.

I left him in the dying man's cabin, and returned to my room much affected by this scene. During the whole day I was haunted by uncomfortable suspicions and at night I slept badly. Between my broken dreams I fancied I heard distant sighs like the notes of a funeral psalm. Were they the prayers of the dead, murmured in that language that I could not understand?

The next morning I went on to the bridge. Captain Nemo was there before me. As soon as he perceived me he came to me.

"Professor, will it be convenient to you to make a submarine excursion today?"

"With my companions?" I asked.

"If they like."

"We obey your orders, Captain."

"Will you be so good then as to put on your cork jackets?"

This had nothing to do with the dead or dying, I thought.

I rejoined Ned Land and Conseil, and told them of Captain Nemo's proposition. Conseil hastened to accept it, and this time the Canadian seemed quite willing to follow our example.

It was eight o'clock in the morning. At half-past eight we were equipped for this new excursion and provided with two contrivances for light and breathing. The double door was open; and, accompanied by Captain Nemo, who was followed by a dozen of the crew, we set foot, at a depth of about thirty feet, on the solid bottom on which the *Nautilus* rested.

A long slope ended in an uneven bed ninety feet deep. This bottom differed entirely from the one I had visited on my first excursion under the waters of the Pacific Ocean. Here there was no fine sand, no submarine prairies, no sea forest. I immediately recognized that marvelous region in which, on that day, the captain did the honors to us. It was the coral kingdom.

The light produced a thousand charming varieties, playing in the midst of the branches that were so vividly colored. I seemed to see the membranous and cylindrical tubes tremble beneath the undulation of the waters. I was tempted to gather their fresh petals, ornamented with delicate tentacles, some just blown, others budding, while a small fish, swimming swiftly, touched them slightly, like flights of birds. But if my hand approached these living flowers, these animated, sensitive plants, the whole colony took alarm. The white petals re-entered their red cases, the flowers faded as I looked, and the bush changed into a block of stony knobs.

Chance had just thrown me among the most precious

specimens of the zoophyte. This coral was more valuable than that found in the Mediterranean, on the coasts of France, Italy or Barbary. Its tints justified the poetical names of *flower of blood* and *blood foam* that trade has given to its most beautiful productions. Coral is sold for $100 per ounce; and in this place the watery beds would make the fortunes of a company of coral divers. This precious matter, often confused with other polyps, formed then an inextricable tangle called "macciota," and on which I noticed several beautiful specimens of pink coral.

Real petrified thickets, long joints of fantastic architecture, were disclosed before us. Captain Nemo stood under a dark gallery where by a steep incline we reached a depth of 300 feet. The light from our lamps produced magical effects, highlighting the rough outlines of the natural arches, and tipping with points of fire the pendant formations.

At last, after walking two hours, we had attained a depth of about 900 feet; that is to say, the extreme limit of the coral formation. But there was no isolated bush, no modest brushwood, at the bottom of these lofty trees. It was an immense forest of large mineral vegetations, enormous petrified trees united by garlands of elegant sea bindweed, all adorned with clouds and reflections. We passed freely under their high branches, lost in the shade of the waves.

Captain Nemo had stopped. I and my companions halted, and, turning around, I saw his men were forming a semicircle around their chief. Watching attentively, I observed that four of them carried on their shoulders an object of an oblong shape.

We occupied, in this place, the center of a vast glade

surrounded by the lofty foliage of the submarine forest. Our lamps threw over this place a sort of clear twilight that singularly elongated the shadows on the ground. At the end of the glade the darkness increased, and was only relieved by little sparks reflected by the points of coral.

Ned Land and Conseil were near me. We watched, and I felt that I was going to witness a strange scene. On observing the ground, I saw that it was raised in certain places by slight excrescences encrusted with limy deposits, and disposed with a regularity that betrayed the hand of man.

In the midst of the glade, on a pedestal of rocks roughly piled up, stood a cross of coral that extended long arms one might have thought were made of petrified blood. At a sign from Captain Nemo one of the men advanced; and at some feet from the cross he began to dig a hole with a pickax that he took from his belt. I understood all! This glade was a cemetery, this hole a tomb, this oblong object the body of the man who had died in the night! The captain and his men had come to bury their companion in this general resting place at the bottom of this inaccessible ocean!

The grave was being dug slowly; the fish fled on all sides while their retreat was being thus disturbed; I heard the strokes of the pickax, which sparkled when it hit upon some flint lost at the bottom of the ocean. The hole was soon large and deep enough to receive the body. Then the bearers approached; the body, enveloped in a tissue of white linen, was lowered into the damp grave. Captain Nemo, with his arms crossed on his breast, and all the friends of him who had loved them, knelt in prayer.

The grave was then filled in with the rubbish taken from the ground, which formed a slight mound. When this was

done, Captain Nemo and his men rose; approaching the
grave, they knelt again and all extended their hands in sign
of a last adieu. Then the funeral procession returned to the
Nautilus, passing under the arches of the forest, through
thickets, beside coral bushes, and still on the ascent. At last
the light of the ship appeared, and its luminous track guided
us to the *Nautilus.* At one o'clock we had returned.

As soon as I had changed my clothes I went up onto the
platform, and, a prey to conflicting emotions, I sat down
near the binnacle. Captain Nemo joined me. I rose and said
to him:

"So, as I said he would, this man died in the night?"

"Yes, Mr. Aronnax."

"And he rests now, near his companions, in the coral
cemetery?"

"Yes, forgotten by all else, but not by us. We dug the
grave, and the polyps undertake to seal our dead for eternity." And, burying his face quickly in his hands, he tried in
vain to suppress a sob. Then he added: "Our peaceful
cemetery is there some hundred feet below the surface of
the waves."

"Your dead sleep quietly, at least, Captain, out of the
reach of sharks."

"Yes, sharks and *men,*" gravely replied the captain.

PART TWO

1. The Indian Ocean

WE NOW come to the second part of our journey under the sea. The first ended with the moving scene in the coral cemetery which left such a deep impression on my mind. Captain Nemo would pass his entire life in the midst of the seas, and had even prepared his grave in one of its deepest abysses. There, no ocean monster would trouble the last sleep of the *Nautilus'* crew, those friends riveted to each other in death as in life. "Nor any man, either," had added the captain, expressing again his fierce, implacable defiance toward human society.

I could no longer content myself with Conseil's theory.

That worthy fellow persisted in visualizing the commander of the *Nautilus* as one of those obscure servants who return mankind's indifference with contempt. To Conseil, the captain was a misunderstood genius tired of earth's deceptions, who had taken refuge in this inaccessible medium where he might follow his instincts freely. To my mind, this explained but one side of Captain Nemo's character. Indeed, the mystery of that last night during which we had

179

been chained in prison, the sleep, and the precaution so violently taken by the captain of snatching from my eyes the glass I had raised to sweep the horizon, the mortal wound of the man due to an unaccountable shock of the *Nautilus*—all put me on a new track. No. Captain Nemo was not satisfied with shunning man. His formidable machine not only suited his instinct of freedom, but perhaps also the design of some terrible retaliation.

At this moment nothing was clear to me; I caught but a glimpse of light amid all the darkness, and had to confine myself to writing as events dictated.

That day, the 24th of January, 1868, at noon, the second officer came to take the altitude of the sun. I mounted the platform, lit a cigar, and watched the operation. It seemed to me that the man did not understand French for several times I made remarks in a loud voice which must have drawn from him some involuntary sign of attention, if he had understood them; but he remained undisturbed and dumb.

As he was taking observations with the sextant, one of the sailors of the *Nautilus*—the strong man who had accompanied us on our first submarine excursion to the Island of Crespo—came to clean the glass of the lantern. I examined the fittings of the lamp, the strength of which was increased a hundredfold by lenticular rings placed similar to those in a lighthouse, and which projected their brilliance in a horizontal plane. The electric lamp was put together in such a way as to give its most powerful light. Indeed, it was produced *in vacuo,* which insured both its steadiness and its intensity. This vacuum economized the graphite points between which the luminous arc was developed—an important point of economy for Captain Nemo, who could not easily have replaced them; and under these conditions their waste was imperceptible. When the *Nautilus* was ready to continue its submarine journey I went down to the lounge. The panel was closed, and the course marked direct west.

We were furrowing the waters of the Indian Ocean, a vast liquid plain with a surface of 28,925,504 square miles, and whose waters are so clear and transparent that anyone leaning over them would turn giddy. The *Nautilus* usually floated between fifty and a hundred fathoms deep. We went on so for some days. To anyone but myself, who had a great love for the sea, the hours would have seemed long and monotonous; but the daily walks on the platform, when I steeped myself in the reviving air of the ocean, the sight of the rich waters through the windows of the lounge, the books in the library, the compiling of my memoirs, took up all my time, and left me not a moment of ennui or weariness.

For some days we saw a great number of aquatic birds, sea mews or gulls. Some were cleverly killed and, prepared in a certain way, made very acceptable water game. Among large-winged birds, carried a long distance from all lands and resting upon the waves from the fatigue of their flight, I saw some magnificent albatrosses, uttering discordant cries like the braying of an ass, and birds belonging to the family of the long wings.

As to the fish, they always provoked our admiration when we surprised the secrets of their aquatic life through the open panels. I saw many kinds which I never before had a chance of observing.

From the 21st to the 23rd of January the *Nautilus* moved

at the rate of 250 leagues in twenty-four hours, that is, 540 miles, or at 22 knots. If we recognized so many different varieties of fish it was because, attracted by the electric light, they tried to follow us; the greater part, however, were soon outdistanced by our speed, though they remained in the area of the *Nautilus* for a time. The morning of the 24th, in 12° 5′ S. lat. and 94° 33′ long. we observed Keeling Island, a coral formation planted with magnificent coconut trees, and which had been visited by Mr. Darwin and Captain Fitzroy. The *Nautilus* skirted the shores of this desert island for a little distance. Its nets brought up numerous specimens of polyps and curious shells of molluscs.

Soon Keeling Island disappeared from the horizon, and our course was toward the northwest in the direction of the Indian Peninsula.

From Keeling Island our course was slower and more variable, often taking us into great depths. Several times the captain used the side fins, which certain internal levers placed obliquely at the water line. In that way we cruised at about two miles, but without ever obtaining the greatest depths of the Indian Sea, whose soundings of 7,000 fathoms have never been reached. As to the temperature of the lower strata, the thermometer invariable indicated 39° Fahrenheit. I did, however, observe that in the upper regions the water was always colder in the high levels than at the surface of the sea.

On the 25th of January the ocean was entirely deserted; the *Nautilus* passed the day on the surface, beating the waves with its powerful propeller and making them rebound to a great height. Who under such circumstances would not have taken it for a gigantic whale? Three parts of this day I spent on the platform. I watched the sea. Nothing on the horizon, till about four o'clock a steamer running west on our counter. Her masts were visible for an instant, but she could not see the *Nautilus,* which lay low in the water. She probably belonged to the Peninsula and Oriental line that runs from Ceylon to Sydney, touching at King George's Point and Melbourne.

At five o'clock in the evening, just before that fleeting twilight which binds night to day in tropical zones, Conseil and I saw a curious spectacle.

It was a shoal of argonauts traveling along on the surface of the ocean. We could count several hundreds. They belonged to a tubular kind which are peculiar to the Indian seas.

These graceful molluscs moved backward by means of their locomotive tube through which they propelled the water already drawn in. Of their eight tentacles, six were elongated and stretched out floating on the water, while the other two, rolled up flat, were spread to the wing like a light sail. I saw their spiral-shaped and fluted shells, which Cuvier justly compares to an elegant skiff. A boat indeed! It bears the creature which secretes it without its adhering to it.

For nearly an hour the *Nautilus* floated in the midst of this shoal of molluscs. Then I know not what sudden fright they took. But as if at a signal every sail was furled, the arms folded, the body drawn in, the shells turned over, changing their center of gravity, and the whole fleet disappeared under the waves. Never did the ships of a squadron maneuver with more uniformity.

At that moment night fell suddenly, and the reeds, scarcely raised by the breeze, lay peaceably under the sides of the *Nautilus*.

The next day, the 26th of January, we cut the equator at

the eighty-second meridian and entered the Northern Hemisphere. During the day a formidable troop of sharks accompanied us, terrible creatures, which multiply in these seas and make them very dangerous. They were the *cestracio philippi* sharks, with brown backs and whitish bellies, armed with eleven rows of teeth—eyed sharks—their throat being marked with a large black spot surrounded with white like an eye. There were also some Isabella sharks, with rounded snouts marked with dark spots. These powerful creatures often hurled themselves at the windows of the lounge with such violence as to make us feel very insecure. At such times Ned Land was no longer master of himself. He wanted to go to the surface and harpoon the monsters, particularly certain smooth-hound sharks, whose mouths are studded with teeth like a mosaic; and large tiger sharks nearly 13 feet long, the last named of which seemed to excite him more particularly. But the *Nautilus,* accelerating her speed, easily left the most rapid of them behind.

The 27th of January, at the entrance of the vast Bay of Bengal, we met repeatedly a forbidding spectacle, dead bodies floating on the surface of the water. They were the dead of the Indian villages, carried by the Ganges to the level of the sea, and which the vultures, the only undertakers of the country, had not been able to devour. But the sharks did not fail to help them at their grisly work.

About seven o'clock in the evening the *Nautilus,* half immersed, was sailing in a milk-white sea. At first sight the ocean seemed filled with milk. Was it the effect of the lunar rays? No, for the moon, scarcely two days old, was still lying hidden under the horizon in the rays of the sun. The whole sky, though lit by the sidereal rays, seemed black by contrast with the whiteness of the waters.

Conseil could not believe his eyes, and questioned me as to the cause of this strange phenomenon. Happily I was able to answer him.

"It is called a milk sea," I explained. "A large extent of white wavelets often to be seen on the coasts of Amboyna, and in these parts of the sea."

"But," said Conseil, "can Monsieur tell me what causes such an effect? For I suppose the water is not really turned into milk."

"No, my boy; and the whiteness which surprises you is caused only by the presence of myriads of infusoria, a sort of luminous little worm, gelatinous and without color, of the thickness of a hair, and whose length is not more than seven-thousandths of an inch. These insects adhere to one another sometimes for several leagues."

"Several leagues!" exclaimed Conseil.

"Yes, my boy; and you need not try to compute the number of these infusoria. You will not be able, for, if I am not mistaken, ships have floated on these milk seas for more than 40 miles."

Toward midnight the sea suddenly resumed its usual color; but behind us, even to the limits of the horizon, the sky reflected the whitened waves, and for a long time seemed impregnated with the vague glimmerings of an aurora borealis.

2. The Novel Proposal of Captain Nemo

ON THE 28th of February, when at noon the *Nautilus* came to the surface of the sea, in 9° 4′ N. lat., there was land in sight about eight miles to westward. The first thing I noticed was a range of mountains about two thousand feet high, whose outlines were most unusual. On taking the bearings, I knew that we were nearing the Island of Ceylon, the pearl which hangs from the lobe of the Indian Peninsula.

Captain Nemo and his second appeared at this moment. The captain glanced at the map. Then, turning to me, he said:

"The Island of Ceylon, noted for its pearl fisheries. Would you like to visit one of them, Mr. Aronnax?"

"Certainly, Captain."

"Well, the thing is easy. Though if we see the fisheries, we shall not see the fishermen. The annual exportation has not yet begun. Never mind, I will give orders to head for the Gulf of Manaar, and we shall reach it tonight."

The captain said something to his second, who immediately went out. Soon the *Nautilus* sank to her native element, and the manometer showed that she was about 30 feet deep.

"Well, sir," said Captain Nemo, "you and your companions shall visit the Bank of Manaar, and if by chance some fisherman should be there, we shall see him at work."

"Agreed, Captain!"

"By the way, Mr. Aronnax, you are not afraid of sharks?"

"Sharks!" I exclaimed.

This question seemed a difficult one.

"Well?" continued Captain Nemo.

"I admit, Captain, that I am not yet very familiar with that kind of fish."

"*We* are accustomed to them," replied Captain Nemo, "and in time you will be, too. However, we shall be armed, and on the road we may be able to hunt some of the tribe. It is interesting. So, till tomorrow, sir, and early."

This said in a careless tone, Captain Nemo left the lounge. Now, if you were invited to hunt the bear in the mountains of Switzerland, what would you say?

"Very well! tomorrow we will go and hunt the bear?"

Were you asked to hunt the lion in the plains of Atlas, or the tiger in the Indian jungles, what would you say?

"Ha! ha! it seems we are going to hunt tiger or lion!"

But if you should be invited to hunt the shark in its native haunt, you would perhaps reflect before accepting the invitation. As for myself, I passed my hand over my forehead, on which stood large drops of cold perspiration. "Let us consider this carefully," said I, "and take our time about it. Hunting otters in submarine forests as we did in the Island of Crespo, is quite all right. But going up and down the bottom of the sea where one is almost certain to meet sharks, that is another matter! I know well that in certain countries, particularly in the Andaman Islands, the natives never hesitate to attack the sharks with a dagger in one hand and a running noose in the other. But I also know that few who affront those creatures ever return alive. However, I am not a native, and if I were I think a little hesitation in this case would not be ill-timed."

At this moment Conseil and the Canadian entered, quite composed, and even joyous. They knew not what awaited them.

"Faith, sir," said Ned Land, "your Captain Nemo—the devil take him!—has just made us a very pleasant offer."

"Ah!" I said, "you know?"

"If agreeable to Monsieur," interrupted Conseil, "the

commander of the *Nautilus* has invited us to visit the magnificent Ceylon fisheries tomorrow in your company; he did it kindly, and behaved like a real gentleman."

"He said nothing more?"

"Nothing more, sir, except that he had already spoken to you of this little walk."

"Would Monsieur," said Conseil, "give us some details of the pearl fishery?"

"As to the fishing itself," I asked, "or the incidents, which?"

"On the fishing," replied the Canadian. "Before entering the ground, it's well to know something about it."

"Very well; sit down, my friends, and I will teach you."

Ned and Conseil seated themselves on an ottoman, and the first thing the Canadian asked was:

"Sir, what is a pearl?"

"My worthy Ned," I answered, "to the poet a pearl is a tear of the sea; to the Orientals, it is a drop of dew solidified; to the ladies, it is a jewel of an oblong shape, of a brilliancy of mother-of-pearl substance, which they wear on their fingers, their necks, or their ears; for the chemist it is a mixture of phosphate and carbonate of lime, with a little gelatin; and lastly, for naturalists, it is simply a morbid secretion of the organ that produces the mother-of-pearl among certain bivalves."

"Branch of mollusca," said Conseil.

"Precisely so, my learned Conseil; and, among these testacea, the ear shell, the tridacnae, the turbos, in a word, all those which secrete mother-of-pearl; that is, the blue, bluish, violet, or white substance which lines the interior of their shells, are capable of producing pearls."

"Mussels, too?" asked the Canadian.

"Yes, mussels of certain waters in Scotland, Wales, Ireland, Saxony, Bohemia, and France."

"Good! I shall be on the lookout, in the future," replied the Canadian.

"But," I continued, "the particular mollusc which yields most of the world's supply of pearls is the pearl oyster. The pearl is nothing but a formation deposited in a globular form, either adhering to the oyster shell or buried in the folds of the creature. On the shell it is fast: in the flesh it is loose; but always has for a kernel a small hard substance, maybe a barren egg, maybe a grain of sand, around which the pearly matter deposits itself year after year successively, and by thin concentric layers."

"Are many pearls found in the same oyster?" asked Conseil.

"Yes, my boy. Some are a perfect casket. One oyster has been mentioned, though I allow myself to doubt it, as having contained no less than 150 sharks."

"A hundred and fifty sharks!" exclaimed Ned Land.

"Did I say sharks?" I said hurriedly. "I meant to say 150 pearls. Shark does not make sense."

"Certainly not," said Conseil; "but will you tell us now by what means they extract these pearls?"

"They proceed in various ways. When they adhere to the shell, the fishermen often pull them off with pincers; but the most common way is to lay the oysters on mats of the seaweed which covers the banks. Thus they die in the open air; and at the end of ten days they are in an advanced state of decomposition. They are then plunged into large reservoirs of sea water; then they are opened and washed."

"The price of these pearls varies according to their size?" asked Conseil.

"Not only according to their size," I answered, "but also according to their shape, their *water*—that is, their color— and their luster, which make them so charming to the eye. The most beautiful are called virgin pearls, or paragons. They form singly in the tissue of the mollusc—white, often opaque, and sometimes with the transparency of an opal. They are generally round or oval. The round ones are made into bracelets, the oval ones into pendants, and, being more precious, are sold singly. Those adhering to the shell of the oyster are more irregular in shape, and are sold by weight. Lastly, in a lower order are classed those small pearls known as seed pearls; they are sold by measure, and are especially used in embroidery for church ornaments."

"But," said Conseil, "is this pearl fishery dangerous?"

"No," I answered quickly; "particularly if certain pre- cautions are taken."

"What does one risk in such a calling?" said Ned Land, "the swallowing of some mouthfuls of sea water?"

"As you say, Ned. By the way," said I, trying to take Captain Nemo's careless tone, "are you afraid of sharks, brave Ned?"

"I!" replied the Canadian; "a harpooner by profession? It is my trade to make light of them."

"But," said I, "it is not a question of fishing for them with an iron swivel, hoisting them into the vessel, cutting off their tails with a blow of a chopper, ripping them up, and throwing their hearts into the sea!"

"Then, it is a question of——"

"Precisely."

"In the water?"

"In the water."

"Faith, with a good harpoon! You know, sir, these sharks are ill-fashioned beasts. They turn on their bellies to seize you, and in that time——"

Ned Land had a way of saying "seize" which made my blood run cold.

"Well, and you, Conseil, what do you think of sharks?"

"Me!" said Conseil. "I will be frank, Monsieur."

"So much the better," thought I.

"If Monsieur means to face the sharks, I do not see why his faithful servant should not face them also."

3. A Pearl Worth Millions

THE NEXT morning at four o'clock I was awakened by the steward whom Captain Nemo had placed at my service. I rose hurriedly, dressed, and went into the lounge.

Captain Nemo was awaiting me.

"Mr. Aronnax," he said, "are you ready to start?"

"I am ready."

"Then please follow me."

"And my companions, Captain?"

"They have been told and are waiting."

"Won't we wear diving suits?" I asked.

"Not yet. I have not brought the *Nautilus* too near this coast, and we are some distance from the Manaar Bank; but the small boat is ready and will take us to the exact point of disembarking, which will save us a long way. It carries our diving outfits, which we will put on when we begin our submarine journey."

Captain Nemo conducted me to the central staircase

which led to the platform. Ned and Conseil were already there, delighted at the idea of the "pleasure party." Five sailors from the *Nautilus* waited with oars in the boat, which had been made fast against the side.

The night was still dark. Layers of clouds covered the sky; only a few stars could be seen. I looked at the coastal side and saw nothing but a dark line enclosing three parts of the horizon, from southwest to northwest. The *Nautilus*, having returned during the night up the western coast of Ceylon, was now west of the bay or rather gulf, formed by the mainland and the Island of Manaar. There, under the dark waters, stretched the pintadine bank, an inexhaustible field of pearls, the length of which is more than twenty miles.

Captain Nemo, Ned Land, Conseil, and I took our places in the stern of the boat. One crew member took the tiller; his four companions leaned on their oars, the painter was cast off, and we moved steadily away from the *Nautilus*.

The boat headed south; the oarsmen did not hurry. I noticed that their strokes, strong in the water, followed each other every ten seconds, according to the method generally adopted in the navy.

We were silent. What was Captain Nemo thinking of? Perhaps of the land he was approaching, and which he found all too close, contrary to the Canadian's opinion, who thought it too far off. As to Conseil, he was there from curiosity.

About half-past five the first streaks of dawn on the horizon revealed the upper line of coast more distinctly. Flat enough in the east, it rose a little to the south. Five miles still lay between it and us. Half an hour later it was suddenly daylight, with that rapidity peculiar to tropical regions that know neither true dawn nor twilight. The solar rays pierced the curtain of clouds piled up on the eastern horizon and the sun rose rapidly. Now I could see land distinctly—a few trees scattered here and there. The boat neared Manaar Island, which rose to the south. Captain Nemo rose from his seat and watched the sea.

At a sign from him we dropped anchor, in water that was little more than three feet deep; this spot was one of the highest points of the pintadine bank.

"Here we are, Mr. Aronnax," said Captain Nemo. "You see that enclosed bay? Here in a month will be assembled the numerous fishing boats of the exporters, and these are the waters their divers will ransack so boldly. Happily, this bay is well situated for that kind of fishing. It is sheltered from the strongest winds; the sea is never very rough here, which makes it favorable for the diver's work. Now we can put on our diving suits and begin our walk."

I did not answer, but kept an eye on the suspicious waters as I began, with the help of the sailors, to put on my heavy diving suit. Captain Nemo and my companions were also dressing. None of the *Nautilus* men were to accompany us on this new excursion.

Soon we were enveloped to the throat in rubber clothing, with our air devices fixed to our backs by braces. As to the Ruhmkorff apparatus, there was no necessity for it. Before putting my head into the copper cap, I had asked the question of the captain.

"They would be useless," he replied. "We are not going very deep, and the solar rays will be enough to light our walk. Besides, it would not be prudent to carry the electric light in these waters; it might attract some of the dangerous inhabitants of the coast most inopportunely."

As Captain Nemo pronounced these words, I turned to Conseil and Ned Land. But my two friends had already encased their heads in their metal helmets, and they could neither hear nor answer.

One last question remained to be asked of Captain Nemo.

"And our arms?" I asked; "won't we need our guns?"

"Guns! What for? Don't mountaineers use a dagger for attacking bears? And isn't steel surer than lead? Here is a strong blade; put it in your belt and we will start."

I looked at my companions; they were armed like us. More than that, Ned Land was brandishing an enormous harpoon which he had placed in the boat before leaving the *Nautilus.*

Following the captain's example, I was fitted with a heavy copper helmet, and our reservoirs of air started working at once. An instant later we were standing in about six feet of water on even sand. Captain Nemo beckoned, and we followed him down a gentle incline into deeper water.

Seven o'clock found us surveying the oyster banks at last, where pearl oysters are reproduced by millions.

Captain Nemo pointed to the enormous mass of oysters. I could well believe that this mine was inexhaustible, for Nature's creative power is far beyond man's instinct of destruction. Ned Land, faithful to his instinct, quickly filled his net with some of the finest specimens. But we could not stop. We had to follow the captain, who seemed to follow paths known only to himself. Sometimes the ground would slope upward, and when I raised my arm it would be above the surface of the sea. Then the level of the bank would sink as capriciously. Often we rounded high rocks scarped into pyramids. In their dark crevices huge crustacea were perched on their great claws like some war machine. They watched us with fixed eyes, while under our feet crawled various kinds of annelids.

Suddenly we saw before us a large grotto, formed by a picturesque arrangement of rocks, and carpeted with the thick warp of submarine flora. At first it seemed completely lightless. The sun's rays were extinguished by successive gradations, until its vague transparency became nothing more than drowned light. Captain Nemo entered; we followed. My eyes soon became accustomed to this relative darkness. I could distinguish arches springing from natural pillars that stood broad upon their granite bases, like the heavy columns of Tuscan architecture. Why had our incomprehensible guide led us to this submarine crypt? I was soon to know. After descending a rather steep slope, we found ourselves at the bottom of a circular pit, formed by the rocks. There Captain Nemo stopped and pointed to a huge object which immediately engrossed me. It was an oyster of extraordinary dimensions, a gigantic clam with a breadth of more than seven feet, even larger than the one in the lounge of the *Nautilus*. I drew closer to this remarkable mollusc. It was fastened by its filaments to a table of granite, and there, isolated, it had developed in the calm waters of the grotto. I estimated the weight of this fabulous clam at 600 pounds. Such an oyster could yield 30 pounds of meat; one would require a gargantuan appetite to demolish one—let alone a dozen of these fellows!

Quite evidently, Captain Nemo already knew of the

existence of this bivalve, and seemed to have a particular reason for checking on its state. The shells were a little open; the captain put his dagger between them to keep them from closing. Then he raised the fringed membrane which formed the creature's cloak. There, among the folds, I saw a loose pearl the size of a coconut! It globular shape, perfect clarity and soft luster made it altogether a jewel of inestimable value. Carried away by curiosity, I reached out to touch it, but the captain stopped me. He quickly withdrew his dagger, and the two shells closed suddenly. I then understood Captain Nemo's intention. In leaving this pearl hidden in the mantle of the clam, he was allowing it to grow slowly. Each year the secretions of the mollusc would add new concentric circles. I estimated its value at $2,500,000, at least.

About ten minutes later, Captain Nemo stopped short. I thought he was about to return. But he motioned us to crouch beside him in a deep crevice of the rock and pointed to one area of the waters, which I watched attentively.

About 15 feet from me a shadow appeared and sank to the ocean floor. The disquieting idea of sharks shot through my mind but I was mistaken; once again it was not a monster of the ocean that we had to do with.

It was a man, a living man, an Indian, a fisherman, a poor devil who, I suppose, had come to glean before the harvest began. I could see the bottom of his canoe anchored some feet above his head. He would dive and go up repeatedly. He held a stone between his feet, which was fastened by a rope to his boat, and this helped him to descend more rapidly. This was all his equipment. Reaching the bottom, about 15 feet deep, he knelt down and filled his bag with oysters picked up at random. Then he went up, emptied it, pulled up his stone, and began the operation once more, which lasted thirty seconds.

The diver did not see us. The shadow of the rock hid us from sight. And how could this poor man ever dream that beings like himself would be there in the water, observing his movements? Several times he went up in this way and dived again. He did not carry away more than ten oysters at each plunge, for he had to pull them from the bank to which they were fastened. And how many of those oysters for which he risked his life had no pearl in them! I watched him closely; his maneuvers were finely coordinated; and for half an hour no danger appeared to threaten him.

I was just getting used to his way of fishing, when suddenly, while the Indian was on the bottom, I saw him make a gesture of terror, rise, and spring toward the ocean's surface.

How well I understood his dread! A gigantic shadow had appeared above the unfortunate diver. A shark of enormous size was cutting in, its eyes on fire and its jaws open. I was numb with horror and unable to move.

The voracious creature shot toward the Indian, who threw himself on one side to avoid the shark's fins—but not its tail, for it struck his chest and knocked him to the ocean floor.

In a few seconds the shark had returned and flipped onto its back, preparing to cut the Indian in two. I saw Captain Nemo rise suddenly, and then, dagger in hand, walk toward the monster, ready for direct combat. Just as the shark was about to snap the unhappy fisherman in two it perceived a new adversary, and, turning over again, made straight toward him.

I can still see Captain Nemo's position. Bracing himself,

he waited for the shark with admirable coolness; and when it rushed at him, threw himself on one side with marvelous quickness and buried his dagger deep into the creature's side. But it wasn't yet over. A terrible struggle ensued.

The shark had seemed to roar, if I might say so. Blood poured from its wound. The sea was dyed red, and through its opacity I could distinguish nothing more. Nothing more until, as the water cleared, I saw the undaunted captain hanging on to one of the creature's fins, struggling, and dealing successive blows at his enemy, yet still unable to give a decisive one.

The shark's struggles churned the water with such fury that it almost upset us who were watching.

I wanted to go to the captain's assistance, but I was rooted to the spot with horror.

Then the captain fell to the earth, overpowered by the enormous mass. The shark's jaws opened wide, and it might have been all over for the captain, if, harpoon in hand, Ned Land had not rushed forward and struck the creature deep with the keen edge of the harpoon.

The waves were red with blood. The shark's movements churned them with indescribable fury. But Ned Land's aim was true. It was the monster's death blow. Struck to the heart, it struggled in fearful convulsions.

Ned Land had meanwhile disentangled the captain, who was not wounded. The captain went over to the Indian, quickly cut the cord which held him to his stone, took him in his arms, and with a sharp blow of his heel, mounted to the surface.

We all three followed in a few seconds, feeling saved by a miracle, and reached the fisherman's boat.

Captain Nemo's first care was to resuscitate the unfortunate man. I wasn't sure he would succeed—the poor man's immersion had not been long, but the blow from the shark's tail could have injured him fatally.

Happily, with both the captain and Conseil giving artificial respiration, consciousness returned, and the man opened his eyes. Imagine his surprise, his terror even, at seeing four great copper heads leaning over him! And what must he have thought when Captain Nemo drew from his pocket a bag of pearls, and placed it in his hand! This munificent charity from the man of the waters to the poor Indian was accepted with a trembling hand. His wondering eyes showed that he knew not to what superhuman beings he owed both fortune and life.

At a sign from the captain we returned to the bank, and retracing our route, came in about half an hour to where the boat of the *Nautilus* was anchored.

Once aboard, with the help of the sailors we got rid of the heavy copper helmets.

Captain Nemo's first word was to the Canadian.

"Thank you, Master Land," he said.

"It was repayment, Captain," replied Ned Land. "I owed you that."

A ghost of a smile passed over the captain's face, then:

"To the *Nautilus*," he said.

The boat flew over the waves. Some minutes later we saw the body of the dead shark floating. By the black marking on the tips of its fins I recognized the terrible melanopteron of the Indian Ocean. It was more than 25 feet long; its enormous mouth occupied one-third of its body. Its six rows of teeth placed in an isosceles triangle in the upper jaw showed it to be an adult.

While I was contemplating this lifeless mass, a dozen

voracious sharks appeared around the boat, and without noticing us, threw themselves upon the dead body and fought with one another for the pieces.

At half-past eight we were again on board the *Nautilus*. Two conclusions I must inevitably draw from our excursion to the Manaar Bank—one bearing on the unparalleled courage of Captain Nemo, the other upon his devotion to a human being, a representative of that race from which he fled beneath the sea. Whatever he might say, this strange man had not yet succeeded in entirely crushing his heart.

When I made this observation to him, he answered in a slightly moved tone:

"That Indian, sir, is an inhabitant of an oppressed country; and I am still, and shall be, to my last breath, one of them!"

4. The Red Sea

ON JANUARY 29 during the course of the day, the Island of Ceylon disappeared under the horizon, and the *Nautilus,* at a speed of 20 knots, slid into the labyrinth of channels which separate the Maldives from the Laccadives. We coasted the Island of Kiltan, a land of coral origin discovered by Vasco da Gama in 1499, and one of the nineteen principal islands of the Laccadive Archipelago, situated between 10° and 14° 30′ N. lat., and 69° 50′ 72″ E. long.

We had traveled 18,675 miles, or 7,500 (French) leagues from our starting point in the Sea of Japan.

The next day, January 30, when the *Nautilus* went to the surface of the ocean, there was no land in sight. Its new course was NNE in the direction of the Sea of Oman, between Arabia and the Indian Peninsula, which serves as an outlet to the Persian Gulf. It was quite evidently without any possible egress. Where was Captain Nemo taking us? I had no idea. This, however, did not satisfy the Canadian, who that day came to me asking where we were going.

"We are going where our captain's fancy takes us, Master Ned."

"His fancy cannot take us far, then," said the Canadian. "The Persian Gulf has no outlet: and, if we do go in, it will not be long before we are out again."

"Very well, then, we will come out again, Master Land; and if, after the Persian Gulf, the *Nautilus* would like to visit the Red Sea, the Strait of Bab el Mandeb is there to give us entrance."

"I need not tell you, sir," said Ned Land, "that the Red Sea is as much closed as the Gulf—the Isthmus of Suez is not yet cut, and, if it was, a boat as mysterious as ours would not risk itself in the locks of a canal. And again, the Red Sea is not the road to take us back to Europe."

"But I never said we were going back to Europe."

"What do you suppose, then?"

"I suppose that, after visiting the interesting coasts of Arabia and Egypt, the *Nautilus* will go down the Indian Ocean again, perhaps cross the Channel of Mozambique, perhaps off the Mascarenes, and so to the Cape of Good Hope."

"And once at the Cape of Good Hope?" asked the Canadian, with peculiar emphasis.

"Well, we shall venture into that Atlantic which we do not yet know. Ah! friend Ned, you are getting tired of this journey under the sea; you are surfeited with the incessantly varying spectacle of submarine wonders. For my part, I shall be sorry to see the end of a voyage which so few men are privileged to make."

For four days, till the 3rd of February, the *Nautilus* scoured the Gulf of Oman, at various speeds and at various depths. The ship seemed to cruise at random almost as if its captain were hesitating over which route to follow, but it never crossed the Tropic of Cancer.

In quitting this gulf we sighted Muscat for an instant, one of the most important towns of the country of Oman. I admired its strange aspect, surrounded by black rocks upon which its white houses and forts stood out in relief. I saw the rounded domes of its mosques, the elegant points of its minarets, its fresh and verdant terraces. But it was only a vision! The *Nautilus* soon sank under the waves at that part of the sea.

We passed along the Arabian coast near Matrah and Hadhramaut, for a distance of six miles; the undulating line of mountains was occasionally relieved by some ancient ruin. The 5th of February we at last entered the Gulf of Aden, a perfect funnel introduced into the neck of Bab el Mandeb, through which the waters of the Indian Ocean enter the Red Sea.

The 6th of February, the *Nautilus* floated in sight of Aden, perched upon a promontory which a narrow isthmus joins to the mainland, a kind of inaccessible Gibraltar, whose fortifications were rebuilt by the English after taking possession in 1839. I caught a glimpse of the octagonal minarets of this town, at one time, according to the historian Edrisi, the richest commercial center on the coast.

I certainly thought that Captain Nemo, now he had reached this point, would go out again; but I was mistaken, for he did no such thing.

The next day, the 7th of February, we entered the Strait of Bab el Mandeb, which, in the Arab tongue, means "The Gate of Tears."

Although 20 miles in breadth, this passage is only 32 in length. For the *Nautilus* at full speed, the crossing was scarcely the work of an hour. But I saw nothing, not even the Island of Perim, with which the British Government has fortified the position of Aden. There were too many English or French steamers of the line of Suez to Bombay, Calcutta, Melbourne, Réunion and Mauritius, furrowing this narrow passage, for the *Nautilus* to venture to show itself. So it remained prudently below the surface. At last, about noon, we were in the waters of the Red Sea.

I would not even seek to understand the caprice which had decided Captain Nemo upon entering the gulf. But I quite approved of the *Nautilus* entering it. Its speed was lessened; sometimes it surfaced, sometimes it dived to avoid a vessel, and thus I was able to observe both the upper and lower regions of this curious sea.

At dawn on the 8th of February, Mocha came in sight. Now a ruined town, its walls would fall at a gunshot, yet it shelters here and there some verdant date trees. It was once an important city containing six public markets and 26 mosques, and whose walls, defended by 14 forts, formed a girdle of two miles in circumference.

The *Nautilus* then approached the African shore, where the depth of the sea was greater. There, in water as clear as crystal, we saw through the open panels the beautiful

bushes of brilliant coral, and great blocks of rock clothed
with splendid green algae and lichens. What an indescribable spectacle, and what a variety of sites and landscapes
along these sand banks and volcanic islands which bound
the Libyan coast! These shrubs appeared in all their glory
on the eastern coast, to which the *Nautilus* soon returned.
There, on the coast of Tehama, not only did this display of
zoophytes flourish beneath the level of the sea, but their
picturesque interlacings unfolded themselves about sixty
feet above the surface, more capricious but less highly colored than those whose freshness was maintained by the vital
power of the waters.

What pleasant hours I passed thus at the window of the
lounge! What new specimens of submarine flora and fauna
I admired under the brightness of our electric lantern!

The 9th of February the *Nautilus* floated in the broadest
part of the Red Sea, which lies between Suakin on the west
coast, and Qunfidha on the east coast, a distance of 90
miles.

That day at noon, after the bearings were taken, Captain
Nemo mounted the platform, where I happened to be, and I
was determined not to let him go down again without at
least pressing him regarding his ulterior projects. As soon as
he saw me he approached and offered me a cigar.

"Well, sir, does this Red Sea please you? Have you sufficiently observed the wonders it covers, its fishes, its zoophytes, its parterres of sponges, and its forests of coral? Did
you catch a glimpse of the towns on its borders?"

"Yes, Captain Nemo," I replied; "and the *Nautilus* is
well fitted for such a study. Ah! it is an intelligent boat!"

"Yes, sir, intelligent and invulnerable. It fears neither the terrible tempests of the Red Sea, nor its currents, nor its sand banks."

"Certainly," I said, "this sea is quoted as one of the worst; in the time of the ancients, if I am not mistaken, its reputation was detestable."

"Detestable, Mr. Aronnax. The Greek and Latin historians do not speak favorably of it, and Strabo says it is very dangerous during the Etesian winds and in the rainy season. The Arabian Edrisi portrays it under the name of the Gulf of Colzoum, and relates that vessels perished there in great numbers on the sand banks and that no one would risk sailing in the night. It is, he pretends, a sea subject to fearful hurricanes, strewn with inhospitable islands, and 'which offers nothing good either on its surface or in its depths.' "

"One may see," I replied, "that these historians never sailed on board the *Nautilus*."

"Just so," replied the captain, smiling; "and in that respect moderns are not more advanced than the ancients. It required many ages to discover the mechanical power of steam. Who knows if in another hundred years we may not see a second *Nautilus?* Progress is slow, Mr. Aronnax."

"It is true," I answered; "your boat is at least a century before its time, perhaps an era. What a misfortune that the secret of such an invention should die with its inventor!"

Captain Nemo did not reply. After some minutes' silence he continued:

"You were speaking of the opinions of ancient historians upon the dangerous navigation of the Red Sea."

"It is true," I said; "but weren't the fears exaggerated?"

"Yes and no, Mr. Aronnax," replied Captain Nemo, who seemed to know the Red Sea by heart. "That which is no

longer dangerous for a modern vessel, well rigged, strongly
built and master of its own course, thanks to obedient
steam, offered all sorts of perils to the ships of the ancients.
Picture to yourself those first navigators venturing in ships
made of planks sewn with the cords of the palm tree,
saturated with the grease of the sea dog, and covered with
powdered resin! They had not even instruments wherewith
to take their bearings, and they went by guess among currents of which they scarcely knew anything. Under such
conditions shipwrecks were, and must have been, numerous. But in our time steamers running between Suez and the
South Seas have nothing more to fear from the fury of this
gulf, in spite of contrary trade winds. The captain and passengers do not prepare for their departure by offering pro-
pitiatory sacrifices; and on their return they no longer go
ornamented with wreaths and gilt fillets to thank the gods in
the neighboring temple."

"I agree with you," I said; "and steam seems to have
killed all gratitude in the hearts of sailors. But, Captain,
since you seem to have especially studied this sea, can you
tell me the origin of its name?"

"There exist several explanations on the subject, Mr.
Aronnax. Would you like to know the opinion of a chron-
icler of the fourteenth century?"

"Willingly."

"This fanciful writer pretends that its name was given to
it after the passage of the Israelites, when Pharaoh perished
in the waves which closed at the voice of Moses."

"A poet's explanation, Captain Nemo," I replied; "but I
cannot content myself with that. I ask you for your opinion."

"Here it is, Mr. Aronnax. According to my idea, we must

see in this appellation of the Red Sea a translation of the Hebrew word 'Edom'; and if the ancients gave it that name, it was on account of the particular color of its waters."

"But up to this time I have seen nothing but transparent waves without any particular color."

"Very likely; but as we advance to the bottom of the gulf you will see this singular appearance. I remember seeing the Bay of Tor entirely red, like a sea of blood."

"And you attribute this color to the presence of a microscopic seaweed?"

"Yes."

"So, Captain Nemo, it is not the first time you have traversed the Red Sea on board the *Nautilus?*"

"No, sir."

"As you spoke a while ago of the passage of the Israelites and of the catastrophe to the Egyptians, I will ask whether you have met with the traces under the water of this great historical fact?"

"No, sir; and for a good reason."

"What is it?"

"It is that the spot where Moses and his people passed is now so blocked up with sand that the camels can barely bathe their legs there. You can well understand that there would not be water enough for my *Nautilus*."

"And the spot?" I asked.

"The spot is situated a little above the Isthmus of Suez, in the arm which formerly made a deep estuary, when the Red Sea extended to the Salt Lakes. Now, whether this passage were miraculous or not, the Israelites, nevertheless, crossed there to reach the Promised Land, and Pharaoh's army perished precisely on that spot; and I think that excavations made in the middle of the sand would bring to light a large number of arms and instruments of Egyptian origin."

"That is evident," I replied; "and for the sake of archaeologists let us hope that these excavations will be made sooner or later, when new towns are established on the isthmus after the construction of the Suez Canal; a canal, however, very useless to a vessel like the *Nautilus*."

"Very likely; but useful to the whole world," said Captain Nemo. "The ancients well understood the utility of a communication between the Red Sea and the Mediterranean for their commercial affairs. But they did not think of digging a canal direct, and took the Nile as an intermediate. Very probably the canal which united the Nile to the Red Sea was begun by Sesostris, if we may believe tradition. One thing is certain, that in the year 615 B.C. Neco undertook the works of a canal, fed by the waters of the Nile, across the plain of Egypt, opposite Arabia. It took four days to go up this canal, and it was so wide that two triremes could go abreast. It was carried on by Darius, the son of Hystaspes, and probably finished by Ptolemy II. Strabo saw it navigated: but its decline from the point of departure, near Bubastis, to the Red Sea was so slight that it was only navigable for a few months in the year. This canal answered all commercial purposes to the age of Antonius, when it was abandoned and blocked up with sand. Restored by order of the Caliph Omar, it was definitely destroyed in 761 or 762 by Caliph Al-Mansur, who wished to prevent the arrival of provisions to Mohammed-ben-Abdallah, who had revolted against him. During the expedition into Egypt, your General Bonaparte discovered traces of the works in the desert of Suez; and, surprised by the tide, he nearly perished before regaining Hadjaroth, at the very place where Moses had encamped three thousand years before."

"Well, Captain, what the ancients dared not undertake, this junction between the two seas, which will shorten the road from Cadiz to India, M. Lesseps has succeeded in doing; and before long he will have changed Africa into an immense island."

"Yes, Mr. Aronnax; you have the right to be proud of your countryman. Such a man brings more honor to a nation than great captains. He began like so many others, with disgust and rebuffs; but he has triumphed, for he has the genius of will. And it is sad to think that a work like that, which ought to have been an international work and which would have sufficed to make a reign illustrious, should have succeeded by the energy of one man. All honor to M. Lesseps!"

"Yes! honor to the great citizen," I replied, surprised by the manner in which Captain Nemo had just spoken.

"Unfortunately," he continued, "I cannot take you through the Suez Canal; but you will be able to see the long jetty of Port Said after tomorrow, when we shall be in the Mediterranean."

"The Mediterranean!" I exclaimed.

"Yes, sir, does that astonish you?"

"What astonishes me is to think that we shall be there the day after tomorrow."

"Indeed?"

"Yes, Captain, although by this time I ought to have accustomed myself to be surprised at nothing since I have been on board your boat."

"But the cause of this surprise?"

"Well, it is the fearful speed you will have to put on the *Nautilus,* if the day after tomorrow it is to be in the Mediterranean, having made the round of Africa and doubled the Cape of Good Hope!"

"Who told you that it would make the round of Africa and double the Cape of Good Hope, sir?"

"Well, unless the *Nautilus* sails on dry land, and passes above the isthmus——"

"Or beneath it, Mr. Aronnax."

"Beneath it?"

"Certainly," replied Captain Nemo quietly. "A long time ago Nature made under this tongue of land what man has this day made on its surface."

"What! Such a passage exists?"

"Yes; a subterranean passage, which I have named the Arabian Tunnel. It takes us beneath Suez and opens into the Gulf of Pelusium."

"But this isthmus is nothing but quicksand!"

"To a certain depth. But at 165 feet there is a solid layer of rock."

"Did you discover this passage by chance?" I asked, more and more surprised.

"Chance and reasoning, sir; and by reasoning even more than by chance. Not only does this passage exist, but I have profited by it several times. Without that I should not have ventured this day into the impassable Red Sea. I noticed that in the Red Sea and in the Mediterranean there existed a certain number of fish of a kind perfectly identical. Certain of the fact, I asked myself was it possible that there was no communication between the two seas? If there was, the subterranean current must necessarily run from the Red

Sea to the Mediterranean, from the sole cause of difference of level. I caught a large number of fishes in the neighborhood of Suez. I passed a copper ring through their tails, and threw them back into the sea. Some months later, on the coast of Syria, I caught some of my fish ornamented with the ring. Thus the communication between the two was proved. I then sought for it with my *Nautilus;* I discovered it, ventured into it, and before long, sir, you, too, will have passed through my Arabian Tunnel!"

5. The Arabian Tunnel

LATE THAT same afternoon in 21° 30′ N. lat. the *Nautilus* surfaced as it approached the Arabian coast. I saw Jiddah, the most commercial center of Egypt, Syria, Turkey, and India. I distinguished clearly enough its buildings, the vessels moored at the docks, and the larger ships whose draught of water obliged them to anchor in the roads. The sun, rather low on the horizon, struck full on the houses of the town, bringing out their whiteness. Outside, some wooden cabins and some made of reeds, showed the quarter inhabited by the Bedouins. Soon Jiddah was shut out from view by the shadows of night, and the *Nautilus* found herself under water slightly phosphorescent.

The next day, the 10th of February, we sighted several ships running to windward. The *Nautilus* returned to its submarine navigation; but at noon when her bearings were taken the sea was deserted, so she cruised again at the waterline.

Accompanied by Ned and Conseil, I seated myself on the

platform. The coast on the eastern side looked like a mass faintly printed on a damp fog.

We were leaning on the side of the pinnace, talking of one thing and another, when Ned Land, stretching out his hand toward a spot on the sea, said:

"Do you see anything there, sir?"

"No, Ned," I replied; "but I have not your eyes, you know."

"Look well," said Ned, "there, on the starboard beam, about the height of the lantern! Do you not see a mass which seems to move?"

"Certainly," I said, after close attention; "I see something like a long black body on the top of the water."

And certainly before long the black object was not more than a mile from us. It looked like a great sandbank deposited in the open sea. It was a gigantic dugong!

Ned Land looked eagerly. His eyes shone with covetousness at the sight of the animal. His hand seemed ready to harpoon it. One would have thought he was awaiting the moment to throw himself into the sea and attack it in its element.

At this instant Captain Nemo appeared on the platform. He saw the dugong, understood the Canadian's attitude, and, addressing him, said:

"If you held a harpoon just now, Master Land, would it not burn your hand?"

"Just so, sir."

"And you would not be sorry to go back, for one day, to your trade of a fisherman and to add this cetacean to the list of those you have already killed?"

"I should not, sir."

"Well, you can try."

"Thank you, sir," said Ned Land, his eyes flaming.

"Only," continued the captain, "I advise you for your own sake not to miss the creature."

"Is the dugong dangerous to attack?" I asked, in spite of the Canadian's shrug of the shoulders.

"Yes," replied the captain; "sometimes the animal turns upon its assailants and overturns their boat. But for Master Land this danger is not to be feared. His eye is prompt, his arm sure."

At this moment seven men of the crew, mute and immovable as ever, mounted the platform. One carried a harpoon and a line similar to those employed in catching whales. The pinnace was lifted from the bridge, pulled from its socket, and let down into the sea. Six oarsmen took their seats, and the coxswain went to the tiller. Ned, Conseil and I went to the back of the boat.

"You are not coming, Captain?" I asked.

"No, sir; but I wish you good sport."

The boat put off, and, with the six rowers working vigorously drew rapidly toward the dugong, which floated about two miles from the *Nautilus.*

Arrived some cable's length from the cetacean, the speed slackened and the oars dipped noiselessly into the quiet waters. Ned Land, harpoon in hand, stood in the fore part of the boat. The harpoon used for striking the whale is generally attached to a very long cord which runs out rapidly as the wounded creature draws it after him. But here the cord was not more than ten fathoms long, and the extremity was attached to a small barrel which, by floating, was to show the course the dugong took under the water.

I stood and carefully watched the Canadian's adversary. This dugong, which also bears the name of the halicore, closely resembles the manatee; its oblong body terminates in a lengthened tail, and its lateral fins in perfect fingers. Its difference from the manatee consists in its upper jaw, which is armed with two long and pointed teeth forming diverging tusks on each side.

This dugong which Ned Land was preparing to attack was of colossal dimensions; it was more than 21 feet long. It did not move, and seemed to be sleeping on the waves, which circumstance made it easier to capture.

The boat approached within 18 feet of the animal. The oars rested on the rowlocks. I half rose. Ned Land, his body thrown a little back, brandished the harpoon in his experienced hand.

Suddenly a hissing noise was heard, and the dugong disappeared. The harpoon, although thrown with great force, had apparently only struck the water.

"Curse it!" exclaimed the Canadian furiously; "I have missed it!"

"No," said I; "the creature is wounded—look at the blood; but your weapon has not stuck in his body."

"My harpoon! My harpoon!" cried Ned Land.

The sailors rowed on, and the coxswain made for the floating barrel. The harpoon regained, we followed in pursuit of the animal.

The latter came now and then to the surface to breathe. Its wound had not weakened it, for it shot onward with great rapidity.

The boat, rowed by strong arms, flew in its track. Several times it approached within some few yards, and the Canadian was ready to strike, but the dugong made off with a sudden plunge, and it was impossible to reach it.

Imagine the passion which excited impatient Ned Land!

He hurled at the unfortunate creature the most energetic expletives in the English tongue. For my part, I was only vexed to see the dugong escape all our attacks.

We pursued it without relaxation for an hour, and I began to think it would prove difficult to capture, when the animal, possessed with the perverse idea of vengeance of which he had cause to repent, turned upon the pinnace and assailed us in its turn.

This maneuver did not escape the Canadian.

"Look out!" he cried.

The coxswain said some words in his outlandish tongue, doubtless warning the men to keep on their guard.

The dugong came within twenty feet of the boat, stopped, sniffed the air briskly with its large nostrils (not at the extremity but in the upper part of its muzzle). Then, taking a spring, he threw himself upon us.

The pinnace could not avoid the shock, and half upset, shipped, it seemed, tons of water which had to be bailed out; but thanks to the coxswain, we took the shock sideways, not full front, so we were not quite overturned. While Ned Land, clinging to the bows, belabored the gigantic animal with blows from his harpoon, the creature's teeth were buried in the gunwale, and it lifted the whole thing out of the water, as a lion does a roebuck. We were spilled over one another, and I know not how the adventure would have ended if the Canadian, still enraged with the beast, had not struck it to the heart.

I heard its teeth grind on the iron plate, and the dugong disappeared, carrying the harpoon with it. But the barrel soon returned to the surface, and shortly after the body of the animal surfaced on its back. The boat caught up with the creature, took it in tow, and made straight for the *Nautilus*.

It required tackle of enormous strength to hoist the dugong onto the platform. It weighed 10,000 pounds.

The next day, the 11th of February, the larder of the *Nautilus* was enriched by some more delicate game. A flight of sea swallows rested on the *Nautilus*. It was a species of the *Sterna nilotica*, peculiar to Egypt; its beak is black, head gray and pointed, the eye surrounded by white spots, the back, wings and tail of a grayish color, the belly and throat white, and claws red. We also took some dozen of Nile ducks, a wild bird of high flavor, its throat and upper part of the head white with black spots.

About five o'clock in the evening we sighted to the north the Cape of Ras Mohammed. This cape forms the extremity of Arabia Petraea, situated between the Gulf of Suez and the Gulf of Akaba.

The *Nautilus* penetrated into the Straits of Jubal, which leads to the Gulf of Suez. I distinctly saw a high mountain, towering between the two gulfs of Ras Mohammed. It was Mount Horeb, or Sinai, where Moses saw God face to face.

At six o'clock the *Nautilus,* sometimes floating, sometimes immersed, passed some distance from Tor, situated at the end of the bay, the waters of which seemed tinted with red, an observation already made by Captain Nemo. Then night fell in the midst of a heavy silence, sometimes broken by the cries of the pelican and other night birds and the noise of the waves breaking upon the shore, chafing against the rocks, or by the panting of some far-off steamer beating the waters of the gulf with its noisy paddles.

From eight to nine o'clock the *Nautilus* remained some fathoms under the water. According to my calculation we must have been very near Suez. Through the panel in the lounge I saw the rocky bottom brilliantly lit up by our electric lamp. We seemed to be leaving the straits farther and farther behind.

At a quarter past nine, the vessel having returned to the surface, I mounted the platform. Most impatient to pass through Captain Nemo's tunnel, I could not stay in one place, so came to breathe the fresh night air.

Soon in the shadow I saw a pale light, half discolored by the fog, shining about a mile from us.

"A floating lighthouse!" said someone near me.

I turned, and saw the captain.

"It is the floating light of Suez," he continued. "It will not be long before we gain the entrance of the tunnel."

"The entrance cannot be easy!"

"No, sir; for that reason I am accustomed to go into the steersman's cage and myself direct our course. And now, if you will go down, Mr. Aronnax, the *Nautilus* is going under the waves and will not return to the surface until we have passed through the Arabian Tunnel."

Captain Nemo led me toward the central staircase; halfway down he opened a door, traversed the upper deck, and landed in the pilot's cage, which it may be remembered rose at the forward part of the platform. It was a cabin measuring six feet square, very much like that occupied by the pilot on the steamboats of the Mississippi or Hudson. In the midst worked a wheel, placed vertically and connected to the tiller rope, which ran to the stern of the *Nautilus*. Four light-ports with lenticular glasses allowed the man at the wheel to see in all directions.

This cabin was dark; but soon my eyes grew accustomed to the obscurity, and I perceived the pilot, a strong man, with his hands resting on the spokes of the wheel. Outside, the sea appeared vividly lit up by the lantern, which shed its rays from the back of the cabin to the other extremity of the platform.

"Now," said Captain Nemo, "let us try to make our passage."

Electric wires connected the pilot's cage with the machinery room, and from there the captain could communicate to his *Nautilus* crew the direction and speed. He pressed a metal knob, and at once the speed of the propeller diminished.

I looked in silence at the high, straight wall we were running by at this moment, the immovable base of a massive sandy coast. We followed it thus for an hour only a few feet off.

Captain Nemo did not take his eye from the knob, suspended by its two concentric circles in the cabin. At a simple gesture the pilot modified the course of the *Nautilus* every instant.

I had placed myself at the port scuttle, and saw some magnificent substructures of coral, zoophytes and seaweed, and giant crustaceans, their enormous claws stretching out from the fissures of the rock.

At a quarter past ten the captain himself took the helm. A large gallery, black and deep, opened before us. The *Nautilus* went boldly into it. A strange roaring was heard around its sides. It was the waters of the Red Sea, which the incline of the tunnel precipitated violently toward the Mediterranean. The *Nautilus* went with the torrent, rapid as an arrow in spite of the efforts of the machinery, which, in order to offer more effective resistance, beat the waves with propeller reversed.

On the walls of the narrow passage I could see nothing but brilliant rays, straight lines, furrows of fire traced by the great speed, under the brilliant electric light. My heart beat fast.

At 10:35 P.M. Captain Nemo quitted the helm, and, turning to me, said:

"The Mediterranean!"

In less than 20 minutes the *Nautilus*, carried along by the torrent, had passed through the Isthmus of Suez.

6. The Grecian Archipelago

THE NEXT day, the 12th of February, at the dawn of day, the *Nautilus* rose to the surface. I hastened onto the platform. Three miles to the south the dim outline of Pelusium was to be seen. A torrent had carried us from one sea to another. About seven o'clock Ned and Conseil joined me.

"Well, Sir Naturalist," said the Canadian, in a slightly jovial tone, "and the Mediterranean?"

"We are floating on its surface, friend Ned."

"What!" said Conseil, "this very night?"

"Yes, this very night; in a few minutes we have passed this impassable isthmus."

"I do not believe it," replied the Canadian.

"Then you are wrong, Master Land," I continued; "this low coast which rounds off to the south is the Egyptian coast. And you who have such good eyes, Ned, you can see the jetty of Port Said stretching into the sea."

The Canadian looked attentively.

"Certainly you are right, sir, and your captain is a first-rate man. We are in the Mediterranean. Good! Now, if you please, let us talk of our own little affair, but so that no one hears us."

I saw what the Canadian wanted, and, in any case, I thought it better to let him talk, as he wished it; so we all three went and sat down near the lantern, where we were less exposed to the spray of the blades.

"Now, Ned, we listen; what have you to tell us?"

"What I have to tell you is very simple. We are in Europe; and before Captain Nemo's caprices drag us once more to the bottom of the Polar Seas or lead us into Oceania I ask to leave the *Nautilus*."

I wished in no way to shackle the liberty of my companions, but I certainly felt no desire to leave Captain Nemo.

Thanks to him and thanks to his apparatus, I was each day nearer the completion of my submarine studies; and I was rewriting my book of submarine depths in its very element. Should I ever again have such an opportunity of observing the wonders of the ocean? No, certainly not! And I could not bring myself to the idea of abandoning the *Nautilus* before the cycle of investigation was accomplished.

"Friend Ned, answer me frankly, are you tired of being on board? Are you sorry that destiny has thrown us into Captain Nemo's hands?"

The Canadian remained some moments without answering. Then, crossing his arms, he said:

"Frankly, I do not regret this journey under the seas. I shall be glad to have made it; but, now that it is made, let us have done with it. That is my idea."

"It will come to an end, Ned."

"Where and when?"

"Where I do not know—when I cannot say; or, rather, I suppose it will end when these seas have nothing more to teach us."

"Then what do you hope for?" demanded the Canadian.

"That circumstances may occur as well six months hence as now by which we may and ought to profit."

"Oh," said Ned Land, "and where shall we be in six months, if you please, Sir Naturalist?"

"Perhaps in China; you know the *Nautilus* is a rapid traveler. It goes through water as swallows through the air, or as an express on the land. It does not fear frequented seas; who can say that it may not beat the coasts of France, England or America, on which flight may be attempted as advantageously as here."

"Mr. Aronnax," replied the Canadian, "your arguments are rotten at the foundation. You speak in the future, 'We shall be there! We shall be here!' I speak in the present, 'We are here, and we must profit by it.'"

Ned Land's logic pressed me hard, and I felt myself beaten on that ground. I knew not what argument would now tell in my favor.

"Sir," continued Ned, "let us suppose an impossibility: if Captain Nemo should this day offer you your liberty, would you accept it?"

"I do not know," I answered, after a slight hesitation.

"And if," he added, "the offer made you this day was never to be renewed, would you accept it?"

"Friend Ned, this is my answer. Your reasoning is against me. We must not rely on Captain Nemo's good will. Common prudence forbids him to set us at liberty. On the other side, prudence bids us profit by the first opportunity to leave the *Nautilus*."

"Well, Mr. Aronnax, that is wisely said."

"Only one observation—just one. The occasion must be serious and our first attempt must succeed; if it fails, we shall never find another, and Captain Nemo will never forgive us."

"All that is true," replied the Canadian. "But your observation applies equally to all attempts at flight, whether in two years' time or in two days'. But the question is still this: if a favorable opportunity presents itself, it must be seized."

"Agreed! And now, Ned, will you tell me what you mean by a favorable opportunity?"

"It will be that which, on a dark night, will bring the *Nautilus* a short distance from some European coast."

"And you will try and save yourself by swimming?"

"Yes, if we were near enough to the bank, and if the vessel was floating at the time. Not if the bank was far away, and the boat was under the water."

"And in that case?"

"In that case, I should seek to make myself master of the pinnace. I know how it is worked. We must get inside, and the bolts once drawn, we shall come to the surface of the water without even the pilot, who is in the bows, perceiving our flight."

"Well, Ned, watch for the opportunity; but do not forget that a hitch will ruin us."

"I will not forget, sir."

"And now, Ned, would you like to know what I think of your project?"

"Certainly, Mr. Aronnax."

"Well, I think—I do not say I hope—I think that this favorable opportunity will never present itself."

"Why not?"

"Because Captain Nemo cannot hide from himself that we have not given up all hope of regaining our liberty, and he will be on his guard, above all, in the seas and in the sight of European coasts."

"We shall see," replied Ned Land, shaking his head determinedly.

"And now, Ned Land," I added, "let us stop here. Not another word on the subject. The day that you are ready, come and let us know, and we will follow you. I rely entirely upon you."

Thus ended a conversation which, at no very distant time, led to such grave results. I must say here that facts seemed to confirm my foresight, to the Canadian's great despair. Did Captain Nemo distrust us in these frequented seas or did he only wish to hide himself from the numerous vessels of all nations, which plowed the Mediterranean? I could not tell; but we were now oftener beneath the waters and farther from the coast. Or, if the *Nautilus* did emerge, nothing was to be seen but the pilot's cage; and sometimes it went to great depths, for, between the Grecian Archipelago and Asia Minor we could not touch the bottom by more than a thousand fathoms.

Thus I only knew we were near the Island of Karpathos, one of the Sporades, by Captain Nemo reciting these lines from Virgil:

> Est Carpathio Neptuni gurgite vates,
> Cæruleus Proteus,[1]

as he pointed to a spot on the planisphere.

It was indeed the ancient abode of Proteus, the old shepherd of Neptune's flocks, now the Island of Scarpanto, situated between Rhodes and Crete. I saw nothing but the granite base through the glass panels of the lounge.

The next day, the 14th of February, I resolved to employ some hours in studying the fishes of the archipelago; but for some reason or other the panels remained hermetically sealed. Upon taking the course of the *Nautilus,* I found that we were going toward Candia, the ancient Isle of Crete. At the time I embarked on the *Abraham Lincoln,* the whole of this island had risen in insurrection against the despotism of the Turks. But of how the insurgents had fared since that time I was absolutely ignorant, and it was not Captain Nemo, deprived of all land communications, who could tell me.

I made no allusion to this event when that night I found myself alone with him in the lounge. Besides, he seemed to be taciturn and preoccupied. Then, contrary to his custom, he ordered both panels to be opened, and, going from one to the other, observed the mass of waters attentively. To what end I could not guess; so, on my side, I employed my time in studying the fish passing before my eyes.

In the midst of the waters a man appeared, a diver, carry-

[1] "In the Carpathian Sea, Proteus, dark prophet of Neptune dwells.

ing at his belt a leather purse. It was not a body abandoned
to the waves; it was a living man, swimming with a strong
hand, disappearing occasionally to take breath at the surface.

I turned toward Captain Nemo, and in an agitated voice
exclaimed:

"A man shipwrecked! He must be saved at any price!"

The captain did not answer me, but came and leaned
against the panel.

The man had approached, and, with his face flattened
against the glass, was looking at us.

To my great amazement, Captain Nemo signed to him.
The diver answered with his hand, mounted immediately to
the surface of the water, and did not appear again.

"Do not be uncomfortable," said Captain Nemo. "It is
Nicholas of Cape Matapan, surnamed Pesca. He is well
known in all the Cyclades. A bold diver! Water is his element, and he lives more in it than on land, going continually from one island to another, even as far as Crete."

"You know him, Captain?"

"Why not, Mr. Aronnax?"

Saying which, Captain Nemo went toward a piece of
furniture standing near the left panel of the lounge. Near
this piece of furniture I saw a chest bound with iron on the
cover of which was a copper plate bearing the cipher of the
Nautilus with its device.

At that moment the captain, without noticing my presence, opened the piece of furniture, a sort of strong box,
which held a great many ingots.

They were ingots of gold. From whence came this precious metal, which represented an enormous sum? Where

did the captain gather this gold from, and what was he going to do with it?

I did not say one word. I looked. Captain Nemo took the ingots one by one, and arranged them methodically in the chest, which he filled entirely. I estimated the contents at more than 4,000 pounds of gold, that is to say, nearly $1,000,000.

The chest was securely fastened, and the captain wrote an address on the lid in characters which must have belonged to modern Greece.

This done, Captain Nemo pressed a knob the wire of which communicated with the quarters of the crew. Four men appeared and, not without some trouble, pushed the chest out of the lounge. Then I heard them hoisting it up the iron staircase by means of pulleys.

At that moment Captain Nemo turned to me.

"And you were saying, sir?" he said.

"I was saying nothing, Captain."

"Then, sir, if you will allow me, I will wish you good night."

Whereupon he turned and left the lounge.

I returned to my room much troubled, as one may believe. I vainly tried to sleep—I sought the connecting link between the apparition of the diver and the chest filled with gold. Soon, I felt by certain movements of pitching and tossing that the *Nautilus* was leaving the depths and returning to the surface.

Then I heard steps upon the platform, and I knew they were unfastening the pinnace and launching it upon the waves. For one instant it struck the side of the *Nautilus,* then all noise ceased.

Two hours after, the same noise, the same going and

coming was renewed; the boat was hoisted on board, replaced in its socket, and the *Nautilus* again plunged under the waves.

So these millions had been transported to their address. To what point of the continent? Who was Captain Nemo's correspondent?

The next day I related to Conseil and the Canadian the events of the night, which had excited my curiosity to the highest degree. My companions were not less surprised than myself.

"But where does he take his millions to?" asked Ned Land.

To that there was no possible answer. I returned to the lounge after having breakfast and set to work. Till five o'clock in the evening I employed myself in arranging my notes. At that moment—ought I to attribute it to some peculiar idiosyncrasy?—I felt so great a heat that I was obliged to take off my coat. It was strange, for we were under low latitudes; and even then the *Nautilus,* submerged as it was, ought to experience no change of temperature. I looked at the manometer; it showed a depth of sixty feet, to which atmospheric heat could never attain.

I continued my work, but the temperature rose to such a pitch as to be intolerable.

"Could there be fire on board?" I asked myself.

I was leaving the lounge when Captain Nemo entered; he approached the thermometer, consulted it, and, turning to me, said:

"One hundred and seven degrees."

"I have noticed it, Captain," I replied; "and if it gets much hotter we cannot bear it."

"Oh, sir, it will not get hotter if we do not wish it."

"You can reduce it as you please, then?"

"No; but I can go farther from the stove which produces it."

"It is outward, then!"

"Certainly; we are floating in a current of boiling water."

"Is it possible?" I exclaimed.

"Look."

The panels opened, and I saw the sea entirely white all around. A sulphurous smoke was curling amid the waves, which boiled like water in a copper. I placed my hand on one of the panes of glass, but the heat was so great that I quickly took it off again.

"Where are we?" I asked.

"Near the Island of Santorin, sir," replied the captain. "I wished to give you a sight of the curious spectacle of a submarine eruption."

"I thought," I said, "that the formation of these new islands was ended."

"Nothing is ever ended in the volcanic parts of the sea," replied Captain Nemo; "and the globe is always being worked by subterranean fires. Already, in the nineteenth year of our era, according to Cassiodorus and Pliny, a new island, Theia, appeared in the very place where these islets have recently been formed. Then they sank under the waves, to rise again in the year 69, when they again subsided. Since that time to our days the Plutonian work has been suspended. But on the 3rd of February, 1866, a new island, which they named George Island, emerged from the midst of the sulphurous vapor near Nea Kaumene, and settled again the 6th of the same month. Seven days later, on the 13th of February the Island of Aphroessa appeared, leaving between Nea Kaumene and itself a channel 30 feet wide. I was in these seas when the phenomenon occurred, and I was able therefore to observe all the different phases. The Island of Aphroessa was round and measured 300 feet in diameter, 30 feet in height. It was composed of black and vitreous lava mixed with fragments of felspar. And lastly, on the 10th of March, a smaller island, called Reka, showed itself near Nea Kaumene, and since then these three have joined together, forming but one and the same island."

"And the channel we are in at this moment?" I asked.

"Here it is," replied Captain Nemo, showing me a map of the archipelago. "You see I have marked the new islands."

I returned to the glass. The *Nautilus* was no longer moving; the heat was becoming unbearable. The sea, which till now had been white, was red, owing to the presence of salts of iron. In spite of the ship's being hermetically sealed, an insupportable smell of sulphur filled the lounge, and the brilliancy of the electricity was entirely extinguished by bright scarlet flames. I was in a bath, I was choking, I was broiled.

"We can remain no longer in this boiling water," said I to the captain.

"No, it would not be prudent," replied the impassive Captain Nemo.

An order was given: the *Nautilus* tacked about and left the intolerable furnace. A quarter of an hour later we were breathing fresh air on the surface. The thought then struck me that, if Ned Land had chosen this part of the sea for our flight, we should never have come out alive.

The next day, the 16th of February, we left that basin between Rhodes and Alexandria which is reckoned at about

1,500 fathoms in depth; the *Nautilus,* passing some distance from Cerigo, quitted the Grecian Archipelago after having doubled Cape Matapan.

7. The Mediterranean in 48 Hours

THE MEDITERRANEAN, the blue sea par excellence, "the great sea" of the Hebrews, "the sea" of the Greeks, the "mare nostrum" of the Romans, bordered by orange trees, aloes, cacti, and sea pines; embalmed with the perfume of the myrtle, surrounded by rude mountains, saturated with pure and transparent air, but incessantly worked by under-ground fires; a perfect battlefield in which Neptune and Pluto still dispute the empire of the world!

It is upon these banks, and on these waters, says Michelet, that man is renewed in one of the most powerful climates of the globe. But, beautiful as it was, I could take only a rapid glance at the basin whose superficial area is 966,757 square miles. Even Captain Nemo's knowledge was lost to me, for this puzzling person did not appear once during our passage at full speed. I estimated the course which the *Nautilus* took under the waves of the sea at about 600 leagues, and it was accomplished in 48 hours. Starting on the morning of the 16th of February from the shores of Greece, we had crossed the Straits of Gibraltar by sunrise on the 18th.

It was plain to me that this Mediterranean, enclosed in the midst of those countries which he wished to avoid, was distasteful to Captain Nemo. Those waves and those breezes brought back too many memories, if not too many regrets. Here he had no longer that independence and that liberty of gait which he had when in the open seas.

Our speed was now 25 knots. It may be well understood that Ned Land, to his great disgust, was obliged to renounce his intended flight. He could not launch the pinnace, going at the rate of 36 to 39 feet every second. To quit the *Nautilus* under such conditions would be as bad as jumping from a train going at full speed—an imprudent thing, to say the least. Besides, our vessel only mounted to the surface of the waves at night to renew its stock of air; it was steered entirely by the compass and the log.

I saw no more of the interior of this Mediterranean than a traveler by express train perceives of the landscape which flies before his eyes; that is to say, the distant horizon, and not the nearer objects which pass like a flash of lightning.

We were then passing between Sicily and the coast of Tunis. In the narrow space between Cape Bon and the Strait of Messina the bottom of the sea rose almost suddenly. There was a perfect bank on which there was not more than nine fathoms of water, while on either side the depth was 90 fathoms.

The *Nautilus* had to maneuver very carefully so as not to strike against this submarine barrier.

I showed Conseil this reef on the map.

"But Monsieur," observed Conseil, "it is like a real isthmus joining Europe to Africa."

"Yes, my boy, it forms a perfect bar to the Straits of Libya, and Smith's soundings have proved that in former times the continents between Cape Boco and Cape Farina were joined."

"I can well believe it," said Conseil.

"I will add," I continued, "that a similar barrier exists between Gibraltar and Ceuta, which in geological times originally cut off the Mediterranean waters."

"What if some volcanic burst should one day raise these two barriers above the waves?"

"It is not probable, Conseil."

"Well, but if Monsieur will permit me to finish, if this phenomenon should take place, it will be troublesome for Mr. Lesseps, who has taken so much pains to pierce the isthmus."

"I agree with you; but I repeat, Conseil, this phenomenon will never happen. The violence of subterranean force is ever diminishing. Volcanoes, so plentiful in the first days of the world, are being extinguished by degrees; the internal heat is weakened, the temperature of the lower strata of the globe is lowered by a perceptible quantity every century to the detriment of our globe, for its heat is its life."

"But the sun?"

"The sun is not sufficient, Conseil. Can it give heat to a dead body?"

"Not that I know of."

"Well, my friend, this earth will one day be that cold corpse; it will become uninhabitable and uninhabited like the moon, which has long since lost all its vital heat."

"In how many centuries?"

"In some hundreds of thousands of years, my boy."

"Then," said Conseil, "we shall have time to finish our journey—that is, if Ned Land does not interfere with it."

And Conseil, reassured, returned to the study of the bank, which the *Nautilus* was skirting at a moderate speed.

During the night of the 16th and 17th of February we had entered the second Mediterranean basin, the greatest depth of which was 1,450 fathoms. The *Nautilus,* by the action of its propeller and its inclined planes, slid down and buried itself in the lowest depths of the sea.

On the 18th of February, at about 3:00 A.M., we were at the entrance of the Straits of Gibraltar. There once existed two currents: an upper one, long since recognized, which conveys the waters of the ocean into the basin of the Mediterranean; and a lower countercurrent, which reasoning has now shown to exist. Indeed, the volume of water in the Mediterranean, incessantly added to by the waves of the Atlantic and by rivers falling into it, would each year raise the level of this sea, for its evaporation is not sufficient to restore the equilibrium. As it is not so, we must necessarily admit the existence of an undercurrent, which empties into the basin of the Atlantic through the Straits of Gibraltar the surplus waters of the Mediterranean. A fact indeed; and it was this countercurrent by which the *Nautilus* profited. It advanced rapidly by the narrow pass. For one instant I caught a glimpse of the beautiful ruins of the temple of Hercules buried in the ground, according to Pliny, with the low island which supported it. A few minutes later we were floating on the Atlantic.

8. Vigo Bay

THE ATLANTIC! A vast sheet of water whose surface area covers 31,839,306 square miles, the length of which is 9,000 miles, with a mean breadth of 2,700—an ocean

whose parallel winding shores embrace an immense circumference, watered by the largest rivers of the world: the St.
Lawrence, the Mississippi, the Amazon, the Plata, the Ori-
noco, the Niger, the Senegal, the Elbe, the Loire, and the
Rhine, which carry water from the most civilized, as well as
from the most savage, countries! Magnificent field of water,
incessantly plowed by vessels of every nation, sheltered by
the flags of every nation, and which terminates in those two
terrible points so dreaded by mariners, Cape Horn and the
Cape of Good Hope.

The *Nautilus* was piercing the water with its sharp spur,
after having accomplished nearly 10,000 leagues in three
months and a half, a distance greater than the great circle
of the earth. Where were we going now, and what was
reserved for the future? The *Nautilus*, leaving the Straits of
Gibraltar, had gone far out from shore, so it returned to the
surface of the waves, and our daily walks on the platform
were restored to us.

I mounted at once, accompanied by Ned Land and Conseil. At a distance of about twelve miles Cape St. Vincent
was dimly to be seen, forming the southwestern point of the
Spanish peninsula. A strong southerly gale was blowing.
The sea was swollen and billowy; it made the *Nautilus* rock
violently. It was almost impossible to keep one's foot on the
platform, which the heavy rolls of the sea beat over every
instant. So we descended after inhaling some mouthfuls of
fresh air.

I returned to my room, Conseil to his cabin; but the
Canadian, with a preoccupied air, followed me. Our rapid
passage across the Mediterranean had not allowed him to
put his project into execution, and he could not help show-

ing his disappointment. When the door of my room was shut, he sat down and looked at me silently.

"Friend Ned," I said, "I understand you; but you cannot reproach yourself. To have attempted to leave the *Nautilus* under the circumstances would have been folly."

Ned Land did not answer; his compressed lips and frowning brow showed the violent possession that his fixed idea had taken over his mind.

"Let us see," I continued; "we need not despair yet. We are going up the coast of Portugal again; France and England are not far off, where we can easily find refuge. Now if the *Nautilus,* on leaving the Straits of Gibraltar, had gone to the south, if it had carried us toward regions where there were no continents, I should share your uneasiness. But we know now that Captain Nemo does not fly from civilized seas, and one of these days I think you can act with security."

Ned Land still looked at me fixedly; at length his lips parted, and he said, "It is for tonight."

I drew myself up suddenly. I was, I admit, little prepared for this communication. I wanted to answer the Canadian, but words would not come.

"We agreed to wait for an opportunity," continued Ned Land, "and the opportunity has arrived. This night we shall be but a few miles from the Spanish coast. It is cloudy. The winds blows freely. I have your word, Mr. Aronnax, and I rely upon you."

As I was silent, the Canadian approached me.

"Tonight, at nine o'clock," said he. "I have warned Conseil. At that moment Captain Nemo will be shut up in his room, probably in bed. Neither the engineers nor the ship's crew can see us. Conseil and I will gain the central staircase, and you, Mr. Aronnax, will remain in the library, two steps from us, waiting my signal. The oars, the mast, and the sail are in the canoe. I have even succeeded in getting some provisions. I have procured an English wrench, to unfasten the bolts which attach it to the shell of the *Nautilus*. So all is ready; till tonight."

"The sea is bad."

"That I allow," replied the Canadian; "but we must risk that. Liberty is worth paying for; besides, the boat is strong, and a few miles with a fair wind to carry us is no great thing. Who knows but by tomorrow we may be a hundred leagues away? Let circumstances only favor us, and by ten or eleven o'clock we shall have landed on some spot of terra firma, alive or dead. But adieu now till tonight."

With these words the Canadian withdrew, leaving me almost dumb. I had imagined that, the chance gone, I should have time to reflect and discuss the matter. My obstinate companion had given me no time; and, after all, what could I have said to him? Ned Land was perfectly right. Here was the opportunity to profit by. Could I retract my word and take upon myself the responsibility of compromising the future of my companions? Tomorrow Captain Nemo might take us far from all land.

At that moment a rather loud hissing noise told me that the reservoirs were filling, and that the *Nautilus* was sinking under the waves of the Atlantic.

A sad day I passed, between the desire of regaining my liberty of action and of abandoning the wonderful *Nautilus* and leaving my submarine studies incomplete.

What dreadful hours I passed thus! Sometimes seeing myself and companions safely landed, sometimes wishing, in spite of my reason, that some unforeseen circumstances would prevent the realization of Ned Land's project.

Twice I went to the lounge. I wished to consult the compass. I wished to see if the direction the *Nautilus* was taking was bringing us nearer or taking us farther from the coast. But the *Nautilus* kept in Portuguese waters.

I must therefore take my part and prepare for flight. My luggage was not heavy; my notes, nothing more.

As to Captain Nemo, I asked myself what he would think of our escape; what trouble it might cause him, and what he might do in case of its discovery or failure. Certainly I had no cause to complain of him; on the contrary, never was hospitality freer than his. In leaving him I could not be taxed with ingratitude. No oath bound us to him. It was on the strength of circumstances he relied, and not upon our word, to fix us forever.

I had not seen the captain since our visit to the Island of Santorin. Would chance bring me to his presence before our departure? I wished it and I feared it at the same time. I listened if I could hear him walking the room contiguous to mine. No sound reached my ear. I felt an unbearable uneasiness. This day of waiting seemed eternal. Hours struck too slowly to keep pace with my impatience.

My dinner was served in my room as usual. I ate but little; I was too preoccupied. I left the table at seven o'clock. A hundred and twenty minutes (I counted them) still separated me from the moment in which I was to join Ned Land. My agitation redoubled. My pulse beat violently. I could not remain quiet. I went and came, hoping to calm my troubled spirit by constant movement. The idea of failure in our bold enterprise was the least painful of my anxieties; but the thought of seeing our project discovered before leaving the *Nautilus,* of being brought before Captain Nemo, irritated, or, what was worse, saddened, at my desertion, made my heart beat.

I wanted to see the lounge for the last time. I descended the stairs and arrived in the museum, where I had passed so many useful and agreeable hours. I looked at all its riches, all its treasures, like a man on the eve of an eternal exile who was leaving never to return.

These wonders of nature, these masterpieces of art, among which for so many days my life had been concentrated, I was going to abandon forever! I should like to have taken a last look through the windows of the lounge into the waters of the Atlantic, but the panels were hermetically closed, and a cloak of steel separated me from that ocean which I had not yet explored.

In passing through the lounge I came near the door which opened into the captain's room. To my great surprise, this door was ajar. I drew back involuntarily. If Captain Nemo should be in his room, he could see me. But, hearing no sound, I drew nearer. The room was deserted. I pushed open the door and took some steps forward. Still the same monklike severity of aspect.

Suddenly the clock struck eight. The first beat of the hammer on the bell awoke me from my dreams. I trembled as if an invisible eye had plunged into my most secret thoughts, and I hurried from the room.

There my eye fell upon the compass. Our course was still north. The log indicated moderate speed, the manometer a depth of about 60 feet.

I returned to my room, clothed myself warmly—sea

boots, an otterskin cap, a great coat lined with sealskin. I was ready, I was waiting. The vibration of the propeller alone broke the deep silence which reigned on board. I listened attentively. Would no loud voice suddenly inform me that Ned Land had been surprised in his projected flight? A mortal dread hung over me, and I vainly tried to regain my accustomed coolness.

At a few minutes to nine I put my ear to the captain's door. No noise. I left my room and returned to the lounge, which was half in obscurity but deserted.

I opened the door communicating with the library. The same insufficient light, the same solitude. I placed myself near the door leading to the central staircase, and there waited for Ned Land's signal.

At that moment the trembling of the propeller sensibly diminished, then it stopped entirely. The silence was now only disturbed by the beatings of my own heart. Suddenly a slight shock was felt, and I knew that the *Nautilus* had stopped at the bottom of the ocean. My uneasiness increased. The Canadian's signal did not come. I felt inclined to join Ned Land and beg of him to put off his attempt. I felt that we were not sailing under our usual conditions.

At this moment the door of the big lounge opened and Captain Nemo appeared. He saw me and without further preamble began in an amiable tone of voice:

"Ah, sir! I have been looking for you. Do you know the history of Spain?"

Now, one might know the history of one's own country by heart, but in the condition I was at the time, distracted and troubled, I could not have remembered a single fact.

"Well," continued Captain Nemo, "you heard my question! Do you know the history of Spain?"

"Very slightly," I answered.

"Well, here are learned men having to learn," said the captain. "Come, sit down, and I will tell you a curious episode in this history. Sir, listen well," said he; "this history will interest you on one side, for it will answer a question which doubtless you have not been able to solve."

"I listen, Captain," said I, not knowing what my interlocutor was driving at, and asking myself if this incident was bearing on our projected flight.

"Sir, if you have no objection, we will go back to 1702. You cannot be ignorant that your king, Louis XIV, thinking that the gesture of a potentate was sufficient to bring the Pyrenees under his yoke, had imposed the Duke of Anjou, his grandson, on the Spaniards. This prince reigned more or less badly under the name of Philip V, and had a strong party against him abroad. Indeed, the preceding year the royal houses of Holland, Austria and England had concluded a treaty of alliance at the Hague, with the intention of plucking the crown of Spain from the head of Philip V and placing it on that of an archduke to whom they prematurely gave the title of Charles III.

"Spain must resist this coalition; but she was almost entirely unprovided with either soldiers or sailors. However, money would not fail them, provided that their galleons, laden with gold and silver from America, once entered their ports. And about the end of 1702 they expected a rich convoy which France was escorting with a fleet of twenty-three vessels, commanded by Admiral Chateau-Renaud, for the ships of the coalition were already beating the Atlantic.

This convoy was to go to Cadiz, but the admiral, hearing that an English fleet was cruising in those waters, resolved to make for a French port.

"The Spanish commanders of the convoy objected to this decision. They wanted to be taken to a Spanish port, and, if not to Cadiz, into Vigo Bay, situated on the northwest coast of Spain, and which was not blocked.

"Admiral Chateau-Renaud had the rashness to obey this injunction, and the galleons entered Vigo Bay.

"Unfortunately, it formed an open road which could not be defended in any way. They had, therefore, to unload the galleons before the arrival of the combined fleet; and time would not have failed them had not a miserable question of rivalry suddenly arisen.

"You are following the chain of events?" asked Captain Nemo.

"Perfectly," I said, not knowing the end proposed by this historical lesson.

"I will continue. This is what passed. The merchants of Cadiz had a privilege by which they had the right of receiving all merchandise coming from the West Indies. Now, to disembark these ingots at the port of Vigo was depriving them of their rights. They complained at Madrid, and obtained the consent of the weak-minded Philip that the convoy, without discharging its cargo, should remain sequestered in the roads of Vigo until the enemy had disappeared.

"But while coming to this decision, on the 22nd of October, 1702, the English vessels arrived in Vigo Bay. Admiral Chateau-Renaud, in spite of inferior forces, fought bravely. But, seeing that the treasure must fall into the enemy's hands, he burned and scuttled every galleon. All went to the bottom with their immense riches."

Captain Nemo stopped. I admit I could not see yet why this history should interest me.

"Well?" I asked.

"Well, Mr. Aronnax," replied Captain Nemo, "we are in that Vigo Bay; and it rests with yourself whether you will penetrate its mysteries."

The captain rose, telling me to follow him. I had had time to recover. I obeyed. The lounge was dark, but through the transparent glass the waves were sparkling. I looked.

For half a mile around the *Nautilus* the waters seemed bathed in electric light. The sandy bottom was clean and bright. Some of the ship's crew in their diving suits were clearing away half-rotten barrels and empty cases from the midst of the blackened wrecks. From these cases and from these barrels escaped ingots of gold and silver, cascades of piastres and jewels. The sand was heaped up with them. Laden with their precious booty, the men returned to the *Nautilus,* disposed of their burden, and went back to this inexhaustible fishery of gold and silver.

I understood now. This was the scene of the battle of the 22nd of October, 1702. Here on this very spot the galleons laden for the Spanish Government had sunk. Here Captain Nemo came, according to his wants, to pack up those millions with which he burdened the *Nautilus*. It was for him and him alone America had given up her precious metals. He was heir direct, without anyone to share, in those treasures torn from the Incas and from the conquered of Ferdinand Cortez.

"Did you know, sir," he asked, smiling, "that the sea contained such riches?"

"I knew," I answered, "that they value money held in suspension in these waters at two millions."

"Doubtless; but to extract this money the expense would be greater than the profit. Here, on the contrary, I have but to pick up what man has lost—and not only in Vigo Bay, but in a thousand other ports where shipwrecks have occurred, and which are marked on my submarine map. Can you understand now the source of the millions I am worth?"

"I understand, Captain. But allow me to tell you that in exploring Vigo Bay you have only been beforehand with a rival society."

"And which?"

"A society which has received from the Spanish Government the privilege of seeking those buried galleons. The shareholders are led on by the allurement of an enormous bounty, for they value these rich shipwrecks at five hundred million."

"Five hundred million they were," answered Captain Nemo, "but they are so no longer."

"Just so," said I; "and a warning to those shareholders would be an act of charity. But who knows if it would be well received? What gamblers usually regret above all is less the loss of their money than of their foolish hopes. After all, I pity them less than the thousands of unfortunates to whom so much riches well distributed would have been profitable, while for them they will be forever barren."

I had no sooner expressed this regret than I felt that it must have wounded Captain Nemo.

"Barren!" he exclaimed, with animation. "Do you think then, sir, that these riches are lost because I gather them? Is it for myself alone, according to your idea, that I take the trouble to collect these treasures? Who told you that I did not make a good use of it? Do you think I am ignorant that there are suffering beings and oppressed races on this earth, miserable creatures to console, victims to avenge? Do you not understand?"

Captain Nemo stopped at these last words, regretting perhaps that he had spoken so much. But I had guessed that, whatever the motive which had forced him to seek independence under the sea, it had left him still a man, that his heart still beat for the sufferings of humanity, and that his immense charity was for oppressed races as well as individuals. And I then understood for whom those millions were destined which were forwarded by Captain Nemo when the *Nautilus* was cruising in the waters of Crete.

9. A Vanished Continent

THE NEXT morning, the 19th of February, I saw the Canadian enter my room. I expected this visit. He looked very disappointed.

"Well, sir?" he said.

"Well, Ned, fortune was against us yesterday."

"Yes; that captain must needs stop exactly at the hour we intended leaving his vessel."

"Yes, Ned, he had business at his banker's."

"His banker's!"

"Or rather his banking house; by that I mean the ocean, where his riches are safer than in the chests of the state."

I then related to the Canadian the incidents of the preceding night, hoping to bring him back to the idea of not
abandoning the captain; but my recital had no other result
than an energetically expressed regret from Ned that he had
not been able to take a walk on the battlefield of Vigo on
his own account.

"However," he said, "all is not ended. It is only a blow
of the harpoon lost. Another time we must succeed; and tonight, if necessary———"

"In what direction is the *Nautilus* going?" I asked.

"I do not know," replied Ned.

"Well, at noon we shall see."

The Canadian returned to Conseil. As soon as I was
dressed, I went into the lounge. The compass was not reassuring. The course of the *Nautilus* was ssw. We were turning our backs on Europe.

I waited with some impatience till the ship's place was
pricked on the chart. At about half-past eleven the reservoirs were emptied and our vessel rose to the surface of the
ocean. I rushed toward the platform. Ned Land had preceded me. No more land in sight. Nothing but an immense
sea. Some sails on the horizon, doubtless those going to San
Roque in search of favorable winds for rounding the Cape
of Good Hope. The weather was cloudy. A gale of wind
was preparing. Ned raved, and tried to pierce the cloudy
horizon. He still hoped that behind all that fog stretched the
land he so longed for.

At noon the sun showed itself for an instant. The second
in command profited by this brightness to take its height.
Then, the sea becoming more billowy, we descended and
the panel closed.

An hour later, upon consulting the chart, I saw the position of the *Nautilus* was marked at 16° 17′ long., and 33° 22′ lat., at 150 leagues from the nearest coast. There was no means of flight, and I leave you to imagine the rage of the Canadian when I informed him of our situation.

For myself, I was not particularly sorry. I felt lightened of the load which had oppressed me, and was able to return with some degree of calmness to my accustomed work.

That night, about eleven o'clock, I received a most unexpected visit from Captain Nemo. He asked me very graciously if I felt fatigued from my watch of the preceding night. I answered in the negative.

"Then, Mr. Aronnax, I propose a curious excursion."

"Propose, Captain?"

"You have hitherto only visited the submarine depths by daylight, under the brightness of the sun. Would it suit you to see them in the darkness of the night?"

"Most willingly."

"I warn you, the way will be tiring. We shall have far to walk, and must climb a mountain. The roads are not well kept."

"What you say, Captain, only heightens my curiosity; I am ready to follow you."

"Come then, sir, we will put on our diving suits."

When I arrived at the robing room I saw that neither of my companions nor any of the ship's crew were to follow us on this excursion. Captain Nemo had not even proposed my taking with me either Ned or Conseil.

In a few moments we had put on our diving suits; crewmen placed on our backs the reservoirs, abundantly filled with air, but no electric lamps were prepared. I called the captain's attention to the fact.

"They will be useless," he replied.

I thought I had not heard aright, but I could not repeat my observation, for the captain's head had already disappeared in its metal case. I finished harnessing myself. I felt an iron-pointed stick put into my hand, and some minutes later, after going through the usual form, we set foot on the bottom of the Atlantic at a depth of 150 fathoms. Midnight was near. The waters were profoundly dark, but Captain Nemo pointed out in the distance a reddish spot, a sort of large light shining brilliantly about two miles from the *Nautilus*. What this fire might be, what could feed it, why and how it lit up the liquid mass, I could not say. In any case, it did light our way, vaguely, it is true, but I soon accustomed myself to the peculiar darkness, and I understood, under such circumstances, the uselessness of the Ruhmkorff apparatus.

As we advanced, I heard a kind of pattering above my head. The noise redoubling, sometimes producing a continual shower, I soon understood the cause. It was rain falling violently, and crisping the surface of the waves. Instinctively the thought flashed across my mind that I should be wet through! By the water! In the midst of the water! I could not help laughing at the odd idea. But, indeed, in the thick diving suit, the liquid element is no longer felt, and one only seems to be in an atmosphere somewhat denser than the terrestrial atmosphere. Nothing more.

After half an hour's walk the soil became stony. Medusae, microscopic crustacea, and pennatulae lit it slightly with their phosphorescent gleam. I caught a glimpse of pieces of stone covered with millions of zoophytes and masses of seaweed. My feet often slipped upon this sticky carpet of seaweed, and without my iron-tipped stick I should have fallen more than once. In turning around, I could still see the whitish lantern of the *Nautilus* beginning to pale in the distance.

But the rosy light which guided us increased and lit up the horizon. The presence of this fire under water puzzled me in the highest degree. Was I going toward a natural phenomenon as yet unknown to the savants of the earth? Or even—for this thought crossed my brain—had the hand of man aught to do with this conflagration? Had he fanned this flame? Was I to meet in these depths companions and friends of Captain Nemo whom he was going to visit, and who, like him, led this strange existence? Should I find down there a whole colony of exiles who, weary of the miseries of this earth, had sought and found independence in the deep ocean? All these foolish and unreasonable ideas pursued me. And in this condition of mind, overexcited by the succession of wonders continually passing before my eyes, I should not have been surprised to meet at the bottom of the sea one of those submarine towns of which Captain Nemo dreamed.

Our road grew lighter and lighter. The white glimmer came in rays from the summit of a mountain about 800 feet high. But what I saw was simply a reflection, developed by the clearness of the waters. The source of this inexplicable light was a fire on the opposite side of the mountain.

In the midst of this stony maze furrowing the bottom of the Atlantic Captain Nemo advanced without hesitation. He knew this dreary road. Doubtless he had often traveled over it, and could not lose himself. I followed him with unshaken confidence. He seemed to me like a genie of the sea; and, as he walked before me, I could not help admiring his stature, which was outlined on the luminous horizon.

It was one in the morning when we arrived at the first slopes of the mountain; but to gain access to them we must venture through the difficult paths of a vast copse.

Yes, a copse of dead trees, without leaves, without sap, trees petrified by the action of the water and here and there overtopped by gigantic pines. It was like a coal pit still standing, holding by the roots to the broken soil, and whose branches, like fine black paper cuttings, showed distinctly on the watery ceiling. Picture to yourself a forest in the Harz hanging onto the sides of the mountain, but a forest swallowed up. The paths were encumbered with seaweed and fuci between which groveled a whole world of crustacea. I went along, climbing the rocks, striding over extended trunks, breaking the sea bindweed which hung from one tree to the other, and frightening the fishes, which flew from branch to branch.

Pressing onward, I felt no fatigue. I followed my guide, who was never tired. What a spectacle! How can I express it? How paint the aspect of those woods and rocks in this medium—their under parts dark and wild, the upper colored with red tints by that light which the reflecting powers of the waters doubled? We climbed rocks which fell directly after with gigantic bounds and the low growling of an avalanche. To right and left ran long dark galleries, where sight was lost. Here opened vast glades which the hand of man seemed to have worked; and I sometimes asked myself if some inhabitant of these submarine regions would not suddenly appear to me.

But Captain Nemo was still climbing. I could not stay behind. I followed boldly. My stick gave me good help. A false step would have been dangerous on the narrow passes sloping down to the sides of the gulfs, but I walked with firm step, without feeling any giddiness. Now I jumped a crevice, the depth of which would have made me hesitate had it been among the glaciers on the land; now I ventured on the unsteady trunk of a tree thrown across from one abyss to the other, without looking under my feet, having only eyes to admire the wild sites of this region.

There, monumental rocks, leaning on their regularly cut bases, seemed to defy all laws of equilibrium. From between their stony knees trees sprang, like a jet under heavy pressure, and upheld others which upheld them. Natural towers, large scarps, cut perpendicularly, like a "curtain," inclined at an angle which the laws of gravitation could never have tolerated in terrestrial regions.

Two hours after quitting the *Nautilus* we had crossed the line of trees, and a hundred feet above our heads rose the top of the mountain, which cast a shadow on the brilliant irradiation of the opposite slope. Some petrified shrubs branched fantastically here and there. Fishes came up under our feet like birds in the long grass. The massive rocks were rent with impenetrable fractures, deep grottos, and unfathomable holes, at the bottom of which formidable creatures might be heard moving. My blood curdled when I saw enormous antennae blocking my road, or some frightful claw snapping closed in the shadow of some cavity. Millions of luminous spots shone brightly in the midst of the darkness. They were the eyes of giant crustacea crouched in their holes; giant lobsters setting themselves up like halberdiers, and moving their claws with the clicking sound of pincers; titanic crabs, pointed like guns on their carriages;

and frightful-looking octopi interweaving their tentacles like a living nest of serpents.

We had now arrived on the first platform, where other surprises awaited me. Before us lay some picturesque ruins, which betrayed the hand of man and not that of the Creator. There were vast heaps of stone among which might be traced the vague and shadowy forms of castles and temples, clothed with a world of blossoming zoophytes, and over which, instead of ivy, seaweed and lichen threw a thick vegetable mantle. But what was this portion of the globe which had been swallowed by cataclysms? Who had placed those rocks and stones like cromlechs of prehistoric times? Where was I? Whither had Captain Nemo's fancy hurried me?

I would fain have asked him; not being able to, I stopped him—I seized his arm. But, shaking his head, and pointing to the highest point of the mountain, he seemed to say:

"Come, come along; come higher!"

I followed, and in a few minutes I had climbed to the top, which for a circle of ten yards commanded the whole mass of rock.

I looked down the side we had just climbed. The mountain did not rise more than seven or eight hundred feet above the level of the plain; but on the opposite side it commanded from twice that height the depths of this part of the Atlantic. My eyes ranged far over a large space lit by violent flashes of light. In fact, the mountain was a volcano.

At fifty feet above the peak, in the midst of a rain of stones and scoriae, a large crater was vomiting forth torrents of lava which fell in a fiery cascade into the midst of the sea. Thus situated, this volcano lit the lower plain like an immense torch, even to the extreme limits of the horizon. I said that the submarine crater threw up lava, but no flames. Flames require the oxygen of the air to feed upon and cannot be developed under water; but streams of lava, having in themselves the principles of their incandescence, can attain a white heat, fight vigorously against the liquid element, and turn it to vapor by contact.

Rapid currents bearing all these gases in diffusion and torrents of lava slid to the bottom of the mountain like an eruption of Vesuvius on another Terra del Greco.

There indeed under my eyes, ruined, destroyed, lay a town—its roofs open to the sky, its temples fallen, its arches dislocated, its columns lying on the ground, from which one would still recognize the massive character of Tuscan architecture. Farther on some remains of a gigantic aqueduct; here the high base of an Acropolis, with the floating outline of a Parthenon; there traces of a quay, as if an ancient port had formerly abutted on the borders of the ocean, and disappeared with its merchant vessels and its war galleys. Farther on again long lines of sunken walls and broad, deserted streets—a perfect Pompeii escaped beneath the waters. Such was the sight that Captain Nemo brought before my eyes!

Where was I? Where was I? I must know at any cost. I tried to speak, but Captain Nemo stopped me by a gesture, and, picking up a piece of chalk stone, advanced to a rock of black basalt, and traced the one word:

ATLANTIS

What a light shot through my mind! Atlantis! the Atlantis of Plato, that continent denied by Origen and Humboldt, who placed its disappearance among the legendary tales. I

had it there now before my eyes, bearing upon it the un-
exceptionable testimony of its catastrophe. The region thus
engulfed was beyond Europe, Asia, and Lybia, beyond the
columns of Hercules, where those powerful people, the At-
lantides, lived, against whom the first wars of ancient
Greeks were waged.

Thus, led by the strangest destiny, I was treading under-
foot the mountains of this continent, touching with my
hand those ruins a thousand generations old and contemporary with the geological epochs. I was walking on the very
spot where the contemporaries of the first man had walked.

While I was trying to fix in my mind every detail of this
grand landscape, Captain Nemo remained motionless, as if
petrified in mute ecstasy, leaning on a mossy stone. Was he
dreaming of those generations long since disappeared? Was
he asking them the secret of human destiny? Was it here
this strange man came to steep himself in historical recollections, and live again this ancient life—he who wanted no
modern one? What would I not have given to know his
thoughts, to share them, to understand them! We remained
for an hour at this place, contemplating the vast plains under the brightness of the lava, which was sometimes wonderfully intense. Rapid tremblings ran along the mountain
caused by internal bubblings; deep rumblings, transmitted
through the waters were echoed with majestic grandeur. At
this moment the moon pierced the ocean depths and threw
her pale rays on the buried continent. It was but a gleam,
but what an indescribable effect! The captain rose, cast one
last look on the immense plain, and then bade me follow
him.

We descended the mountain rapidly, and, the mineral

forest once passed, I saw the lantern of the *Nautilus* shining like a star. The captain walked straight to it, and we got on board as the first rays of light whitened the surface of the ocean.

10. The Submarine Coal Mines

THE NEXT day, the 20th of February, I awoke very late: the fatigues of the previous night had prolonged my sleep until eleven o'clock. I dressed quickly, and hastened to find the course the *Nautilus* was taking. The instruments showed it to be still toward the south, with a speed of twenty miles an hour and a depth of fifty fathoms.

The species of fishes here did not differ much from those already noticed. There were rays of giant size, five yards long, and endowed with great muscular strength, which enabled them to shoot above the waves; sharks of many kinds; among others, one fifteen feet long, with triangular sharp teeth, and whose transparency rendered it almost invisible in the water.

Among bony fish Conseil noticed some about three yards long, armed at the upper jaw with a piercing sword; other bright-colored creatures, known in the time of Aristotle by the name of the sea dragon, which are dangerous to capture on account of the spikes on their back.

About four o'clock the soil, generally composed of a thick mud mixed with petrified wood, changed by degrees, and it became more stony, and seemed strewn with conglomerate and pieces of basalt, with a sprinkling of lava. I thought that a mountainous region was succeeding the long plains; and accordingly, after a few evolutions of the *Nautilus,* I saw the southerly horizon blocked by a high wall which seemed to close all exit. Its summit evidently passed the level of the ocean. It must be a continent, or at least an island—one of the Canaries, or of the Cape Verde Islands. As the bearings had not yet been taken, perhaps designedly, I was ignorant of our exact position. In any case, such a wall seemed to me to mark the limits of that Atlantis, of which we had in reality passed over only the smallest part.

Much longer should I have remained at the window admiring the beauties of sea and sky, but the panels closed. At this moment the *Nautilus* arrived at the side of this high, perpendicular wall. What it would do, I could not guess. I returned to my room; it no longer moved. I lay down with the full intention of waking after a few hours' sleep; but it was eight o'clock the next day when I entered the lounge. I looked at the manometer. It told me that the *Nautilus* was floating on the surface of the ocean. Besides, I heard steps on the platform. I went to the panel. It was open; but, instead of broad daylight, as I expected, I was surrounded by profound darkness. Where were we? Was I mistaken? Was it still night? No; not a star was shining and night has not that utter darkness.

I knew not what to think, when a voice near me said:

"Is that you, Professor?"

"Ah, Captain," I answered, "where are we?"

"Underground, sir."

"Underground!" I exclaimed. "And the *Nautilus* floating still?"

"It always floats."

"But I do not understand."

"Wait a few minutes. Our lantern will be lit, and if you prefer light places, you will be satisfied."

I stood on the platform and waited. The darkness was so complete that I could not even see Captain Nemo; but, looking to the zenith, exactly above my head, I seemed to catch an undecided gleam, a kind of twilight filling a circular hole. At this instant the lantern was lit, and its vividness dispelled the faint light. I closed my dazzled eyes for an instant, and then looked again. The *Nautilus* was stationary, floating near a mountain which formed a sort of quay. The lake, then, supporting it was a lake imprisoned by a circle of walls, measuring two miles in diameter and six in circumference. Its level (the manometer showed) could only be the same as the outside level, for there must necessarily be a communication between the lake and the sea. The high partitions, leaning forward on their base, grew into a vaulted roof bearing the shape of an immense funnel turned upside down, the height being about five or six hundred yards. At the summit was a circular orifice by which I had caught the slight gleam of light, evidently daylight.

"Where are we?" I asked.

"In the very heart of an extinct volcano, the interior of which has been invaded by the sea after some great convulsion of the earth. While you were sleeping, Professor, the *Nautilus* penetrated to this lagoon by a natural canal, which opens about ten yards beneath the surface of the ocean. This is our harbor of refuge, a sure, commodious, and mysterious one, sheltered from all gales. Show me, if you can, on the coasts of any of your continents or islands, a road which can give such perfect refuge from all storms."

"Certainly," I replied, "you are in safety here, Captain

Nemo. Who could reach you in the heart of a volcano? But did I not see an opening at its summit?"

"Yes, its crater, formerly filled with lava, vapor and flames, now gives entrance to the life-giving air we breathe."

"But what is this volcanic mountain?"

"It belongs to one of the numerous islands with which this sea is strewn—to vessels a simple sand bank—to us an immense cavern. Chance led me to discover it, and chance served me well."

"But of what use is this refuge, Captain? The *Nautilus* wants no port."

"No, sir; but it wants electricity to make it move, and the wherewithal to make the electricity—sodium to feed the elements, coal from which to get the sodium, and a coal mine to supply the coal. And exactly on this spot the sea covers entire forests embedded during the geological periods, now mineralized and transformed into coal; for me they are an inexhaustible mine."

"Your men follow the trade of miners here, then, Captain?"

"Exactly so. These mines extend under the waves like the mines of Newcastle. Here, in their diving suits, pickax and shovel in hand, my men extract the coal which I obtain freely, without recourse to the mines of the earth. When I burn this combustible for the manufacture of sodium, the smoke, escaping from the crater of the mountain, gives it the appearance of a still-active volcano."

"And we shall see your companions at work?"

"No, not this time at least, for I am in a hurry to continue our submarine tour of the earth. So I shall content myself with drawing from the reserve of sodium I already possess. The time for loading is one day only, and we continue our voyage. So, if you wish to go over the cavern and make the round of the lagoon, you must take advantage of today, Mr. Aronnax."

I thanked the captain and went to get my companions, who had not yet left their cabin. I invited them to follow me without saying where we were. They mounted the platform. Conseil, who was astonished at nothing, seemed to think it was quite natural that he should wake under a mountain, after having fallen asleep under the waves. But Ned Land thought only of finding an exit from the cavern. After breakfast, about ten o'clock, we left the *Nautilus* to explore the shore and the mountain walls surrounding the lagoon.

"Here we are, once more on land," said Conseil.

"I do not call this land," said the Canadian. "And besides, we are not on it, but beneath it."

Between the walls of the mountain and the waters of the lake lay a sandy shore which, at its greatest breadth, measured 500 feet. On this soil one might easily make the tour of the lake. But the base of these high partitions was stony ground, with volcanic rocks and enormous pumice stones lying in picturesque piles. All these detached masses, enameled and polished by the great heat of subterraneous fires, glistened in the light of our electric lantern, and the mica dust along the shore stirred up by our feet flew like a cloud of sparks. The ground now rose steeply, and we soon arrived at the long, sloping wall of the mountain which, by a circuitous route and inclined planes, led us higher by degrees; but we were obliged to walk carefully among these loosely piled rocks, our feet slipping on the glassy crystal, feldspar, and quartz.

The volcanic nature of this enormous excavation was confirmed on all sides, and I pointed it out to my companions.

"Picture to yourselves," I said, "what this crater must have been when filled with boiling lava, and when the level of the incandescent liquid rose to the orifice of the mountain, as though melted on the top of a hot plate."

"I can picture it perfectly," said Conseil. "But will Monsieur tell me why the Great Architect has suspended operations, and how it is that the furnace is replaced by the quiet waters of the lake?"

"Most probably, Conseil, because some convulsion beneath the ocean produced that very opening which has served as a passage for the *Nautilus*. Then the waters of the Atlantic rushed into the interior of the mountain. There must have been a terrible struggle between the two elements, a struggle which ended in the victory of Neptune. But many ages have run out since then, and the submerged volcano is now a peaceful grotto."

"Very well," replied Ned Land; "I accept the explanation, sir; but in our own interests I regret that the opening of which you speak was not made above the level of the sea."

"But, friend Ned," said Conseil, "if the passage had not been under the sea, the *Nautilus* could not have gone through it."

We continued ascending. The steps became more and more perpendicular and narrow, and difficult to negotiate. There were deep excavations which we were obliged to jump across; and sloping masses were piled up which we had to go around. We slid to our knees and crawled along.

But Conseil's dexterity and the Canadian's strength sur-mounted all obstacles.

At a height of about 100 feet the nature of the ground changed without becoming any easier. The loose stones and rough volcanic rock were succeeded by black basalt, the first spread out in layers full of bubbles like rock sponge, the latter forming regular prisms, placed like a colonnade supporting the "spring" of the immense vault, an admirable specimen of natural architecture. Between the blocks of basalt wound long streams of lava, long since grown cold, encrusted with streaks of bituminous coal; and in some places there were spread large carpets of sulphur. A more powerful light shone through the upper crater, shedding a vague glimmer over these volcanic depressions forever bur-ied in the bossom of this extinguished mountain. But our upward march was soon stopped at a height of about 250 feet by impassable obstacles. There was a complete vaulted arch overhanging us, and our ascent was changed to a cir-cular walk. At this level the vegetable kingdom began a struggle with the mineral. Some shrubs, and even some trees, grew from the crevices in the walls. I recognized some euphorbias, with the caustic sugar coming from them; helio-tropes, quite incapable of justifying their name, sadly drooped their clusters of flowers, both their color and per-fume half gone. Here and there some chrysanthemums grew timidly at the foot of an aloe with long, sickly-looking leaves. But between the streams of lava I saw some little violets still slightly perfumed, and I admit that I smelled them with delight. Perfume is the soul of the flower, and sea flowers have no soul.

We had arrived at the foot of some sturdy dragon trees,

which had pushed aside the rocks with their strong roots, when Ned Land exclaimed:

"Ah, sir, a hive! A hive!"

"A hive!" I replied, with a gesture of incredulity.

"Yes, a hive," repeated the Canadian, "and bees humming around it."

I approached, and was bound to believe my own eyes. There at a hole bored in one of the dragon trees were some thousands of these ingenious insects, so common in all the Canaries, and whose produce is so much esteemed. Naturally enough, the Canadian wished to gather the honey, and I could not well oppose his wish. He lit a quantity of dry leaves mixed with sulphur, with a spark from his flint and he began to smoke out the bees. The humming ceased by degrees, and the hive eventually yielded several pounds of the sweetest honey, with which Ned Land filled his haversack.

"When I have mixed this honey with the paste of the breadfruit," said he, "I shall be able to offer you a succulent cake."

" 'Pon my word," said Conseil, "it will be gingerbread."

"Never mind the gingerbread," I said; "let us continue our interesting walk."

At every turn of the path we were following the lake appeared in all its length and breadth. The lantern lit up the whole of its peaceful surface, which knew neither ripple nor wave. The *Nautilus* remained perfectly immovable. On the platform and on the mountain, the ship's crew were working like black shadows clearly carved against the luminous atmosphere. We were now going around the highest crest of the first layers of rock which upheld the roof. I then saw that bees were not the only representatives of the animal kingdom in the interior of this volcano. Birds of prey hovered here and there in the shadows, or fled from their nests on the top of the rocks. There were sparrow hawks, with white breasts, and kestrels, and down the slopes scampered, with their long legs, several fine fat bustards. I leave anyone to imagine the covetousness of the Canadian at the sight of this savory game, and whether he did not regret having no gun. But he did his best to replace the lead by stones, and, after several fruitless attempts, he succeeded in wounding a magnificent bird. To say that he risked his life twenty times before reaching it is but the truth; but he managed so well that the creature joined the honey in his bag.

We were now obliged to descend toward the shore; the crest had become impracticable. Above us the crater seemed to gape like the mouth of a well. From this place we could see the sky; and clouds, scattered by the west wind left behind them, even on the summit of the mountain, their misty remnants—certain proof that they were only moderately high, for the volcano did not rise more than 800 feet above the level of the ocean. Half an hour after the Canadian's last exploit we had regained the inner shore. Here the flora was represented by large carpets of marine crystal, a little umbelliferous plant very good to pickle, which also bears the name of pierce stone and sea fennel. Conseil gathered some bundles of it. As to the fauna, it might be counted by thousands in crustacea of all sorts—lobsters, crabs, spider crabs, chameleon shrimps, and a large number of shells, rockfish, and limpets. Three-quarters of an hour later we had finished our circuitous walk and were on board. The crew had just finished loading the sodium, and the *Nautilus* could have left that instant. But Captain Nemo gave no order. Did he wish to wait until night, and leave the submarine passage secretly? Perhaps so. Whatever it might be, the next day, the *Nautilus,* having left its port, steered clear of all land at a few yards beneath the waves of the Atlantic.

11. The Sargasso Sea

THAT DAY the *Nautilus* crossed a singular part of the Atlantic Ocean. No one can be ignorant of the existence of a current of warm water known by the name of the Gulf Stream. After leaving the Gulf of Florida we went in the direction of Spitzbergen. But before entering the Gulf of Mexico, about 45° of N. lat., this current divides into two arms, the principal one going toward the coast of Ireland and Norway, while the second bends to the south about the height of the Azores; then, touching the African shore and describing a lengthened oval, returns to the Antilles. This second arm—it is rather a collar than an arm—surrounds with its circles of warm water that portion of the cold, quiet, immovable ocean called the Sargasso Sea, a perfect lake in the open Atlantic; it takes no less than three years for the great current to pass around it.

Such was the region the *Nautilus* was now visiting, a perfect meadow, a close carpet of seaweed, rockweed and tropical berries, so thick and so compact that the stem of a vessel could hardly tear its way through it. And Captain Nemo, not wishing to entangle the *Nautilus'* propeller in this herbaceous mass, kept some yards beneath the surface of the waves. The name Sargasso comes from the Spanish word "sargazzo" which means kelp. This kelp or berry plant is the main ingredient of the immense bed.

As to why these plants unite in the peaceful basin of the
Atlantic: the only explanation which can be given, Maury
says in his *Physical Geography*, seems the result of a reaction known to all the world. Place in a vase some fragments
of cork or other floating body, and give to the water in the
vase a circular movement. The scattered fragments will
unite in a group in the center of the liquid surface, that is to
say, in the part least agitated. In the phenomenon we are
considering, the Atlantic is the vase, the Gulf Stream the
circular current, and the Sargasso Sea the central point at
which the floating bodies unite.

I share Maury's opinion, and I was able to study the
phenomenon in the very midst, where vessels rarely penetrate. Above us floated debris of all kinds. Heaped up
among these brownish plants were trunks of trees torn from
the Andes or the Rocky Mountains, and floated by the
Amazon or the Mississippi; numerous wrecks, remains of
keels, or ships' bottoms, side planks stove in, and so
weighted with shells and barnacles that they could not again
rise to the surface. And time will one day justify Maury's
other opinion, that these substances thus accumulated for
ages will become petrified by the action of the water and
will then form inexhaustible coal mines—a precious reserve
prepared by farseeing Nature for the moment when men
shall have exhausted the mines of continents.

In the midst of this inextricable mass of plants and seaweed I noticed some charming pink halcyons and actiniae,
with their long tentacles trailing after them, and medusae,
green, red, and blue.

We passed all the day of February 22nd in the Sargasso
Sea, where such fish as are partial to marine plants find

abundant nourishment. The next day the ocean had returned to its accustomed aspect. From this time for nineteen days, from the 23rd of February to the 12th of March,
the *Nautilus* kept in the middle of the Atlantic, carrying us
at a constant speed of 100 leagues in 24 hours. Captain
Nemo evidently intended accomplishing his submarine pro-
gram, and I imagined that he intended, after rounding the
Horn, to return to the Australian seas of the Pacific. Ned
Land had cause for fear. In these large seas, devoid of islands, we could not attempt to leave the boat. Nor had we
any means of opposing Captain Nemo's will. Our only
course was to submit; but what we could gain by neither
force nor cunning I liked to think might be obtained by
persuasion. This voyage ended, would he not consent to
restore our liberty, under an oath never to reveal his existence—an oath of honor which we should have religiously
kept. We must consider that delicate question with the captain. But was I free to claim this liberty? Had he not himself
said from the beginning, in the firmest manner, that the
secret of his life exacted from him our lasting imprisonment
on board the *Nautilus?* And would not my four months'
silence appear to him a tacit acceptance of our situation?
And would not a return to the subject result in raising suspicions which might be hurtful to our projects, if at some
future time a favorable opportunity offered to return to
them?

During the nineteen days mentioned above no incident
of any kind happened to signalize our voyage. I saw little of
the captain; he was at work. In the library I often found his
books left open, especially those on natural history. My
work on submarine depths, conned over by him, was cov-

ered with marginal notes, often contradicting my theories
and systems; but the captain contented himself with thus
purging my work; it was very rare for him to discuss it with
me. Sometimes I heard the melancholy tones of his organ,
but only at night, in the midst of the deepest obscurity,
when the *Nautilus* slept upon the deserted ocean. During
this part of our voyage we sailed whole days on the surface
of the waves. The sea seemed abandoned. A few sailing
vessels, on the road to India, were making for the Cape of
Good Hope. One day we were followed by the boats of a
whaler, who, no doubt, took us for some enormous whale
of great price; but Captain Nemo did not wish the worthy
fellows to lose their time and trouble, so ended the chase by
plunging under the water. Our navigation continued until
the 13th of March; that day the *Nautilus* was employed in
taking soundings, which greatly interested me. We had then
traveled about 13,000 leagues since our departure from the
high seas of the Pacific. The bearings gave us 45° 37′ S.
lat., and 37° 53′ W. long. It was the same water in which
Captain Denham of the *Herald* sounded 7,000 fathoms, or
35,000 feet, without finding the bottom. Here, too, it was
that Lieutenant Parker of the American frigate *Congress*
had been unable to touch the bottom with soundings of
40,000 feet. Captain Nemo intended seeking the bottom of
the ocean at a diagonal, by means of the *Nautilus'* side fins,
placed at an angle of 45° with the water line. Then the
propeller set to work at its maximum speed, its four blades
beating the waves with indescribable force. Under this powerful pressure the hull of the *Nautilus* quivered like a
sonorous chord, and sank steadily under the water.

At 7,000 fathoms I saw some blackish tops rising from
the midst of the waters; but these summits might belong to

high mountains like the Himalayas or Mount Blanc, even higher; and the depth of the abyss remained incalculable. The *Nautilus* descended still lower, in spite of the great pressure. I felt the steel plates tremble at the fastenings of the bolts; its bars bent, its partitions groaned; the windows of the lounge seemed to curve under the pressure of the waters. And this firm structure would doubtless have yielded, if, as its captain had said, it had not resisted like a solid block. I still saw some shells, some serpulae and spin-orbes, still living, and some specimens of asteriads. But soon this last representative of animal life disappeared; and at the depth of more than three leagues, the *Nautilus* had passed the limits of submarine existence. We had attained a depth of 16,000 fathoms, or 80,000 feet under the sea! The sides of the *Nautilus* then bore a pressure of 1600 atmospheres, that is to say, 3200 pounds to each square two-fifths of an inch of its surface.

"What a situation to be in!" I exclaimed, "To be in these deep regions where man has never trod! Look, Captain, look at these magnificent rocks, these uninhabited grottos, these lowest receptacles of the globe where life is no longer possible! What unknown sights are here! Surely, we will always remember them!"

"Would you like to carry away more than a memory?" asked Captain Nemo.

"What do you mean?"

"I mean to say that nothing is easier than to take a photographic view of this submarine region."

I had not time to express my surprise at this new proposition, when, at Captain Nemo's call, a camera was brought into the lounge. Through the widely opened panel, the liquid mass was bright with electricity, which was distrib-

uted with such uniformity, that not a shadow, not a gradation, was to be seen in our manufactured light. The *Nautilus* remained motionless, the force of its propeller
counteracted by the angle of its side fins. The camera was
aimed at the bottom of the ocean, and in a few seconds we
had obtained a perfect negative. The positive shows those
primitive rocks, which have never looked upon the light of
heaven; that lowest granite which forms the foundation of
the globe; those deep grottos. I cannot describe the effect of
these smooth, black, polished rocks, those strange lifeless
forms, standing solidly on the sandy carpet of the bottom.

The operation over Captain Nemo said, "Let us go up;
we must not expose the *Nautilus* too long to such great
pressure."

"Go up again!" I exclaimed.

"Hold on tight."

I had not time to understand why the captain cautioned
me thus, when I was thrown suddenly forward. At a signal
from the captain, the propeller was disengaged and the side
fins raised vertically. The *Nautilus* rose with stunning rapidity, cutting the mass of waters with a sonorous agitation.
Nothing was visible; in four minutes it had shot through the
four-odd miles which separated it from the ocean's surface,
and after emerging like a flying-fish, fell back, making the
waves rebound to an enormous height.

12. Right Whales and Sperm Whales

DURING THE nights of March 13th and 14th the *Nautilus*
returned to its southerly course. I fancied that at Cape Horn

the captain would turn the helm westward to the Pacific seas, and so complete the tour of the world. He did nothing of the kind, but continued on his way to the southern regions. Where was he going? To the pole? It was madness! I began to think that the captain's temerity justified Ned Land's fears. For some time past the Canadian had not spoken to me of his projects of flight; he was less communicative, almost silent. I could see that this lengthened imprisonment was weighing upon him, and I felt that rage was burning within him. When he met the captain his eyes lit up with suppressed anger, and I feared that his natural violence would lead him to extremes. That day, the 14th of March, he and Conseil came to me in my room. I inquired the cause of their visit.

"A simple question to ask you, sir."

"Speak, Ned."

"How many men are there on board the *Nautilus*, do you think?"

"I cannot tell, my friend."

"I should say that its working does not require a large crew."

"Certainly, under existing conditions, ten men at the most ought to be enough."

"Well, why should there be any more?"

"Why?" I replied, looking fixedly at Ned Land, whose meaning was easy to guess. "Because," I added, "if my surmises are correct, and if I have well understood the captain's existence, the *Nautilus* is not only a vessel: it is also a place of refuge for those who, like its commander, have broken every tie upon earth."

"Perhaps so," said Conseil; "but, in any case, the *Nautilus* can only contain a certain number of men. Could not Monsieur estimate their maximum?"

"How, Conseil?"

"By calculation; given the size of the vessel, which you know, sir, and consequently the quantity of air it contains, knowing also how much each man expands at a breath, and comparing these results with the fact that the *Nautilus* is obliged to go to the surface every twenty-four hours."

Conseil had not finished the sentence before I saw what he was driving at.

"I understand," said I; "but that calculation, though simple enough, can give but a very uncertain result."

"Never mind," said Ned Land, urgently.

"Here it is, then," I said. "In one hour each man consumes the oxygen contained in twenty gallons of air; and in twenty-four, that contained in 480 gallons. We must, therefore, find how many times 480 gallons of air the *Nautilus* contains."

"Just so," said Conseil.

"Well," I continued, "the size of the *Nautilus* is 3,100 tons. Now, allowing 1600 tons for displacement and weight of its equipment, furnishings, etc., we arrive at an estimated 1500 tons of air. Since one ton equals 200 gallons of air, it contains 300,000 gallons, which, divided by 480, gives a quotient of 625. Which means to say, strictly speaking, that the air contained in the *Nautilus* would suffice for 625 men for twenty-four hours."

"Six hundred and twenty-five!" repeated Ned.

"But remember that all of us, passengers, sailors, and officers included, would not form a tenth of that number."

"Still too many for three men," murmured Conseil.

The Canadian shook his head, passed his hand across his forehead, and left the room without answering.

"Will Monsieur permit me to make one observation?" asked Conseil. "Poor Ned is longing for everything that he can't have. His past life is always present to him; everything that we are forbidden he regrets. His head is full of old recollections. And we must understand him. What has he to do here? Nothing. He is not learned like Monsieur; he has not the same taste for the beauties of the sea that we have. He would risk everything to be able to go once more into a tavern in his own country."

Certainly the monotony on board must seem intolerable to the Canadian, accustomed as he was to a life of liberty and activity. Events were rare which could rouse him to any show of spirit; but that day an event did happen which recalled the bright days of the harpooner. About eleven in the morning, being on the surface of the ocean, the *Nautilus* fell in with a herd of whales—an encounter which did not astonish me, knowing that these creatures, hunted to death, had taken refuge in high latitudes.

We were seated on the platform, with a quiet sea. The month of October in those latitudes gave us some lovely autumnal days. It was the Canadian—he could not be mistaken—who signaled a whale on the eastern horizon. Looking attentively, one might see its black back rise and fall with the waves, five miles from the *Nautilus*.

"Ah," exclaimed Ned Land, "if I was on board a whaler now, such a meeting would give me pleasure. It is a large one. See it spouting! Confound it, why am I bound to these steel plates?"

"What, Ned," I said, "you have not forgotten your old ideas of fishing?"

"Can a whale fisher ever forget his old trade, sir? Can he ever tire of the excitement of such a chase?"

"You have never fished in these seas, Ned?"

"Never, sir; in the northern only, and as much in the Bering as in the Davis Strait."

"Then the southern right whale is still unknown to you. It is the Greenland whale you have hunted up to this time, one not found in the warm waters of the equator. Whales are localized, according to their kind, in certain seas which they never leave. And if one of these creatures went from the Bering to the Davis Strait, it must be simply because there is a passage from one sea to the other, either on the American or the Asiatic side."

"In that case, as I have never fished in these seas, I do not know the kind of whale frequenting them!"

"I have told you, Ned."

"A greater reason for making their acquaintance," said Conseil.

"Look! Look!" exclaimed the Canadian. "It is getting nearer! They aggravate me; he knows I cannot go after him!"

Ned stamped his foot. His hand trembled as he grasped an imaginary harpoon.

"Are these whales as large as those of the northern seas?" he asked.

"Very nearly, Ned."

"Because I have seen large whales, sir, whales measuring a hundred feet. I have even been told that those around the Aleutian Islands are sometimes 150 feet long."

"That seems to me an exaggeration. These creatures are generally much smaller than the Greenland whale."

"Ah," exclaimed the Canadian, whose eyes had never left the ocean, "they are coming nearer; they are in the same water as the *Nautilus*."

Then, returning to our discussion, he said:

"You spoke of the cachalot, the sperm whale, as a small creature. I have heard of gigantic ones. They are intelligent animals. It is said that some will cover themselves with seaweed and lichens and then are mistaken for islands. People encamp on them and settle there, light a fire——"

"And build houses," said Conseil.

"Yes, joker," said Ned Land. "And one fine day the creature plunges, carrying with it all the inhabitants to the bottom of the sea."

"Something like the travels of Sindbad the Sailor," I replied, laughing.

"Ah," suddenly exclaimed Ned Land, "it is not one whale; there are ten—there are twenty—it is a whole troop! And I not able to do anything!"

"But, friend Ned," said Conseil, "why do you not ask Captain Nemo's permission to chase them?"

Conseil had not finished his sentence when Ned Land had lowered himself through the panel to seek the captain. A few minutes afterward the two appeared together on the platform.

Captain Nemo watched the herd of whales playing on the waters about a mile from the *Nautilus*.

"They are southern right whales," he said; "there goes the fortune of a whole fleet of whalers."

"Well, sir," asked the Canadian, "can I not chase them, if only to remind me of my old trade of harpooner?"

"And to what purpose?" replied Captain Nemo; "only to destroy! We have no use for whale oil on board."

"But, sir," continued the Canadian, "in the Red Sea you allowed us to follow the dugong."

"Then it was to procure fresh meat for my crew. Here it would be killing for killing's sake. I know that is a privilege reserved for man, but I do not approve of such murderous pastime. In destroying the southern whale—like the Greenland whale, an inoffensive creature—your traders do a culpable action, Master Land. They have already depopulated the whole of Baffin Bay and are annihilating a class of useful animals. Leave these unfortunate whales alone. They have plenty of natural enemies—cachalots, swordfish and sawfish—without *you* troubling them."

The captain was right. The barbarous and inconsiderate greed of these fishermen will one day cause the disappearance of the last whale in the ocean. Ned Land whistled "Yankee Doodle" between his teeth, thrust his hands into his pockets, and turned his back on us. But Captain Nemo watched the herd, and addressing me, said:

"I was right in saying that these whales have enough natural enemies without counting man. They will have plenty to do before long. Do you see, Mr. Aronnax, about eight miles to leeward, those blackish moving points?"

"Yes, Captain," I replied.

"Those are cachalots [sperm whales]—terrible animals, which I have met in herds of two or three hundred. As to *them*, they are cruel, mischievous creatures; it would be right to exterminate them."

The Canadian turned quickly at the last words.

"Well, Captain," he said, "it is still time, in the interest of the right whales."

"It is useless to expose one's self. The *Nautilus* will disperse them. It is armed with a steel spur as good as Master Land's harpoon, I imagine."

The Canadian did not put himself out enough to shrug his shoulders. Attack whales with blows of a spur! Who had ever heard of such a thing?

"Wait, Mr. Aronnax," said Captain Nemo. "We will show you something you have never yet seen. We have no pity for these ferocious creatures. They are nothing but mouth and teeth."

Mouth and teeth! No one could better describe the macrocephalous sperm whale, which is sometimes more than seventy-five feet long. Its enormous head occupies one-third of its entire body. Better armed than the other whales, whose upper jaw is furnished only with whalebone, it is supplied, on the lower jaw, with twenty-five large tusks, about eight inches long, cylindrical and conical at the top, each weighing two pounds. In the upper part of this enormous head, in great cavities divided by cartilages, is to be found from six to eight hundred pounds of that precious oil called spermaceti. The sperm whale is a disagreeable creature, more tadpole than fish, according to Fredol's description. It is badly formed, the whole of its left side being, if we may say it, a "failure," it is only able to see with its right eye.

But the formidable herd was nearing us. They had seen the right whales and were preparing to attack them. One could judge beforehand that the sperm whales would be victorious, not only because they were better built for attack than their inoffensive adversaries, but also because they could remain longer under water without coming to the surface. There was only just time to go to the help of the right whales.

The *Nautilus* went under water. Conseil, Ned Land and I took our places before the window in the lounge, and Captain Nemo joined the pilot in his cage to work his ship as an engine of destruction. Soon I felt the beatings of the propeller quicken, and our speed increased.

The battle between the sperm and right whales had already begun when the *Nautilus* arrived. They did not at first show any fear at the sight of this new monster joining in the conflict. But they soon had to guard against its blows. What a battle! The *Nautilus* was nothing but a formidable harpoon, brandished by the hand of its captain. It hurled itself against the fleshy mass, passing clean through the animal, leaving behind it two quivering halves. The *Nautilus* could not feel the formidable blows from their tails upon its sides, nor the shock which the ship itself produced. One sperm whale killed, it rammed the next, tacked so that it might not miss its prey, going forward and backward, answering to the helm, plunging when the cetacean dived into the deep waters, coming up with it when it returned to the surface, striking it front or sideways, cutting or tearing in all directions and at any pace, piercing it with the terrible spur. What carnage! What a noise on the surface of the waves! What sharp hissing and snorting peculiar to these enraged animals! In the midst of these waters, generally so peaceful, their tails made perfect billows.

For one hour this wholesale massacre continued, from

which the sperm whales could not escape. Several times ten
or twelve united tried to crush the *Nautilus* by their weight.
From the window we could see their enormous mouths,
studded with tusks, and their wicked eyes. Ned Land could
not contain himself; he threatened and swore at them. We
could feel them clinging to our vessel like dogs worrying a
wild boar in a copse. But the *Nautilus,* its propeller churn-
ing steadily, carried them here and there, or to the upper
levels of the ocean, without feeling their enormous weight,
nor the powerful strain on the vessel. At length the mass of
sperm whales disappeared; the waves became quiet, and I
felt that we were rising to the surface. The panel opened
and we hurried on to the platform. The sea was covered
with mutilated bodies. A formidable explosion could not
have divided and torn this fleshy mass with more violence.
We were floating amid gigantic bodies, bluish on the back
and white underneath, covered with enormous protuber-
ances. Some terrified sperm whales were flying toward the
horizon. The waves were dyed red for several miles, and the
Nautilus floated in a sea of blood. Captain Nemo joined us.

"Well, Master Land?" he said.

"Well, sir," replied the Canadian, whose enthusiasm had
somewhat calmed, "it is a terrible spectacle, certainly. But I
am not a butcher. I am a hunter, and I call this a butchery."

"It is a massacre of mischievous creatures," replied the
captain; "the *Nautilus* is not a butcher's knife."

"I like my harpoon better," said the Canadian.

"Everyone to his own taste," answered the captain, looking fixedly at Ned Land.

I feared the Canadian would commit some act of violence which would end in sad consequences. But his anger

was turned by the sight of a whale which the *Nautilus* had just come up with. The creature had not quite escaped from the sperm whale's teeth. I recognized the southern right whale by its flat head, which is entirely black. Anatomically, it is distinguished from the white whale and the North Cape whale by the seven cervical vertebrae, and it has two more ribs than its congeners. The unfortunate cetacean was lying on its side, riddled with holes from the bites, and quite dead. From its mutilated fin still hung a young whale which it could not save from the massacre. Its open mouth let the water flow in and out, murmuring like the waves breaking on the shore. Captain Nemo steered close to the corpse of the creature. Two of his men mounted its side, and I saw, not without surprise, that they were drawing from its breasts all the milk which they contained, that is to say, about two or three tons. The captain offered me a cup of the milk, which was still warm. I could not help showing my repugnance to the drink, but he assured me that it was excellent, and not to be distinguished from cow's milk. I tasted it, and was of his opinion. It was a useful reserve to us, for in the shape of salt butter or cheese it would form an agreeable variety from our ordinary food. From that day I noticed with uneasiness that Ned Land's ill-will toward Captain Nemo increased, and I resolved to watch the Canadian's gestures closely.

13. The Great Ice Barrier

THE *Nautilus* was steadily pursuing its southerly course, following the fiftieth meridian with considerable speed. Did Captain Nemo wish to reach the pole? I did not think so, for every attempt to reach that point had hitherto failed. Again, the season was far advanced, for in the Antarctic regions the 13th of March corresponds with the 13th of September of northern regions, which begins the equinoctial season. On the 14th of March I saw floating ice in latitude 55°, merely pale bits of debris 20 to 25 feet long, forming banks over which the sea curled. The *Nautilus* remained on the surface of the ocean.

Ned Land, who had fished in the Arctic waters, was familiar with icebergs; but Conseil and I admired them for the first time. In the atmosphere toward the southern horizon stretched a white dazzling band. English whalers have given it the name of "ice blink." However thick the clouds may be, it is always visible, and announces the presence of an ice pack or bank. Accordingly, larger blocks soon appeared whose brilliancy changed with the caprices of the fog. Some of these masses showed green veins, as if long, undulating lines had been traced with sulphate of copper; others resembled enormous amethysts with the light shining through them. Some reflected the light of day upon a thousand crystal facets. Others shaded with vivid calcareous reflections resembled a perfect town of marble. The nearer we drew to the South Pole the more these floating islands increased both in number and size.

At 60° lat. every passage was blocked. Then, seeking carefully, Captain Nemo found a narrow opening through which he boldly slipped, knowing that it would soon close behind him. Thus guided by this clever hand, the *Nautilus* passed through all that ice with a precision which quite charmed Conseil. We saw icebergs, or mountains; ice fields, or smooth plains seeming to have no limits; drift ice or floating ice packs; plains broken up, called palchs when they are circular and streams when they are made up of long strips. The temperature was very low; the thermometer exposed to the air marked 27° or 28° above zero, but we were warmly clad in seal or polar-bear fur. The interior of the *Nautilus,* warmed evenly by its electric system, defied the most intense cold. Besides, it would have been necessary only to go a few feet beneath the waves to find a more bearable temperature. Two months earlier we should have had perpetual daylight in these latitudes; but already we had had three or four hours of night; soon the six months of darkness would settle on these polar regions.

On the 15th of March we were in the latitude of New Shetland and South Orkney. The captain told me that formerly numerous tribes of seals inhabited them, but that English and American whalers, in their rage for destruction, massacred both old and young; thus, where there were once life and animation they had left silence and death.

About eight o'clock on the morning of March 16th, the *Nautilus,* following the 55th meridian, crossed the Antarctic polar circle. Ice surrounded us on all sides, and closed the horizon. But Captain Nemo found one opening after another, always heading south. I cannot express my astonishment at the beauties of these new regions. The ice took on surprising shapes. Here the grouping formed an oriental town, with innumerable mosques and minarets; there a fallen city toppled by some convulsion of nature. The whole aspect was constantly changed by the oblique rays of the sun, or lost in grayish fogs and blizzards. We heard cracking and splitting on all sides, as icebergs tumbled over, constantly altering the landscape. Often seeing no exit, I thought we were hopeless prisoners; but guided by a kind of instinct, Captain Nemo would discover a new pass. He was never mistaken in the thin threads of bluish water trickling along the ice fields; and I had no doubt that he had already ventured into Antarctic waters. On the 16th of March, however, the ice fields absolutely blocked our route. It was not the Great Ice Barrier itself as yet, but vast fields cemented by the cold. But this obstacle could not stop Captain Nemo: he hurled himself against it with frightful violence. The *Nautilus* entered the brittle mass like a wedge, and split it with frightful crackings. It was the battering ram of the ancients hurled by infinite strength. The ice, thrown high in the air, fell like hail around us. By its own power of impulsion our vessel made a path for itself; sometimes carried away by its own impetus, it lodged on the ice field, crushing it with its own weight, or sometimes, when it became embedded, would free itself by a simple pitching movement. Violent gales assailed us from every angle, and thick fogs, through which we could see nothing. The snow was piled so deep and so hard-packed that we had to break it with blows of a pickax; the temperature stayed at 22°, and the *Nautilus* was sheathed in ice. The rigging of a sailing vessel would have frozen up and been unmanageable. Only a vessel without sails, with electricity for its motive power, could brave such high latitudes. Even so, on the 18th of March after many useless attempts the *Nautilus* itself was completely blocked. Now it was no longer a question of an ice stream, palch, or ice field, but an interminable and immovable chain of ice mountains.

"The Great Ice Barrier!" said the Canadian to me.

I knew that to Ned Land, as well as to all other navigators who had preceded us, this was an inevitable obstacle.

The sun appeared for an instant at noon, and Captain Nemo took an observation which gave our situation as approximately 51° 30′ long. and 67° 39′ of S. lat. We had advanced one degree farther in this Antarctic region. Open water was no longer visible. Under the spur of the *Nautilus* lay stretched a vast plain, entangled with confused blocks. Here and there sharp points and slender needles rose to a height of 200 feet; farther on, a steep shore, rough as though hewn with an ax and clothed with grayish tints, reflected a few rays of sunshine, half drowned in the fog. And over this desolate face of nature a stern silence reigned, scarcely broken by the flapping wings of petrels and puffins. Everything—even sound—was frozen.

The *Nautilus* was halted in its adventurous course in the midst of these ice fields. In spite of our efforts, in spite of its powerful means of breaking up the ice, the *Nautilus* remained immovable. Generally, when we can proceed no farther, we can still retreat. But here return was as impossible as advance, for every pass had closed behind us. For the few moments when we were stationary, we were likely to be entirely blocked, which did indeed happen about two o'clock in the afternoon, the fresh ice forming around the vessel's sides with astonishing rapidity. I was obliged to admit that Captain Nemo was more than imprudent. I was on the platform at that moment. The captain had been observing our situation for some time past, when he said to me:

"Well, sir, what do you think of this?"

"I think that we are caught, Captain."

"So, Mr. Aronnax, you really think that the *Nautilus* cannot disengage itself?"

"With difficulty, Captain, for the season is already too far advanced for you to reckon on further breaking up of the ice."

"Ah, sir," said Captain Nemo, in an ironical tone, "you will always be the same. You see nothing but difficulties and obstacles. I affirm that not only can the *Nautilus* disengage itself, but also that it can go farther still."

"Farther to the south?" I asked, looking at the captain.

"Yes, sir; we shall go to the pole."

"To the pole!" I exclaimed, unable to repress a gesture of incredulity.

"Yes," replied the captain coldly, "to the Antarctic pole —to that unknown point from whence springs every meridian of the globe. *You* know whether I can do as I please with the *Nautilus!*"

Yes, I knew that. I knew that this man was bold, even to rashness. But to conquer those obstacles which bristled around the South Pole, rendering it more inaccessible than the North Pole—and even that had not yet been reached by the boldest navigators—was it not a mad enterprise, one which only a maniac would have conceived? It then came into my head to ask Captain Nemo if he had ever discovered that pole which had never yet been trodden by a human creature?

"No, sir," he replied; "but we will discover it together. Where others have failed, *I* will not fail. I have never yet led my *Nautilus* so far into southern seas; but, I repeat, it shall go farther yet."

"I can well believe you, Captain," I said, in a slightly ironical tone. "I believe you! Let us go ahead! There are no obstacles for us! Let us smash this barrier! Let us blow it up; and, if it resists, the *Nautilus* has wings to fly over it!"

"Over it, sir!!" said Captain Nemo quietly. "No, not over it, but *under* it!"

"Under it!" I exclaimed, a sudden idea of the captain's projects flashing upon my mind. I understood; the wonderful qualities of the *Nautilus* were going to serve us in this superhuman enterprise.

"I see we are beginning to understand one another, sir," said the captain, half-smiling. "You begin to see the possibility—I should say the success—of this attempt. That which is impossible for an ordinary vessel is easy to the *Nautilus*. If a continent lies before the pole, it must stop before the continent; but if, on the contrary, the pole is washed by open sea, it will go even to the pole."

"Certainly," I said, carried away by the captain's reasoning; "if the surface of the sea is solidified by the ice, the lower depths are free by the providential law which has placed the maximum of density of the ocean waters at two degrees above freezing point; and, if I am not mistaken, the portion of this barrier which is above the water is as one to four to that which is below."

"Very nearly, sir, for one foot of iceberg above the sea there are three below it. If these ice mountains are not more than 300 feet above the surface, they are not more than 900 beneath. And what are 900 feet to the *Nautilus?*"

"Nothing, sir."

"It could even seek at greater depths that uniform temperature of sea water, and there be impervious to the surface cold."

"Just so, sir—just so," I replied, getting animated.

"The only difficulty," continued Captain Nemo, "is that of remaining several days without renewing our provision of fresh air."

"Is that all? The *Nautilus* has vast reservoirs; we can fill them, and they will supply us with all the oxygen we want."

"Well thought of, Mr. Aronnax," replied the captain, smiling. "But, not wishing you to accuse me of rashness, I will first give you all my objections."

"Have you any more to make?"

"Only one. It is possible, if the sea exists at the South Pole, that it may be covered; and consequently we shall be unable to come to the surface."

"Good, sir! But are you forgetting that the *Nautilus* is armed with a powerful spur, that we could send diagonally against these ice fields?"

"Ah, sir, you are full of ideas today."

"Besides, Captain," I added enthusiastically, "why should we not find the sea open at the South Pole as well as at the North? The frozen poles of the earth do not coincide, either in the southern or in the northern regions; and, until it is proved to the contrary, we may suppose either a continent or an ocean free from ice at these two points of the globe."

"I think so, too, Mr. Aronnax," replied Captain Nemo. "I only wish you to observe that, after having made so many objections to my project, you are now crushing me with arguments in its favor!"

The preparations for this audacious attempt now began. The powerful pumps of the *Nautilus* were working air into the reservoirs and storing it at high pressure. About four o'clock Captain Nemo announced the closing of the panels on the platform. I threw one last look at the massive ice barrier which we were going to cross. The air was clear and pure, and cold, only 8° above zero; but as the wind had died down this temperature was not so unbearable. About ten men mounted the sides of the *Nautilus,* armed with pickaxes to break the ice around the vessel, which was soon free. The operation was quickly performed, for the fresh ice was still very thin. We all went below. The reservoirs were filled with water and the *Nautilus* soon descended.

I had taken my place with Conseil in the lounge; through the open window we could see the lower beds of the Southern Ocean. The thermometer went up, the needle of the compass deviated on the dial. At about 900 feet, as Captain Nemo had foreseen, we were floating beneath the undulating bottom of the ice barrier. But the *Nautilus* went lower still—to the depth of 2,400 feet. The temperature of the water at the surface had registered eight degrees; it was now ten; we had gained two. Of course, the temperature inside the *Nautilus* was raised by its heating system to a much higher degree.

Every maneuver was carried out with wonderful precision.

"We shall pass it, I believe, Monsieur," said Conseil.

"I believe we shall," I said, in a tone of firm conviction.

In this open sea the *Nautilus* had taken a course direct to the pole, along the 52nd meridian. We had a distance still to travel of from 67° 30' to 90°—22.5° of latitude, or over 1,000 miles. The *Nautilus* maintained a speed of 26 knots. If we kept that up, in 40 hours we should reach the pole.

For part of the night the novelty of the situation kept us at the window. The sea was lit by the electric lamp, but it was deserted; fish did not live in these imprisoned waters, but found a passage there to take them from the Antarctic Ocean to the open polar sea.

About two in the morning I went to my room to rest, and

Conseil did the same. In crossing the waist I did not meet Captain Nemo. I supposed him to be in the pilot's cage.

The next morning, the 19th of March, I took my post once more in the lounge. The electric log told me that the speed of the *Nautilus* had been slackened. It was then moving toward the surface, but emptying its reservoirs very slowly. My heart beat fast. Were we going to emerge and regain the open polar atmosphere? No! A shock told me that the *Nautilus* had struck the bottom of the ice barrier, still very thick to judge from the dull sound of the blow. We had indeed "struck," to use a sea expression, but in an inverse sense, and at 1,000 feet. This meant there were more than 1,000 feet of ice above us, over 300 feet of it above the water mark.

The barrier was higher here than at its borders, then— not a very reassuring fact. Several times that day the *Nautilus* tried again, and every time it struck the wall which lay like a ceiling above it. Sometimes the ice was 2,700 feet in depth of which 900 feet rose above the surface. This was more than twice the height of the ice where the *Nautilus* had gone under the waves. I carefully noted the different depths, and thus obtained a submarine profile of the ice-mountain chain. That night no change took place in our situation. Still ice between 1,200 to 1,500 feet in depth! It was evidently diminishing, but still, what a thickness between us and the surface of the ocean!

It was then eight o'clock. According to the daily custom on board the *Nautilus,* the air should have been renewed four hours ago. As yet I did not suffer much, and Captain Nemo had not made any demand on his oxygen reserve.

My sleep was painful that night; hope and fear besieged

me by turns. I arose several times. The groping of the *Nautilus* continued. About three in the morning I noticed that the lower surface of the ice barrier was only about fifty feet deep. One hundred and fifty feet now separated us from the surface of the waters. The ice barrier was slowly becoming an ice field, the mountain a plain. My eyes never left the manometer. We were still rising diagonally to the surface, which sparkled under the electric rays. The barrier was beginning to slope upward on its underside (and probably downward above the water). Mile by mile it grew longer and thinner. Finally at six in the morning of that memorable day, the 19th of March, the door of the lounge opened and Captain Nemo appeared.

"The sea is open!!" was all he said.

14. The South Pole

I RUSHED onto the platform. Yes, here indeed was the open sea, with but a few scattered ice floes and moving icebergs—a long stretch of sea; a world of birds in the air, and myriads of fish under those waters, which varied from intense blue to olive green, according to the depth. The thermometer registered 37° above zero. It was comparative spring to us, shut up as we had been behind the ice barrier, whose lengthened mass we could dimly see on our northern horizon.

"Are we at the pole?" I asked the captain, with a beating heart.

"I do not know," he replied. "At noon I will take our bearings, and we shall see."

"But will the sun shine through this fog?" I asked.

"Even a little will be enough," replied the captain.

About ten miles to the south a solitary island rose to a height of 312 feet. We made for it, but carefully, for the sea might conceal shallow banks. One hour afterward we had reached it; two hours later we had rounded it. The island measured four or five miles in circumference. A narrow canal separated it from a considerable stretch of land, perhaps a continent, for we could not see its limits. The existence of this land seemed to give some color to Maury's theory. The ingenious American has remarked that between the South Pole and the 60th parallel the sea is covered with floating ice of enormous size, which is never met with in the North Atlantic. From this fact he has drawn the conclusion that the Antarctic Circle encloses considerable continents, as icebergs cannot form in open sea, but only on the coasts. According to these calculations, the mass of ice surrounding the southern pole forms a vast cap at least 2,500 miles in circumference.

But the *Nautilus,* for fear of running aground, had stopped about three cable lengths from a strand over which reared a lofty pile of rocks. The pinnace was launched; the captain, two of his men, bearing instruments, Conseil, and myself were in it. It was ten in the morning. I had not seen Ned Land. Doubtless the Canadian did not wish to admit the presence of the South Pole. A few strokes of the oar brought us to the sand, where we ran ashore. Conseil was going to jump on to the land, when I held him back.

"Sir," said I to Captain Nemo, "to you belongs the honor of first setting foot on this land."

"Yes, sir," said the captain. "And if I do not hesitate to

be first to tread this South Pole, it is because, up to this time, no human being has left a trace here."

Saying this he jumped lightly onto the sand. How his heart must have beat with emotion! He climbed a rock that formed a little promontory, and there, with his arms crossed, mute and motionless and with an eager look, he seemed to take possession of these southern regions. After five minutes passed in silent ecstasy he turned to us.

"When you like, sir."

I landed, followed by Conseil; the two men stayed in the boat. For some distance we walked over ground that seemed to be composed of reddish sandstone, something like crushed brick, and bits of lava and pumice stone of unmistakable volcanic origin. From cracks in the ground, wisps of sulphurous smoke still issued, although even from a height I could see no volcano in a radius of several miles. Yet we know that in these Antarctic countries James Ross found two craters, the Erebus and Terror, in full activity on the 167th meridian, latitude 77° 32'.

The vegetation of this desolate continent seemed to me quite limited. There were some lichens of the species *Unsnea Melanoxantha* on the black rocks, some microscopic plants such as rudimentary diatoms, a kind of cell, placed between two quartz shells, and long purple and scarlet sea lichen, supported on little swimming bladders, which the breaking waves brought to the shore. These constituted the meager flora of the region.

The shore was strewn with molluscs, little mussels, limpets, smooth bucards in the shape of a heart, and particularly some clios with oblong membranous bodies, the heads of which were formed of two rounded lobes. I also saw myriads of northern clios, one and a quarter inches long, which the whale swallows by the hundreds at a mouthful; and some charming pteropods, perfect sea butterflies, brightening the waters along the shore.

Amongst other zoophytes, there appeared on the shallow bottom some coral shrubs, of that kind which, according to James Ross, live in the Antarctic seas to the depth of more than 3,000 feet. Then there were little kingfishers and starfish studding the soil.

But it was in the air where life most abounded. There thousands of birds of all kinds fluttered, deafening us with their cries; others crowded the rock, looking at us as we passed by without fear, and pressing familiarly close by our feet. There were penguins, so agile in the water, heavy and awkward as they are on the ground; they were uttering harsh cries—a large assembly, sober in gesture but extravagant in clamor. Albatrosses passed in the air, their wingspan at least 12 feet wide, and justly called the vultures of the ocean; gigantic petrels, and some damiers, a kind of small duck, the under part of whose body is black and white. Then there were various species of petrels, some whitish, with brown-bordered wings; others, blue, are peculiar to the Antarctic seas. Petrels are so oily, as I told Conseil, that the inhabitants of the Faeroe Islands have only to put in a wick before lighting them.

"A little more," said Conseil, "and they would be perfect lamps. But I suppose we cannot expect Nature to furnish them with wicks!"

About half a mile farther on, the soil was riddled with auks' nests, a sort of laying ground, out of which countless birds issued, braying like donkeys. They were about the size of geese, slate-colored on the body, white beneath, with a yellow line around their throats. They allowed themselves to be killed with a stone, never trying to escape, and Captain Nemo had hundreds killed, for they are good to eat.

The fog did not lift, and at eleven the sun had not yet shown itself. Its absence made me uneasy. Without it no observations were possible. How, then, could we decide whether we had reached the pole? When I rejoined Captain Nemo I found him leaning on a piece of rock, silently watching the sky. He seemed impatient and vexed. But what was to be done? This rash and powerful man could not command the sun as he did the sea. Noon arrived, and still no sun. We could not even tell its position behind the curtain of fog; and soon the fog turned to snow.

"Till tomorrow," said the captain quietly, and we returned to the *Nautilus*.

The snow continued till the next day. It was impossible to remain on the platform. From the lounge, where I was taking notes of incidents happening during this excursion to the polar continent, I could hear the cries of petrels and albatrosses sporting in the midst of this violent storm. The *Nautilus* did not remain motionless, but skirted the coast, advancing ten miles farther to the south, in the half-light left by the sun as it skirted the edge of the horizon.

The next day, the 20th of March, the snow had ceased. The cold was greater, about 28° above zero. The fog was rising, and I hoped that today we might take observations. Captain Nemo having not yet appeared, the boat took Conseil and myself to land. The soil was still of the same volcanic nature: everywhere were traces of lava, scoriae, and basalt; but the crater which had vomited them I could not

see. Here, as lower down, this continent was alive with
myriads of birds. But now, in addition, we saw large troops
of sea mammals, looking at us with their soft eyes. There
were several kinds of seals, some stretched on the earth,
some on flakes of ice, many going in and out of the sea.
They did not flee at our approach, never having known
man; and I reckoned that there were provisions there for
hundreds of vessels.

"Will Monsieur," said Conseil, "tell me the names of
these creatures?"

"They are seals and walruses."

It was now eight in the morning—four hours before the
sun could be observed with advantage. I directed our steps
toward a vast bay cut in the steep granite shore. There, I
can aver that earth and ice were lost to sight by the numbers of sea mammals covering them, and I involuntarily
sought for old Proteus, the mythological shepherd who
watched these immense flocks of Neptune. There were more
seals than anything else, forming distinct groups, male and
female, the father watching over his family, the mother
suckling her little ones, some already strong enough to go a
few steps. When they wished to move, they took little
jumps, made by the contraction of their bodies, and helped
awkwardly enough by their imperfect fin, which, as with the
manatee their cousin, forms a perfect forearm. I should say
that, in the water, which is their element—the spine of these
creatures is flexible, and they have a smooth, tight skin and
webbed feet—they swim admirably. On land they take the
most graceful attitudes.

Thus the ancients, observing their soft and expressive
looks, which cannot be surpassed by the most beautiful look

a woman can give, their clear, voluptuous eyes, their charming positions, and the poetry of their manners, metamorphosed them, the male into a triton and the female into a mermaid. I made Conseil notice the considerable development of the brain area in these interesting cetaceans. No mammal, except man, has such a quantity of brain matter; they are also capable of receiving a certain amount of education, are easily domesticated, and I think, with other naturalists, that if properly taught they would be of great service as fishing dogs. The greater part of them slept on the rocks or on the sand. Among these seals, that have no external ears (in which they differ from the otter, whose ears are prominent), I noticed several varieties about nine feet long, with white coats, bulldog heads, armed with teeth in both jaws, four incisors at the top and four at the bottom, and two large canine teeth in the shape of a fleur-de-lis. Among them glided sea elephants, a kind of seal, with short, flexible trunks. The giants of this species measured 20 feet around and about 31 feet in length; but they did not move as we approached.

"These creatures are not dangerous?" asked Conseil.

"No, not unless you attack them. When they have to defend their young their rage is terrible, and it is not uncommon for them to break the fishing boats to pieces."

"They are quite right," said Conseil.

"I do not say they are not."

Two miles farther on we were stopped by the promontory which shelters the bay from the southerly winds. Beyond it we heard loud bellowings such as a troop of ruminants would produce.

"Good!" said Conseil; "a concert of bulls!"

"No, a concert of walruses."

"They are fighting!"

"They are either fighting or playing."

We now began to climb the treacherous black rocks, over stones made slippery by the ice. More than once I rolled over, bruising my loins. Conseil, more prudent or more steady, did not stumble, and helped me up, saying:

"If Monsieur would have the kindness to take wider steps, he would preserve his equilibrium better."

At the upper ridge of the promontory, I saw a vast white plain covered with walruses. They were playing among themselves; what we had heard were bellowings of pleasure.

As I passed these curious animals I could examine them at leisure, for they did not move. Their skins were thick and rugged, of a yellowish tint deepening to red; their hair was short and scant. Some of them were over 12 feet long. Quieter and less timid than their cousins of the north, they did not, like them, place sentinels around the outskirts of their encampment. After examining this settlement of walruses, I began to think of returning. It was eleven o'clock, and if Captain Nemo found the conditions favorable for observations, I wished to be present at the operation. We followed a narrow pathway running along the summit of the steep shore. At half-past eleven we had reached the place where we landed. The boat had run aground, bringing the captain. I saw him standing on a block of basalt, his instruments near him, his eyes fixed on the northern horizon near which the sun was then describing a lengthened curve. I took my place beside him, and waited without speaking. Noon arrived, and, as before, the sun did not appear. It was a fatality. Observations were still wanting. If not accomplished tomorrow, we must give it up. We were indeed exactly at the 20th of March. Tomorrow, the 21st, would be the equinox; the sun would disappear behind the horizon for six months, and with its disappearance the long polar night would begin. Since the September equinox it had emerged from the northern horizon, rising by lengthened spirals up to the 21st of December. At this period, the summer solstice of the northern regions, it had begun to descend; and tomorrow it was to shed its last rays. I communicated my fears and observations to Captain Nemo.

"You are right, Mr. Aronnax," he said; "if tomorrow I cannot take the altitude of the sun, I shall not be able to do it for six months. But precisely because chance has led me into these seas on the 21st of March, my bearings will be easy to take, if at twelve we can see the sun."

"Why, Captain?"

"Because then the orb of day describes such lengthened curves that it is difficult to measure exactly its height above the horizon, and grave errors may be made with instruments."

"What will you do then?"

"I shall use only my chronometer," replied Captain Nemo. "If tomorrow, the 21st of March, the disc of the sun, allowing for refraction, is exactly cut by the northern horizon, it will show that I am at the South Pole."

"Just so," said I. "But this statement is not mathematically correct, because the equinox does not necessarily begin at noon."

"Very likely, sir, but the error will not involve more than a hundred yards, and we do not need to be more exact. Till tomorrow, then!"

Captain Nemo returned on board. Conseil and I remained to survey the shore, observing and studying until five o'clock. Then I went to bed, not, however, without invoking, like the Indian, the favor of the radiant orb. The next day, the 21st of March, at five in the morning I mounted the platform. I found Captain Nemo there.

"The weather is lightening a little," he said. "I have some hope. After breakfast we will go on shore and choose a post for observation."

That point settled, I sought Ned Land. I wanted to take him with me. But the obstinate Canadian refused, and I saw that his taciturnity and bad humor grew day by day. After all, I was not sorry for his obstinacy under the circumstances. Indeed, there were too many seals on shore, and we ought not to lay such temptation in this unreflecting fisherman's way. Breakfast over, we went on shore. The *Nautilus* had gone some miles farther up in the night. It was a whole league from the coast, above which reared a sharp peak about 1,500 feet high. Besides me, the boat took Captain Nemo, two men of the crew, and the instruments, which consisted of a chronometer, a telescope, and a barometer. While crossing, I saw numerous whales belonging to the three kinds peculiar to the southern seas; the right whale, which has no dorsal fin; the humpback, with reeved chest and large, whitish fins; and the finback, of a yellowish brown, the liveliest of all the cetacea. This powerful creature is heard a long way off for he spouts to a great height. These various cetaceans were disporting themselves in the quiet waters, and I could see that this basin of the Antarctic Pole serves as a place of refuge to the cetacea too closely tracked by the hunters. I also noticed large medusae floating between the reeds.

At nine we landed; the sky was brightening, the clouds were flying to the south, and the fog seemed to be leaving the cold surface of the waters. Captain Nemo went toward the peak, which he doubtless meant to be his observatory. It was a painful ascent over the sharp lava and the pumice stones, in an atmosphere often impregnated with a sulphurous smell from the smoking cracks. For a man unaccustomed to walk on land, the captain climbed the steep slopes with an agility I never saw equaled, and which a hunter would have envied. We were two hours getting to the summit of this peak, which was half porphyry and half basalt. From thence we looked upon a vast sea which, toward the north, distinctly traced its boundary line upon the sky. At our feet lay fields of dazzling whiteness. Over our heads a pale azure, free from fog. To the north the disc of the sun seemed like a ball of fire, already horned by the cutting of the horizon. From the bosom of the water rose sheaves of liquid jets by hundreds. In the distance lay the *Nautilus* like a cetacean asleep on the water. Behind us, to the south and east, an immense country and a chaotic heap of rocks and ice, the limits of which were not visible. On arriving at the summit Captain Nemo carefully toook the mean height of the barometer, for he would have to consider that in taking his observations. At a quarter to twelve the sun, then seen only by refraction, looked like a golden disc shedding its last rays upon this deserted continent and sea. Captain Nemo, furnished with a lenticular glass which, by means of a mirror, corrected the refraction, watched the orb sinking below the horizon by degrees, following a lengthened diagonal. I held the chronometer. My heart beat fast. If the disappearance of the half disc of the sun coincided with twelve o'clock on the chronometer, we were at the pole itself.

"Twelve!" I exclaimed.

"The South Pole!" replied Captain Nemo, in a grave voice, handing me the glass, which showed the orb cut in exactly equal parts by the horizon.

I looked at the last rays crowning the peak and the shadows mounting by degrees up its slopes. At that moment Captain Nemo, resting his hand on my shoulder, said:

"I, Captain Nemo, on this 21st day of March, 1868, have reached the South Pole on the ninetieth degree; and I take possession of this part of the globe, equal to one-sixth of the known continents."

"In whose name, Captain?"

"In my own, sir!"

Saying which, Captain Nemo unfurled a black banner bearing an "N" in gold quartered on its bunting. Then, turning toward the orb of day, whose last rays lapped the horizon of the sea, he exclaimed:

"Farewell, sun! Disappear, thou radiant orb! Rest beneath this open sea, and let a night of six months spread its shadows over my new domains!"

15. Accident or Incident?

THE NEXT day, the 22nd of March, at six in the morning, preparations for departure were begun. The last gleams of twilight were melting into night. The cold was great, the constellations shone with wonderful intensity. In the zenith glittered that wondrous Southern Cross—the polar star of

Antarctic regions. The thermometer showed 10° above zero, and when the wind freshened it was most biting. Flakes of ice increased on the open water. Numerous blackish patches spread on the surface, showing the formation of fresh ice. Evidently the southern basin, frozen during the six winter months, was absolutely inaccessible. What became of the whales in that time? Doubtless they went beneath the icebergs, seeking more practicable seas. As to the seals and walruses, accustomed to live in a hard climate, they remained on these icy shores. These creatures have the instinct to break holes in the ice field and to keep them open. To these holes they come for breath; when the birds, driven away by the cold, have emigrated to the north, these sea mammals remain sole masters of the polar continent.

But the reservoirs were filling with water, and the *Nautilus* was slowly descending. At 1,000 feet deep it stopped. Then, as the propeller beat the ocean's depths, we advanced straight toward the north at 15 knots. Toward night we were already floating under the immense body of the iceberg. At three in the morning I was awakened by a violent shock. I sat up in my bed and listened in the darkness, when I was thrown into the middle of the room. The *Nautilus*, after having struck, had rebounded violently. I groped along the partition, and by the staircase to the lounge, which was lit by the luminous ceiling. The furniture was overturned. Fortunately the windows were firmly set, and had held fast. The pictures on the starboard side, no longer vertical, hung by the wallpaper. The *Nautilus* was lying on its starboard side perfectly motionless. I heard footsteps and a confusion of voices; but Captain Nemo did not appear. As I was leaving the lounge, Ned Land and Conseil entered.

"What is the matter?" I said, at once.

"We came to ask Monsieur," replied Conseil.

"Confound it!" exclaimed the Canadian, "I know well enough! The *Nautilus* has struck; and judging by the way it lies, I do not think it will right itself as it did the first time in Torres Straits."

"But," I asked, "has it at least come to the surface of the sea?"

"We do not know," said Conseil.

"It is easy to decide," I answered. I consulted the manometer. To my great surprise, it showed a depth of more than 180 fathoms. "What does that mean?" I exclaimed.

"We must ask Captain Nemo," said Conseil.

"But where shall we find him?" said Ned Land.

"Follow me," I said to my companions.

We left the lounge. There was no one in the library. At the center staircase, by the berths of the ship's crew, there was no one. I thought that Captain Nemo must be in the pilot's cage. It was best to wait. We all returned to the lounge. For twenty minutes we remained thus, listening for the slightest noise which might indicate the plight of the *Nautilus,* when Captain Nemo entered. He seemed not to see us; his face, generally so impassive, showed signs of uneasiness. He watched the compass silently, then the manometer; and going to the planisphere, placed his finger on a spot representing the southern seas. I would not interrupt him; but some minutes later, when he turned toward me, I said, using one of his own expressions in the Torres Strait:

"An incident, Captain?"

"No, sir; an accident this time."

"Serious?"

"Perhaps."

"Is the danger immediate?"

"No." In spite of this reassurance, however, the captain's evident agitation indicated a grave situation.

"The *Nautilus* is stranded?"

"Yes."

"And this has happened—how?"

"From a caprice of nature, not from the ignorance of man. This was no error of operation. But we cannot prevent equilibrium from producing its effects. We may brave human laws, but we cannot resist natural ones."

Captain Nemo had chosen a strange moment for uttering this philosophical reflection. On the whole, his answer helped me little.

"May I ask, sir, the cause of this accident?"

"An enormous block of ice, a whole mountain, has turned over," he replied. "When icebergs are undermined at their base by warmer water or reiterated shocks, their center of gravity rises and the whole thing turns over. This is what has happened; one of these blocks, as it overturned, struck the *Nautilus*. Then, gliding under its hull, raised it with irresistible force, bringing it into beds which are not so thick, where it is lying on its side."

"But can't we get the *Nautilus* off by emptying its reservoirs to regain equilibrium?"

"That, sir, is being done at this moment. You can hear the pump working. Look at the needle of the manometer; it shows that the *Nautilus* is rising, but the block of ice is rising with it; and, until some obstacle stops its ascending motion, our position cannot be altered."

Indeed, the *Nautilus* still held the same position to starboard; doubtless it would right itself when the block stopped. But at any moment we might be frightfully crushed between the two glassy surfaces. I reflected on the possible consequences of our position.

Captain Nemo never took his eyes from the manometer. Since the fall of the iceberg, the *Nautilus* had risen about a hundred and fifty feet, but it was still at the same angle with the perpendicular. Suddenly a slight movement was felt in the hold. Evidently it was righting a little. The partitions of the lounge were nearly upright. No one spoke. With beating hearts we watched and felt the straightening. The boards became horizontal under our feet. Ten minutes passed.

"At last we have righted!" I exclaimed.

"Yes," said Captain Nemo, going to the door of the lounge.

"But are we floating?" I asked.

"Certainly," he replied; "since the reservoirs are empty; when empty, the *Nautilus* must rise to the surface of the sea."

We were floating, but at a distance of about ten yards on either side of the *Nautilus* rose a dazzling wall of ice. Above and beneath the same wall. Above, because the lower surface of the iceberg stretched over us like an immense ceiling. Beneath, because the overturned block, having slid by degrees, had found a resting place on the lateral walls, which kept it in that position. The *Nautilus* was really imprisoned in a perfect tunnel of ice more than twenty yards in breadth, filled with quiet water. It was easy to get out of it by going either forward or backward, and then make a free passage under the iceberg some hundreds of yards deeper. The luminous ceiling had been extinguished, but the lounge was still resplendent with intense light. It was the powerful reflection from the glass partition sent violently back to the sheets of the lantern. I cannot describe the effect of the voltaic rays upon the great blocks so capriciously cut; upon every angle, every ridge, every facet was thrown a different light, according to the nature of the veins running through the ice; a dazzling mine of gems, the blue rays of sapphires crossing with emerald green. Here and there were opal shades of wonderful softness, running through bright spots like diamonds of fire, the brilliancy of which the eye could not bear. The power of the lantern seemed to increase a hundredfold, like a lamp through the lenticular plates of a first-class lighthouse.

"How beautiful! How beautiful!" cried Conseil.

"Yes," I said, "it is a wonderful sight. Is it not, Ned?"

"Yes, confound it! Yes," answered Ned Land, "it is superb! I hate to admit it. No one has ever seen anything like it; but the sight may cost us dear. And, I must say it, I think we are seeing here things which God never intended man to see."

Ned was right; it was too beautiful. Suddenly a cry from Conseil made me turn.

"What is it?" I asked.

"Monsieur must shut his eyes, and not look!" Saying which, Conseil clapped his hands over his eyes.

"But what is the matter, my boy?"

"I am dazzled, blinded."

My eyes turned involuntarily toward the glass, but I could not stand the fire which seemed to devour them. I understood what had happened. The *Nautilus* had put on full speed. All the quiet luster of the ice walls was at once changed into flashes of lightning. The fire from these myriads of diamonds was blinding. It required some time to calm our troubled looks. At last the hands were taken down.

"Faith, I should never have believed it," said Conseil.

It was then five in the morning, and at that moment a shock was felt at the bows of the *Nautilus*. I knew that its spur had struck a block of ice. It must have been a false maneuver, for this submarine tunnel, obstructed by blocks, was not easy to navigate. I thought that Captain Nemo by changing his course would either turn these obstacles or else follow the windings of the tunnel. In any case, the road before us could not be entirely blocked. But, contrary to my expectations, the *Nautilus* took a decided retrograde motion.

"We are going backward," said Conseil.

"Yes," I replied. "This end of the tunnel can have no egress."

"And then?"

"Then," I said, "the working is easy. We must go back again, and go out at the southern opening. That is all."

In speaking thus, I wished to appear more confident than I really was. But the retrograde motion of the *Nautilus* was increasing; and, reversing the propeller, it carried us at great speed.

"It means more delay," said Ned.

"What does it matter, some hours more or less, provided we get out at last?"

"Yes," repeated Ned Land, "provided we do get out at last!"

I walked from the lounge to the library. My companions were silent. I soon threw myself on an ottoman, and took a

book, which my eyes scanned mechanically. A quarter of
an hour later Conseil, approaching me, said, "Is what Monsieur is reading very interesting?"

"Very interesting!" I replied.

"I should think so. It is Monsieur's own book he is reading."

"My book?"

And indeed I was holding in my hand the work on the
Great Submarine Depths. I had not even noticed. I closed
the book and returned to my walking. Ned and Conseil rose
to go.

"Stay here, my friends," I said, detaining them. "Let us
remain together until we are out of this block."

"As Monsieur pleases," Conseil replied.

Some hours passed. How often I looked at the instruments hanging from the partition. The manometer showed
that the *Nautilus* kept at a constant depth of more than 900
feet; the compass still pointed to south; the log indicated a
speed of 20 knots, which, in such a cramped space, was
very great. But Captain Nemo knew that he could not
hasten too much, and that minutes were worth ages to us.
At 8:25 A.M. a second shock took place, this time from
behind. I turned pale. My companions were close by my
side. I seized Conseil's hand. Our looks expressed our feelings better than words. At this moment the captain entered
the lounge. I went up to him.

"Our course is barred southward?" I asked.

"Yes, sir. The iceberg has shifted and closed every outlet."

"We are blocked up then?"

"Yes, sir, we are."

16. Want of Air

THUS AROUND the *Nautilus,* above and below, was an impenetrable wall of ice; we were prisoners of the iceberg. I watched the captain. His countenance had resumed its habitual imperturbability.

"Gentlemen," he said calmly, "there are two ways of dying in the circumstances in which we are placed." The strange man at this moment had the air of a mathematical professor lecturing to his pupils. "The first is to be crushed; the second is to die of suffocation. I do not speak of the possibility of dying of hunger, for the supply of provisions in the *Nautilus* will certainly last longer than we shall. Let us, then, calculate our chances."

"As to suffocation, Captain," I replied, "that is not to be feared, because our reservoirs are full."

"Just so, but they will yield only two days' supply of air. Now, for 36 hours we have been hidden under the water, and already the heavy atmosphere of the *Nautilus* requires renewal. In 48 hours our reserve will be exhausted."

"Well, Captain, can we be delivered before 48 hours?"

"We will attempt it, at least, by piercing the wall that surrounds us."

"On which side?"

"Sound will tell us. I am going to run the *Nautilus* aground on the lower bank, and my men will attack the iceberg on the side that is least thick."

Captain Nemo went out. Soon I discovered by a hissing noise that the water was entering the reservoirs. The *Nau-*

tilus sank slowly, and rested on the ice at a depth of 1,000 feet, the depth at which the lower bank was immersed.

"My friends," I said, "our situation is serious, but I rely on your courage and energy."

"Sir," replied the Canadian, "I am ready to do anything for the general safety."

"Good!" and I held out my hand to the Canadian.

"I will add," he continued, "that I am as handy with the pickax as with the harpoon; if I can be useful to the captain, he can command my services."

"He will not refuse your help. Come, Ned!"

I led him to the room where the crew of the *Nautilus* were putting on their cork jackets, and told the captain of Ned's proposal, which he accepted. The Canadian put on his diving suit, and was soon ready to go with his companions. When I re-entered the drawing-room the panes of glass were open, and posted near Conseil, I examined the ice beds that supported the *Nautilus*. A few moments later, we saw a dozen of the crew step out on the bank of ice, tall Ned Land prominent among them.

Captain Nemo was also with them. Before proceeding to dig the walls he took soundings, to be sure of working in the right direction. Long sounding leads were sunk in the side walls, but beyond 45 feet the men were again stopped by the thick wall. It was useless to attack the "ceiling" surface, since the iceberg itself was over 1200 feet high. Captain Nemo then sounded the lower surface. There only 30 feet of wall separated us from the water. The captain decided, therefore, to cut out a piece there, equal in area to the *Nautilus* at the water line. About 60,000 cubic yards must be dug out to make a hole large enough for us to escape by.

The work was begun immediately, and carried on with indefatigable energy. Instead of digging around the *Nautilus,* which would have involved greater difficulty, Captain Nemo had an immense trench made at eight yards from the port quarter. Then the men set to work simultaneously with their picks on several points of its circumference. This compact matter was attacked so vigorously that soon large blocks were detached from the mass. By a curious effect of specific gravity, these blocks, lighter than water, rose to the vault of the tunnel so that it increased in thickness at the top in proportion as it diminished at the base. But that mattered little, as long as the lower part grew thinner. After two hours' hard work Ned Land came in exhausted. He and his comrades were replaced by new workers, and Conseil and I joined them. The second lieutenant of the *Nautilus* superintended us. The water seemed singularly cold, but I soon got warm handling the pickax. My movements were free enough, although they were made under a pressure of thirty atmospheres.

When I re-entered, after working two hours, to take some food and rest, I found a perceptible difference between the pure fluid with which the Rouquayrol engine supplied me and the atmosphere of the *Nautilus,* already charged with carbonic acid. The air had not been renewed for forty-eight hours, and its vivifying qualities were considerably enfeebled. And in a twelve-hour period, we had removed only a three-foot layer of ice from the marked surface area of 6000 feet! It was 18,000 cubic feet, but reckoning that it took twelve hours to accomplish this much, it would take five nights and four days to bring this enterprise to a satisfactory conclusion. Five nights and four

days! And we had only air enough for two days in the
reservoirs.

"Without taking into account," said Ned, "that even if
we get out of this infernal prison, we shall also be imprisoned under the iceberg, shut out from all possible communication with the atmosphere."

True enough! Who could then foresee the minimum of
time necessary for our deliverance? We might be suffocated
before the *Nautilus* could regain the surface of the waves!
Was the ship and all those it supported destined to perish in
this ice tomb? The situation was frightful. But everyone had
faced the danger, and each was determined to do his duty to
the last.

As I expected, during the night another three-foot layer
of the ice wall was carried away, and still further sank the
immense hollow. But in the morning when, dressed in my
cork-jacket, I traversed the slushy mass at a temperature of
20° above zero, I remarked that the side walls were gradually closing in. The beds of water farthest from the trench,
that were not warmed by the men's work, showed a tendency to solidification. In presence of this new and imminent danger, what were our chances of safety, and how
hinder the solidification of this liquid medium, that would
eventually burst the partitions of the *Nautilus* like glass?

I did not tell my companions of this new danger. What
was the good of damping the energy they displayed in the
painful work of escape? But when I went on board again, I
told Captain Nemo of this grave complication.

"I know it," he said, in that calm tone which could coun-
teract the most terrible apprehensions. "It is one danger
more; but I see no way of escaping it; the only chance of

safety is to go quicker than solidification. We must be beforehand with it, that is all."

On this day for several hours I used my pickax vigorously. The work kept me up. Besides, to work was to breathe directly the pure air drawn from the reservoirs and supplied by our apparatus, and to quit the impoverished and vitiated atmosphere of the *Nautilus*. Toward evening the trench was dug four feet deeper. When I returned on board, I was nearly suffocated by the carbonic acid in the air—Ah! if we only had the chemical means to drive away this deleterious gas. We had plenty of oxygen; all this water contained a considerable quantity, and by our electrical equipment we could restore the vivifying fluid to the air. I thought about it; but what was the good, since the carbonic acid produced by our respiration had invaded every part of the vessel? To absorb this, it was necessary to fill some jars with caustic potash, and to shake them incessantly. Now this substance was wanting on board, and nothing could replace it. On that evening I felt that Captain Nemo should open the taps of his reservoirs, and let some pure air into the interior of the *Nautilus*. Without this precaution we could not get rid of the sense of suffocation.

The next day, March 26th, I resumed my miner's work in beginning the fifth yard-deep area. The side walls and the lower surface of the iceberg had thickened visibly. It was evident that they would meet before the *Nautilus* was able to disengage itself. Despair seized me for an instant; my pickax nearly fell from my hands. What was the good of digging if I must be suffocated, crushed by the water that was turning into stone—a punishment that the ferocity of the savages even would not have invented! Just then Captain Nemo passed near me. I touched his hand and showed him the walls of our prison. The wall to port had advanced to at least four yards from the hull of the *Nautilus*. The captain understood me and signaled to me to follow him. We went on board. I took off my cork jacket and accompanied him into the lounge.

"Mr. Aronnax, we must attempt some desperate means or we shall be sealed up in this solidified water as in cement."

"Yes. But what is to be done?"

"Ah! if my *Nautilus* were strong enough to bear this pressure without being crushed!"

"Well?" I asked, not catching the captain's idea.

"Do you not understand," he replied, "that this congelation of water will help us? Do you not see that by its solidification it could burst through this field of ice that imprisons us, as, when it freezes, it bursts the hardest stones? Do you not perceive that it would be an agent of safety instead of destruction?"

"Yes, Captain, perhaps. But, whatever resistance to crushing the *Nautilus* possesses, it cannot support this terrible pressure. The ship will be flattened like an iron plate."

"I know it, sir. Therefore we must not reckon on the aid of nature, but on our own exertions. We must stop this solidification. Not only will the side walls be pressed together, but there is not ten feet of water before or behind the *Nautilus*. The congelation gains on us on all sides."

"How long will the air in the reservoirs last for us to breathe on board?"

The captain looked in my face. "After tomorrow they will be empty."

A cold sweat came over me. But why should I have been astonished at the answer? On March 22, the *Nautilus* had last surfaced in the open polar seas. It was now the 26th. For five days we had lived on the reserve on board. And what was left of the respirable air must be kept for the workers. Even now, as I write, my recollection is still so vivid, that an involuntary terror seizes me, and my lungs seem to be without air. Meanwhile Captain Nemo reflected silently. Evidently an idea had struck him, but he seemed to reject it. At last these words escaped his lips:

"Boiling water!" he muttered.

"Boiling water?" I cried.

"Yes, sir. We are enclosing in a space that is relatively confined. Would not jets of boiling water, constantly injected by the pumps, raise the temperature enough to stave off the congelation?"

"Let us try it," I said resolutely.

"Let us try it, Professor."

The thermometer then stood at 18° outside. Captain Nemo took me to the galleys, where the vast distillatory machines stood that furnished the drinking water by evaporation. They filled these with water, and all the electric heat from the piles was thrown through the worms bathed in the liquid. In a few minutes this water reached 212°. It was directed toward the pumps, while fresh water replaced it in proportion. The heat developed by the troughs was such that cold water, drawn up from the sea after only having gone through the machines, came boiling into the body of the pump. The injection was begun, and three hours later, the thermometer marked 20° outside. One degree was gained. Two hours later the thermometer registered 24°.

"We shall succeed," I said to the captain after having anxiously watched the result of the operation.

"I think," he answered, "that we shall not be crushed. Now we have only suffocation to fear."

During the night the temperature of the water rose to 30°. The injections could not carry it to a higher point. But, as sea water freezes at 28.4°, I was at least reassured against the dangers of solidification.

The next day, March 27th, a layer of six yards of the ice wall had been cleared, a layer of twelve feet only remaining to be cleared away. There was yet 48 hours' work. The air could not be renewed inside the *Nautilus,* and this day would make it worse. An intolerable weight oppressed me. Toward 3:00 P.M. this feeling became almost unbearable. Enormous yawns almost dislocated my jaws. I panted as I inhaled the burning gas. A moral torpor seized me. I was powerless, almost unconscious. My brave Conseil, though exhibiting the same symptoms and suffering in the same manner, never left me. He took my hand and encouraged me, and I heard him murmur, "Oh! if I could only not breathe, so as to leave more air for Monsieur!"

Tears came to my eyes, hearing him speak thus. If our situation to all was intolerable in the interior, with what haste and gladness would we put on our cork jackets to work in our turn! Pickaxes sounded on the frozen ice beds. Our arms ached, the skin was torn off our hands. But what were these fatigues, what did the wounds matter? Vital air came to the lungs! We breathed! We breathed!

All this time no one prolonged his voluntary task beyond the prescribed time. His task accomplished, each one handed in turn to his panting companions the apparatus that supplied him with life. Captain Nemo set the example, and submitted first to this severe discipline. When the time came, he gave up his apparatus to another and returned to the vitiated air on board, calm, unflinching, unmurmuring.

On that day the ordinary work was accomplished with unusual vigor. Only two yards remained to be raised from the surface. Two yards only separated us from the open sea. But the reservoirs were nearly emptied of air. The little that remained ought to be kept for the workers; not a particle for the *Nautilus*. When I went back on board, I was half suffocated. What a night! I know not how to describe it. The next day my breathing was oppressed. Dizziness accompanied the pain in my head and made me like a drunken man. My companions showed the same symptoms. Some of the crew had rattling in the throat.

On that day, the sixth of our imprisonment, Captain Nemo, finding the pickaxes worked too slowly, resolved to crush the ice bed that still separated us from the liquid sheet. This man's coolness and energy never forsook him. He subdued his physical pains by moral force.

By his orders the vessel was lightened, that is to say, raised from the ice bed by a change of specific gravity. When the ship was afloat, the crew towed it over until it was directly above the immense trench made on the level of the water line. Then the reservoirs were filled with water, and the vessel descended into the trench.

All the crew came on board and the outside double door was shut. The *Nautilus* now rested on the bed of ice which was not one yard thick, and which the sounding leads had perforated in a thousand places. The taps of the reservoirs were then opened, and 100 cubic yards of water were let in, increasing the weight of the *Nautilus* to 3,400 tons. We waited, we listened, forgetting our sufferings in hope. Our safety depended on this last chance. Notwithstanding the buzzing in my head, I soon heard the humming sound under the hull of the *Nautilus*. The ice cracked with a singular noise, like tearing paper, and the *Nautilus* sank.

"We are off!" murmured Conseil in my ear.

I could not answer him. I seized his hand, and pressed it convulsively. All at once, carried away by its frightful overcharge, the *Nautilus* sank like a bullet under the waters, that is to say, it fell as if it were in a vacuum. Then all the electric force was put on the pumps that soon began to let the water out of the reservoirs. After some minutes our fall was stopped. Soon, too, the manometer indicated an ascending movement. The propeller made the iron hull vibrate to its very bolts and drew us toward the north. But if this floating under the iceberg was to last another day before we reached the open sea, we should be dead first.

Half stretched upon a divan in the library, I was suffocating. My face was purple, my lips blue, my faculties suspended. I neither saw nor heard. All notion of time had gone from my mind. My muscles could not contract. I do not know how many hours passed thus, but I was conscious of the agony that was coming over me. I felt as if I were going to die. Suddenly I came to. Some breaths of air penetrated my lungs. Had we risen to the surface of the waves? Were we free of the iceberg? No! Ned and Conseil, my two brave friends, were sacrificing themselves to save me. Some particles of air still remained at the bottom of one apparatus. Instead of using it, they had kept it for me, and, while they were being suffocated, they gave me life, drop by drop.

I wanted to push back the thing; they held my hands, and for some moments I breathed freely. I looked at the clock; it was 11:00 A.M. It ought to be the 28th of March. The *Nautilus* went at the frightful rate of 40 knots. It literally tore through the water. Where was Captain Nemo? Had he succumbed? Were his companions dead with him? At the moment the manometer indicated that we were not more than 20 feet from the surface. A mere plate of ice separated us from the atmosphere. Could we not break it? Perhaps. In any case, the *Nautilus* was going to attempt it. I felt that it was in an oblique position, lowering the stern, and raising the bows. The introduction of water had been the means of changing the equilibrium. Then, impelled by its powerful propeller, the ship attacked the ice field from beneath like a formidable battering ram, and broke it by backing and then rushing forward against the field, which gradually gave way. At last, dashing suddenly against it, the ship shot forward on the ice field that crushed beneath the ship's weight. The panel was opened—one might say torn off—and the pure air came in in abundance to all parts of the *Nautilus*.

17. From Cape Horn to the Amazon

How I got onto the platform I have no idea; perhaps the Canadian had carried me there. But I breathed, I inhaled the vivifying sea air. My two companions were delirious with the fresh draughts. The other unhappy men had been so long without food that they were not able to take the simplest foods that were given them. We, on the contrary, had nothing to restrain ourselves about; we could draw this air freely into our lungs, and it was the breeze, the breeze alone, that filled us with this keen enjoyment.

"Ah," said Conseil, "how delightful this oxygen is! Master need not fear to breathe it. There is enough for everybody."

Ned Land did not speak, but he opened his jaws wide enough to frighten a shark. Our strength soon returned, and when I looked around me, I saw we were alone on the platform. The foreign seamen in the *Nautilus* were contented with the air that circulated in the interior; none of them had come to drink of it in the open.

The first words I spoke were words of gratitude and thankfulness to my two companions. Ned and Conseil had prolonged my life during the last hours of this long agony. All my gratitude could not repay such devotion.

"My friends," I said, "we are bound one to the other forever, and I am under infinite obligations to you."

"And I shall take advantage of it," exclaimed the Canadian.

"What do you mean?" said Conseil.

"I mean that I shall take you with me when I leave this infernal *Nautilus*."

"If," said Conseil, "after all this, we're going in the right direction. Are we, Monsieur?"

"Yes," I replied, "for we are going the way of the sun, and here the sun is in the north."

"No doubt," said Ned Land; "but it remains to be seen whether the captain will head for the Pacific or the Atlantic Ocean; that is, into frequented or deserted seas."

I could not answer that question, and I feared that Captain Nemo would rather take us to the vast ocean that touches the coasts of Asia and America at the same time. He would thus complete the tour around the submarine world, and return to those waters in which the *Nautilus* could sail freely. We ought, before long, to settle this important point. The *Nautilus* went at a rapid pace. The polar circle was soon passed, and the course shaped for Cape Horn. We were off the American point, March 31st, at seven o'clock in the evening. Then all our past sufferings were forgotten. The remembrance of that imprisonment in the ice disappeared in our thoughts of the future. Captain Nemo did not appear again either in the lounge or on the platform. The point shown each day on the planisphere and marked by the lieutenant, showed me the exact direction of the *Nautilus*. Now, on that evening it was evident, to my great satisfaction, that we were going back to the north by the Atlantic. The next day, April 1st, when the *Nautilus* ascended to the surface some minutes before noon, we sighted land to the west. It was Tierra del Fuego, which the first navigators named thus from seeing the quantity of smoke that rose from the natives' huts. The coast seemed low to me, but in the distance rose high mountains. I even thought I had a glimpse of Mount Sarmiento, that rises 6,210 feet above the level of the sea, with a very pointed summit which, according to whether it is misty or clear, is a sign of fine or of wet weather. At this moment the peak was clearly defined against the sky. The *Nautilus,* diving again under the water, approached the coast, which was only some few miles off. From the glass windows in the lounge, I saw long seaweeds and gigantic varech, of which the open polar sea contains so many specimens, with their sharp polished filaments; they measured about 900 feet in length—

real cables, thicker than one's thumb; having great tenacity, they are often used as ropes for vessels. Another weed known as velp, with leaves four feet long, buried in the coral concretions, hung at the bottom. It served as nest and food for myriads of crustacea and molluscs, crabs and cuttlefish. There seals and otters had splendid repasts, eating the flesh of fish with sea vegetables, according to the English fashion. Over this fertile and luxuriant ground the *Nautilus* passed with great rapidity. Toward evening it approached the Falkland group, the rough summits of which I recognized the following day. The depth of the sea was moderate. On the shores our nets brought in beautiful specimens of seaweed, and particularly a certain plant whose roots were filled with the best mussels in the world. Geese and ducks fell by dozens on the platform and soon took their places in the pantry on board.

When the last heights of the Falklands had disappeared from the horizon, the *Nautilus* sank to between 60 and 75 feet, and followed the American coast. Captain Nemo did not appear. Until the 3rd of April we did not quit the shores of Patagonia, sometimes under the ocean, sometimes at the surface. The *Nautilus* passed beyond the large estuary formed by the Uruguay. Our direction was northward and followed the long windings of the coast of South America. At about 11:00 A.M. we crossed the Tropic of Capricorn on the 37th meridian, and passed Cape Frio standing out to sea. Captain Nemo, to Ned Land's great displeasure, did not care for the inhabited coasts of Brazil, and we went at a giddy rate.

This speed was kept up for several days. On April 9th in the evening we sighted the most westerly point of South

America that forms Cape San Roque. Then the *Nautilus* swerved again and sought the lowest depth of a submarine valley lying between the cape and Sierra Leone on the African coast. This valley bifurcates to the parallel of the Antilles, and terminates at the mouth by the enormous depression of 9,000 yards. In this place the geological basin of the ocean forms, as far as the Lesser Antilles, a cliff to three and a half miles perpendicular in height, and, at the parallel of the Cape Verde Islands, another wall not less considerable, that encloses thus all the sunk continent of the Atlantic. The bottom of this immense valley is dotted with some mountains that give to these submarine places a picturesque aspect. I speak, moreover, from the manuscript charts that were in the library of the *Nautilus*—charts evidently due to Captain Nemo's hand, and made after his personal observations. For two days we visited the deep waters. But on the 11th of April we rose suddenly and land appeared at the mouth of the Amazon River, a vast estuary, the embouchure of which is so considerable that it freshens the sea water for the distance of several leagues.

18. Octopi and Cuttlefish

FOR SEVERAL days the *Nautilus* held off the American coast. Evidently the captain did not wish to risk the tides of the Gulf of Mexico or of the sea of the Antilles. On April 16th we sighted Martinique and Guadaloupe from a distance of about 30 miles. I saw their tall peaks for an instant. The Canadian, who counted on carrying out his projects in the gulf, by either landing or hailing one of the numerous boats that coast from one island to another, was quite disheartened. Flight would have been quite practicable, if Ned Land had been able to take possession of the boat without the captain's knowledge. But in the open sea it could not be thought of. The Canadian, Conseil, and I had a long conversation on this subject.

For six months we had been prisoners on board the *Nautilus*. We had traveled 75,000 miles; and, as Ned Land said, there was no reason why it should come to an end. We could hope for nothing from the captain of the *Nautilus*, but only from ourselves. Besides, for some time past he had become graver, more retired, less sociable. He seemed to shun me. I met him rarely. Formerly he was pleased to explain the submarine marvels to me; now he left me to my studies, and came no more to the lounge. What change had come over him? For what cause? For my part, I did not wish to bury with me my curious and novel studies. I now had the power to write the true book of the sea; and this book, sooner or later, I wished to see daylight.

The land nearest us was the archipelago of the Bahamas. There rose high submarine cliffs covered with large weeds.

"Well," I said, "these are proper caverns for octopi, and I should not be astonished to see some of these monsters."

"What!" said Conseil. "Cuttlefish, real cuttlefish of the cephalopod class?"

"No," I said, "octopi of huge dimensions."

"I will never believe that such animals exist," said Ned.

"Well," said Conseil, with the most serious air in the world, "I remember perfectly having seen a large vessel drawn under the waves by an octopus's arm."

"You saw that?" asked the Canadian, incredulously.

"Yes, Ned."

"With your own eyes?"

"With my own eyes."

"Where, pray, might that be?"

"At St. Malo," answered Conseil.

"In the port?" said Ned ironically.

"No; in a church," replied Conseil.

"In a church!" cried the Canadian.

"Yes, friend Ned. In a picture representing this octopus."

"Good!" said Ned Land, bursting out laughing.

"He is quite right," I said. "I have heard of this picture; but the subject represented is taken from a legend, and you know what to think of legends in the matter of natural history. Besides, when it is a question of monsters, the imagination is apt to run wild. Not only is it supposed that these octopi can draw down vessels, but a certain Olaüs Magnus speaks of an octopus a mile long that is more like an island than an animal. It is also said that the Bishop of Nidros once built an altar on an immense rock. When Mass was finished, the rock began to walk and returned to the sea. The rock was an octopus. Another bishop, Pontoppidan, speaks also of an octopus on which a regiment of cavalry could maneuver. Lastly, the ancient naturalists speak of monsters whose mouths were like gulfs, and which were too large to pass through the Straits of Gibraltar."

"But how much is true of these stories?" asked Conseil.

"Nothing, my friends; at least none of that which passes over the limit of truth into fable. Nevertheless, there must be some ground for the imagination of the storytellers. One cannot deny that octopi and cuttlefish exist of a large species, inferior, however, to the cetaceans. Aristotle has stated the dimensions of a cuttlefish as five cubits, or nine feet two inches. Our fishermen frequently see some that are more than four feet long. Some skeletons of octopi are preserved in the museums of Trieste and Montpelier that measure six feet in length. Besides, according to the calculations of some naturalists, one of these animals only six feet long would have tentacles 27 feet long. That would be a formidable monster."

"Do they fish for them in these days?" asked Ned.

"If they do not fish for them, sailors see them at least. One of my friends, Captain Paul Bos of Havre, has often affirmed that he met one of these monsters of colossal dimensions in the Indian seas. But the most astonishing fact, and which does not permit of the denial of the existence of these gigantic animals, happened some years ago, in 1861."

"What is the fact?" asked Ned Land.

"This is it. In 1861, to the northeast of Teneriffe, very nearly in the same latitude we are in now, the crew of the despatch boat *Alector* perceived a monstrous cuttlefish swimming in the waters. Captain Bouguer went near to the animal and attacked it with harpoon and guns, without much success, for balls and harpoons glided over the soft flesh. After several fruitless attempts the crew tried to pass a slipknot around its body. The noose slipped as far as the tail fins and there stopped. They tried then to haul it on board, but its weight was so considerable that the tightness of the cord separated the tail from the body, and, deprived of this ornament, it disappeared under the water."

"Indeed! Is that a fact?"

"An indisputable fact, my good Ned. They proposed to name it 'Bouguer's cuttlefish.' "

"What length was it?" asked the Canadian.

"Did it not measure about 18 feet?" said Conseil, who, posted at the window, was again examining the irregular windings of the cliff.

"Precisely," I replied.

"Its head," rejoined Conseil, "was it not crowned with eight tentacles that beat the water like a nest of serpents?"

"Precisely."

"Had not its eyes, placed at the back of its head, considerable development?"

"Yes, Conseil."

"And was not its mouth like a parrot's beak?"

"Exactly, Conseil."

"Very well, no offense to Monsieur," he replied quietly; "if this is not Bouguer's cuttlefish, it is, at least, one of its brothers."

I looked at Conseil. Ned Land hurried to the window.

"What a horrible beast!" he cried.

I looked in my turn, and could not repress a gesture of disgust. Before my eyes was a horrible monster worthy to figure in the legends of the marvelous. It was an immense cuttlefish 24 feet long. It swam crossways in the direction of the *Nautilus* with great speed, watching us with its enormous staring green eyes. Its eight arms, or rather feet, fixed to its head, that have given the name of cephalopod to these animals, were twice as long as its body, and were twisted like the Furies' hair. One could see the 250 air holes on the inner side of the tentacles. The monster's mouth, a horned beak like a parrot's, opened and shut vertically. Its tongue, a horned substance, furnished with several rows of pointed teeth, came out quivering from this veritable pair of shears. What a freak of nature, a bird's beak on a mollusc! Its spindle-like body formed a fleshy mass that might weigh 4,000 to 5,000 pounds; the varying color changing with great rapidity, according to the irritation of the animal, passed successively from livid gray to reddish brown. What irritated this mollusc? No doubt the presence of the *Nautilus,* more formidable than itself, and on which its suckers or its jaws had no hold. Yet, what monsters these creatures are! What vitality the Creator has given them! What vigor in their movements, and they possess three hearts! Chance had brought us into the presence of this cuttlefish, and I did not wish to lose the opportunity of carefully studying this specimen of cephalopods. I overcame the horror that inspired me, and, taking a pencil, began to draw it.

"Perhaps this is the same which the *Alector* saw," said Conseil.

"No," replied the Canadian; "for this is whole, and the other had lost its tail."

"That is no reason," I replied. "The arms and tails of these animals are re-formed by renewal; and in seven years the tail of Bouguer's cuttlefish has no doubt had time to grow."

By this time other cephalopods appeared at the port light. I counted seven. They formed a procession after the *Nautilus,* and I heard their beaks gnashing against the iron hull. I continued my work. The monsters kept to our speed with such precision that they seemed immovable. Suddenly the *Nautilus* stopped. A shock made it tremble in every plate.

"Have we struck anything?" I asked.

"In any case," replied the Canadian, "we shall be free, for we are floating."

The *Nautilus* was floating, no doubt, but it did not move.

A minute passed. Captain Nemo, followed by his lieutenant, entered the lounge. I had not seen him for some time. He seemed dull. Without noticing or speaking to us, he went to the panel, looked at the creatures, and said something to his lieutenant. The latter went out. Soon the panels were shut. The ceiling was lighted. I went toward the captain.

"A curious collection of cephalopods," I said.

"Yes, indeed, Mr. Naturalist," he replied; "and we are going to fight them, man to beast."

I looked at him. I thought I had not heard aright.

"Man to beast?" I repeated.

"Yes, sir. The propeller is stopped. I think that the horny jaws of one of the cuttlefish are entangled in the blades. That is what prevents our moving."

"What are you going to do?"

"Rise to the surface, and slaughter this vermin."

"A difficult enterprise."

"Yes, indeed. The electric bullets are powerless against the soft flesh, where they do not find resistance enough to go off. But we shall attack them with the hatchet."

"And the harpoon, sir," said the Canadian, "if you do not refuse my help."

"I will accept it, Master Land."

"We will follow you," I said, and, following Captain Nemo, we went toward the central staircase.

There, about ten men with boarding hatchets were ready for the attack. Conseil and I took two hatchets; Ned Land seized a harpoon. The *Nautilus* had then risen to the surface. One of the sailors, posted on the top ladder step, unscrewed the bolts of the panels. But hardly were the screws loosed when the panel rose with great violence, evidently drawn by the suckers of an octopus's arm. Immediately one of these arms slid like a serpent down the opening and twenty others were above. With one blow of the ax, Captain Nemo cut this formidable tentacle, that slid wriggling down the ladder. Just as we were pressing one on the other to reach the platform, two other arms, lashing the air, came down on the seaman just in front of Captain Nemo and lifted him up with irresistible power. Captain Nemo uttered a cry, and rushed out. We hurried after him.

What a scene! The unhappy man, seized by the tentacle and fixed to the suckers, was balanced in the air at the caprice of this enormous trunk. He rattled in this throat, he was stifled, he cried, "Help! Help!" These words, *spoken in French,* startled me! I had a fellow countryman on board, perhaps several! That heartrending cry! I shall hear it all my life. The unfortunate man was lost. Who could rescue him from that powerful pressure? However, Captain Nemo had rushed to the poulp, and with one blow of the ax had cut through one arm. His lieutenant struggled furiously against other monsters that crept on the flanks of the *Nautilus.* The crew fought with their axes. The Canadian, Conseil, and I buried our weapons in the fleshy masses; a strong smell of musk penetrated the atmosphere. It was horrible!

For one instant I thought the unhappy man, entangled with the octopus, would be torn from its powerful suction. Seven of the eight arms had been cut off. One only wriggled in the air, brandishing the victim like a feather. But just as Captain Nemo and his lieutenant threw themselves on it, the animal ejected a stream of black liquid. We were blinded with it. When the cloud dispersed, the cuttlefish had disappeared, and my unfortunate countryman with it. Ten or twelve octopi now invaded the platform and sides of the

Nautilus. We rolled pell-mell into the midst of this nest of serpents that wriggled on the platform in the waves of blood and ink. It seemed as though these slimy tentacles sprang up like the hydra's heads. Ned Land's harpoon, at each stroke, was plunged into the staring eyes of the creature. But my bold companion was suddenly overturned by the tentacles of a cuttlefish he had not been able to avoid.

Ah! how my heart beat with emotion and horror! The formidable beak of the creature was open over Ned Land. The unhappy man would be cut in two. I rushed to his succor. But Captain Nemo was before me; his ax disappeared between the two enormous jaws, and, miraculously saved, the Canadian, rising, plunged his harpoon deep into the triple heart of the monster.

"I owed myself this revenge!" said the captain to the Canadian.

Ned bowed without replying. The combat had lasted a quarter of an hour. The monsters, vanquished and mutilated, left us at last, and disappeared under the waves. Captain Nemo, covered with blood, nearly exhausted, gazed upon the sea that had swallowed up one of his companions, and great tears gathered in his eyes.

19. The Gulf Stream

THIS TERRIBLE scene of the 20th of April none of us can ever forget. I have written it under the influence of violent emotion. Since then I have revised the recital; I have read it to Conseil and to the Canadian. They found it exact as to facts but insufficient as to effect. To paint such pictures one must have the pen of the most illustrious of our poets, the author of *The Toilers of the Deep*.

I have said that Captain Nemo wept while watching the waves; his grief was great. It was the second companion he had lost since our arrival on board, and what a death! That friend, crushed, stifled, bruised by the dreadful arms of a poulp, pounded by its iron jaws, would not rest with his comrades in the peaceful coral cemetery! In the midst of the struggle it was the despairing cry uttered by the unfortunate man that had torn my heart. The poor Frenchman, forgetting his conventional language, had taken to his own mother tongue, to utter a last appeal! Among the crew of the *Nautilus,* associated with the body and soul of the captain, recoiling like him from all contact with men, I had a fellow countryman. Did he alone represent France in this mysterious association, evidently composed of individuals of divers nationalities? It was one of these insoluble problems that rose up unceasingly before my mind!

Captain Nemo entered his room, and I saw him no more for some time. But that he was sad and irresolute I could see by the vessel, of which he was the soul, and which received all his impressions. The *Nautilus* did not keep on in its settled course; it floated about like a corpse at the will of the waves. It went at random. The captain could not tear himself away from the scene of the last struggle, from this sea that had devoured one of his men. Ten days passed thus. It was not till the 1st of May that the *Nautilus* resumed its northerly course, after having sighted the Bahamas at the mouth of the Bahama Canal. We were then following the current from the largest river to the sea, that has its banks, its fish, and its proper temperatures. I mean the Gulf Stream. It is really a river that flows freely to the

middle of the Atlantic, and whose waters do not mix with
the ocean waters. It is a salt river, saltier than the surrounding sea. Its mean depth is 1,500 fathoms, its mean breadth
ten miles. In certain places the current flows with the speed
of two miles and a half an hour. The body of its waters is
more considerable than that of all the rivers in the globe. It
was on this ocean river that the *Nautilus* then sailed.

I must add that, during the night, the phosphorescent
waters of the Gulf Stream rivaled the electric power of our
watch light, especially in the stormy weather that threatened us so frequently. On the 8th of May we were still
crossing Cape Hatteras, at the height of the North Caro-
line. The width of the Gulf Stream there is about 75
miles and its depth 210 yards. The *Nautilus* still went at
random; all supervision seemed abandoned. I thought that,
under these circumstances, escape would be possible. Indeed, the inhabited shores offered anywhere an easy refuge.
The sea was incessantly plowed by the steamers that ply
between New York or Boston and the Gulf of Mexico, and
overrun day and night by the little schooners coasting about
the several parts of the American coast. We could hope to
be picked up. It was a favorable opportunity, notwithstanding the thirty miles that separated the *Nautilus* from the
coasts of the Union. One unfortunate circumstance
thwarted the Canadian's plans. The weather was very bad.
We were nearing those shores where tempests are so frequent, that country of waterspouts and cyclones actually
engendered by the current of the Gulf Stream. To tempt the
sea in a frail boat was certain destruction. Ned Land owned
this himself. He fretted, seized with a fever that only flight
could cure.

"Master," he said that day to me, "this must come to an

end. I must make a clean breast of it. This Nemo is leaving land and going up to the north. But I declare to you that I have had enough of the South Pole, and I will not follow him to the North."

"What is to be done, Ned, since flight is impracticable just now?"

"We must speak to the captain," he said; "you said nothing when we were in your native seas. I will speak, now we are in mine. When I think that before long the *Nautilus* will be by Nova Scotia, and that there near Newfoundland is a large bay, and into that bay the St. Lawrence empties itself, and that the St. Lawrence is my river, the river by Quebec, my native town—when I think of this, I feel furious, it makes my hair stand on end. Sir, I would rather throw myself into the sea! I will not stay here! I am stifled!"

The Canadian was evidently losing all patience. His vigorous nature could not stand this prolonged imprisonment. His face altered daily; his temper became more surly. I knew what he must suffer, for I was seized with homesickness myself. Nearly seven months had passed without our having had any news from land; Captain Nemo's isolation, his altered spirits, especially since the fight with the octopi, his taciturnity, all made me view things in a different light.

"Well, sir?" said Ned, seeing I did not reply.

"Well, Ned, do you wish me to ask Captain Nemo his intentions concerning us?"

"Yes, sir."

"Although he has already made them known?"

"Yes; I wish it settled finally. Speak for me, in my name only, if you like."

"But I so seldom meet him. He avoids me."

"That is all the more reason for you to go to see him."

I went to my room. From thence I meant to go to Captain Nemo's. It would not do to let this opportunity of meeting him slip. I knocked at the door. No answer. I knocked again, then turned the handle. The door opened. I went in. The captain was there. Bending over his worktable, he had not heard me. Resolved not to go without having spoken, I approached him. He raised his head quickly, frowned, and said roughly, "You here! What do you want?"

"To speak to you, Captain."

"But I am busy, sir; I am working. I leave you at liberty to shut yourself up. Cannot I be allowed the same?"

This reception was not encouraging, but I was determined to hear and answer everything.

"Sir," I said coldly, "I have to speak to you on a matter that admits of no delay."

"What is that, sir?" he replied ironically. "Have you discovered something that has escaped me, or has the sea delivered up any new secrets?"

We were at cross-purposes. But before I could reply he showed me an open manuscript on his table, and said, in a more serious tone, "Here, Mr. Aronnax, is a manuscript written in several languages. It contains the sum of my studies of the sea; and, if it please God, it shall not perish with me. This manuscript, signed with my name, complete with the history of my life, will be shut up in a little floating case. The last survivor of all of us on board the *Nautilus* will throw this case into the sea, and it will go whither it is borne by the waves."

This man's name, his history written by himself! His mystery would then be revealed some day.

"Captain," I said, "I can but approve of the idea that makes you act thus. The result of your studies must not be lost. But the means you employ seem to me to be primitive. Who knows where the winds will carry this case, and in whose hands it will fall? Could you not use some other means? Could not you, or one of yours——"

"Never, sir!" he said, hastily interrupting me.

"But I and my companions are ready to keep this manuscript in store, and, if you will put us at liberty——"

"At liberty?" said the captain, rising.

"Yes, sir; that is the subject on which I wish to question you. For seven months we have been here on board, and I ask you today, in the name of my companions and in my own, if your intention is to keep us here always?"

"Mr. Aronnax, I will answer you today as I did seven months ago: Whoever enters the *Nautilus* must never quit it."

"You impose actual slavery upon us!"

"Give it what name you please."

"But everywhere the slave has the right to regain his liberty."

"Who denies you this right? Have I ever tried to chain you with an oath?"

He looked at me with his arms crossed.

"Sir," I said, "to return a second time to this subject will be neither to your nor to my taste; but, as we have entered upon it, let us go through with it. I repeat, it is not only myself whom it concerns. Study is to me a relief, a diversion, a passion that could make me forget everything. Like you, I am willing to live obscure, in the frail hope of bequeathing one day, to future time, the result of my labors.

But it is otherwise with Ned Land. Every man worthy of the name deserves some consideration. Have you thought that love of liberty, hatred of slavery, can give rise to schemes of revenge in a nature like the Canadian's; that he could think, attempt, and try——"

I was silenced; Captain Nemo rose.

"Whatever Ned Land thinks of, attempts, or tries, what does it matter to me? I did not seek him! It is not for my pleasure that I keep him on board! As for you, Mr. Aronnax, you are one of those who can understand everything, even silence. I have nothing more to say to you. Let this first time you have come to treat of this subject be the last! For a second time I will not listen to you."

I retired. Our situation was critical. I related my conversation to my two companions.

"We know now," said Ned, "that we can expect nothing from this man. The *Nautilus* is nearing Long Island. We will escape, whatever the weather may be."

But the sky became more and more threatening. Symptoms of a hurricane became manifest. The atmosphere was becoming white and misty. On the horizon fine streaks of cirrus clouds were succeeded by masses of cumuli. Other low clouds passed swiftly by. The swollen sea rose in huge billows. The birds disappeared with the exception of the petrels, those friends of the storm. The barometer fell sensibly, and indicated an extreme extension of the vapors. The mixture of the storm glass was decomposed under the influence of the electricity that pervaded the atmosphere. The tempest burst on the 18th of May, just as the *Nautilus* was floating off Long Island, some miles from the port of New York. I can describe this strife of the elements, for, instead of fleeing to the depths of the sea, Captain Nemo, by an unaccountable caprice, would brave it at the surface. The wind blew from the southwest at first. During the squalls Captain Nemo had taken his place on the platform. He had made himself fast, to prevent being washed overboard by the monstrous waves. I had hoisted myself up, and made myself fast also, dividing my admiration between the tempest and this extraordinary man who was coping with it. The raging sea was swept by huge cloud drifts, which were actually saturated with the waves. The *Nautilus,* sometimes lying on its side, sometimes standing up like a mast, rolled and pitched terribly. About five o'clock a torrent of rain fell that lulled neither sea nor wind. The hurricane winds had a velocity of 160 miles an hour. On land it must have overturned houses, broken iron gates, displaced twenty-four-pounders. However, the *Nautilus,* in the midst of the tempest, confirmed the words of a clever engineer, "There is no well-constructed hull that cannot defy the sea." This was not a resisting rock; it was a steel spindle, obedient and movable, without rigging or masts, that braved the fury.

I watched the raging waves. They were 15 feet high, 300 to 525 feet long, and their rate of speed was 30 feet per second. Their bulk and power increased with the depth of the water. Such waves as these, at the Hebrides, have displaced a mass weighing 8,400 pounds. They are the waves which, in the tempest of December 23, 1864, after destroying the town of Yeddo, Japan, broke the same day on the shores of America. The intensity of the tempest increased with the night. The barometer, as in 1860 at Réunion during a cyclone, fell seven-tenths at the close of day. I saw a large vessel pass on the horizon struggling painfully. She was trying to lie to under half steam, to keep up above the waves. It was probably one of the steamers of the line from New York to Liverpool, or Havre. She soon disappeared in the gloom.

At ten o'clock in the evening the sky was on fire. The atmosphere was streaked with vivid lightning. I could not bear the brightness of it; while the captain, looking at it, seemed to envy the spirit of the tempest. A terrible noise filled the air, a complex noise made up of the howls of the crushed waves, the roaring of the wind, and the thunder. The wind veered suddenly to all points of the horizon; and the cyclone, rising in the east, returned after passing by the north, west, and south, in the inverse course pursued by the circular storm of the Southern Hemisphere. Ah, that Gulf Stream! It deserves its name of the King of Tempests. It is that which causes those formidable cyclones by the difference of temperature between its air and its currents. A shower of fire had succeeded the rain. The drops of water were changed to sharp spikes. One would have thought that Captain Nemo was courting a death worthy of himself, a death by lightning. As the *Nautilus,* pitching dreadfully, raised its steel spur in the air, it seemed to act as a conductor, and I saw long sparks burst from it. Crushed and without strength I crawled to the panel, opened it, and descended to the lounge. The storm was then at its height. It was impossible to stand upright in the interior of the *Nautilus.* Captain Nemo came down about twelve. I heard the reservoirs filling by degrees, and the *Nautilus* sank slowly beneath the waves. Through the open windows in the lounge I saw large fish terrified, passing like phantoms in the water. Some were struck before my eyes. The *Nautilus* was still descending. I thought that at about eight fathoms deep we should find a calm. But no, the upper beds were too violently agitated for that. We had to seek repose at more than 25 fathoms in the bowels of the deep. But there, what quiet, what silence, what peace! Who could have told that such a hurricane had been let loose on the surface of that ocean?

20. From Lat. 47° 24′ to Long. 17° 28′

IN CONSEQUENCE of the storm, we had been thrown eastward once more. All hope of escape on the shores of New York or the St. Lawrence had faded away; and poor Ned, in despair, had isolated himself like Captain Nemo. Conseil and I, however, never left each other. I said that the *Nautilus* had gone aside to the east. I should have said, to the northeast. For some days it wandered first on the surface, and then beneath it, amid those fogs so dreaded by sailors. What accidents are due to these thick fogs! What shocks upon these reefs when the wind drowns the breaking of the waves! What collisions between vessels, in spite of their warning lights, whistles, and alarm bells! And the bottoms of these seas look like a field of battle, where still lie all the conquered of the ocean; some old and already encrusted, others fresh and reflecting from their iron bands and copper plates the brilliancy of our lantern.

On the 15th of May we were at the extreme south of the Bank of Newfoundland. This bank consists of alluvia, or large heaps of organic matter, brought either from the equator by the Gulf Stream or from the North Pole by the counter-current of cold water which skirts the American coast. There also are heaped up those erratic blocks which are carried along by the broken ice; and close by, a vast charnel house of molluscs, which perish here by millions. The depth of the sea is not great at Newfoundland—not more than some hundreds of fathoms; but toward the south is a depression of 1,500 fathoms. There the Gulf Stream widens. It loses some of its speed and some of its temperature, but it becomes a sea.

It was on the 17th of May, about 500 miles from Heart's Content, at a depth of more than 1,400 fathoms, that I saw the electric cable lying on the bottom. Conseil, to whom I had not mentioned it, thought at first that it was a gigantic sea serpent. But I undeceived the worthy fellow, and by way of consolation related several particulars in the laying of this cable. The first one was laid in the years 1857 and 1858; but after transmitting about 400 telegrams, would not act any longer. In 1863 the engineers constructed another one, measuring 2,000 miles in length, and weighing 4,500 tons, which was embarked on the *Great Eastern*. This attempt also failed.

On the 25th of May the *Nautilus,* being at a depth of more than 1,918 fathoms, was on the precise spot where the rupture occurred which ruined the enterprise. It was within 638 miles of the coast of Ireland; and at half-past two in the afternoon they discovered that communication with Europe had ceased. The electricians on board resolved to cut the cable before fishing it up, and at eleven o'clock at night they had recovered the damaged part. They made another point and spliced it, and it was once more submerged. But some days after it broke again, and in the depths of the ocean could not be recaptured. The Americans, however, were not discouraged. Cyrus Field, the bold promoter of the enterprise, as he had sunk all his own fortune, set a new subscription on foot, which was at once answered, and another cable was constructed on better principles. The bundles of conducting wires were each enveloped in gutta-percha and protected by a wadding of hemp contained in a metallic covering. The *Great Eastern* sailed on the 13th of July, 1866. The operation worked well. But one incident occurred. Several times in unrolling the cable they observed that nails had recently been forced into it, evidently with the motive of destroying it. Captain Anderson, the officers, and engineers consulted together, and had it posted up that, if the offender was surprised on board, he would be thrown without further trial into the sea. From that time the criminal attempt was never repeated.

On the 23rd of July the *Great Eastern* was not more than 500 miles from Newfoundland, when they telegraphed from Ireland the news of the armistice concluded between Prussia and Austria. On the 27th, in the midst of heavy fogs, they reached the port of Heart's Content. The enterprise was successfully terminated; and for its first dispatch young America addressed old Europe in these words of wisdom, so rarely understood: "Glory to God in the highest, and on earth peace, good will toward men."

I did not expect to find the electric cable in its primitive state, such as it was on leaving the manufactory. The long serpent, covered with the remains of shells, bristling with foraminiferae, was encrusted with a strong coating which served as a protection against all boring molluscs. It lay quietly sheltered from the motions of the sea, and under a favorable pressure for the transmission of the electric spark which passes from Europe to America in .32 of a second. Doubtless this cable will last for a great length of time, for they find that the gutta-percha covering is improved by the sea water. Besides, on this level, so well chosen, the cable is never so deeply submerged as to cause it to break. The *Nautilus* followed it to the lowest depth, which was more than 2,212 fathoms, and there it lay without any anchorage; and then we reached the spot where the accident had taken place in 1863. The bottom of the ocean then formed a valley about 100 miles broad in which Mont Blanc might have been placed without its summit appearing above the waves. This valley is closed at the east by a perpendicular wall more than 6,000 feet high. We arrived there on the 28th of May, and the *Nautilus* was then not more than 120 miles from Ireland.

Was Captain Nemo going to land on the British Isles? No. To my great surprise he made for the south, once more coming back toward European seas. In rounding the Emerald Isle, for one instant I caught sight of Cape Clear, and the light which guides the thousands of vessels leaving Glasgow or Liverpool. An important question then arose in my mind. Did the *Nautilus* dare entangle itself in the Channel? Ned Land, who had reappeared since we had been nearing land, did not cease to question me. How could I answer? Captain Nemo remained invisible. After having shown the Canadian a glimpse of American shores, was he going to show me the coast of France?

But the *Nautilus* was still going southward. On the 30th of May it passed in sight of Land's End, between the extreme point of England and the Scilly Isles, which were left to starboard. If he wished to enter the Channel, he must go straight to the east. He did not do so.

During the whole of May 31 the *Nautilus* described a series of circles on the water, which greatly interested me. It seemed to be seeking a spot that there was some trouble in finding. At noon Captain Nemo himself came to work the ship's log. He spoke no word to me, but seemed gloomier than ever. What could sadden him thus? Was it his proximity to European shores? Had he some recollections of his abandoned country? If not, what did he feel? Remorse or regret? For a long while this thought haunted my mind, and I had a kind of presentiment that before long chance would betray the captain's secrets.

The next day, the 1st of June, the *Nautilus* continued the same process. It was evidently seeking some particular spot in the ocean. Captain Nemo took the sun's altitude as he had done the day before. The sea was beautiful, the sky clear. About eight miles to the east a large steam vessel could be discerned on the horizon. No flag fluttered from its mast, and I could not discover its nationality. Some minutes before the sun passed the meridian Captain Nemo took his sextant, and watched with great attention. The perfect rest of the water greatly helped the operation. The *Nautilus* was motionless, it neither rolled nor pitched.

I was on the platform when the altitude was taken, and the captain pronounced these words: "It is here."

He turned and went below. Had he seen the vessel which was changing its course and seemed to be nearing us? I could not tell. I returned to the lounge. The panels closed, I heard the hissing of the water in the reservoirs. The *Nautilus* began to sink, following a vertical line, for the propel-

ler was still. Some minutes later it stopped at a depth of
more than 420 fathoms, resting on the ground. The luminous ceiling was darkened, then the panels were opened,
and through the glass I saw the sea brilliantly illuminated
by the rays of our lantern for at least half a mile around us.

I looked to the port side, and saw nothing but an immensity of quiet waters. But to starboard, on the bottom,
appeared a large protuberance, which at once attracted my
attention. One would have thought it a ruin buried under a
coating of white shells, much resembling a covering of
snow. Upon examining the mass attentively, I could recognize the ever-thickening form of a vessel bare of its masts,
which must have sunk. It certainly belonged to past times.
This wreck, to be thus encrusted with the lime of the water,
must already be able to count many years passed at the
bottom of the ocean.

What was this vessel? Why did the *Nautilus* visit its
tomb? Could it have been aught but a shipwreck which had
drawn it under the water? I knew not what to think, when
near me in a low voice I heard Captain Nemo say:

"At one time this ship was called the *Marseillaise*. She
carried 74 guns and was launched in 1762. On August 13,
1778, commanded by La Poype-Vertrieux, she fought
boldly against the *Preston*. In 1779, on the 4th of July, she
was at the taking of Grenada, with the squadron of Admiral
Estaing. In 1781, on the 5th of September, she took part in
the battle of Comte de Grasse, in Chesapeake Bay. In 1794
the French Republic changed her name. On the 16th of
April, in the same year, she joined the squadron of Villaret
Joyeuse, at Brest, being entrusted with the escort of a cargo
of corn coming from America, under the command of Ad-

miral Van Stebel. Then this squadron met with an English vessel. Sir, today is the first of June, 1868. It is now 74 years, day for day, on this very spot, in lat. 47° 24′, long. 17° 28′, since this vessel, after fighting heroically, losing her three masts, with the water in her hold, and a third of her crew disabled, preferred sinking with her 356 sailors to surrendering; and, nailing her colors to the poop, disappeared under the waves to the cry of 'Long live the Republic!' "

"The *Avenger!*" I exclaimed.

"Yes, sir, the *Avenger!* A good name!" muttered Captain Nemo, crossing his arms.

21. A Hecatomb

THE WAY of describing this unlooked-for scene, the history of the patriot ship, told at first so coldly, and the emotion with which this strange man pronounced the last words, the name of the *Avenger,* the significance of which could not escape me, all impressed themselves deeply on my mind. My eyes did not leave the captain, who, with his hand stretched out to sea, was watching with a glowing eye the glorious wreck. Perhaps I was never to know who he was, from whence he came, or where he was going to, but I saw the man moved, and no longer the savant. It was no common misanthropy which had shut Captain Nemo and his companions within the *Nautilus,* but a hatred, either monstrous or sublime, which time could never weaken. Did this hatred still seek for vengeance? The future would soon teach me that. But the *Nautilus* was rising slowly to the surface of the sea, and the form of the *Avenger* disappeared by degrees from my sight. Soon a slight rolling told me that we were in the open air. At that moment a dull boom was heard. I looked at the captain. He did not move.

"Captain?" I said.

He did not answer. I left him and mounted the platform. Conseil and the Canadian were already there.

"Where did that sound come from?" I asked.

"It was a gunshot," replied Ned Land.

I looked in the direction of the vessel I had already seen. She was nearing the *Nautilus,* and we could see that she was putting on steam. She was within six miles of us.

"What is that ship, Ned?"

"By her rigging and the height of her lower masts," said the Canadian, "I bet she is a ship of war. May she reach us; and, if necessary, sink this cursed *Nautilus.*"

"Friend Ned," replied Conseil, "what harm can she do to the *Nautilus?* Can she attack beneath the waves? Can she cannonade us at the bottom of the sea?"

"Tell me, Ned," said I, "can you tell what country she belongs to?"

The Canadian knitted his eyebrows, dropped his eyelids, and screwed up the corners of his eyes, and for a few moments fixed a piercing look upon the vessel.

"No, sir," he replied; "I cannot tell what nation she belongs to, for she shows no colors. But I can declare she is a man-of-war, for a long pennant flutters from her mainmast."

For a quarter of an hour we watched the ship which was steaming toward us. I could not, however, believe that she could see the *Nautilus* from that distance; and still less that

she could know what this submarine engine was. Soon the
Canadian informed me that she was a large, armored, two-
decker ram. A thick black smoke was pouring from her two
funnels. Her sails were furled. She hoisted no flag at her
mizzen peak. The distance prevented us from distinguishing
the colors of her pennant, which floated like a thin ribbon.
She advanced rapidly. If Captain Nemo allowed her to approach, there was a chance of salvation for us.

"Sir," said Ned Land, "if that vessel passes within a mile
of us I shall throw myself into the sea, and I should advise
you to do the same."

I did not reply to the Canadian's suggestion, but continued watching the ship. Whether English, French, American, or Russian, she would be sure to take us in if we could
only reach her. Presently a white smoke burst from the fore
part of the vessel; some seconds later the water, agitated by
the fall of a heavy body, splashed the stern of the *Nautilus,*
and shortly afterward a loud explosion struck my ear.

"What! They are firing at us!" I exclaimed.

"So please you, sir," said Ned, "they have recognized the
unicorn, and they are firing at us."

"But," I exclaimed, "surely they can see that there are
men in the case?"

"It is, perhaps, because of that," replied Ned Land, looking at me.

A whole flood of light burst upon my mind. Doubtless
they knew now how to believe the stories of the supposed
monster. No doubt on board the *Abraham Lincoln,* when
the Canadian struck it with the harpoon, Commander Farragut had recognized in the supposed narwhal a submarine
vessel more dangerous than a supernatural cetacean. Yes, it

must have been so; and on every sea they were now seeking this engine of destruction. Terrible, indeed, if, as we supposed, Captain Nemo employed the *Nautilus* in works of vengeance. On the night when we were imprisoned in that cell, in the midst of the Indian Ocean, had he not attacked some vessel? The man buried in the coral cemetery, had he not been a victim to the shock caused by the *Nautilus*? Yes, I repeat it, it must be so. One part of the mysterious existence of Captain Nemo had been unveiled; and, if his identity had not been recognized, at least the nations united against him were no longer hunting a chimerical creature, but a man who had vowed a deadly hatred against them. All the formidable past rose before me. Instead of meeting friends on board the approaching ship, we could expect only pitiless enemies. But the shot rattled about us. Some of them struck the sea and ricocheted, losing themselves in the distance. But none touched the *Nautilus*. The vessel was not more than three miles from us. In spite of the serious cannonade, Captain Nemo did not appear on the platform; but if one of the conical projectiles had struck the shell of the *Nautilus*, it would have been fatal. The Canadian then said, "Sir, we must do all we can to get out of this dilemma. Let us signal them. They will then, perhaps, understand that we are honest folks."

Ned Land took his handkerchief to wave in the air, but he had scarcely displayed it, when he was struck down by an iron hand, and fell, in spite of his great strength, upon the deck.

"Fool," exclaimed the captain, "do you wish to be pierced by the spur of the *Nautilus* before it is hurled at this vessel?"

Captain Nemo was terrible to hear; he was still more

terrible to see. His face was deadly pale, as though a spasm clutched at his heart. For an instant it must have ceased to beat. His pupils were fearfully contracted. He did not speak; he roared as, with his body thrown forward, he wrung the Canadian's shoulders. Then leaving him and turning to the ship of war, whose shot was still raining around him, he exclaimed with a powerful voice, "Ah, ship of an accursed nation, you know who I am! I do not want your colors to know you by! Look, and I will show you mine!"

And on the fore part of the platform Captain Nemo unfurled a black flag similar to the one he had placed at the South Pole. At that moment a shot struck the shell of the *Nautilus* obliquely, without piercing it; and, rebounding near the captain, was lost in the sea. He shrugged his shoulders; and, addressing me, said shortly, "Go down, you and your companions, go down!"

"Sir," I cried, "are you going to attack this vessel?"

"Sir, I am going to sink it."

"You will not do that?"

"I shall do it," he replied coldly. "And I advise you not to judge me, sir. Fate has shown you what you ought not to have seen. The attack has begun. Go down."

"What is this vessel?"

"You do not know? Very well, so much the better! Its nationality to you, at least, will be a secret. Go down!"

We could but obey. About 15 of the sailors surrounded the captain, looking with implacable hatred at the vessel nearing them. One could feel that the same desire of vengeance animated every soul. I went down at the moment another projectile struck the *Nautilus,* and I heard the captain exclaim:

"Strike, mad vessel! Shower your useless shot! And then, you will not escape the spur of the *Nautilus.* But it is not here that you shall perish! I would not have your ruins mingle with those of the *Avenger!*"

I reached my room. The captain and his second had remained on the platform. The propeller was set in motion, and the *Nautilus,* moving with speed, was soon beyond the reach of the ship's guns. But the pursuit continued, and Captain Nemo contented himself with keeping his distance.

About four in the afternoon, being no longer able to contain my impatience, I went to the central staircase. The panel was open, and I ventured on to the platform. The captain was still walking up and down with an agitated step. He was looking at the ship, which was five or six miles to leeward.

He was going around it like a wild beast, and, drawing it eastward, he allowed them to pursue. But he did not attack. Perhaps he still hesitated? I wished to mediate once more. But I had scarcely spoken when Captain Nemo imposed silence, saying:

"I am the law, and I am the judge! I am the oppressed, and there is the oppressor! Through him I have lost all that I loved, cherished, and venerated—country, wife, children, father, and mother. I saw all perish! All that I hate is there! Say no more!"

I cast a last look at the man of war, which was putting on steam, and rejoined Ned and Conseil.

"We will fly!" I exclaimed.

"Good!" said Ned. "What is this vessel?"

"I do not know; but, whatever she is, she will be sunk before night. In any case, it is better to perish with her than be made accomplices in a retaliation the justice of which we cannot judge."

"That is my opinion, too," said Ned Land coolly. "Let us wait for night."

Night arrived. Deep silence reigned on board. The compass showed that the *Nautilus* had not altered its course. It was on the surface, rolling slightly. My companions and I resolved to fly when the vessel should be near enough either to hear us or to see us; for the moon, which would be full in two or three days, shone brightly. Once on board the ship, if we could not prevent the blow which threatened it, we could, at least we would, do all that circumstances would allow. Several times I thought the *Nautilus* was preparing for attack; but Captain Nemo contented himself with allowing his adversary to approach, and then fled once more before it.

Part of the night passed without any incident. We watched the opportunity for action. We spoke little, for we were too much moved. Ned Land would have thrown himself into the sea, but I forced him to wait. According to my idea, the *Nautilus* would attack the ship at her water line, and then it would not only be possible, but easy, to fly.

At three in the morning, full of uneasiness, I mounted the platform. Captain Nemo had not left it. He was standing at the forepart near his flag, which a slight breeze displayed above his head. He did not take his eyes from the vessel. The intensity of his look seemed to attract, and fascinate, and draw her onward more surely than if he had been towing her. The moon was then passing the meridian.

Jupiter was rising in the east. Amid this peaceful scene of nature sky and ocean rivaled each other in tranquillity, the sea offering to the orbs of night the finest mirror they could ever have in which to reflect their image. As I thought of the deep calm of these elements, compared with all those passions brooding imperceptibly within the *Nautilus,* I shuddered.

The vessel was within two miles of us. She was ever nearing that phosphorescent light which showed the presence of the *Nautilus.* I could see her green and red lights, and her white lantern hanging from the large foremast. An indistinct vibration quivered through her rigging, showing that the furnaces were heated to the uttermost. Sheaves of sparks and red ashes flew from the funnels, shining in the atmosphere like stars.

I remained thus until six in the morning, without Captain Nemo noticing me. The ship stood about a mile and a half from us, and with the first dawn of day the firing began afresh. The moment could not be far off when, the *Nautilus* attacking its adversary, my companions and myself should forever leave this man. I was preparing to go down to remind them, when the second mounted the platform, accompanied by several sailors. Captain Nemo either did not or would not see them. Some steps were taken which might be called the signal for action. They were very simple. The iron balustrade around the platform was lowered, and the lantern and pilot cages were pushed within the shell until they were flush with the deck. The long surface of the steel cigar no longer offered a single point to check its maneuvers. I returned to the lounge. The *Nautilus* still floated; some streaks of light were filtering through the liquid beds.

With the undulations of the waves the windows were brightened by the red streaks of the rising sun, and this dreadful day of the 2nd of June had dawned.

At five o'clock the log showed that the speed of the *Nautilus* was slackening, and I knew that it was allowing them to draw nearer. Besides, the reports were heard more distinctly, and the projectiles, laboring through the ambient water, were extinguished with a strange hissing noise.

"My friends," I said, "the moment is come. One grasp of the hand, and may God protect us!"

Ned Land was resolute, Conseil calm, myself so nervous that I knew not how to contain myself. We all passed into the library; but the moment I pushed the door opening on to the central staircase I heard the upper panel close sharply. The Canadian rushed onto the stairs, but I stopped him. A well-known hissing noise told me that the water was running into the reservoirs, and in a few minutes the *Nautilus* was some yards beneath the surface of the waves. I understood the maneuver. It was too late to act. The *Nautilus* did not wish to strike at the impenetrable cuirass, but below the water line, where the metallic covering no longer protected it.

We were again imprisoned, unwilling witnesses of the dreadful drama that was preparing. We had scarcely time to reflect. Taking refuge in my room, we looked at each other without speaking. A deep stupor had taken hold of my mind: thought seemed to stand still. I was in that painful state of expectation preceding a dreadful report. I waited, I listened, every sense was merged in that of hearing! The speed of the *Nautilus* was accelerated. It was preparing to rush. The whole ship trembled. Suddenly I screamed. I felt the shock, but comparatively light. I felt the penetrating power of the steel spur. I heard rattlings and scrapings. But the *Nautilus,* carried along by its propelling power, passed through the mass of the vessel like a needle through sailcloth!

I could stand it no longer. Mad, out of my mind, I rushed from my room into the lounge. Captain Nemo was there, mute, gloomy, implacable; he was looking through the port panel. A large mass cast a shadow on the water, and, that it might lose nothing of her agony, the *Nautilus* was going down into the abyss with her. Ten yards from me I saw the open shell through which the water was rushing with the noise of thunder, then the double line of guns and the netting. The bridge was covered with black, agitated shadows.

The water was rising. The poor creatures were crowding the ratlines, clinging to the masts, struggling under the water. It was a human ant heap overtaken by the sea. Paralyzed, stiffened with anguish, my hair standing on end, with eyes wide open, panting, without breath, and without voice, I, too, was watching! An irresistible attraction glued me to the glass! Suddenly an explosion took place. The compressed air blew up her decks, as if the magazines had caught fire. Then the unfortunate vessel sank more rapidly. Her topmast, laden with victims, now appeared; then her spars, bending under the weight of men; and, last of all, the top of her mainmast. Then the dark mass disappeared, and with it the dead crew, drawn down by the strong eddy.

I turned to Captain Nemo. That terrible avenger, a perfect archangel of hatred, was still looking. When all was over, he turned to his room, opened the door, and entered. I followed him with my eyes. On the end wall beneath his heroes I saw the portrait of a woman, still young, and two little children. Captain Nemo looked at them for some moments, stretched his arms toward them, and, kneeling down, burst into deep sobs.

22. The Last Words of Captain Nemo

THE PANELS had closed on this dreadful vision, but light had not returned to the lounge; all was silence and darkness within the *Nautilus*. At wonderful speed 100 feet beneath the water it was leaving this desolate spot. Whither were we headed? To the north or south? Where was the man flying to after such dreadful retaliation? I had returned to my room, where Ned and Conseil had remained silent enough. I felt an insurmountable horror for Captain Nemo. Whatever he had suffered at the hands of these men, he had no right to punish thus. He had made me, if not an accomplice, at least a witness of his vengeance. At eleven the electric light reappeared. I passed into the lounge. It was deserted. I consulted the different instruments. The *Nautilus* was flying northward at the rate of 25 knots, now on the surface, and now 30 feet below it. On taking the bearings by the chart I saw that we were passing the mouth of the Channel, and that our course was hurrying us toward the northern seas at a frightful speed.

That night we crossed 200 leagues of the Atlantic. The shadows fell, and the sea was covered with darkness until the rising of the moon. I went to my room, but could not sleep. I was troubled with dreadful nightmare. The horrible scene of destruction was continually before my eyes. From that day who could tell into what part of the North Atlantic basin the *Nautilus* would take us? Still with unaccountable speed. Still in the midst of these northern fogs. Would we touch at Spitzbergen, or on the shores of Nova Zembla? Should we explore those unknown seas, the White Sea, the Sea of Kara, the Gulf of Obi, the Archipelago of Liarrov, and the unknown coast of Asia? I could not say. I could no longer judge of the time that was passing. The clocks had been stopped on board. It seemed, as in polar countries, that night and day no longer followed their regular course. I felt myself being drawn into that strange region where the foundered imagination of Edgar Allan Poe roamed at will. Like the fabulous Gordon Pym, at every moment I expected to see "that veiled human figure, of larger proportions than those of any inhabitant of the earth, thrown across the cataract which defends the approach to the pole." I estimated—though perhaps I may be mistaken—I estimated this adventurous course of the *Nautilus* to have lasted fifteen or twenty days. And I know not how much longer it might have lasted had it not been for the catastrophe which ended this voyage. Of Captain Nemo I saw nothing whatever now, nor of his second. Not a man of the crew was visible for an instant. The *Nautilus* was almost incessantly under water. When we came to the surface to renew the air, the panels opened and shut mechanically. There were no more marks on the planisphere. I knew not where we were. And the Canadian, too, his strength and patience at an end, appeared no more. Conseil could not draw a word from him; and, fearing that, in a dreadful fit of madness, he might kill himself, watched him with constant devotion. One morning, what date it was I could not say, I had fallen into a heavy sleep toward the early hours, a sleep both painful and unhealthy, when I suddenly awoke. Ned Land was leaning over me, saying, in a low voice, "We are going to fly."

I sat up.

"When shall we go?" I asked.

"Tonight. All inspection on board the *Nautilus* seems to have ceased. All appear to be stupefied. You will be ready, sir?"

"Yes. Where are we?"

"In sight of land. I took the reckoning this morning in the fog—twenty miles to the east."

"What country is it?"

"I do not know; but, whatever it is, we will take refuge there."

"Yes, Ned, yes. We will fly tonight, even if the sea should swallow us up."

"The sea is bad, the wind violent, but twenty miles in that light boat of the *Nautilus* does not frighten me. Unknown to the crew I have been able to procure food and some bottles of water."

"I will follow you."

"But," continued the Canadian, "if I am surprised, I will defend myself; I will force them to kill me."

"We will die together, friend Ned."

I had made up my mind to all. The Canadian left me. I reached the platform on which I could with difficulty support myself against the shock of the waves. The sky was threatening; but, as land was in those thick brown shadows, we must fly. I returned to the lounge, fearing and yet hoping to see Captain Nemo, wishing and yet not wishing to see

him. What could I have said to him? Could I hide the involuntary horror with which he inspired me? No. It was
better that I should not meet him face to face; better to
forget him. And yet—— How long seemed that day, the
last that I should pass in the *Nautilus*. I remained alone. Ned
Land and Conseil avoided speaking, for fear of betraying
themselves. At six I dined, but I was not hungry; I forced
myself to eat in spite of my disgust, that I might not weaken
myself. At half-past six Ned Land came to my room, saying, "We shall not see each other again before our departure. At ten the moon will not be risen. We will profit by
the darkness. Come to the boat; Conseil and I will wait for
you."

The Canadian went out without giving me time to answer. Wishing to verify the course of the *Nautilus,* I went to
the lounge. We were running NNE at frightful speed, and
more than fifty yards deep. I cast a last look on these wonders of nature, on the riches of art heaped up in this
museum, upon the unrivaled collection destined to perish at
the bottom of the sea with him who had formed it. I wished
to fix an indelible impression of it in my mind. I remained
an hour thus, bathed in the light of that luminous ceiling,
and passing in review those treasures shining under their
glasses. Then I returned to my room.

I dressed myself in strong sea clothing. I collected my
notes, placing them carefully about me. My heart beat
loudly. I could not check its pulsations. Certainly my
trouble and agitation would have betrayed me to Captain
Nemo's eyes. What was he doing at this moment? I listened
at the door of his room. I heard steps. Captain Nemo was
there. He had not gone to rest. At every moment I expected

to see him appear and ask me why I wished to fly. I was constantly on the alert. My imagination magnified everything. The impression became at last so poignant that I asked myself if it would not be better to go to the captain's room, see him face to face, and brave him with look and gesture.

It was the inspiration of a madman; fortunately I resisted the desire, and stretched myself on my bed to quiet my bodily agitation. My nerves were somewhat calmer, but in my excited brain I saw over again all my existence on board the *Nautilus;* every incident, either happy or unfortunate, which had happened since my disappearance from the *Abraham Lincoln*—the submarine hunt, the Torres Strait, the savages of Papua, the running ashore, the coral cemetery, the passage of Suez, the Island of Santorin, the Cretan diver, Vigo Bay, Atlantis, the iceberg, the South Pole, the imprisonment in the ice, the fight among the octopi, the storm in the Gulf Stream, the *Avenger,* and the horrible scene of the vessel sunk with all her crew. All these events passed before my eyes like scenes in a drama. Then Captain Nemo seemed to grow enormously, his features to assume superhuman proportions. He was no longer my equal, but a man of the waters, the genie of the sea.

It was then half-past nine. I held my head between my hands to keep it from bursting. I closed my eyes; I would not think any longer. There was another half-hour to wait, another half-hour of a nightmare which might drive me mad.

At that moment I heard the distant strains of the organ, a sad harmony to an undefinable chant, the wail of a soul longing to break these earthly bonds. I listened with every sense, scarcely breathing; plunged, like Captain Nemo, in that musical ecstasy, which was drawing him in spirit to the end of life.

Then a sudden thought terrified me. Captain Nemo had left his room. He was in the lounge, which I must cross to fly. There I should meet him for the last time. He would see me, perhaps speak to me. A gesture of his might destroy me, a single word chain me on board.

But ten was about to strike. The moment had come for me to leave my room and join my companions.

I must not hesitate, even if Captain Nemo himself should rise before me. I opened my door carefully; and even then, as it turned on its hinges, it seemed to me to make a dreadful noise. Perhaps it only existed in my own imagination.

I crept along the dark stairs of the *Nautilus,* stopping at each step to check the beating of my heart. I reached the door of the lounge, and opened it gently. It was plunged in profound darkness. The strains of the organ sounded faintly. Captain Nemo was there. He did not see me. In the full light I do not think he would have noticed me, so entirely was he absorbed in the ecstasy.

I crept along the carpet, avoiding the slightest sound which might betray my presence. I was at least five minutes reaching the door, at the opposite side, opening into the library.

I was going to open it when a sigh from Captain Nemo nailed me to the spot. I knew that he was rising. I could even see him, for the light from the library came through to the lounge. He came toward me silently, with his arms crossed, gliding like a specter rather than walking. His

breast was swelling with sobs, and I heard him murmur
these words, the last which ever struck my ear:

"Almighty God! Enough! Enough!"

Was it a confession of remorse which thus escaped from
this man's conscience?

In desperation I rushed through the library, mounted the
central staircase, and, following the upper flight, reached
the boat. I crept through the opening, which had already
admitted my two companions.

"Let us go! Let us go!" I exclaimed.

"Directly," replied the Canadian.

The orifice in the plates of the *Nautilus* was first closed,
and fastened down by means of a false key, with which Ned
Land had provided himself; the opening in the boat was
also closed. The Canadian began to loosen the bolts which
still held us to the submarine boat.

Suddenly a noise was heard. Voices were answering each
other loudly. What was the matter? Had they discovered
our flight? I felt Ned Land slipping a dagger into my hand.

"Yes," I murmured, "we know how to die!"

The Canadian had stopped in his work. But one word
many times repeated, a dreadful word, revealed the cause
of the agitation spreading on board the *Nautilus*. It was not
we the crew were looking after!

"The Maelstrom! The Maelstrom!" Could a more dreadful word in a more dreadful situation have sounded in our
ears! We were then upon the dangerous coast of Norway.
Was the *Nautilus* being drawn into this gulf at the moment
our boat was going to leave its sides? We knew that at the
tide the pent-up waters between the islands of Faeroe and

Lofoten rush with irresistible violence, forming a whirl-pool from which no vessel ever escapes. From every point of the horizon enormous waves were meeting, forming a gulf justly called the "Navel of the Ocean," whose power of attraction extends to a distance of twelve miles. There, not only vessels but whales are sacrificed, as well as white bears from the northern regions.

It is thither that the *Nautilus,* voluntarily or involuntar-ily, had been run by the captain.

The ship was describing a spiral, the circumference of which was lessening by degrees, and the small boat, which was still fastened to *Nautilus'* side, was carried along with giddy speed. I felt that sickly giddiness which arises from long-continued whirling around.

We were in dread. Our horror was at its height, circula-tion had stopped, all nervous influence was annihilated, and we were covered with cold sweat, like a sweat of agony! And what noise around our frail bark! What roarings re-peated by the echo miles away! What an uproar was that of the waters broken on the sharp rocks at the bottom, where the hardest bodies are crushed, and trees worn away, "with all the fur rubbed off," according to the Norwegian phrase!

What a situation to be in! We rocked frightfully. The *Nautilus* defended itself like a human being. Its steel muscles cracked. Sometimes it seemed to stand upright, and we with it!

"We must hold on," said Ned, "and look after the bolts. We may still be saved if we stick to the *Nautilus.*"

He had not finished the words when we heard a crashing noise, the bolts gave way, and the boat, torn from its

groove, was hurled like a stone from a sling into the midst
of the whirlpool.

My head struck on a piece of iron, and with the violent
shock I lost all consciousness.

23. Conclusion

THUS ENDS the voyage under the seas. What passed during
that night—how the boat escaped from the eddies of the
maelstrom—how Ned Land, Conseil, and myself ever came
out of the gulf I cannot tell.

But when I returned to consciousness, I was lying in a
fisherman's hut, on the Lofoten Isles. My two companions,
safe and sound, were near me holding my hands. We em-
braced one another heartily.

At that moment we could not think of returning to
France. The means of communication between the north of
Norway and the south are rare. And I am therefore obliged
to wait for the steamboat running monthly from Cape
North.

And among the worthy people who have so kindly received us, I revise my record of these adventures once
more. Not a fact has been omitted, not a detail exaggerated.
It is a faithful narrative of this incredible expedition in an
element inaccessible to man but to which Progress will one
day open a road.

Shall I be believed? I do not know. And it matters little,
after all. What I now affirm is that I have a right to speak of
these seas, under which, in less than ten months, I have
crossed 20,000 leagues in that submarine tour of the world,
which has revealed so many wonders.

But what has become of the *Nautilus?* Did it resist the pressure of the Maelstrom? Does Captain Nemo still live? And does he still follow under the ocean those frightful retaliations? Or did he stop after the last hecatomb?

Will the waves one day carry to him this manuscript containing the history of his life? Shall I ever know the name of this man? Will the missing vessel tell us by its nationality that of Captain Nemo?

I hope so. And I also hope that his powerful vessel has conquered the sea at its most terrible gulf, and that the *Nautilus* has survived where so many other vessels have been lost! If it be so—if Captain Nemo still inhabits the ocean, his adopted country, may hatred be appeased in that savage heart! May the contemplation of so many wonders extinguish forever the spirit of vengeance! May the judge disappear, and the philosopher continue the peaceful exploration of the sea! If his destiny be strange, it is also sublime. Have I not understood it myself? Have I not lived ten months of this unnatural life? And to the question asked by Ecclesiastes three thousand years ago, "That which is far off and exceeding deep, who can find it out?" two men alone of all now living have the right to give an answer—

Captain Nemo and myself.

AROUND
THE
MOON

⊙

*

AROUND THE MOON

Prologue

DURING THE year 186– the whole world was greatly excited by an experiment unprecedented in the annals of science. The members of the Gun Club, a circle of artillerymen formed at Baltimore after the Civil War, conceived the idea of putting themselves in communication with the moon —yes, with the moon—by sending up a projectile. Their president, Barbicane, the promoter of the enterprise, consulted the astronomers of the Cambridge Observatory upon the subject. They declared the project practicable, and Barbicane thereupon took all the necessary means to insure the success of this extraordinary enterprise. After setting on foot a public subscription which realized nearly five and one-half million dollars, they began the gigantic work.

According to the advice forwarded from the Observatory, the gun destined to launch the projectile had to be fixed in a country situated between 0° and 28° N. or S. lat., in order to aim at the moon when at the zenith; and its initial velocity was fixed at 36,000 feet to the second.

367

Launched on the 1st of December, at precisely 13 minutes
and 20 seconds before 11:00 P.M., it ought to reach the
moon four days after departure, on the 5th of December at
midnight precisely, at the moment when the moon attained
its perigee, or its nearest distance from the earth (about
228,000 miles).

The principal members of the Gun Club, President Barbicane, Major Elphinstone, the secretary Joseph T. Maston,
and other learned men, held several meetings, at which the
shape and composition of the projectile were discussed, also
the position and nature of the gun, and the quality and
quantity of the powder to be used. It was decided first, that
the projectile should be a shell made of aluminum with a
diameter of 108 inches and a thickness of twelve inches to
its walls, and should weigh 19,250 pounds. Second, the
gun should be a columbiad cast in iron, 900 feet long, and
run perpendicularly into the earth. Third, the charge should
contain 400,000 pounds of guncotton, which, giving out
6,000,000,000 liters of gas in the rear of the projectile,
would easily carry it toward the moon.

These considerations led President Barbicane, assisted by
Murchison the engineer, to choose a spot situated in Florida called Stones Hill, in 27° 7′ N. lat., and 77° 3′ W.
long. It was on this spot, after stupendous labor, that the
columbiad was cast with full success. Things stood thus
when an incident took place which greatly increased the
interest attached to this great enterprise.

A Frenchman, an enthusiastic Parisian, as witty as he
was bold, asked to be enclosed in the projectile, in order
that he might reach the moon and reconnoiter this terrestrial satellite. The name of this intrepid adventurer was

Michel Ardan. He landed in America, was received with enthusiasm, and was able to reconcile President Barbicane to his mortal enemy, Captain Nicholl, and even persuaded them both to start with him in the projectile.

The shape of the projectile was then slightly altered to become a hollow conical cylinder. This aerial car was lined with strong springs and partitions to deaden the shock of departure. It was provided with food for a year, water for some months, and gas for some days. A self-acting apparatus supplied the three travelers with air to breathe. At the same time, on one of the highest points of the Rocky Mountains the Gun Club had a gigantic telescope erected in order to follow the course of the projectile through space. All was then ready.

On December 1st, at the appointed hour, from the midst of an extraordinary crowd of spectators the departure took place, and for the first time three human beings quitted the terrestrial globe and launched into interplanetary space with almost a certainty of reaching their destination. These bold travelers, Michel Ardan, President Barbicane, and Captain Nicholl, were expected to make the passage in 97 hours, 13 minutes, and 20 seconds, reaching the lunar surface on the 5th of December at midnight, at the exact moment when the moon would be full.

Unfortunately, the detonation produced by the columbiad had the immediate effect of disturbing the earth's atmosphere. Such an amount of mist and vapor was thereby created that the moon was hidden from the eyes of the watchers for several nights.

Meanwhile, Joseph T. Maston, the staunchest friend of the three travelers, started for the Rocky Mountains, accompanied by Professor Belfast, director of the Cambridge Observatory. They soon reached the station of Longs Peak, where the telescope had been erected to bring the moon within a range of visibility equal to five miles. Maston made the journey because he wished to observe for himself the course of the projectile in which his daring friends were making their space journey.

The accumulation of the clouds in the atmosphere prevented all observations on the 5th, 6th, 7th, 8th, 9th, and 10th of December.

At length, to the general satisfaction, a heavy storm cleared the atmosphere on the night of the 11th and 12th of December, and the moon's half-illuminated disc was plainly seen in the black sky.

That very night a telegram was sent from the station of Long's Peak by Joseph T. Maston and Belfast to the gentlemen of the Cambridge Observatory, announcing that, on the 11th of December at 8:47 P.M., the projectile had been detected by Belfast and Maston—that it had deviated from its course from some unknown cause and had not reached its destination but that it had passed near enough to be held by the lunar attraction; that it was now following an elliptical orbit around the moon, becoming in effect its satellite. The telegram added that the distance separating the projectile from the lunar surface "might" be reckoned at about 2,833 miles.

It ended with this double hypothesis: either the attraction of the moon would draw the projectile down to the moon's surface, and the travelers would thus attain their end; or that the projectile, held in immutable orbit, would gravitate around the moon to all eternity.

With such alternatives, what would be the fate of travelers? Certainly they had food for some time. But supposing they did succeed in their rash enterprise, how would they return? Could they ever return? Should those on earth hear from them? These questions, debated by the most learned pens of the day, strongly occupied the public attention.

It is advisable here to make a remark which ought to be well considered by hasty observers. When a purely speculative discovery is announced to the public, it cannot be done with too much prudence. No one is obliged to discover either a planet, a comet, or a satellite; and whoever makes a mistake in such a case exposes himself justly to the derision of the mass. Far better is it to wait; and that is what the impatient Joseph T. Maston should have done before sending this telegram forth to the world, which, according to his idea, told the whole result of the enterprise. Indeed this telegram contained two sorts of errors, as was proved eventually. First, errors of observation, concerning the distance of the projectile from the surface of the moon, for on the 11th of December the projectile could not be seen. What Joseph T. Maston had seen, or thought he saw, could not have been the projectile. Second, errors of theory on what the projectile's fate might be, for declaring that it might become a satellite of the moon was directly contrary to all mechanical laws.

One single hypothesis of Maston and Belfast was accurate, that which foresaw the case of the travelers, if still alive, attaining the surface of the moon.

Now these men, as clever as they were daring, had survived the terrible shock consequent on their departure, and it is their journey in the projectile car which is here related in its most dramatic details. This recital will destroy many illusions and surmises. But it will give a true idea of the singular adventures in store for such an enterprise. It will bring out the scientific instincts of Barbicane, the industrious resources of Nicholl, and the audacious humor of Michel Ardan. Besides this, it will prove that their worthy friend, Joseph T. Maston, was wasting his time as he watched, over the gigantic telescope, the course of the moon through starry space.

1. From 10:00 P.M. to 10:47 P.M.

As TEN o'clock struck Michel Ardan, Barbicane, and Nicholl said goodbye to the numerous friends they were leaving on the earth. The two dogs, destined to propagate the canine race on the lunar continents, were already shut up in the projectile.

The three travelers approached the enormous cast-iron tube, and a crane let them down to the conical top of the projectile. There an opening made for the purpose gave them access to the aluminum car. The tackle belonging to the crane was hauled away and the mouth of the columbiad was instantly cleared of its last supports.

Nicholl, once introduced with his companions inside the projectile, began to close the opening by means of a strong plate held in position by powerful screws. Other plates, closely fitted, covered the glass windows and the travelers, hermetically enclosed in their metal prison, were plunged in profound darkness.

"And now, my dear companions," said Michel Ardan, "let us make ourselves at home; I am a domesticated man and strong in housekeeping. We are bound to make the best of our new lodgings, and make ourselves comfortable. And first let us try and see a little. Gas was not invented for moles."

So saying, he lit a match by striking it on the sole of his boot, and approached the burner fixed to the gas tank, in which was carbonized hydrogen, stored at high pressure, sufficient for the lighting and warming of the projectile for 146 hours, or six days and six nights. The gas caught fire, and thus lighted, the projectile looked like a comfortable room with thickly padded walls, furnished with a circular divan, and a roof rounded in the shape of a dome.

The objects it contained—arms, instruments and utensils —were securely fastened against the rounds of padding to bear the shock of departure. Humanly speaking, every possible precaution had been taken to bring this rash experiment to a successful termination.

Michel Ardan examined everything and declared himself satisfied with his installation.

"It is a prison," he said, "but a traveling prison; and, with the right of putting my nose to the window, I could well stand a lease of a hundred years. You smile, Barbicane. Have you any last thoughts? Do you say to yourself, 'This prison may be our tomb?' Tomb, perhaps; still I would not change it for Mahomet's, which floats in space but never advances an inch!"

While Michel Ardan was speaking, Barbicane and Nicholl were making their last preparations.

Nicholl's chronometer marked 10:20 P.M. when the

three travelers were finally enclosed in their projectile. This chronometer was set within the tenth of a second by that of Murchison the engineer. Barbicane consulted it.

"My friends," he said, "it is now 10:20. At 10:47 Murchison will launch the electric spark on the wire connected with the charge of the columbiad. At that precise moment we shall leave the earth. We still have 27 minutes remaining."

"No, 26 minutes, 13 seconds," replied the methodical Nicholl.

"Well" exclaimed Michel Ardan, in a good-humored tone, "much may be done in 26 minutes. The gravest questions of morals and politics may be discussed, and even solved; 26 minutes well employed are worth more than 26 years in which nothing is done. Some seconds of a Pascal or a Newton are more precious than the whole existence of a crowd of raw simpletons——"

"And you conclude, then, you everlasting talker?" asked Barbicane.

"I conclude that we have 26 left," replied Ardan.

"Only 24," said Nicholl.

"Well, 24 if you like, my noble captain," said Ardan; "24 minutes in which to investigate——"

"Michel," said Barbicane, "during the passage we shall have plenty of time to investigate the most difficult questions. For the present we must concern ourselves with our departure."

"Are we not ready?"

"Doubtless; but there are still some precautions to be taken, to deaden as much as possible the first shock."

"Haven't we water cushions between the partition breaks, whose elasticity will sufficiently protect us?"

"I hope so, Michel," replied Barbicane gently, "but I am not sure."

"Ah, the joker!" exclaimed Michel Ardan. "He hopes! He is not sure! And he waits for the moment when we are encased to make this deplorable admission! I beg to be allowed to get out!"

"And how?" asked Barbicane.

"Humph!" said Michel Ardan, "it is not easy; we are in the train, and the guard's whistle will sound before 24 minutes are over."

"Now 20," said Nicholl.

For some moments the three travelers looked at one another. Then they began to examine the objects imprisoned with them.

"Everything is in its place," said Barbicane. "We have now to decide how we can best place ourselves to resist the shock. Position cannot be an indifferent matter; and we must, as much as possible, prevent the rush of blood to the head."

"Just so," said Nicholl.

"Then," replied Michel Ardan, ready to suit the action to the word, "let us put our heads down and our feet in the air, like the clowns in the grand circus."

"No," said Barbicane, "let us stretch ourselves on our sides; we shall resist the shock better that way. Remember that when the projectile starts, it matters little whether we are in it or before it; it amounts to much the same thing."

"If it is only 'much the same thing,' I may cheer up," said Michel Ardan.

"Do you approve of my idea, Nicholl?" asked Barbicane.

"Entirely," replied the captain. "We've still thirteen minutes and a half."

"That Nicholl is not a man," exclaimed Michel; "he is a chronometer with seconds, an escape, and eight holes."

But his companions were not listening; they were taking up their last positions with the most perfect coolness. They were like two methodical travelers in a car, seeking to place themselves as comfortably as possible.

We might well ask ourselves of what materials are the hearts of these Americans made, when the approach of the most frightful danger seemed not to affect them.

Three thick and solidly-made couches had been placed in the projectile. Nicholl and Barbicane placed them in the center of the disc forming the floor. There the three travelers were to stretch themselves some moments before their departure.

During this time Ardan, not being able to keep still, turned in his narrow prison like a wild beast in a cage, chatting with his friends, speaking to the dogs Diana and Satellite, to whom, as may be seen, he had given significant names.

"Ah, Diana! Ah, Satellite!" he exclaimed, teasing them; "so you are going to show the moon dogs the good habits of the dogs of the earth! That will do honor to the canine race! If ever we do come down again, I will bring a cross type of 'moon dogs,' which will make a stir!"

"If there *are* dogs on the moon," said Barbicane.

"There are," said Michel Ardan, "just as there are horses, cows, donkeys, and chickens. I bet that we shall find chickens."

"A hundred dollars we shall find none!" said Nicholl.

"Done, my captain!" replied Ardan, clasping Nicholl's hand. "But you have already lost three bets with our president, as the necessary funds for the enterprise have been found, as the operation of casting has been successful, and, lastly, as the columbiad has been loaded without accident —a total of $6,000."

"Yes," replied Nicholl.

"And," Ardan went on, "before another quarter of an hour you will have to pay $9,000 more to the president; $4,000 because the columbiad will not burst, and $5,000 because the projectile will rise more than six miles in the air."

"I have the dollars," replied Nicholl, slapping the pocket of his coat. "I only ask to be allowed to pay."

"Come, Nicholl, I see that you are a man of method, which I could never be; but indeed you have made a series of bets of very little advantage to yourself, allow me to tell you."

"And why?" asked Nicholl.

"Because, if you gain the first, the columbiad will have burst, and the projectile with it; and Barbicane will no longer be there to reimburse your dollars."

"My stake is deposited at the bank in Baltimore," replied Barbicane simply, "and if Nicholl is not there, it will go to his heirs."

"Ah, you practical men," exclaimed Michel Ardan. "I admire you the more for not being able to understand you."

"Forty-two minutes past ten!" said Nicholl.

"Only five minutes more!" answered Barbicane.

"Yes, five little minutes!" replied Michel Ardan; "and we are enclosed in a projectile, at the bottom of a gun 900 feet long! And under this projectile are rammed 400,000 pounds of guncotton, which is equal to 1,600,000 pounds of ordinary powder! And friend Murchison, with his chronometer in hand, his eye fixed on the needle, his finger on the electric apparatus, is counting the seconds preparatory to launching us into interplanetary space."

"Enough, Michel, enough!" said Barbicane in a serious voice. "Let us prepare. A few instants alone separate us from an eventful moment. One clasp of the hand, my friends."

"Yes," exclaimed Michel Ardan, more moved than he wished to appear.

"God preserve us!" said the religious Barbicane.

Michel Ardan and Nicholl stretched themselves on the couches placed in the center of the disc.

"Forty-seven minutes past ten!" murmured the captain.

"Twenty seconds more!" Barbicane quickly put out the gas and lay down by his companions, and the profound silence was broken only by the ticking of the chronometer marking the seconds.

Suddenly a dreadful shock was felt, and the projectile, under the force of 6,000,000,000 liters of gas, developed by the combustion of pyroxylin, mounted into space.

2. The First Half Hour

WHAT HAD happened? What effect had this frightful shock produced? Had the ingenuity of the constructors of the projectile obtained any happy result? Had the shock been deadened, thanks to the springs, the four plugs, the water cushions, and the partition breaks? Had they been able to subdue the frightful pressure of the initiatory speed of 36,000 feet per second? This was evidently the question suggested to the thousand spectators of this moving scene. They forgot the aim of the journey, and thought only of the travelers. And if one among them—Joseph T. Maston, for example—could have cast one glimpse into the projectile, what would he have seen?

Nothing then. The darkness was profound. But the projectile's partitions had resisted wonderfully. Not a rent nor a dent anywhere! The wonderful projectile was not even heated under the intense deflagration of the powder, nor liquefied, as they seemed to fear, in a shower of aluminum.

The interior showed but little disorder. Indeed, only a few objects had been violently thrown toward the roof; but the most important seemed not to have suffered from the shock at all; their fixtures were intact.

On the movable disc, the projectile's floor, three bodies lay apparently lifeless. Barbicane, Nicholl, and Michel Ardan—did they still breathe? or was the projectile nothing now but a metal coffin bearing three corpses into space?

Some minutes after the departure of the projectile one of the bodies moved, shook its arms, lifted its head, and finally succeeded in getting on its knees. It was Michel Ardan. He felt himself all over, gave a sonorous "Hem!" and then said:

"Michel Ardan is whole. How about the others?"

The courageous Frenchman tried to rise, but could not stand. His head swam from the rush of blood; he was blind; he was like a drunken man.

"Bur-r!" he said. "It produces the same effect as two bottles of wine, though perhaps less agreeable to swallow."

Then, passing his hand several times across his forehead and rubbing his temples, he called in a firm voice:

"Nicholl! Barbicane!"

He waited anxiously. No answer; not even a sigh to show that the hearts of his companions were still beating. He called again. The same silence.

"The devil!" he exclaimed. "They look as if they had fallen from a fifth story on their heads. Bah!" he added, with that imperturbable confidence which nothing could check, "if a Frenchman can get on his knees, two Americans ought to be able to get on their feet. But first let us put some light on the scene."

Ardan felt the tide of life return by degrees. His blood became calm, and returned to its accustomed circulation. Another effort restored his equilibrium. He succeeded in rising, drew a match from his pocket, and approaching the burner lighted it. The tank had not suffered at all. The gas had not escaped. Besides, the smell would have betrayed it; and in that case Michel Ardan could not have carried a lighted match with impunity through the space filled with hydrogen. The gas mixing with the air would have produced a detonating mixture, and the explosion would have finished what the shock had perhaps begun. When the burner was lit, Ardan leaned over the bodies of his companions: they were lying one on the other, an inert mass, Nicholl above, Barbicane underneath.

Ardan lifted the captain, propped him up against the divan, and began to rub vigorously. This means, used with judgment, restored Nicholl, who opened his eyes, and instantly recovering his presence of mind, seized Ardan's hand and looked around him.

"And Barbicane?" he said.

"Each in turn," replied Michel Ardan. "I began with you, Nicholl, because you were on the top. Now let us look to Barbicane."

Ardan and Nicholl raised the president of the Gun Club and laid him on the divan. He seemed to have suffered more than either of his companions; he was bleeding, but Nicholl was reassured by finding that the hemorrhage came from a slight wound on the shoulder, a mere contusion, which he bound up carefully.

Still, Barbicane was a long time coming to himself, which frightened his friends, who continued to rub him.

"He breathes, though," said Nicholl, putting his ear to the chest of the wounded man.

"Yes," replied Ardan, "he breathes like a man who has some notion of that daily operation. Rub, Nicholl; let us rub harder." And the two improvised practitioners worked so hard and so well that Barbicane recovered his senses.

He opened his eyes, sat up, took his two friends by the hands, and his first words were: "Nicholl, are we moving?"

Nicholl and Ardan looked at each other. They had not yet troubled themselves about the projectile; their first thought had been for the traveler, not for the car.

"Well, are we really moving?" repeated Michel Ardan.

"Or quietly resting on the soil of Florida?" asked Nicholl.

"Or at the bottom of the Gulf of Mexico?" added Michel Ardan.

"What an idea!" exclaimed the president.

And this double hypothesis suggested by his companions had the effect of recalling him to his senses. In any case they could not decide on the position of the projectile. Its apparent immovability, and the want of communication with the outside, prevented them from solving the question. Perhaps the projectile was unwinding its course through space. Perhaps after a short rise it had fallen upon the earth, or even in the Gulf of Mexico—a fall which the narrowness of the peninsula of Florida would render not impossible.

The case was serious, the problem interesting, and one that must be solved as soon as possible. Thus, highly excited, Barbicane's moral energy triumphed over physical weakness and he rose to his feet. He listened. Outside was perfect silence—the thick padding was enough to intercept all sounds coming from the earth. But one circumstance struck Barbicane: the temperature inside the projectile was singularly high. The president drew a thermometer from its case and consulted it. The instrument showed 81° Fahrenheit.

"Yes," he exclaimed, "yes, we are moving! This stifling heat, penetrating through the partitions of the projectile, is produced by its friction on the atmospheric strata. It will soon diminish, because we are already floating in space, and after having been nearly stifled, we shall have to suffer intense cold."

"What!" said Michel Ardan. "According to your showing, Barbicane, we are already beyond the limits of the terrestrial atmosphere?"

"Without a doubt, Michel. Listen to me. It is 10:55; we have been gone about eight minutes. If our initiatory speed has not been checked by the friction, six seconds would be enough for us to pass through the forty miles of atmosphere which surrounds the globe."

"Just so," replied Nicholl; "but in what proportion do you estimate the reduction of speed by friction?"

"In the proportion of one-third, Nicholl. This reduction is considerable, but according to my calculations it is nothing less. If, then, we had an initial speed of 36,000 feet, on leaving the atmosphere this speed would be reduced to 27,500. In any case we have already passed through this interval, and——"

"And then," said Michel Ardan, "friend Nicholl has lost his two bets: $4,000 because the columbiad did not burst; $5,000 because the projectile has risen more than six miles. Now, Nicholl, pay up."

"Let us prove it first," said the captain, "and we will pay afterward. It is quite possible that Barbicane's reasoning is correct, and that I have lost my nine thousand dollars. But a new hypothesis presents itself to my mind, and it annuls the wager."

"What is that?" asked Barbicane quickly.

"The hypothesis that, for some reason or other, fire was never set to the powder, and we have not started at all."

"My goodness, Captain," exclaimed Michel Ardan, "that hypothesis is worthy of my brain! It cannot be a serious one. For have we not been half annihilated by the shock? Did I not recall you to life? Is not the president's shoulder still bleeding from the blow it has received?"

"Granted," replied Nicholl; "but one question."

"Well, Captain?"

"Did you hear the detonation, which certainly ought to be loud?"

"No," replied Ardan, much surprised; "certainly I did not hear the detonation."

"And you, Barbicane?"

"Nor I, either."

"Very well," said Nicholl.

"Well, now," murmured the president, "why did we not hear the detonation?"

The three friends looked at one another with a disconcerted air. It was quite an inexplicable phenomenon. The projectile had started, and consequently there must have been a detonation.

"Let us first find out where we are," said Barbicane, "and let down the window panel."

This very simple operation was soon accomplished.

The nuts which held the bolts to the outer plates of the right-hand window gave way under the pressure of the wrench. These bolts were pushed outside, and buffers covered with rubber stopped up the holes which let them through. Immediately the outer plate fell back upon its hinges like a porthole, and they could look out through the glass. A similar glass was set into the thick partition on the opposite side of the projectile, another in the top of the dome, and, finally, a fourth in the middle of the base. They could, therefore, make observations in four different directions: the firmament by the side windows, the earth or the moon by the upper and under openings in the projectile.

Barbicane and his two companions immediately rushed to the uncovered window. But it was lit by no ray of light. Profound darkness surrounded them, which, however, did not prevent the president from exclaiming:

"No, my friends, we have not fallen back upon the earth; no, nor are we submerged in the Gulf of Mexico. Yes, we are mounting into space. See those stars shining in the night, and that impenetrable darkness heaped up between the earth and us!"

"Hurrah! Hurrah!" exclaimed Michel Ardan and Nicholl in one voice.

Indeed, this thick darkness proved that the projectile had left the earth, for the ground, brilliantly lit by moonlight, would have been visible to the travelers if they had been lying on its surface. This darkness also showed that the projectile had passed out of the earth's atmospheric strata, for the diffused light spread in the air would have been reflected on the metal walls, and this reflection was not present. The window was dark. Doubt was no longer possible: the travelers had left the earth.

"I have lost," said Nicholl.

"I congratulate you," replied Ardan.

"Here is the $9,000," said the captain, drawing a roll of paper dollars from his pocket.

"Will you have a receipt for it?" asked Barbicane, taking the sum.

"If you do not mind," answered Nicholl; "it is more businesslike."

And coolly and seriously, as if he had been at his strong-box, the president drew forth his notebook, tore out a blank leaf, wrote a proper receipt in pencil, dated and signed it with the usual flourish, and gave it to the captain, who carefully placed it in his pocketbook. Michel Ardan, taking off his hat, bowed to his two companions without speaking. So much formality under such circumstances left him speechless. He had never before seen anything so "American."

This affair settled, Barbicane and Nicholl had returned to

the window, and were watching the constellations. The stars looked like bright points on the black sky. But from that side they could not see the moon which, traveling from east to west, would rise by degrees toward the zenith. Its absence drew the following remark from Ardan:

"And the moon; will she perchance fail at our rendezvous?"

"Do not alarm yourself," said Barbicane, "our future globe is at its post. But we cannot see her from this side; let us open the other."

As Barbicane was about to leave the window to open the opposite one, his attention was attracted by the approach of a brilliant object. It was an enormous disc whose colossal dimension could not be estimated. Its face, which was turned to the earth, was very bright. One might have thought it a small moon reflecting the light of the large one. It advanced with great speed, and seemed to describe an orbit around the earth which would intersect the passage of the projectile. This body revolved upon its axis, and exhibited the phenomena of all celestial bodies abandoned in space.

"Ah," exclaimed Michel Ardan, "what is that? another projectile?"

Barbicane did not answer. The appearance of this enormous body surprised and troubled him. A collision was possible, and might be attended with deplorable results. Either the projectile would deviate from its path, or its impetus broken, it might fall to the earth. Or conceivably, it might be irresistibly drawn away by the powerful asteroid. The president was instantly aware of the consequences of these three hypotheses, any of which would, one way or the other, bring their experiment to an unsuccessful and fatal termination. His companions stood silently looking into space. The object grew rapidly as it approached them, and by an optical illusion the projectile seemed to be throwing itself before it.

"By Jove," exclaimed Michel Ardan, "we shall run into one another!"

Instinctively the travelers drew back. Their dread was great, but it did not last many seconds. The asteroid passed several hundred yards from the projectile and disappeared, not so much from the rapidity of its course, as that its face being opposite the moon, it was suddenly merged into the perfect darkness of space.

"A happy journey to you," exclaimed Michel Ardan, with a sigh of relief. "Surely infinity of space is large enough for a poor little projectile to walk through without fear. Now, what is this portentous globe which nearly struck us?"

"I know," replied Barbicane.

"Oh, indeed! You know everything."

"It is," said Barbicane, "a simple meteorite, but an enormous one, which the attraction of the earth has retained as a satellite."

"Is it possible," exclaimed Michel Ardan, "the earth then has two moons like Neptune?"

"Yes, my friend, two moons, though it passes generally for having only one. But this second moon is so small, and its speed so great, that the inhabitants of the earth cannot see it. A French astronomer, Petit, was able to determine the existence of this second satellite and calculate its elements. According to his observations, this meteorite will accomplish its revolution round the earth in three hours and twenty minutes, which implies a wonderful rate of speed."

"Do all astronomers admit the existence of this satellite?" asked Nicholl.

"No," replied Barbicane; "but if, like us, they had met it, they could no longer doubt it. Indeed, I think that this meteorite will give us the means of deciding what our position in space is."

"How?" said Ardan.

"Because its distance is known, and when we met it, we were exactly 4,650 miles from the surface of the terrestrial globe."

"That beats the express trains of the pitiful globe called the earth," exclaimed Michel Ardan.

"I should think so," replied Nicholl, consulting his chronometer; "it is eleven o'clock, only 13 minutes since we left the American continent."

"Only 13 minutes?" said Barbicane.

"Yes," said Nicholl; "and if our initial speed of 36,000 feet has been kept up, we shall have made about 20,000 miles in the hour."

"That is all very well, my friends," said the president, "but the insoluble question still remains. Why didn't we hear the detonation of the columbiad?"

For want of an answer the conversation dropped, and Barbicane began thoughtfully to let down the shutter of the second side. He succeeded, and through the uncovered glass the moon filled the projectile with a brilliant light. Nicholl, as an economical man, put out the gas, whose brilliancy prevented any observation of the interplanetary space.

The moon shone with wonderful purity. No longer filtered through the vapory atmosphere of the earth, its rays shone through the glass, filling the interior of the projectile with silvery reflections. The black curtain of the firmament in reality heightened the moon's brilliancy. Yet the ether being unfavorable to diffusion, the neighboring stars still shone brightly. The heavens, thus seen, presented quite a new aspect, and one which the human eye could never dream of. One may conceive the interest with which these bold men watched the moon, the great goal of their journey.

In its motion the moon was by insensible degrees nearing the zenith, the mathematical point which it ought to attain 96 hours later. Its mountains, its plains, every projection was as clearly discernible to their eyes as if they were observing it from some spot upon the earth. But its light was developed through space with wonderful intensity, and it shone like a platinum mirror. Of the earth flying from under their feet the travelers had lost all recollection.

It was Captain Nicholl who first recalled their attention to the vanishing globe.

"Yes," said Michel Ardan, "do not let us be ungrateful to it. Since we are leaving our country, let our last looks be directed to it. I wish to see the earth once more before it is quite hidden from my eyes."

To satisfy his companions, Barbicane began to uncover the window at the bottom of the projectile, which would allow them directly to observe the earth. The disc, which the force of the projection had shattered, was removed, not without difficulty. Its fragments, placed carefully against the wall, might serve again upon occasion. Then a circular gap appeared, 19 inches in diameter, hollowed out of the lower part of the projectile. A glass cover, six inches thick and strengthened with upper fastenings, closed it tightly. Beneath was fixed an aluminum plate, held in place by bolts. The screws being undone, and the bolts let go, the plate fell down, and visible communication was established between the interior and the exterior.

Michel Ardan knelt by the glass. It was cloudy, seemingly opaque.

"Well," he exclaimed, "and the earth?"

"The earth?" said Barbicane. "There it is."

"What! that little thread, that silver crescent?"

"Doubtless, Michel. In four days, when the moon will be full, at the very time we shall reach it, the earth will be new, and will only appear to us as a slender crescent which will soon disappear, and for some days will be enveloped in utter darkness."

"That is the earth?" repeated Michel Ardan, looking with all his eyes at the thin slip of his native planet.

The explanation given by President Barbicane was correct. The earth, with respect to the projectile, was entering its last phase. It was in its octant, and showed a crescent finely traced on the dark background of the sky. Its light, rendered bluish by the thick strata of the atmosphere, was less intense than that of the crescent moon, but it was of considerable dimensions, and looked like an enormous arch stretched across the firmament. Some parts brilliantly lighted, especially on its concave part, showed the presence of high mountains, often disappearing behind thick spots. They were rings of clouds placed concentrically around the terrestrial globe.

While the travelers were trying to pierce the profound darkness, a brilliant cluster of shooting stars burst upon their eyes. Hundreds of meteorites, ignited by the friction of the atmosphere, streaked the darkness with their luminous trails. At this period the earth was in its perihelion, and the month of December is so propitious to these shooting stars that astronomers have counted as many as 24,000 in an hour. But Michel Ardan, disdaining scientific reasonings, preferred thinking that the earth was thus saluting the departure of her three children with her most brilliant fireworks.

Indeed this was all they saw of the earth, lost in the solar world, rising and setting to the great planets like a simple morning or evening star. This globe, where they had left all their affections, was nothing more than a fugitive crescent!

Long did the three friends look without speaking, although united in heart, while the projectile sped onward with an ever-decreasing speed. Then an irresistible drowsiness crept over their brains. Was it weariness both of body and mind? No doubt. After the overexcitement of those last hours on earth, reaction was inevitable.

"Well," said Nicholl, "since we must sleep, let us sleep."

And stretching themselves on their couches, they were all three soon in a profound slumber.

But they had not forgotten themselves for more than a quarter of an hour when Barbicane sat up suddenly, and rousing his companions with a loud voice, exclaimed: "I have found it!"

"What have you found?" asked Michel Ardan, jumping from his bed.

"The reason why we did not hear the detonation of the columbiad."

"And it is——?" said Nicholl.

"Because our projectile traveled faster than the sound!"

3. Their Place of Shelter

WITH THIS curious but certainly correct explanation, the three friends returned to their slumbers. Could they have found a calmer or more peaceful spot to sleep in? On the earth, houses, towns, cottages, and country feel every shock given to the exterior of the globe. On the sea, vessels rocked by the waves are still in motion; in the air, the balloon oscillates incessantly. This projectile alone, floating in perfect space, in the midst of perfect silence, offered perfect repose.

Thus the sleep of our adventurous travelers might have been indefinitely prolonged, if an unexpected noise had not awakened them at about seven o'clock in the morning of the 2nd of December, eight hours after their departure.

This noise was a very natural barking.

"The dogs! It is the dogs!" exclaimed Michel Ardan, rising at once.

"They are hungry," said Nicholl.

"By Jove!" replied Michel, "we have forgotten them."

"Where are they?" asked Barbicane.

They looked and found one of the animals crouched under the divan. Terrified and shaken by the initiatory shock, it had remained in the corner till its voice returned with the pangs of hunger. It was the amiable Diana, still very confused, who crept out of her retreat, though not without much persuasion, Michel Ardan encouraging her with most gracious words.

"Come, Diana," he said. "Come, my girl. You who are destined for a lofty place in the annals of canine glory, you who are rushing into interplanetary space, and will perhaps be the Eve of all future lunar dogs, come, Diana, come here."

Diana, flattered or not, advanced by degrees, uttering plaintive cries.

"Good," said Barbicane. "I see Eve, but where is Adam?"

"Adam?" replied Michel. "Adam cannot be far off. He is there somewhere; we must call him. Satellite! Here, Satellite!"

But Satellite did not appear. Diana would not leave off howling. They found, however, that she was not bruised, and they gave her a pie, which silenced her complaints. As to Satellite, he seemed quite lost. They had to hunt a long time before finding him in one of the upper compartments of the projectile, whither some unaccountable shock must have violently hurled him. The poor beast, much hurt, was in a piteous state.

"The devil!" said Michel.

They brought the unfortunate dog down with great care. Its skull had been broken against the roof, and it seemed unlikely that he could recover from such a shock. Meanwhile, he was stretched comfortably on a cushion. Once there, he heaved a sigh.

"We will take care of you," said Michel. "We are responsible for your existence. I would rather lose an arm than a paw of my poor Satellite."

Saying which, he offered some water to the wounded dog, who swallowed it with avidity.

This attention paid, the travelers watched the earth and the moon attentively. The earth was now only discernible by a cloudy disc ending in a crescent, rather more contracted than that of the previous evening. But its expanse was still enormous, compared with that of the moon, which was approaching nearer and nearer to a perfect circle.

"By Jove," said Michel Ardan, "I am really sorry that we did not start when the earth was full, that is to say, when our globe was in opposition to the sun."

"Why?" asked Nicholl.

"Because we should have seen our continents and seas in a new light—the continents resplendent under the solar rays, the seas cloudy as represented on some maps of the world. I should like to have seen those poles of the earth on which the eye of man has never yet rested."

"I dare say," replied Barbicane; "but if the earth had been *full*, the moon would have been *new*; that is to say, invisible, because of the rays of the sun. It is better for us to see the destination we wish to reach than the point of departure."

"You are right, Barbicane," replied Captain Nicholl; "and, besides, when we have reached the moon, we shall have time during the long lunar nights to consider at our leisure the globe on which our fellow beings swarm."

"Our fellow beings!" exclaimed Michel Ardan. "They are no more that, than the beings on the moon are! We inhabit a new world, peopled by ourselves—the projectile! I am Barbicane's likeness, and Barbicane is Nicholl's. Beyond us, around us, human nature is at an end, and we are the only population of this microcosm until we become pure lunar people."

"In about 88 hours," replied the captain.

"Which means to say?" asked Michel Ardan.

"That it is half-past eight," replied Nicholl.

"Very well," retorted Michel. "Then it is impossible for me to find even the shadow of a reason why we should not go to breakfast."

Indeed the inhabitants of the new star could not live without eating, and their stomachs were suffering from the imperious laws of hunger. Michel Ardan, as a Frenchman, was declared chief cook, an important function gladly surrendered by the others. The gas gave sufficient heat for the culinary apparatus, and the provision box furnished the elements of this first feast.

The breakfast began with three bowls of excellent soup, prepared by dissolving in hot water those precious cakes of Liebig, made from the best beef of the pampas. After the soup came beefsteaks, compressed by a hydraulic press, as tender and succulent as if brought straight from the kitchen of an English eating house. Michel, who was imaginative, maintained that they were even "red."

Preserved vegetables ("fresher than nature," said the amiable Michel) succeeded the meat and was followed by some cups of tea with bread and butter, after the American fashion.

The beverage was declared exquisite.

It was made of choice leaves which the emperor of Russia had donated for the benefit of the travelers.

And last, to crown the repast, Ardan brought out a fine bottle of Nuits, which was found "by chance" in the provision box. The three friends toasted the union of the earth and her satellite.

And, as if he had not already done enough for the generous wine which he had distilled on the slopes of Burgundy, the sun chose to be of the party. At this moment the projectile emerged from the shadow cast by the terrestrial globe, and the rays of the sun struck the lower portion of the projectile, its rays perpendicular because of the oblique angle which the moon's orbit makes with that of the earth.

"The sun!" exclaimed Michel Ardan.

"No doubt," replied Barbicane. "I expected it."

"But," said Michel, "does the conical shadow, which the earth leaves in space, extend beyond the moon?"

"Far beyond it, if the atmospheric refraction is not taken into consideration," said Barbicane. "But when the moon is enveloped in this shadow, it is because the centers of the three stars, the sun, the earth, and the moon, are all in one and the same straight line. Then the *nodes* coincide with the *phases* of the moon, and there is an eclipse. If we had started when there was an eclipse of the moon, all our passage would have been in the shadow, which would have been a pity."

"Why?"

"Because, though we are floating in space, our projectile, bathed in the solar rays, will receive their light and heat. It economizes the gas, which is in every respect a good economy."

Indeed, under these rays which no atmosphere can temper, either in temperature or brilliancy, the projectile grew warm and bright, as if it had passed suddenly from winter to summer. The moon above, the sun beneath, were inundating it with their fire.

"It is pleasant here," said Nicholl.

"I should think so," said Michel Ardan. "With a little earth spread on our aluminum planet we should have green peas in twenty-four hours. I have but one fear, which is that the walls of the projectile might melt."

"Calm yourself, my worthy friend," replied Barbicane. "The projectile withstood a very much higher temperature than this as it slid through the layers of the atmosphere. I should not be surprised if it did not look like a meteor on fire to the eyes of the spectators in Florida."

"But then Joseph T. Maston will think we are roasted!"

"What astonishes me," said Barbicane, "is that we have not been. That was a danger we had not provided for."

"I feared it," said Nicholl simply.

"And you never mentioned it, my sublime captain," exclaimed Michel Ardan, clasping his friend's hand.

Barbicane now began to settle himself in the projectile as if he were never to leave it. One must remember that this aerial car had a base with an area of 54 square feet. Its height to the roof was 12 feet. Carefully laid out in the inside, and little encumbered by instruments and traveling utensils, each of which had its particular place, the projectile left the three travelers a certain freedom of movement. The thick window inserted in the bottom could bear any amount of weight, and Barbicane and his companions walked upon it as if it were solid plank; but the sun striking it directly with its rays lit the interior of the projectile from beneath, thus producing singular effects of light.

The travelers' first task now was to investigate their store of water and provisions. They found neither had suffered, thanks to the care taken to deaden the shock. Their provisions were abundant, and plentiful enough to last the three travelers for more than a year. Barbicane wished to be cautious, in case the projectile should land on a part of the moon which was utterly barren. As to water and the reserve of brandy, which consisted of 50 gallons, there was only enough for two months. But according to the last observations of astronomers, the moon had a low, dense, and thick atmosphere, at least in the deep valleys, and there springs and streams could not fail. Thus, during their passage, and for the first year of their settlement on the lunar continent, these adventurous explorers would suffer neither hunger nor thirst.

Now about the air in the projectile. There, too, they were secure. Reiset and Regnaut's apparatus for producing oxygen was supplied with chlorate of potassium for two months. They consumed a certain quantity of gas, to keep the oxygen-producing substance at a temperature of about 400°. But there again they were all safe. The apparatus only wanted a little care. Of course they had to do more than just renew the oxygen. They must also absorb the carbonic acid produced by exhaling. During the last 12 hours the atmosphere of the projectile had become charged with this deleterious gas. Nicholl discovered the state of the air by observing Diana panting painfully. The carbonic acid, by a phenomenon similar to that produced in the famous Grotto del Cane near Naples had collected at the bottom of the projectile owing to its weight. Poor Diana, with her head low, would suffer before her masters from the presence of this gas. But Captain Nicholl hastened to remedy this state of things by placing on the floor several receivers containing caustic potash, which he shook about for a time, and this substance, greedy for carbonic acid, soon completely absorbed it, thus purifying the air.

An inventory of instruments was then begun. The thermometers and barometers had resisted, all but one minimum thermometer, the glass of which was broken. An excellent aneroid barometer was drawn from the wadded box which contained it and hung on the wall. Of course it was only affected by and marked the pressure of the air inside the projectile, but it also showed the quantity of moisture which the air contained. At that moment its needle oscillated between 25.24 and 25.08.

It was fine weather.

Barbicane had also brought several compasses, which he found intact. It must be understood that under present conditions their needles were acting *wildly,* that is without any *constant* direction. Indeed, at the distance they were from the earth, the magnetic pole could have no perceptible action upon the apparatus. But the box placed on the lunar disc might perhaps exhibit some strange phenomena. In any case it would be interesting to see whether the moon, like the earth, submitted to magnetic influence.

A hypsometer to measure the height of the lunar mountains, a sextant to take the height of the sun, glasses which would be useful as they neared the moon—all these instruments were carefully looked over and pronounced in good order despite the violent shock.

The pickaxes and different tools which were Nicholl's special choice, as well as the sacks of different kinds of grain and shrubs which Michel Ardan hoped to transplant into Selenite ground were stowed away in the upper part of

the projectile. There was a sort of granary there, loaded
with things which the extravagant Frenchman had heaped
up. What they were no one knew, and the good-tempered
fellow did not explain. Now and then he climbed up by
cramp irons riveted to the walls, but kept the inspection to
himself. He arranged and rearranged, he plunged his hand
rapidly into certain mysterious boxes, singing in one of the
falsest of voices an old French refrain to enliven the situation.

Barbicane observed with some interest that his guns and
other arms had not been damaged. These were important,
because, heavily loaded, they were to help lessen the fall of
the projectile, when drawn by the lunar attraction (after
having passed the point of neutral attraction) onto the
moon's surface. This fall ought to be six times less rapid
than it would have been on the earth's surface, thanks to the
difference of bulk.

The inspection ended with general satisfaction, each returned to watch space through the side windows and the
lower glass coverlid. There was the same view. The whole
extent of the celestial sphere swarmed with stars and constellations of wonderful purity, enough to delight any
astronomer. On one side the sun, like the mouth of a lighted
oven, a dazzling disc without a halo, standing out on the
dark background of the sky. On the other, the moon returning its fire by reflection, and apparently motionless in the
midst of the starry world. Then, a large spot seemingly
nailed to the firmament, bordered by a silvery cord: it was
the earth. Here and there nebulous masses like large flakes
of starry snow; and above and below, an immense ring
formed by an impalpable dust of stars, the "Milky Way," in
the midst of which the sun ranks only as a star of the fourth

magnitude. The observers could not take their eyes from this novel spectacle, of which no description could give an adequate idea. What reflections it suggested. What emotions hitherto unknown awoke in their souls. Barbicane wished to begin the relation of his journey while under its first impressions, and hour after hour took notes, writing quietly with his large square writing in a businesslike style.

During this time Nicholl, the calculator, looked over the minutes of their passage, and worked out figures with unparalleled dexterity. Michel Ardan chatted first with Barbicane, who did not answer him, and then with Nicholl, who did not hear him, with Diana, who understood none of his theories, and lastly with himself, questioning and answering, going and coming, busy with a thousand details, at one time bent over the lower glass, at another roosting in the heights of the projectile, and always singing. In this microcosm he represented French loquacity and excitability, and we beg you to believe that they were well represented. The day, or rather (for the expression is not correct) the lapse of 12 hours, which forms a day upon earth, closed with a plentiful supper carefully prepared. No accident of any nature had yet happened to shake the travelers' confidence. So, full of hope, already sure of success, they slept peacefully while the projectile under a uniformly decreasing speed was crossing the sky.

4. A Little Algebra

THE NIGHT passed without incident. The word "night," however, is scarcely applicable.

The position of the projectile with regard to the sun did

not change. Astronomically, it was daylight on the lower part and night on the upper; when, in this narrative, these words are used, they represent the lapse of time between the rising and setting of the sun upon the earth.

The travelers' sleep was rendered more peaceful by the projectile's excessive speed, for it seemed absolutely motionless. Not a motion betrayed its onward course through space. The rate of progress, however rapid it may be, cannot produce any sensible effect on the human frame when it takes place in a vacuum, or when the encircling air moves at the same rate as the body in it. What inhabitant of the earth perceives its speed, which, however, is at the rate of 68,000 miles per hour? Motion under such conditions is "felt" no more than repose. When a body is in repose it will remain so as long as no strange force displaces it; if moving, it will not stop unless an obstacle comes in its way. This indifference to motion or repose is called inertia.

Barbicane and his companions might have believed themselves perfectly stationary, being shut up in the projectile. Indeed, the effect would have been the same if they had been on the outside of it. Had it not been for the moon, which was increasing above them, they might have sworn that they were floating in complete stagnation.

That morning, the 3rd of December, the travelers were awakened by a joyous but unexpected noise: it was the crowing of a cock which sounded through the car. Michel Ardan, who was the first on his feet, climbed to the top of the projectile, and shutting a box, the lid of which was partly open, said in a low voice, "Will you hold your tongue? That creature will spoil my design!"

But Nicholl and Barbicane were awake.

"A cock!" said Nicholl.

"Why no, my friends," Michel answered quickly. "It was I who wished to awake you by this rural sound." So saying, he gave vent to a splendid cock-a-doodle-do which would have done honor to the proudest of poultry yards.

The two Americans could not help laughing.

"Fine talent that," said Nicholl, looking suspiciously at his companion.

"Yes," said Michel. "A joke in my country. It is very Gallic. They play the cock so in the best society."

Then, turning the conversation, Ardan said: "Barbicane, do you know what I have been thinking of all night?"

"No," answered the president.

"Of our Cambridge friends. You have already remarked that I am an ignoramus in mathematical subjects, and it is impossible for me to find out how the savants of the observatory were able to calculate what initial speed the projectile ought to have on leaving the columbiad in order to attain the moon."

"You mean to say," replied Barbicane, "to attain that neutral point where the terrestrial and lunar attractions are equal. Starting from that point, situated about nine-tenths of the distance traveled over, the projectile would simply fall upon the moon, on account of its weight."

"So be it," said Michel. "But, once more, how could they calculate the initial speed?"

"Nothing can be easier," replied Barbicane.

"And you knew how to make that calculation?" asked Michel Ardan.

"Perfectly. Nicholl and I would have made it, if the observatory had not saved us the trouble."

"Very well, old Barbicane," replied Michel. "They might have cut off my head, beginning at my feet, before they could have made me solve that problem."

"Because you do not know algebra," answered Barbicane quietly.

"Ah, there you are, you eaters of x^1. You think you have said all when you have said 'algebra.' "

"Michel," said Barbicane, "can you use a forge without a hammer, or a plow without a plowshare?"

"Hardly."

"Well, algebra is a tool, like the plow or the hammer, and a good tool to those who know how to use it."

"Seriously?"

"Quite seriously."

"And can you use that tool in my presence?"

"If it will interest you."

"And show me how they calculated the initiatory speed of our car?"

"Yes, my worthy friend. Taking into consideration all the elements of the problem, the distance from the center of the earth to the center of the moon, of the radius of the earth, of its bulk, and of the bulk of the moon, I can tell exactly what ought to be the initiatory speed of the projectile, and that by a simple formula."

"Let us see."

"You shall see it, only I shall not give you the real course drawn by the projectile between the moon and the earth in considering their motion around the sun. No, I shall consider these two orbs as perfectly motionless, which will answer all our purpose."

"And why?"

"Because to do otherwise would be trying to solve the

problem called 'the problem of the three bodies,' for which the integral calculus is not yet far enough advanced."

"Then," said Michel Ardan, in his sly tone, "mathematics has not said its last word?"

"Certainly not," replied Barbicane.

"Well, perhaps the moon beings have carried integral calculus farther than you have. But tell me, what is this 'integral calculus?' "

"It is a calculation which is the opposite of the differential," replied Barbicane seriously.

"Much obliged. It is all very clear, no doubt."

"And now," continued Barbicane, "a slip of paper and a bit of pencil, and before a half-hour is over I will have found the required formula."

Half an hour had not elapsed before Barbicane, raising his head, showed Michel Ardan a page covered with algebraical signs, in which the general formula for the solution was contained.

"Well, and does Nicholl understand what that means?"

"Of course, Michel," replied the captain. "All these signs, which seem obscure to you, form the plainest, the clearest, and the most logical language to those who know how to read it."

"And you pretend, Nicholl," asked Michel, "that by means of these hieroglyphics, more incomprehensible than the Egyptian ibis, you can find what initiatory speed it was necessary to give to the projectile?"

"Incontestably," Nicholl replied. "Even by this same formula I can tell you its speed at any point of its transit."

"On your word?"

"On my word."

"Then you are as clever as our president."

"No, Michel. The difficult part is what Barbicane has done, that is, to get an equation which shall satisfy all the conditions of the problem. The remainder is only a question of arithmetic, requiring merely the knowledge of the four rules."

"That is something!" replied Michel Ardan, who for his life could not do addition right, and who defined the rules of this activity as a Chinese puzzle which allowed one to obtain all sorts of totals.

"The expression v zero, which you see in that equation, is the speed which the projectile will have on leaving the atmosphere."

"Just so," said Nicholl. "It is from that point that we must calculate the velocity, since we know already that the velocity at departure was exactly one and a half times more than on leaving the atmosphere."

"I understand no more," said Michel.

"It is a very simple calculation," said Barbicane.

"Not as simple as I am," retorted Michel.

"That means that when our projectile reached the limits of the terrestrial atmosphere it had already lost one-third of its initiatory speed."

"As much as that?"

"Yes, my friend, merely by friction against the atmospheric strata. You understand that the faster it goes the more resistance it meets with from the air."

"That I admit," answered Michel, "and I understand it, although your x's and zero's, and algebraic formula are rattling in my head like nails in a bag."

"First effects of algebra," replied Barbicane. "And now,

to finish, we are going to prove the given number of these different expressions, that is, work out their value."

"Finish it!" replied Michel.

Barbicane took the paper, and began again to make his calculations with great rapidity. Nicholl looked over and greedily read the work as it proceeded.

"That's it! That's it!" at last he cried.

"It is clear?" asked Barbicane.

"It is written in letters of fire," said Nicholl.

"Wonderful fellows!" muttered Ardan.

"Do you understand it at last?" asked Barbicane.

"Do I understand it?" cried Ardan. "My head is splitting with it."

"And now," said Nicholl, "to find out the speed of the projectile when it left the atmosphere we have only to calculate that."

The captain, as a practical man equal to all difficulties, began to write with frightful rapidity. Divisions and multiplications grew under his fingers. The figures were like hail on the white page. Barbicane watched him, while Michel Ardan nursed a growing headache with both hands.

"Very well?" asked Barbicane, after some minutes' silence.

"Well!" replied Nicholl. "Every calculation made, *v* zero, that is to say, the speed necessary for the projectile on leaving the atmosphere, to enable it to reach the equal point of attraction, ought to be——"

"Yes?" said Barbicane.

"Thirty-six thousand feet per second."

"What!" exclaimed Barbicane, starting. "You say——"

"Thirty-six thousand feet."

"The devil!" cried the president, making a gesture of despair.

"What is the matter?" asked Michel Ardan, much surprised.

"What is the matter! Why, if at this moment our speed had already diminished one-third by friction, the initial speed ought to have been——"

"Forty-eight thousand feet."

"And the Cambridge Observatory declared that 36,000 feet was enough at starting, and our projectile, which only started with that speed——"

"Well?" asked Nicholl.

"Well, it will not be enough."

"Good."

"We shall not be able to reach the neutral point."

"The deuce!"

"We shall not even get halfway."

"In the name of the projectile!" exclaimed Michel Ardan, jumping as if it were already on the point of striking the terrestrial globe.

"And we shall fall back upon the earth!"

5. The Cold of Space

THIS REVELATION came like a thunderbolt. Who could have expected such an error in calculation? Barbicane would not believe it. Nicholl revised his figures: they were exact. As to the formula which had determined them, they could not doubt its validity: it was evident that an initial velocity of 48,000 feet in the first second was necessary to enable them to reach the neutral point.

The three friends looked at each other silently. There was no thought of breakfast. Barbicane, with clenched teeth, knitted brows, and hands clasped convulsively, was watching through the window. Nicholl had crossed his arms, and was examining his calculations. Michel Ardan was muttering:

"That is just like those scientific men: they never do anything else. I would give 20 pistoles if we could fall upon the Cambridge Observatory and crush it, together with the whole lot of dabblers in figures which it contains."

Suddenly a thought struck the captain, which he at once communicated to Barbicane.

"It is seven o'clock in the morning," he said, "we have already been gone 32 hours. More than half our passage is over, and we are not falling that I am aware of."

Barbicane did not answer, but, after a rapid glance at the captain, picked up a pair of compasses to measure the angular distance of the terrestrial globe. Then, from the lower window, he took an exact observation and noticed that the projectile was apparently stationary. Rising and wiping his forehead, on which large drops of perspiration were standing, he put some figures on paper. Nicholl understood that the president was deducting from the terrestrial diameter the projectile's distance from the earth. He watched him anxiously.

"No," exclaimed Barbicane, after some moments, "no, we are not falling! No, we are already more than 125,000 miles from the earth. We have passed the point at which the projectile would have stopped if its speed had only been 36,000 feet at starting. We are still going up."

"That is evident," replied Nicholl, "and we must conclude that our initial speed, under the power of the 400,000 pounds of guncotton, must have exceeded the required 36,000 feet. Now I can understand how, after 13 minutes only, we met the second satellite, which gravitates around the earth at close to 5,000 miles' distance."

"And this explanation is the more probable," added Barbicane, "because, in throwing off the water enclosed between its partition breaks, the projectile found itself lightened of a considerable weight."

"Just so," said Nicholl.

"Ah, my brave Nicholl, we are saved!"

"Very well, then," said Michel Ardan quietly. "As we are safe, let us have breakfast."

Nicholl was not mistaken. The initial speed had been, very fortunately, much above that estimated by the Cambridge Observatory; but the Cambridge Observatory had nevertheless made a mistake.

The travelers, recovered from this false alarm, breakfasted merrily. If they ate a great deal, they talked more. Their confidence was greater after than before "the incident of the algebra."

"Why should we not succeed?" said Michel Ardan; "why should we not arrive safely? We are launched; we have no obstacle before us, no stones in our way. The road is open, more so than that of a ship battling with the sea, more open than that of a balloon battling with the wind. And if a ship can reach its destination, a balloon go where it pleases, why cannot our projectile attain its end and aim?"

"It *will* attain it," said Barbicane.

"If only to do honor to the Americans," added Michel Ardan, "the only people who could bring such an enterprise to a happy termination, and the only one which could produce a President Barbicane. Ah, now we are no longer uneasy, I began to think, What will become of us? We shall get right royally weary."

Barbicane and Nicholl made a gesture of denial.

"But I have provided for the contingency, my friends," replied Michel, "you have only to speak and I have chess, draughts, cards, and dominoes at your disposal. Nothing is wanting but a billiard table."

"What!" exclaimed Barbicane. "You brought such trifles?"

"Certainly," replied Michel, "and not only to distract ourselves, but also with the laudable intention of endowing the moon beings' smoking divans with them."

"My friend," said Barbicane, "if the moon is inhabited, its inhabitants must have appeared some thousands of years before those of the earth, for we cannot doubt that their star is much older than ours. If, then, these Selenites have existed their hundreds of thousands of years, and if their brain is of the same organization as the human brain, they have already invented all that we have invented, and even what we may invent in future ages. They have nothing to learn from *us,* and we have everything to learn from *them.*"

"What!" said Michel. "You believe that they have artists like Phidias, Michelangelo, or Raphael?"

"Yes."

"Poets like Homer, Virgil, Milton, Shakespeare, and Hugo?"

"I am sure of it."

"Philosophers like Plato, Aristotle, Descartes, Kant?"

"I have no doubt of it."

"Scientific men like Archimedes, Euclid, Pascal, Newton?"

"I could swear it."

"Then, friend Barbicane, if they are strong as we are, and even stronger—these Selenites—why have they not tried to communicate with the earth? Why have they not launched a lunar projectile to our terrestrial regions?"

"Who told you that they have never done so?" said Barbicane seriously.

"Indeed," added Nicholl, "it would be easier for them than for us, for two reasons. First, because the attraction on the moon's surface is six times less than on that of the earth, which would allow a projectile to rise more easily. Second, because it would be enough to send such a projectile only at 20,000 miles instead of 200,000 which would require the force of projection to be ten times less strong."

"Then," continued Michel, "I repeat it, why have they not done it?"

"And I repeat," said Barbicane, "who told you that they have not done it?"

"When?"

"Thousands of years before man appeared on earth."

"And the projectile—where is the projectile? I demand to see the projectile."

"My friend," replied Barbicane, "the sea covers five-sixths of our globe. From that we may draw five good reasons for supposing that the lunar projectile, if ever launched, is now at the bottom of the Atlantic or the Pacific, unless it sped into some crevasse at that period when the crust of the earth was not yet hardened."

"Old Barbicane," said Michel, "you have an answer for

everything, and I bow before your wisdom. But there is one hypothesis that would suit me better than all the others, which is, that the Selenites, being older than we, are wiser, and have not invented gunpowder."

At this moment Diana joined in the conversation by a sonorous barking. She was asking for her breakfast.

"Ah," said Michel Ardan, "in our discussion we have forgotten Diana and Satellite."

Immediately a good-sized pie was given to the dog, who devoured it hungrily.

"Do you see, Barbicane," said Michel, "we should have made a second Noah's ark of this projectile, and borne with us to the moon a couple of every kind of domestic animal."

"I dare say, but room would have failed us."

"Oh," said Michel, "we might have squeezed a little."

"The fact is," replied Nicholl, "that cows, bulls, and horses would have been very useful on the lunar continent, but unfortunately the car could neither have been made a stable nor a shed."

"Well, we might at least have brought a donkey, only a little donkey, I love those old donkeys. They are the least favored animals in creation; they are not only beaten while alive, but even after they are dead."

"How do you make that out?" asked Barbicane.

"Why," said Michel, "they make their skins into drums."

Barbicane and Nicholl could not help laughing at this ridiculous remark. But a cry from their merry companion stopped them. The latter was leaning over the spot where Satellite lay. He rose, saying: "My good Satellite is no longer ill."

"Ah!" said Nicholl.

"No," answered Michel, "he is dead! There," added he,

in a piteous tone, "that is embarrassing. I much fear, my poor Diana, that you will leave no progeny in the lunar regions!"

Indeed the unfortunate Satellite had not survived his wound. He was quite dead. Michel Ardan looked at his friends with a rueful countenance.

"One question presents itself," said Barbicane. "We cannot keep the dead body of this dog with us for the next forty-eight hours."

"No, certainly not," replied Nicholl. "But our windows are fixed on hinges—they can be let down. We will open one and throw the body out into space."

The president thought for some moments, and then said:

"Yes, we must do so, but at the same time taking very great precautions."

"Why?" asked Michel.

"For two reasons which you will understand," answered Barbicane. "The first relates to the air shut up in the projectile, and of which we must lose as little as possible."

"But we manufacture the air?"

"Only in part. We make only the oxygen, my worthy Michel. And with regard to that, we must watch that the apparatus does not furnish the oxygen in too great a quantity, for an excess would bring us very serious physiological troubles. But if we make the oxygen, we do not make the azote, the medium which the lungs do not absorb, and which ought to remain intact. That azote will escape rapidly through the open window."

"Oh, the little time required for throwing out poor Satellite?" said Michel.

"Agreed. But we must act quickly."

"And the second reason?" asked Michel.

"The second reason is that we must not let the outer cold, which is exceedingly great, penetrate the projectile or we shall be frozen to death."

"But the sun?"

"The sun warms our projectile, which absorbs its rays, but it does not warm the vacuum in which we are floating at this moment. Where there is no air, there can be neither heat nor diffused light. The same with darkness: it is both cold and dark where the sun's rays do not strike directly. The temperature up here is produced only by the radiation of the stars. It is very low and that is what the terrestrial globe would undergo if the sun disappeared one day."

"Which is not to be feared," replied Nicholl.

"Who knows?" said Michel Ardan. "But, in admitting that the sun does not go out, might it not happen that the earth might move away from it?"

"There!" said Barbicane. "There is Michel with his ideas."

"And," continued Michel, "do we not know that in 1861 the earth passed through the tail of a comet? Or let us suppose there exists a comet whose power of attraction is greater than that of the sun. The earth's orbit will bend toward the wandering star, and the earth, becoming its satellite, will be drawn such a distance that the rays of the sun will have no action on its surface."

"That *might* happen, indeed," replied Barbicane, "but the consequences of such a displacement need not be so formidable as you suppose."

"And why not?"

"Because the heat and the cold would be equalized on

our globe. It has been calculated that, had our earth been carried along in its course by the comet of 1861, at its nearest approach to the sun, it would have undergone a heat 28,000 times greater than that of summer. But this heat, which is sufficient to evaporate the waters, would have formed a thick ring of cloud, which would have modified that excessive temperature. Hence the compensation between the cold of the earth when it is farthest from the sun, and the heat when it is closest. This compensation probably makes the mean temperature bearable."

"How many degrees," asked Nicholl, "is the temperature of the planetary spaces?"

"Formerly," replied Barbicane, "it was greatly exaggerated. But now, after the calculations of Fourier, of the French Academy of Science, it is not supposed to exceed 70° or 80° Fahrenheit below zero."

"No more?" asked Michel.

"No more," replied Barbicane. "Yet the temperature which was observed in the polar regions, at Melville Island and Fort Reliance, that is, was 76° Fahrenheit below zero."

"If I mistake not," said Nicholl, "Pouillet, another savant, estimates the temperature of space at 250° Fahrenheit below zero. We shall, however, be able to verify these calculations for ourselves."

"Not at present, because the solar rays, beating directly upon our thermometer, would, on the contrary, give a very high temperature. But when we arrive in the moon, during its fifteen days of night at either face, we shall have leisure to make the experiment, for our satellite lies in a vacuum."

"You mean it is a perfect vacuum?" asked Michel.

"It is absolutely void of air."

"And is the air replaced by nothing whatever?"

"By the ether only," replied Barbicane.

"And pray what is the ether?"

"The ether, my friend, is an agglomeration of imponderable atoms, which, relative to their dimensions, are as far removed from one another as the celestial bodies are in space. It is these atoms which, by their vibratory motion, produce both light and heat in the universe."

They now proceeded to the burial of Satellite. They had merely to drop him into space, in the same way that sailors drop a body into the sea. But, as President Barbicane suggested, they must act quickly, so as to lose as little as possible of that air whose elasticity would rapidly have spread it into space. The bolts of the right scuttle, the opening of which measured about 12 inches across, were carefully drawn, while Michel, quite grieved, prepared to launch his dog into space. The glass, raised by a powerful lever, which enabled it to overcome the pressure of the inside air on the walls of the projectile, turned rapidly on its hinges, and Satellite was thrown out. Scarcely a particle of air could have escaped, and the operation was so successful that later on Barbicane did not fear to dispose of the rubbish which encumbered the car.

6. Question and Answer

ON THE 4th of December, when the travelers awoke after 54 hours' journey, the chronometer marked five o'clock of the terrestrial morning. In time it was just over five hours and 40 minutes, half of that assigned to their sojourn in the projectile. But they had already accomplished nearly seven tenths of the way. This peculiarity was due to their regularly decreasing speed.

Now when they observed the earth through the lower window it looked like nothing more than a dark spot drowned in the solar rays. No more crescent, no more cloudy light. The next day, at midnight, the earth would be *new*, at the very moment when the moon would be full. Above, the orb of night was nearing the line followed by the projectile, so as to meet it at the given hour. All around the black sky was studded with brilliant points, which seemed to move slowly. But, at the great distance the travelers were from them, their relative size did not seem to change. The sun and stars appeared exactly as they do to us upon earth. As to the moon, it was considerably larger. But the travelers' glasses, not very powerful, did not allow them as yet to make any useful observations upon its surface, or reconnoiter it topographically or geologically.

Thus the time passed in never-ending conversations about the moon. Each one brought forward his own contingent of particular facts: Barbicane and Nicholl always serious, Michel Ardan always enthusiastic. The projectile, its situation, its direction, incidents which might happen, the precautions necessitated by their fall onto the moon, were inexhaustible matters of conjecture.

As they were breakfasting, a question of Michel's, relating to the projectile, provoked rather a curious answer from Barbicane, which is worth repeating. Michel, supposing it to be roughly stopped, while still under its formidable initial speed, wished to know what the consequences of the stoppage would have been.

"But," said Barbicane, "I do not see how it could have been stopped."

"But let us suppose so," said Michel.

"It is an impossible supposition," said the practical Barbicane, "unless the impulsive force had failed. But even then its speed would diminish by degrees, and it would not have stopped suddenly."

"Suppose it had struck a body in space."

"What body?"

"Why, that enormous meteor which we met."

"Then," said Nicholl, "the projectile would have been broken into a thousand pieces, and we with it."

"More than that," replied Barbicane, "we should have been burned to death."

"Burned?" exclaimed Michel. "By Jove! I am sorry it did not happen, 'just to see.'"

"And you would have seen," replied Barbicane. "It is known now that heat is only a modification of motion. When water is warmed—that is to say, when heat is added to it—its particles are set in motion."

"Well," said Michel, "that is an ingenious theory!"

"And a true one, my worthy friend, for it explains every phenomenon of caloric action. Heat is but the motion of atoms, a simple oscillation of the particles of a body. When they apply the brake to a train, the train comes to a stop. But what becomes of the motion which it had previously possessed? It is transformed into heat, and the brake becomes hot. Why do they grease the axles of the wheels? To prevent their heating, because this heat would be generated by the motion which is thus lost by transformation."

"Yes, I understand," replied Michel, "perfectly. For example, when I have run a long time, when I am swimming, when I am perspiring in large drops, why am I obliged to stop? Simply because my motion is changed into heat."

Barbicane could not help smiling at Michel's reply. Then, returning to his theory, said:

"Thus, in case of a shock, it would have been with our projectile as with a bullet, which is twisted out of shape or even melted into a thin film when it strikes a metal plate; it is its motion which is turned into heat. Consequently, I affirm that if our projectile had struck the meteor, its speed thus suddenly checked would have raised a heat great enough to turn it into vapor instantaneously."

"Then," asked Nicholl, "what would happen if the earth's motion were to stop suddenly?"

"Its temperature would be raised to such a pitch," said Barbicane, "that it would be at once reduced to vapor."

"Well," said Michel, "that is a way of ending the earth which will greatly simplify things."

"And if the earth fell upon the sun?" asked Nicholl.

"According to calculation," replied Barbicane, "the fall would develop a heat equal to that produced by 16,000 globes of coal, each equal in bulk to our globe."

"Good additional heat for the sun," replied Michel Ardan, "of which the inhabitants of Uranus or Neptune would doubtless not complain. They must be perishing with cold on their planets."

"Thus, my friends," said Barbicane, "all motion suddenly stopped produces heat. And this theory allows us to infer that the heat of the solar disc is fed by a hail of meteors falling incessantly on its surface. They have even calculated——"

"Oh, dear," murmured Michel, "the figures are coming."

"They have even calculated," continued the imperturbable Barbicane, "that the shock of each meteor on the sun ought to produce a heat equal to that of 4,000 masses of coal of an equal bulk."

"And what is the solar heat?" asked Michel.

"It is equal to that produced by the combustion of a layer of coal surrounding the sun to a depth of forty-seven miles."

"And it does not roast us!" exclaimed Michel.

"No," replied Barbicane, "because the terrestrial atmosphere absorbs four-tenths of the solar heat. Besides, the quantity of heat intercepted by the earth is but a billionth part of the entire radiation."

"I see that all is for the best," said Michel, "and that this atmosphere is a useful invention for it not only allows us to breathe, but it prevents us from roasting."

"Yes," said Nicholl, "unfortunately, it will not be the same in the moon."

"Bah!" said Michel, always hopeful. "If there are inhabitants, they must breathe. If there are no longer any, they must have left enough oxygen for three people, if only at the bottom of ravines, where its own weight will cause it to accumulate, and we will not climb the mountains. That is all." And Michel, rising, went to look at the moon, which shone with intolerable brilliancy.

"By Jove," said he, "it must be hot up there!"

"Without considering," replied Nicholl, "that the day lasts 360 hours!"

"And to compensate that," said Barbicane, "the nights have the same length. And since heat escapes by radiation, the temperature is not much greater than that of the planetary space."

"A pretty country, that!" exclaimed Michel. "Never mind! I wish I was there! Ah! my dear comrades, it will be rather curious to have the earth for our moon, to see it rise on the horizon, to recognize the shape of its continents, and to say to oneself, 'There is America, there is Europe.' And to follow the earth when it is about to lose itself in the sun's rays! By the way, Barbicane, are there eclipses on the moon?"

"Yes, eclipses of the sun," replied Barbicane, "when the centers of the three orbs are on a line, the earth being in the middle. But they are only partial, during which the earth allows the greater portion of the sun to be seen."

"And why," asked Nicholl, "is there no total eclipse? Does not the cone of the shadow cast by the earth extend beyond the moon?"

"Yes, if we do not take into consideration the refraction produced by the terrestrial atmosphere. No, if we take that refraction into consideration. Thus let δ be the horizontal parallel and p the apparent semidiameter——"

"Oh!" said Michel. "Do speak plainly, you man of algebra!"

"Very well," replied Barbicane. "In popular language the mean distance from the moon to the earth being sixty times the earth's radius, the length of the cone of the shadow, on account of the refraction, is reduced to less than forty-two radii. The result is that when there are eclipses, the moon finds itself beyond the cone of pure shadow, and that the sun sends the moon its rays, not only from its edges, but also from its center."

"Then," said Michel, in a merry tone, "why are there eclipses, when there ought not to be any?"

"Simply because the solar rays are weakened by this refraction, and the atmosphere through which they pass extinguishes the greater part of them!"

"That reason satisfies me," replied Michel. "Besides, we shall see when we get there. Now, tell me, Barbicane, do you believe that the moon is an old comet?"

"There's an idea!"

"Yes," replied Michel, with an amiable swagger, "I have a few ideas of that sort."

"But that idea does not spring from Michel," answered Nicholl.

"Well, then, I am a plagiarist."

"No doubt about it. According to the ancients, the Arcadians pretend that their ancestors inhabited the earth before the moon became its satellite. Starting from this fact, some scientific men have seen in the moon a comet whose orbit will one day bring it so near to the earth that it will be held there by its attraction."

"Is there any truth in this hypothesis?" asked Michel.

"None whatever," said Barbicane, "and the proof is that the moon has preserved no trace of the gaseous envelope which always accompanies comets."

"But," continued Nicholl, "before becoming the earth's satellite, could not the moon pass so near the sun as by evaporation to get rid of all those gaseous substances?"

"It is possible, friend Nicholl, but not probable."

"Why not?"

"Because—— Faith, I do not know."

"Ah," exclaimed Michel, "what hundreds of volumes we might make of all that we do not know!"

"Ah, indeed! What time is it?" asked Barbicane.

"Three o'clock," answered Nicholl.

"How time goes," said Michel, "in the conversation of scientific men such as we are! Certainly, I feel I know too much. I feel that I am becoming a well!"

Saying which, Michel hoisted himself to the roof of the projectile, "to observe the moon better," he pretended. During this time his companions were watching through the lower glass. Nothing new to note.

When Michel Ardan came down, he went to the side window, and suddenly they heard an exclamation of surprise!

"What is it?" asked Barbicane.

The president approached the window, and saw a sort of flattened sack floating some yards from the projectile. This object seemed as motionless as the projectile, and the travelers consequently deduced that it must have the same rate of speed as the projectile.

"What is that machine?" continued Michel Ardan. "Is it one of the bodies of space which our projectile keeps within its attraction, and which will accompany it to the moon?"

"What astonishes me," said Nicholl, "is that the specific weight of the body, which is certainly less than that of the projectile, allows it to keep so perfectly on a level with it."

"Nicholl," replied Barbicane, after a moment's reflection, "I do not know what the object is, but I do know why it maintains our level."

"And why?"

"Because we are floating in space, my dear captain, and in space bodies fall or move, which is the same thing, with equal speed whatever be their weight or form; it is the air which by its resistance creates these differences in weight. When you create a vacuum in a tube, the objects you send through it, grains of dust or grains of lead, fall with the same rapidity. Here in space is the same cause and the same effect."

"Just so," said Nicholl, "and everything we throw out of the projectile will accompany it until it reaches the moon."

"Ah, fools that we are!" exclaimed Michel.

"Why that expletive?" asked Barbicane.

"Because we might have filled the projectile with useful objects, books, instruments, tools, etc. We could have thrown them all out, and all would have followed in our train. But happy thought! Why cannot we walk outside like the meteor? Why cannot we launch into space through the window? What enjoyment it would be to feel oneself thus suspended in ether, more favored than the birds who must use their wings to keep themselves up!"

"Granted," said Barbicane, "but how to breathe?"

"Hang the air, to fail so inopportunely!"

"But if it did not fail, Michel, your density being less than that of the projectile, you would soon be left behind."

"Then we must remain in our car?"

"We must!"

"Ah!" exclaimed Michel, in a loud voice.

"What is the matter?" asked Nicholl.

"I know, I guess, what this pretended meteor is! It is no asteroid accompanying us! It is not a piece of a planet."

"What is it then?" asked Barbicane.

"It is our unfortunate dog! It is Diana's husband!"

Indeed, this deformed, unrecognizable object, reduced to nothing, was the body of Satellite, flattened like a bagpipe without wind, and ever mounting, mounting.

7. A Moment of Intoxication

THUS A new phenomenon, curious but explicable, was presented to the travelers' view. Every object thrown from the projectile would follow the same course and never stop until it did. This was a subject for conversation which the whole evening could not exhaust.

Besides, the excitement of the three travelers increased as they drew near the end of their journey. They expected unforeseen incidents and new phenomena. Nothing would have astonished them in the frame of mind they then were in. Their overexcited imaginations went faster than the projectile, whose speed was evidently diminishing, though insensibly to themselves. But the moon grew larger to their eyes, and they fancied if they stretched out their hands they could seize it.

The next day, the 5th of December, all three travelers were up at five in the morning. That day was to be the last of their journey, if all calculations were true. That very night, at twelve o'clock, in 18 hours, exactly at the full moon, they would reach their destination. The next midnight would see that journey ended, the most extraordinary of ancient or modern times. Thus from the first of the morning, through the scuttles silvered by its rays, they saluted the moon with a confident and joyous hurrah.

The moon was advancing majestically along the starry firmament. A few more degrees, and it would reach the exact point of rendezvous with the projectile.

According to his own observations, Barbicane reckoned that they would land on its northern hemisphere, where immense plains stretched and where mountains were rare. A favorable circumstance if, as they thought, the lunar atmosphere was stored only in its depths.

"Besides," Michel Ardan observed, "a plain is easier to disembark on than a mountain. A moon being, deposited in Europe on the summit of Mont Blanc, or in Asia on the top of the Himalayas, would not be quite in the right place."

"And," added Captain Nicholl, "on a flat ground the projectile will remain motionless once it has touched; whereas on a declivity it would roll like an avalanche, and not being squirrels we should not come out safe and sound. So it is all for the best."

Indeed, the success of the audacious attempt no longer appeared doubtful. But Barbicane was preoccupied with one thought. Not wishing to make his companions uneasy, however, he kept silence on the subject.

The direction the projectile was taking toward the moon's northern hemisphere showed that its course had been slightly altered. According to the original calculations, the projectile should have hit the moon at its center. If it did not land there, there must have been some deviation. What had caused it? Barbicane could neither imagine nor determine the importance of the deviation, for there were no points to go by.

He hoped, however, that it would have no other result

than that of bringing them near the upper border of the moon, a region more suitable for landing.

Without imparting his uneasiness to his companions, Barbicane contented himself with constantly observing the moon, in order to see whether the course of the projectile would be altered. It would be terrible if the projectile failed in its aim and, being carried beyond the disc, was launched into interplanetary space. At that moment the moon, instead of appearing flat like a disc, began to show its convexity. If the sun's rays had struck it obliquely, the shadow thrown would have brought out the high mountains, which would have been clearly detached. The eye might have gazed into the crater's gaping abysses, and followed the capricious fissures which wound through the immense plains. But all relief was as yet leveled in intense brilliancy. They could scarcely distinguish those large spots which give to the moon the appearance of a human face.

"Face, indeed!" said Michel Ardan. "But I am sorry for the amiable sister of Apollo. A very pitted face!"

The travelers, now so near the end of their journey, were incessantly observing this new world. They imagined themselves walking through its unknown countries, climbing its highest peaks, descending into its lowest depths. Here and there they fancied they saw vast seas, scarcely kept together under so rarefied an atmosphere, and watercourses emptying the mountain tributaries. Leaning over the abyss, they hoped to catch some sounds from that orb forever mute in the solitude of space.

A vague uneasiness took possession of them as they neared the end. This uneasiness would have been doubled had they felt how their speed had decreased. It would have seemed to them quite insufficient to carry them to the end. It was because the projectile then "weighed" almost nothing. Its weight was ever decreasing, and would be entirely annihilated on that line where the lunar and terrestrial attractions would neutralize each other.

But in spite of his preoccupation, Michel Ardan did not forget to prepare the morning repast with his accustomed punctuality. They ate with good appetites. Nothing was so excellent as the soup liquefied by the heat of the gas; nothing better than the preserved meat. Some glasses of good French wine crowned the repast, causing Michel Ardan to remark that the lunar vines, warmed by that intense sun, ought to distill even more generous wines—that is, if they existed. In any case, the far-seeing Frenchman had taken care not to forget in his collection some precious cuttings of vines from the Médoc and Côte d'Or, upon which he founded his hopes.

The air-purifying apparatus worked with great regularity. Not an atom of carbonic acid resisted the potash; and as to the oxygen, Captain Nicholl said "it was of the first quality." The little watery vapor enclosed in the projectile mixing with the air tempered the dryness: many apartments in London, Paris, or New York, and many theaters, were certainly not in such a healthy condition.

But to keep it functioning properly, the apparatus must be kept in perfect order. Each morning Michel visited the escape regulators, tried the taps, and regulated the heat of the gas by the pyrometer. Everything had gone well up to that time, and the travelers began to acquire a degree of *embonpoint* which would have rendered them unrecognizable if their imprisonment had been prolonged to some months. In a word, they behaved like chickens in a coop: they were getting fat.

In looking through the window Barbicane saw the specter of the dog and other divers objects which had been thrown from the projectile obstinately following them. Diana howled lugubriously on seeing the remains of Satellite, which seemed as motionless as if they reposed on the solid earth.

"Do you know, my friends," said Michel Ardan, "that if one of us had succumbed to the shock consequent on departure we should have had a great deal of trouble to bury him? What am I saying? To *etherize* him, as here ether takes the place of earth. You see, the accusing body would have followed us into space like a remorse."

"That would have been sad," said Nicholl.

"Ah," continued Michel, "what I regret is not being able to take a walk outside. What voluptuousness to float amid this radiant ether, to bathe oneself in it, to wrap oneself in the sun's pure rays. If Barbicane had only thought of furnishing us with a diving apparatus and an air pump, I could have ventured out and assumed fanciful attitudes of feigned monsters on the top of the projectile."

"Well, old Michel," replied Barbicane, "you would not have made a feigned monster long, for in spite of your diver's dress, the air inside your body would have expanded and you would have burst like a shell, or rather like a balloon which has risen too high. So do not regret it, and do not forget this—as long as we float in space, all sentimental walks beyond the projectile are forbidden."

Michel Ardan allowed himself to be convinced to a certain extent. He admitted that the thing was difficult but not impossible, a word which he never uttered.

The conversation passed from this subject to another, not failing for an instant. It seemed to the three friends as though, under present conditions, ideas shot up in their brains as leaves shoot at the first warmth of spring. They felt bewildered. In the middle of the questions and answers which crossed each other Nicholl put one question which did not find an immediate solution.

"Ah, indeed!" said he. "It is all very well to go to the moon, but how to get back again?"

His two interlocutors looked surprised. One would have thought that this possibility now occurred to them for the first time.

"What do you mean by that, Nicholl?" asked Barbicane gravely.

"To ask for means to leave a country," added Michel, "when we have not yet arrived there, seems to me rather inopportune."

"I do not say that wishing to draw back," replied Nicholl. "But I repeat my question, and I ask, 'How shall we return?'"

"I know nothing about it," answered Barbicane.

"And I," said Michel, "if I had known how to return, I would never have started."

"There's an answer!" cried Nicholl.

"I quite approve of Michel's words," said Barbicane, "and add that the question has no real interest. Later, when we think it advisable to return, we will take counsel together. If the columbiad is not there, the projectile will be."

"That is a step certainly. A ball without a gun!"

"The gun," replied Barbicane, "can be manufactured. The powder can be made. Neither metals, saltpeter, nor coal can fail in the depths of the moon, and we need only shoot 20,000 miles in order to overcome the moon's attraction. Then we would fall back on the terrestrial globe by virtue of the mere laws of weight."

"Enough," said Michel with animation. "Let it be no longer a question of returning: we have already entertained it too long. As to communicating with our former earthly colleagues, that will not be difficult."

"And how?"

"By means of meteors launched by lunar volcanoes."

"Well thought of, Michel," said Barbicane in a convinced tone of voice. "Laplace has calculated that a force five times greater than that of our gun would suffice to send a meteor from the moon to the earth, and there is not one volcano which has not a greater power of propulsion than that."

"Hurrah!" exclaimed Michel. "These meteors are handy postmen and cost nothing. And how we shall be able to laugh at the post-office administration! But now I think of it——"

"What do you think of?"

"A capital idea. Why did we not fasten a thread to our projectile, and we could have exchanged telegrams with the earth?"

"The deuce!" answered Nicholl. "Do you consider as nothing weight of a thread 250,000 miles long?"

"As nothing. They could have trebled the columbiad's charge, they could have quadrupled or quintupled it!" exclaimed Michel, with whom the verb took a higher intonation each time.

"There is but one little objection to your proposition," replied Barbicane, "which is that, during the rotary motion of the globe, our thread would have wound itself around it like a chain on a capstan, and that it would inevitably have brought us to the ground."

"By the 39 stars of the Union," said Michel, "I have nothing but impracticable ideas today, ideas worthy of J. T. Maston. But I have a notion that, if we do not return to earth, J. T. Maston will be able to come to us."

"Yes, he'll come," replied Barbicane; "he is a worthy and a courageous comrade. Besides, what is easier? Is not the columbiad still buried in the soil of Florida? Isn't there plenty of cotton and nitric acid to manufacture the pyroxilin? Will not the moon again pass to the zenith of Florida? In 18 years' time will it not occupy exactly the same place as today?"

"Yes," continued Michel, "yes, Maston will come, and with him our friends Elphinstone, Blomsberry, all the members of the Gun Club, and they will be well received. And by and by they will run trains of projectiles between the earth and the moon! Hurrah for J. T. Maston!"

It is probable that, if the Hon. J. T. Maston did not hear the hurrahs uttered in his honor, his ears at least tingled. What was he doing then? Doubtless, posted in the Rocky Mountains, at the station of Longs Peak, he was trying to find the invisible projectile gravitating in space. If he was thinking of his dear companions, we must allow that they were not far behind him, and that, under the influence of a strange excitement, they were devoting to him their best thoughts.

But what was the source of this excitement, which was evidently growing upon the tenants of the projectile? Their sobriety could not be doubted. This strange irritation of the brain, must it be attributed to the peculiar circumstances under which they found themselves, to their proximity to the moon, from which only a few hours separated them, to some secret influence of the moon acting upon their nervous systems? Their faces were as rosy as if they had been exposed to the roaring flames of an oven; their voices resounded in loud accents; their words escaped like champagne corks driven out by carbonic gas; their gestures became alarmingly violent, considering the small amount of space in the capsule; and, strange to say, none of them noticed this great tension of the mind.

"Now," said Nicholl, in a short tone, "now that I do not know whether we shall ever return from the moon, I want to know what we are going to do there?"

"What we are going to do there?" replied Barbicane, stamping with his foot as if he were in a fencing match. "I do not know."

"You do not know!" exclaimed Michel, with a bellow which provoked a sonorous echo in the projectile.

"No, I have not even thought about it," retorted Barbicane, in the same loud tone.

"Well, I know," replied Michel.

"Speak, then," cried Nicholl, who could no longer contain the growling of his voice.

"I shall speak if it suits me!" exclaimed Michel, seizing his companions' arms with violence.

"It *must* suit you," said Barbicane, with an eye on fire and a threatening hand. "It was you who drew us into this frightful journey, and we want to know what for."

"Yes," said the captain, "now that I do not know *where* I am going, I want to know *why* I am going."

"Why?" exclaimed Michel, jumping a yard high. "Why? To take possession of the moon in the name of the United States; to colonize the lunar regions; to cultivate them, to people them, to transport thither all the prodigies of art, of science, and industry; to civilize the Selenites, unless they are more civilized than we are; and to constitute them a republic, if they are not already one!"

"And if there are no Selenites?" retorted Nicholl, who, under the influence of this unaccountable intoxication, was very contradictory.

"Who says there are no Selenites?" exclaimed Michel in a threatening tone.

"I do," howled Nicholl.

"Captain," said Michel, "do not repeat that insolence, or I will knock your teeth down your throat!"

The two adversaries were going to fall upon each other, and the incoherent discussion threatened to merge into a fight, when Barbicane intervened with one bound.

"Stop, miserable men," said he, separating his two companions. "If there are no moon beings, we will do without them."

"Yes," exclaimed Michel, who was not particular, "yes, we will do without them. Down with the Selenites!"

"The empire of the moon belongs to us," said Nicholl.

"Let us three constitute the republic."

"I will be the congress!" cried Michel.

"And I the senate," retorted Nicholl.

"And Barbicane, the president," howled Michel.

"Not a president elected by the nation," replied Barbicane.

"Very well, a president elected by the congress," cried

Michel. "And since I am the congress, you are unanimously elected!"

"Hurrah! Hurrah! Hurrah! for President Barbicane," exclaimed Nicholl.

"Hip! Hip! Hip!" vociferated Michel Ardan.

Then the president and the senate struck up in a tremendous voice the popular song "Yankee Doodle," while from the congress resounded the masculine tones of the "Marseillaise."

Then they began a frantic dance, with maniacal gestures, idiotic stampings, and somersaults like those of the boneless clowns in the circus. Diana, joining in the dance, and howling in her turn, jumped to the top of the projectile. An unaccountable flapping of wings was then heard amid most fantastic cockcrows, while five or six hens fluttered like bats against the walls.

Then the three traveling companions, acted upon by some mysterious influence above that of intoxication, inflamed by the air which had set their respiratory apparatus on fire, fell motionless to the bottom of the projectile.

8. The Weightless State

WHAT HAD happened? Whence the cause of this singular intoxication, the consequences of which might have been very disastrous? The answer lay in a simple blunder of Michel's, which, fortunately, Nicholl was able to correct.

After a perfect swoon, which lasted some minutes, the captain, recovering first, soon collected his scattered senses. Although he had breakfasted only two hours before, he felt a gnawing hunger, as if he had not eaten anything for several days. Everything about him, stomach and brain, was overexcited to the highest degree. He got up and demanded from Michel a supplementary repast. Michel, utterly done in, did not answer.

Nicholl then tried to prepare some tea which he intended to drink while eating a dozen sandwiches. He first tried to get some fire, and struck a match sharply. What was his surprise to see the sulphur shine with so extraordinary a brilliancy as to be almost unbearable to the eye. From the gas burner which he lit rose a flame like an electric light.

A revelation dawned on Nicholl's mind. That intensity of light, the physiological troubles which had arisen in him, the overexcitement of all his moral and quarrelsome faculties—he understood all.

"The oxygen!" he exclaimed.

And leaning over the air apparatus, he saw that the tap was allowing scentless, colorless oxygen to escape freely, life-giving, but in its pure state producing the gravest disorders in the system. Michel had blunderingly opened the tap of the apparatus to the full.

Nicholl hastened to stop the escape of oxygen with which the atmosphere was saturated, which would have been the death of the travelers, not by suffocation, but by combustion. Within an hour their lungs were restored to a normal condition. By degrees the three friends recovered from their intoxication, but they were obliged to sleep themselves sober over their oxygen-binge as a drunkard does over his wine.

When Michel learned his share of the responsibility of this incident, he was not really disconcerted. From his point

of view, the unexpected drunkenness broke the monotony
of the journey. Many foolish things had been said while
under its influence, but they were also quickly forgotten.

"And then," added the merry Frenchman, "I am not
sorry to have tasted a little of this heady gas. Do you know,
my friends, that a curious establishment might be founded
with rooms of oxygen, where people whose system is weakened could for a few hours live a more active life? Fancy
parties where the room was saturated with this heroic fluid,
theaters where it should be kept at high pressure. What
passion in the souls of the actors and spectators! What fire!
What enthusiasm! And if, instead of an assembly only a
whole people could be saturated, what activity in its func-
tions, what a supplement to life it would derive. From an
exhausted nation they might make a great and strong one,
and I know more than one state in old Europe which ought
to put itself under the regime of oxygen for the sake of its
health!"

Michel spoke with so much animation that one might
have fancied the oxygen tap was still open too wide. But a
few words from Barbicane soon scattered his enthusiasm.

"That is all very well, friend Michel," he said, "but will
you inform us where these chickens came from which have
mixed themselves up in our concert?"

"These chickens?"

"Yes."

Indeed, half-a-dozen chickens and a fine cock were walking about, flapping their wings and chattering.

"Ah, the awkward things!" exclaimed Michel. "The oxygen has made them revolt."

"But what do you want to do with these chickens?" asked
Barbicane.

"To acclimatize them on the moon, by Jove!"

"Then why did you hide them?"

"A joke, my worthy president, a simple joke, which has proved a miserable failure. I wanted to set them free on the lunar continent without saying anything. Oh, what would have been your amazement on seeing these earthly-winged animals pecking in the lunar fields?"

"You rascal, you unmitigated rascal," replied Barbicane, "you do not need oxygen to make your brain spin. You are always what we were under the influence of the gas, you are always foolish!"

"Well, at least you were wise enough to rescue us from my foolishness," replied Michel Ardan.

The three friends now set about restoring the order of the projectile. Chickens and cock were reinstated in their coop. While proceeding with this operation, Barbicane and his two companions discovered a new phenomenon. As they put the cock and hens back in their cages, they found that the birds, though good-sized, hardly felt heavier than sparrows.

From the moment of leaving the earth their own weight, that of the projectile, and the objects it enclosed, had been subject to an increasing diminution. In the case of the projectile, they might never have become aware of the fact. But the lightness of the birds made them realize that this same phenomenon must apply to their own bodies and to all the utensils and instruments they had aboard.

It is needless to say that a scale would not show this loss, since the scale weight balancing the object would have lost exactly as much as the object itself. But a spring balance for example, in which the tension was independent of the weight, would have given a just estimate of this loss.

We know that the attraction—otherwise called the weight—of a body varies in direct proportion to its density, and in inverse proportion to the square of the distance. Hence this effect: If the earth had been alone in space, if the other celestial bodies had been suddenly annihilated, the projectile, according to Newton's laws, would weigh less as it got farther from the earth, but without ever losing its weight entirely, for the terrestrial attraction would always have made itself felt, at whatever distance.

But, in reality, a time must come when the projectile would no longer be subject to the law of weight, since there did exist other celestial bodies whose effect could not be set down as zero. The projectile's flight was of course being traced between the earth and the moon. As it got farther from the earth and the terrestrial attraction diminished, the lunar attraction rose in proportion. There must then come a point where these two attractions would neutralize each other and the projectile would no longer possess any weight. If the moon's and the earth's densities had been equal, this point would have been at an equal distance between the two orbs. But taking the different densities into consideration, it was easy to reckon that this point would be situated at forty-seven-sixtieths of the whole journey, that is, 187,000 miles from the earth. At this point a body having no principle of speed or displacement in itself would remain immovable forever, being attracted equally by both planets, and not being drawn more toward one than toward the other.

Now if the projectile's impulsive force had been correctly calculated, it would attain this point without speed, having lost all trace of weight. What would happen then? Three hypotheses presented themselves.

1. Either it would retain a certain amount of motion, and pass the point of equal attraction, and fall upon the moon by virtue of the excess of the lunar attraction over the terrestrial.

2. Or, its speed failing, and unable to reach the point of equal attraction, it would fall upon the moon by virtue of the excess of the lunar attraction over the terrestrial.

3. Or, last, animated with sufficient speed to enable it to reach the neutral point, but not sufficient to pass it, it would remain forever suspended in that spot, moving closer to neither the earth nor the moon, though of course following them both in their orbits around the sun.

Such was their situation; and Barbicane clearly explained the consequences to his traveling companions, who listened with great interest. But how should they know when the projectile had reached this neutral point, especially when neither themselves nor the objects enclosed in the projectile would be any longer subject to the laws of weight?

That would be easy, Barbicane explained. It would be at the very moment when they and every other object in the projectile would cease to have any weight at all.

Up to this time the travelers, while admitting that the force of gravity was constantly decreasing, had not yet become sensible to its total absence.

But that day, about eleven o'clock in the morning, Nicholl having accidentally let a glass slip from his hand, the glass, instead of falling, remained suspended in the air.

"Ah," exclaimed Michel Ardan, "that is rather an amusing piece of natural philosophy."

And immediately Michel placed other objects, firearms and bottles in the air, fascinated by the way they held themselves up, as if by enchantment. Diana, too, placed in space by Michel, reproduced, but without any trick, the wonderful suspension practiced by Robert Houdin and other first-class magicians. Indeed the dog did not seem to know that she was floating in air.

The three adventurous companions were surprised and stupefied, despite their scientific reasonings. They felt themselves being carried into the domain of wonders. They felt that weight was really wanting to their bodies. Their arms stretched out remained in that position. Their heads shook on their shoulders. Their feet no longer clung to the floor of the projectile. They were like drunken men, having no stability in themselves.

Fanciful tales have depicted men without the power of reflecting light, others without shadow. But here reality, by the neutralizations of attractive forces, produced men in whom nothing had any weight and who weighed nothing themselves.

Suddenly Michel, taking a spring, left the floor and remained suspended in the air.

The two friends joined him instantly, and all three formed a miraculous levitation in the center of the projectile.

"Is it to be believed? Is it probable? Is it possible?" exclaimed Michel. "And yet it is so. Ah, if Raphael had seen us thus, what an 'Assumption' he would have thrown upon canvas!"

"The 'Assumption' cannot last," replied Barbicane. "If the projectile passes the neutral point, the lunar attraction will draw us to the moon."

"Then our feet will be upon the roof," replied Michel.

"No," said Barbicane, "because the projectile's center of gravity is very low. It will only turn by degrees."

"Then all our portables will be upset from top to bottom, that is a fact."

"Calm yourself, Michel," replied Nicholl, "no upset is to be feared; not a thing will move, for the projectile's evolution will be imperceptible."

"Just so," continued Barbicane, "and when it has passed the point of equal attraction, the neutral line, then its base, being the heavier, will draw it perpendicularly to the moon."

"Pass the neutral line!" cried Michel. "Then let us do as the sailors do when they cross the equator."

A slight side movement brought Michel to the projectile's side. Opening a cupboard, he took a bottle and glasses, placed them "in space" before his companions, and, drinking merrily, they saluted the line with a triple hurrah.

The weightless state scarcely lasted an hour; then the travelers felt themselves insensibly drawn toward the floor. Barbicane noticed that the conical end of the projectile was varying a little from its normal direction toward the moon, while the base was turning toward it. The lunar attraction was prevailing over the terrestrial; the fall toward the moon was beginning, almost imperceptibly as yet, but by degrees the attractive force would become stronger, the fall would be more decided. The projectile, drawn to the moon by its base, would turn its cone to the earth and fall with ever-increasing speed onto the moon's surface and their destination would be attained. Now nothing could prevent the success of their enterprise, and Nicholl and Michel Ardan shared Barbicane's joy.

Then they chatted of all the phenomena which had astonished them one after the other, particularly the neutralization of the laws of weight. Michel Ardan, always enthusiastic, drew conclusions which were purely fanciful.

"Ah, my worthy friends," he exclaimed, "what progress we should make if on earth we could throw off some of that weight, some of that chain which binds us to her. It would be like the prisoner set at liberty: no more fatigue of either arms or legs. In order to fly on the earth's surface, to keep oneself suspended in the air merely by the play of the muscles, there requires a strength 150 times greater than that which we possess. Yet a simple act of volition, a caprice, would bear us into space, if gravity did not exist."

"Just so," said Nicholl, smiling. "If we could succeed in suppressing weight as they suppress pain by anesthesia, that would change the face of modern society!"

"Yes," cried Michel, full of his subject, "destroy weight, and no more burdens!"

"Well said," replied Barbicane, "but if nothing had any weight, nothing would keep in its place, not even your hat on your head, worthy Michel; not your house, whose stones only adhere by weight; not a boat, whose stability on the water is caused only by weight; not even the ocean, whose waves would no longer be equalized by terrestrial attraction; not even the atmosphere, whose atoms, being no longer held in their places, would disperse in space."

"That is tiresome," retorted Michel. "Nothing like these matter-of-fact people for bringing one back to the bare reality."

"But console yourself, Michel," continued Barbicane, "for if no planet exists where all laws of weight are banished, you are at least going to visit one where it is much less than on the earth."

"The moon?"

"Yes, the moon, on whose surface objects weigh six times less than on the earth."

"And we shall feel it?" asked Michel.

"Definitely, 200 pounds will weigh only 30 on the surface of the moon."

"And our muscular strength will not diminish?"

"Not at all. Instead of jumping one yard high, you will be able to leap 18 feet into the air."

"But we shall be regular Herculeses in the moon!" exclaimed Michel.

"That's right," Nicholl replied. "Don't forget that if the height of the Selenites is in proportion to the density of their globe, they will be scarcely a foot high."

"Lilliputians!" Michel said. "I shall play the part of Gulliver. We are going to realize the fable of the giants. This is the advantage of leaving one's own planet and overrunning the solar world."

"One moment, Michel," answered Barbicane. "If you wish to play the part of Gulliver, only visit the inferior planets, such as Mercury, Venus, or Mars, whose density is a little less than that of the earth. Do not venture into the great planets, Jupiter, Saturn, Uranus, Neptune, for there the order will be changed, and you will become Lilliputian."

"And in the sun?"

"In the sun, if its density is 24,013 times greater, and the attraction is twenty-seven times greater than on the surface of our globe, keeping everything in proportion, the inhabitants ought to be at least 200 feet high."

"By Jove," exclaimed Michel, "I should be nothing more than a pigmy, a shrimp!"

"Gulliver with the giants," said Nicholl.

"Just so," replied Barbicane.

"Then it would be wise to carry some pieces of artillery to defend oneself."

"Not so," replied Nicholl. "Your projectiles would have no effect on the sun, they would fall back on the earth after some minutes.

"That is a strong remark."

"It is certain," replied Barbicane. "Everything on the sun weighs an enormous amount. It would require fantastic amounts of powder to propel a ball weighing 500 pounds on earth, which is 30 times heavier on the sun. If you were to fall upon the sun you would weigh—let me see—about 5,000 pounds, a weight which you would never be able to raise again."

"The devil!" said Michel. "One would want a portable crane. However, we will be satisfied with the moon for the present; there at least we shall cut a great figure. We will see about the sun by and by."

9. The Consequences of a Deviation

BARBICANE HAD now no fear of the issue of the journey, at least as far as the projectile's impulsive force was concerned. Its own speed would carry it beyond the neutral line; it would certainly not return to the earth; it would certainly not remain motionless on the line of attraction.

One single hypothesis remained to be realized, the arrival of the projectile at its destination by the action of the lunar attraction.

It was in reality a fall of 20,740 miles to the moon's surface. It is true that weight on the moon could only be reckoned at one-sixth of terrestrial weight. Yet, a formidable fall, nevertheless, and one against which every precaution must be taken without delay.

These precautions were of two sorts, some to deaden the shock when the projectile should touch the lunar soil, others to delay the fall, and consequently make it less violent.

To deaden the shock, it was a pity that Barbicane was no longer able to employ the means which had so ably weakened the shock at departure, that is to say, by water used as springs.

There was a lack of water, for they could not use their reserve, in case during the first days the liquid element should be found wanting on lunar soil. And indeed this reserve would have been quite insufficient for a spring. They must therefore give up this efficient means of deadening the shock of arrival.

Happily, Barbicane, not content with employing water alone, had furnished the movable disc with strong spring plugs, destined to lessen the shock against the base after the breaking of the horizontal partitions. These plugs still existed; they had only to readjust them and replace the movable disc; every piece, easy to handle, as their weight was now scarcely felt, was quickly mounted.

The different pieces were fitted without trouble; tools were not wanting, and soon the reinstated disc lay on steel plugs, like a table on its legs. One inconvenience resulted from the replacing of the disc, the lower window was blocked up; thus it was impossible for the travelers to observe the moon from that opening while they were being precipitated perpendicularly upon it. But by the side openings they could still see vast lunar regions, as a balloonist sees the earth over the side of his car.

This replacing of the disc took at least an hour. It was after twelve when all preparations were finished. Barbicane took fresh observations on the inclination of the projectile, but to his annoyance it had not turned over sufficiently for its fall: it seemed to take a curve parallel to the lunar disc. The moon shone splendidly into space while, opposite, the sun blazed with fire.

Their situation began to make them uneasy.

"Are we reaching our destination?" said Nicholl.

"Let us act as if we were about reaching it," replied Barbicane.

"You are skeptical," retorted Michel Ardan. "We shall arrive, and that, too, quicker than we like."

This answer brought Barbicane back to his preparations, and he occupied himself with placing the contrivances intended to break their descent.

Earlier, before the projectile had been launched, at a meeting held at Tampa Town, in Florida, Captain Nicholl had maintained that the projectile would smash like glass into 1000 pieces when it fell on the moon. To this, Michel Ardan had replied that he would break their fall by means of rockets properly placed.

Thus, powerful fireworks, taking their starting point from the base and bursting outside, could, by producing a recoil, check to a certain degree the projectile's speed. These rockets were to burn in space, it is true, but oxygen would not fail them, for they could supply themselves with it, like the lunar volcanoes, the burning of which has never yet been stopped by the want of atmosphere around the moon.

Barbicane had accordingly supplied himself with these fireworks, enclosed in little steel guns, which could be screwed on to the base of the projectile. Inside, these guns were flush with the bottom; outside, they protruded about 18 inches. There were 20 of them. An opening left in the disc allowed them to light the match with which each was provided. All the effect was felt outside. The burning mixture already had been rammed into each gun. They had, then, nothing to do but to raise the metallic buffers fixed in the base, and replace them by the guns, which fitted closely in their places.

This new work was finished about three o'clock, and after taking all these precautions there remained but to wait. But the projectile was perceptibly nearing the moon, and had already turned over considerably under the moon's influence, though its own velocity also drew it in an oblique direction. From these conflicting influences resulted a line which might become a tangent. But it was certain that the projectile would not fall directly on the moon; its base was still turned away from the perpendicular.

Barbicane's uneasiness increased as he saw his projectile resist the influence of gravitation. The Unknown was opening before him, the Unknown in interplanetary space. The man of science thought he had foreseen the only three hypotheses possible—the return to the earth, the return to the moon, or stagnation on the neutral line; and here a fourth hypothesis, loaded with all the terrors of the Infinite, surged up inopportunely. To face it without flinching, one must be a resolute savant like Barbicane, a phlegmatic being like Nicholl, or an audacious adventurer like Michel Ardan.

Conversation was started upon this subject. Other men would have considered the question from a practical point of view; they would have asked themselves whither their projectile carriage was carrying them. Not so with these: they sought for the cause which produced this effect.

"So we have become diverted from our route," said Michel; "but why?"

"I very much fear," answered Nicholl, "that, in spite of all precautions taken, the columbiad was not fairly pointed. An error, however small, would be enough to throw us out of the moon's attraction."

"Then they must have aimed badly?" asked Michel.

"I do not think so," replied Barbicane. "The perpendicularity of the gun was exact, its aiming at the zenith incontestible; therefore we ought to reach the moon when the moon comes to the zenith. There is another reason, but it escapes me."

"Are we not arriving too late?" asked Nicholl.

"Too late?" said Barbicane.

"Yes," continued Nicholl. "The Cambridge Observatory's note says that the transit ought to be accomplished in ninety-seven hours thirteen minutes and twenty seconds; which means to say that *sooner* the moon will *not* be at the point indicated, and that *later* it will have passed it."

"True," replied Barbicane. "But we started the 1st of December, at 13 minutes and 25 seconds to eleven at night; and we are supposed to arrive on the 5th at midnight, at the exact moment when the moon is full. It is now the 5th of December, 3:30 P.M.; eight and a half hours more ought to see us at the end of our journey. Why shouldn't we arrive?"

"Suppose we have an excess of speed?" queried Nicholl; "we know now that our initial velocity was greater than they supposed."

"No, a hundred times, no!" replied Barbicane. "An excess of speed, if the direction of the projectile had been right, would not have prevented us reaching the moon. No, there has been a deviation. We have been turned off our course."

"By whom? By what?" asked Nicholl.

"I cannot say," replied Barbicane.

"Very well, then, Barbicane," said Michel, "do you wish to know my opinion on the subject of finding out this deviation?"

"Speak."

"I would not give half a dollar to know it. That we have deviated is a fact. Where we are going to matters little; we shall soon see. Since we are being borne along in space we shall end by falling into some center of attraction or other."

Michel Ardan's indifference did not content Barbicane. Not that he was uneasy about the future, but he wanted to know at any cost *why* his projectile had deviated.

But the projectile continued its course sideways to the moon, throwing everything inside in a tangled mass. Barbicane could even prove, by the elevations which served as landmarks upon the moon, which was only 5,000 miles distant, that its speed was becoming uniform—fresh proof that there was no fall. Its impulsive force still prevailed over the lunar attraction, but the projectile's course was certainly bringing it nearer to the moon, and they might hope that at a nearer point the weight, predominating, would cause a decided fall.

The three friends, having nothing better to do, continued

their observations, but they could not yet determine the topographical position of the satellite. Every relief was leveled under the reflection of the solar rays.

They watched thus through the side windows until 8:00 P.M. The moon had then grown so large in their eyes that it filled half of the firmament. The sun on one side, and the moon on the other, flooded the projectile with light.

At that moment Barbicane thought he could estimate the distance which separated them from their aim at not much more than 2,000 miles. The speed of the projectile seemed to him to be more than 600 feet a second. Under the centripetal force, the base of the projectile tended toward the moon. But the centrifugal still prevailed, and it was probable that its rectilineal course would be changed to a curve of some sort, the nature of which they could not at present determine.

Barbicane was still seeking the solution of his insoluble problem. Hours passed without any result. The projectile was evidently nearing the moon, but it was also evident that it would never reach it. As to the nearest distance at which it would pass it, that must be the result of the two forces, attraction and repulsion, affecting its motion.

"I ask but one thing," said Michel: "that we may pass near enough to penetrate its secrets."

"Cursed be the thing that has caused our projectile to deviate from its course," cried Nicholl.

And, as if a light had suddenly broken in upon his mind, Barbicane answered, "Then cursed be the meteor which crossed our path."

"What?" said Michel Ardan.

"What do you mean?" exclaimed Nicholl.

"I mean," said Barbicane in a decided tone, "I mean that our deviation is owing solely to our meeting with this erring body."

"But it did not even brush us as it passed," said Michel.

"What does that matter? Its mass, compared to that of our projectile, was enormous, and its attraction was enough to influence our course."

"So little?" cried Nicholl.

"Yes, Nicholl; but however little it might be," replied Barbicane, "in a distance of 210,000 miles, it wanted no more to make us miss the moon."

10. The Observers of the Moon

BARBICANE HAD evidently hit upon the only plausible reason for the deviation. However slight it might have been, it had sufficed to modify the course of the projectile. It was a fatality. The bold attempt had miscarried by a fortuitous circumstance. Unless some exceptional event occurred, they could now never reach the moon.

Would they pass near enough to be able to solve certain physical and geological questions until then insoluble? This was the question, and the only one, which occupied the minds of these bold travelers. As to the fate in store for themselves, they did not even dream of it.

But what would become of them amid these infinite solitudes. Soon they would need air. A few more days, and they would fall to the floor, stifled in this wandering projectile. But a few days to these intrepid fellows was a century. Undaunted by misfortune, they devoted all their time to observe that moon which they no longer hoped to reach.

The distance which then separated the projectile from the satellite was estimated at about 500 miles. Under these conditions, as far as being able to see its details, the travelers were farther from the moon than are the inhabitants of the earth with their powerful telescopes.

Indeed, we know that the instrument mounted by Lord Rosse at Parsonstown, which magnifies 6,500 times, brings the moon to within an apparent distance of 40 miles. And more than that, with the powerful one set up at Longs Peak, the moon, magnified 48,000 times, is brought to within less than five miles, and objects having a diameter of 30 feet are seen very distinctly. So that, at this distance, the topographical details of the moon, observed without glasses, could not be determined with precision. The eye caught the vast outline of those immense depressions inappropriately called "seas," but they could not recognize their nature. The prominence of the mountains disappeared under the dazzling radiation produced by the reflection of the solar rays. The eye, dazzled as if it were leaning over a bath of molten silver, turned from it involuntarily.

But the oblong form of the moon was quite clear. It appeared like a gigantic egg, with the small end turned toward the earth. Liquid and pliable in the first days of its formation, the moon was originally a perfect sphere. But, being soon drawn within the attraction of the earth, it became elongated under the influence of gravitation. In becoming a satellite, it lost its native purity of form; its center of gravity was in advance of the center of its figure. From this fact some scientists have drawn the conclusion that the air and water had taken refuge on the opposite surface of the moon, which is never seen from the earth.

The oblong shape of the moon was perceptible for only a few moments. The travelers were getting too close to notice it. The distance of the projectile from the moon diminished very rapidly under its speed, which, though much less than its initial velocity was still eight or nine times greater than that which propels our express trains. The oblique course of the projectile gave Michel Ardan some hopes of striking the lunar disc at some point or other. He could not think that they would never reach it. No, he could not believe it; and this opinion he often repeated. But Barbicane, who was a better judge, always answered him with merciless logic.

"No, Michel, no! We can only reach the moon by a fall, and we are not falling. The centripetal force keeps us under the moon's influence, but the centrifugal force draws us irresistibly away from it."

This was said in a tone which quenched Michel Ardan's last hope.

The portion of the moon which the projectile was nearing was the Northern Hemisphere, found usually in the lower part of moon maps. These maps are generally drawn after the outline given by telescopes, and we know that they reverse the objects. This Northern Hemisphere presented vast plains, dotted with isolated mountains.

At midnight the moon was full. At that precise moment the travelers should have alighted upon it, if the mischievous meteor had not diverted their course. The moon was exactly in the condition determined by the Cambridge Observatory. It was mathematically at its perigee, and at the zenith of the 28th parallel. An observer placed at the bottom of the enormous columbiad, pointed perpendicularly to the horizon, would have framed the moon in the mouth of the gun. A straight line drawn through the axis of the piece would have passed through the center of the moon. It is needless to say that during the night of the 5th–6th of December the travelers took not an instant's rest. Could they close their eyes when so near this new world? No! All their feelings were concentrated in one single thought. See! Representatives of the earth, of humanity, past and present, all centered in them. It was through their eyes that the human race would look at these lunar regions and penetrate the secrets of their satellite. A strange emotion filled their hearts as they went from one window to the other. Their observations, reproduced by Barbicane, were rigidly determined. To take them, they had telescopes; to correct them, maps.

As regards the optical instruments at their disposal, they had excellent marine telescopes specially constructed for this journey, possessing magnifying powers of 100. They would thus have brought the moon to within a distance (apparent) of less than 5000 miles from the earth. But then, at a distance which for three hours in the morning did not exceed 65 miles, and in a medium free from all atmospheric disturbances, these instruments could reduce the lunar surface to within less than 4500 feet!

11. Fancy and Reality

HAVE YOU ever seen the moon?" asked a professor, ironically, of one of his pupils.

"No, sir," replied the pupil, still more ironically, "but I must say I have heard it spoken of."

In one sense, the pupil's witty answer might be given by a large majority of sublunary beings. How many people have heard talk of the moon who have never seen it—at least through a glass or a telescope! How many have never examined the map of their satellite!

In looking at a moon map, one peculiarity strikes us. Contrary to the situation on earth and Mars, the continents occupy more particularly the Southern Hemisphere of the lunar globe. These continents do not show such decided, clear, and regular boundary lines as South America, Africa, and the Indian peninsula. Their angular, capricious and deeply indented coasts are rich in gulfs and peninsulas. They remind one of the confusion in the islands of the Sound, where the land is excessively indented. If navigation ever existed on the surface of the moon, it must have been exceedingly difficult and dangerous. We may well pity the sailors and map-makers: the sailors, when they come upon these perilous coasts, the map-makers when they take the sounding of its stormy banks.

We may also notice that, on the moon, the South Pole is much more continental than the North Pole. On the North Pole there is but one slight strip of land separated from other continents by vast seas. Toward the south, continents clothe almost the whole of the hemisphere. It is even possible that the Selenites have already planted the flag on one of their poles, while Franklin, Ross, Kane, Dumont, d'Urville, and Lambert have never yet been able to attain that unknown point of our terrestrial globe.

As to islands, they are numerous on the surface of the moon. Nearly all oblong or circular, and as if traced with the compass, they seem to form one vast archipelago, equal to that charming group lying between Greece and Asia Minor, and which mythology in ancient times adorned with most graceful legends.

After wandering over these vast continents, the eye is attracted by still greater seas. Not only their formation, but their situation and aspect remind one of the terrestrial oceans. Again, as on earth, these seas occupy the greater portion of the globe. But in point of fact, these are not liquid spaces, but plains, the nature of which the travelers hoped soon to determine. Astronomers, we must allow, have graced these pretended seas with at least odd names, which science has respected up to the present time. Michel Ardan was right when he compared this to one of those "maps of matrimony" he had seen in a book by Scudary or Cyrano de Bergerac. "Only," he said, "it is no longer the sentimental map of the seventeenth century, it is the map of life, very neatly divided into two parts, one feminine, the other masculine. The right hemisphere for woman, the left for man."

At Michel's speech his prosaic companions shrugged their shoulders. Barbicane and Nicholl looked upon the lunar map from a very different point of view than that of their fantastic friend. Nevertheless, their fantastic friend was a little in the right. Judge for yourselves.

In the left hemisphere stretches the "Sea of Clouds," where human reason is so often shipwrecked. Not far off lies the "Sea of Rains," fed by all the fever of existence. Near this is the "Sea of Storms," where man is ever fighting against his passions, which too often gain the victory. Then, worn out by deceit, treasons, infidelity, and the whole body of terrestrial misery, what does he find at the end of his career? That vast "Sea of Humors," barely softened by some drops of the waters from the "Gulf of Dew." Clouds, rain, storms, and humors—does the life of man contain more than this? And is it not summed up in these four words?

The right hemisphere, "dedicated to the ladies," encloses smaller seas, whose significant names contain every incident of a feminine existence. There is the "Sea of Serenity," over which the young girl bends; "The Lake of Dreams," reflecting a joyous future; "The Sea of Nectar," with its waves of tenderness and breezes of love; "The Sea of Fruitfulness"; "The Sea of Crises"; then the "Sea of Vapors," whose dimensions are perhaps a little too confined; and, lastly, that vast "Sea of Tranquillity," in which every false passion, every useless dream, every unsatisfied desire is at length absorbed, and whose waves emerge peacefully into the "Lake of Death."

What a strange succession of names! What a singular division of the moon's two hemispheres, joined to one another like man and woman, reflecting in space an image of our terrestial existence. And was not the fantastic Michel right in thus interpreting the fancies of the ancient astronomers? But while his imagination thus roved over "the seas," his grave companions were considering things more geographically. They were learning this new world by heart. They were measuring angles and diameters.

12. Orographic Details

THE COURSE taken by the projectile, as we have before remarked, was bearing it toward the moon's northern hemisphere. The travelers were far from the central point which they would have struck had their course not been subject to an irremediable deviation. It was past midnight; and Barbicane then estimated the distance at 750 miles, which was a little greater than the length of the lunar radius, and which would diminish as it advanced nearer to the North Pole. The projectile was then not at the altitude of the equator, but across the tenth parallel, and from that latitude, Barbicane and his two companions were able to observe the moon under the most favorable conditions. Indeed, by means of glasses, the above-named distance was reduced to little more than 14 miles. The telescope of the Rocky Mountains brought the moon much nearer, but the terrestrial atmosphere singularly lessened its power. Thus Barbicane, posted in his projectile, with the telescope to his eyes, could seize upon details which were almost imperceptible to earthly observers."

"My friends," said the president, in a serious voice, "I do not know whither we are going. I do not know if we shall ever see the terrestrial globe again. Nevertheless, let us proceed as if our work would one day be useful to our fellow men. Let us keep our minds free from every other consideration. We are astronomers, and this projectile is a room in the Cambridge University, carried into space. Let us make our observations."

This said, work was begun with great exactness; and they faithfully reproduced the different aspects of the moon at the different distances which the projectile reached.

At the time that the projectile was as high as the tenth parallel, north latitude, it seemed rigidly to follow the twentieth degree, east longitude. We must here make one important remark with regard to the map by which they were taking observations. In the selenographical maps where, on account of the reversing of the objects by the glasses, the south is above and the north below, it would seem natural that, on account of that inversion, the east should be to the left hand and the west on the right. But this is not so. If the map were turned upside down, showing the moon as we see it, the east would be to the left, and the west to the right, contrary to that which exists on terrestrial maps. The reason for this anomaly is that observers in the Northern Hemisphere, say in Europe, see the moon in the south—according to them. When they take observations, they turn their backs to the north, the reverse position to that which they occupy when they study a terrestrial map. As they turn their backs to the north, the east is on their left, and the west to their right. To observers in the Southern Hemisphere—Patagonia, for example—the moon's west would be quite to their left, and the east to their right, as the south is behind them. Such is the reason of the apparent reversing of these two cardinal points, and we must bear it in mind in order to be able to follow President Barbicane's observations.

With the help of Boer and Moedler's *Mappa Selenographica,* the travelers were able at once to recognize that portion of the disc enclosed within the field of their glasses.

"What are we looking at right now?" asked Michel.

"At the northern part of the 'Sea of Clouds,' " answered Barbicane. "We are too far off to recognize its nature. Are these plains composed of arid sand, as the first astronomer maintained? Or are they nothing but immense forests, according to de la Rue's opinion, who gives the moon an atmosphere, though a very low and a very dense one? That we shall know by and by. We must affirm nothing until we are in a position to do so."

This "Sea of Clouds" was rather doubtfully marked out upon the maps. It is supposed that these vast plains are strewn with blocks of lava from the neighboring volcanoes on their right, Ptolemy, Purbach, Arzachel. Now the projectile was coming close enough for the travelers to make out details. Soon there appeared the heights which bound this sea at this northern limit. Before them rose a mountain radiant with beauty, the top of which seemed lost in an eruption of solar rays.

"That is——?" asked Michel.

"Copernicus," replied Barbicane.

This mountain, situated in 9° N. lat. and 20° E. long. rose to a height of 10,600 feet above the surface of the moon. It is quite visible from the earth, and astronomers can study it with ease, particularly during the phase between the last quarter and the new moon, because then the shadows are thrown lengthways from east to west, allowing them to measure the heights.

Copernicus rises isolated like a gigantic lighthouse on that portion of the "Sea of Clouds" which is bounded by the "Sea of Tempests," thus lighting by its splendid rays two oceans at a time. It was a sight without an equal, those long luminous streaks, so dazzling in the full moon, and which, passing the boundary chain on the north, extend to the "Sea of Rains." At one o'clock of the terrestrial morning, the projectile, like a balloon borne into space, overlooked the top of this magnificent mountain. Barbicane could recognize perfectly its chief features. Like Kepler and Aristarchus, the mountains that overlook the "Ocean of Tempests," sometimes Copernicus appeared like a brilliant point through the cloudy light, and was taken for a volcano in activity. But it is only an extinct one—like all on that side of the moon. Its circumference showed a diameter of about 55 miles. The telescope pinpointed traces of stratification produced by successive eruptions, and the surrounding area was strewn with volcanic debris, which still choked some of the craters.

"There exist," said Barbicane, "several kinds of circular mountains on the surface of the moon, and it is easy to see that Copernicus belongs to the radiating class. If we were nearer, we should see the cones bristling on the inside, which in former times were so many fiery mouths spewing out volcanic matter. A curious arrangement, and one without an exception in mountains of the moon. This inside plateau of cones lies at a lower level than the plains surrounding the mountain, quite different from terrestrial craters, where the bottom is almost always higher than the surrounding country."

"And why this peculiar disposition?" asked Nicholl.

"We do not know," replied Barbicane.

"What splendid radiation!" said Michel. "One could hardly see a finer spectacle, I think."

"What would you say, then," replied Barbicane, "if chance should bear us toward the Southern Hemisphere?"

"Well, I should say that it was still more beautiful," retorted Michel Ardan.

At this moment the projectile hung perpendicularly over the center of the mountain. The circumference of Copernicus formed almost a perfect circle, and its steep escarpments were clearly defined. They could even distinguish a

second ringed enclosure. Around spread a grayish plain of
a wild aspect, where every relief was outlined in yellow. At
the bottom of the circle, as if enclosed in a jewel case,
sparkled for one instant two or three eruptive cones, like
enormous dazzling gems. Toward the north the escarpments were lowered by a depression which would probably
have given access to the interior of the crater.

In passing over the surrounding plains Barbicane noticed
a great number of less important mountains. Among others
was a little ringed one called Guy Lussac, the breadth of
which measured twelve miles.

Toward the south, the plain was very flat, without one
elevation, without one projection. Toward the north, on the
contrary, until where it was bounded by the "Sea of
Storms," the plain resembled a liquid surface agitated by a
storm, of which the hills and hollows formed a succession of
waves suddenly congealed. Over the whole of this, and in
all directions, lay the luminous lines, all converging to the
summit of Copernicus.

The travelers discussed the origin of these strange rays,
but they could not determine their nature any more than
terrestrial observers.

"But why," said Nicholl, "should not these rays be simply
spurs of mountains which reflect more vividly the light of
the sun?"

"No," replied Barbicane. "If that were so, under certain
conditions of the moon these ridges would cast shadows,
and they do not cast any."

And indeed, these rays only appeared when the sun's
rays shone directly on the moon, and disappeared as soon
as its rays became oblique.

"But how have they endeavored to explain these lines of light?" asked Michel. "I cannot believe the savants would ever be stranded for want of an explanation."

"As a matter of fact," replied Barbicane, "Herschel has put forward an opinion, but he did not venture to affirm it."

"Never mind. What was the opinion?"

"He thought that these rays might be streams of cooled lava which shone when the sun beat straight upon them. It may be so, but nothing can be less certain. Besides, if we pass nearer to the mountain called Tycho, we shall be in a better position to find out the cause of this radiation."

"Do you know, my friends, what that plain, seen from the height we are at, resembles?" said Michel.

"No," replied Nicholl.

"Very well; with all those pieces of lava lengthened like rockets, it resembles an immense game of jackstraws thrown pell-mell. There wants but the hook to pull them out one by one."

"Do be serious," said Barbicane.

"Well, let us be serious," replied Michel quietly; "and instead of jackstraws, let us put bones. This plain would then be nothing but an immense cemetery on which would repose the mortal remains of thousands of extinct generations. Do you prefer that high-flown comparison?"

"One is as good as the other," retorted Barbicane.

"My word, you are difficult to please," answered Michel.

"My worthy friend," continued the matter-of-fact Barbicane, "it matters but little what it *resembles*, when we do not know what it *is*."

"Well answered," exclaimed Michel. "That will teach me to reason with savants."

But the projectile continued to advance with almost uniform speed around the lunar disc. The travelers, we may easily imagine, did not dream of taking a moment's rest. Every minute changed the landscape which fled from beneath their gaze. About half-past one o'clock in the morning they caught a glimpse of the tops of another mountain. Barbicane, consulting his map, recognized Eratosthenes.

It was a ringed mountain 9000 feet high, and one of those circles so numerous on this satellite. With regard to this, Barbicane related Kepler's singular opinion on the formation of circles. According to that celebrated mathematician, these craterlike cavities had been dug by the hand of man.

"For what purpose?" asked Nicholl.

"For a very natural one," replied Barbicane. "The Selenites might have undertaken these immense works and dug these enormous holes for a refuge and shield from the solar rays which beat upon them during fifteen consecutive days."

"The Selenites are not fools," said Michel.

"A singular idea," replied Nicholl. "But it is probable that Kepler did not know the true dimensions of these circles, for the digging of them would have been the work of giants quite impossible for the Selenites."

"Why? If weight on the moon's surface is six times less than on the earth?" said Michel.

"But if the Selenites are six times smaller?" retorted Nicholl.

"And if there are *no* Selenites?" added Barbicane.

This put an end to the discussion.

Soon Eratosthenes disappeared under the horizon without the projectile being sufficiently near to allow close observation. This mountain separated the moon range called the Apennines from the Carpathians. On the moon there are few chains of mountains, and they are chiefly distributed over the Northern Hemisphere. Some, however, occupy certain portions of the Southern Hemisphere also.

About two o'clock in the morning Barbicane found that they were above the 20th lunar parallel. The distance of the projectile from the moon was not more than 600 miles. Barbicane, now perceiving that the projectile was steadily approaching the lunar disc, did not despair. If they did not reach it, they might at least discover the secrets of its configuration.

13. Lunar Landscapes

AT HALF-PAST two in the morning the projectile was over the 13th lunar parallel and at the effective distance of 500 miles, reduced by the glasses to just five miles. It still seemed impossible, however, that it could ever touch any part of the disc. Its motive speed, comparatively so moderate, was inexplicable to President Barbicane. At that distance from the moon its speed should have been considerable to enable it to bear up against the moon's attraction. Here was a phenomenon the cause of which escaped them again. Besides, they did not have the time to investigate the cause. All of the moon's surface was under the eyes of the travelers, and they would not lose a single detail.

Through the telescope the moon appeared at the distance

of five miles. What would a balloonist, borne to this distance from the earth, distinguish on its surface? We cannot say, since the greatest ascension has not been more than 25,000 feet.

This, however, is an exact description of what Barbicane and his companions saw at this height. Large patches of different colors appeared on the disc. Selenographers are not agreed upon the nature of these colors. There are several, and rather vividly marked. Schmidt says that, if the terrestrial oceans were dried up, a Selenite observer could not distinguish more clearly the ocean beds and continental plains on the earth than man can perceive similiar features on the moon. According to him, the color common to the moon's vast plains known by the name of "seas" is a dark gray mixed with green and brown. Some of the large craters present the same appearance.

Barbicane knew this opinion of the German astronomer, an opinion shared by Boer and Moedler. Observation has proved that right was on their side, and not on that of some astronomers who admit the existence of only gray on the moon's surface. In some parts green was very distinct, particularly, according to Schmidt, in the seas of "Serenity and Humors." Barbicane also noticed large craters, without any interior cones, which shed a bluish tint similar to the reflection of a sheet of steel freshly polished. These colors belonged really to the lunar disc, and did not result, as some astronomers say, either from the imperfection in telescopes or from the interposition of the terrestrial atmosphere.

Not a doubt existed in Barbicane's mind with regard to it, as he observed it through space and so could not commit any optical error. He considered the establishment of this fact as an acquisition to science. Now, were these shades of green, belonging to tropical vegetation, kept up by a low, dense atmosphere? He could not yet say.

Farther on he noticed a reddish tint, quite defined. The same shade had before been observed at the bottom of an isolated enclosure, known by the name of Lichtenburg's circle, which is situated near the Hercynian Mountains, on the borders of the moon. But they could not tell the nature of it.

They were not more fortunate with regard to another peculiarity of the disc, for they could not decide upon the cause of it.

Michel Ardan was watching near the president when he noticed long white lines, vividly lighted up by the direct rays of the sun. It was a succession of luminous furrows, very different from the radiation of Copernicus not long before; these ran parallel with each other.

Michel, with his usual readiness, hastened to exclaim: "Look there! Cultivated fields!"

"Cultivated fields!" replied Nicholl, shrugging his shoulders.

"Plowed, at all events," retorted Michel Ardan. "But what laborers those Selenites must be, and what giant oxen they must harness to their plow to cut such furrows!"

"They are not furrows," said Barbicane, "they are *rifts*."

"Rifts? Stuff!" replied Michel mildly. "But what do you mean by 'rifts' in the scientific world?"

Barbicane immediately enlightened his companion as to what he knew about lunar rifts. He knew that they were a kind of furrow found on every part of the moon which was not mountainous. These furrows, generally isolated, mea-

sured from 400 to 500 leagues in length and their breadth
varied from 1,000 to 1,500 yards. Their borders were
stricty parallel. But he knew nothing more either of their
formation or their nature.

Barbicane, through his glasses, observed these rifts with
great attention. He noticed that their borders were formed
of steep declivities. They were long, parallel ramparts, and
with some small amount of imagination he might have admitted the existence of long lines of fortifications, raised by
Selenite engineers. Of these different rifts some were perfectly straight, as if cut by a line; others were slightly
curved, though still keeping their borders parallel; some
crossed each other, some cut through craters; here they
wound through plateaus such as Posidonius or Petavius;
there they wound through the seas such as the "Sea of Serenity."

These rifts naturally excited the imaginations of terrestrial astronomers. The first observers do not seem to have
noticed them. Neither Hevelius, Cassin, La Hire, nor Herschel seemed to have known them. It was Schroeter who in
1789 first drew attention to them. Others followed who
studied them, such as Pastorff, Gruithuysen, Boer, and
Moedler. At this time the number of these rifts amounts to
70; but, if they have been counted, their nature has not yet
been determined. They are certainly *not* fortifications any
more than they are the ancient beds of dried-up rivers, for
two reasons. One, the waters, so slight on the moon's surface, could never have worn such drains for themselves
and, two, they often cross craters of great elevation.

We must, however, allow that Michel Ardan had "an
idea," and that, without knowing it, he coincided in that
respect with Schmidt.

"Why," said he, "should not these unaccountable appearances be simply phenomena of vegetation?"

"What do you mean?" asked Barbicane quickly.

"Do not excite yourself, my worthy president," replied Michel. "But might it not be possible that the dark lines forming that bastion were rows of trees regularly placed?"

"You stick to your vegetation, then?" said Barbicane.

"I like," retorted Michel Ardan, "to explain what you savants cannot explain. At least my hypothesis has the advantage of indicating why these rifts disappear, or seem to disappear, at certain seasons."

"And for what reason?"

"For the reason that the trees become invisible when they lose their leaves, and visible when they regain them."

"Your explanation is ingenious, my dear companion," replied Barbicane, "but inadmissible."

"Why?"

"Because there are no seasons as such on the moon's surface. Consequently, the phenomena of vegetation of which you speak cannot occur."

Indeed, the slight obliquity of the lunar axis keeps the sun at an almost equal height in every latitude. Above the equatorial regions the sun almost invariably occupies the zenith, and does not pass the limits of the horizon in the polar regions. Thus, according to each region, there reigns a perpetual winter, spring, summer, or autumn, as in the planet Jupiter, whose axis is but little inclined upon its orbit.

To what origin can we attribute these rifts? That is a question difficult to solve. They certainly came after the formation of craters and rings, for several have introduced themselves by breaking through their circular ramparts.

Thus it may be that, contemporary with the later geological epochs, they are due to the expansion of natural forces.

But the projectile had now attained 40° lunar latitude, at a distance not exceeding forty miles. Through the telescope objects appeared to be only four miles distant.

At this point, under their feet, rose Mount Helicon, 1,520 feet high, and round about the left rose moderate elevations, enclosing a small portion of the "Sea of Rains," under the name of the Gulf of Iris. The terrestrial atmosphere would have to be 170 times more transparent than it is to allow astronomers to make perfect observations on the moon's surface. But in the void in which the projectile floated no fluid interposed itself between the eye of the observer and the object observed. And more, Barbicane found himself able to observe more than the most powerful telescopes had ever done before, either that of Lord Rosse or that of the Rocky Mountains. He was, therefore, under extremely favorable conditions for solving that great question of the habitability of the moon. But the solution still escaped him: he could distinguish nothing but desert beds, immense plains, and toward the north arid mountains. Not a work betrayed the hand of man; not a ruin marked his course; not a group of animals was to be seen indicating life, even in an inferior degree. In no part was there life, in no part was there an appearance of vegetation. Of the three kingdoms which share the terrestrial globe between them, one alone was represented on the lunar: that was the mineral.

"Ah, indeed!" said Michel Ardan, a little out of countenance. "Then you see no one?"

"No," answered Nicholl, "up to this time not a man, not

an animal, not a tree! Whether the atmosphere has taken refuge at the bottom of cavities, in the midst of the circles, or even on the opposite face of the moon—that is something we cannot decide."

"Besides," added Barbicane, "even to the most piercing eye a man cannot be distinguished farther than three and a half miles off, so that, if there are any Selenites, they can see our projectile but we cannot see them."

Toward four in the morning, at the height of the 50th parallel, the distance was reduced to 300 miles. To the left ran a line of mountains capriciously shaped, lying in the full light. To the right, on the contrary, lay a black hollow resembling a vast well, unfathomable and gloomy, drilled into the lunar soil.

This hole was the "Black Lake"; it was Plato, a deep circle which can be conveniently studied from the earth, between the last quarter and the new moon when the shadows fall from west to east.

This black color is rarely met with on the surface of the satellite. As yet it has only been recognized in the depths of the circle of Endymion, to the east of the "Cold Sea," in the Northern Hemisphere, and at the bottom of Grimaldi's circle, on the equator, toward the eastern border of the orb.

Plato is a mountain, situated in 51° N. lat. and 9° E. long. Its circuit is 47 miles long and 32 broad.

Barbicane regretted that they were not passing directly above this vast opening. There was an abyss to fathom, perhaps some mysterious phenomenon to be observed. But the projectile's course could not be altered. They must rigidly submit. They could not guide a balloon, still less a

projectile, when once enclosed within its walls. Toward five
in the morning the northern limits of the "Sea of Rains" was
at length passed. The mounts of Condamine and Fontenelle
remained—one on the right, the other on the left. That part
of the disc beginning with the 60th parallel was becoming
quite mountainous. The glasses brought them to within two
miles, less than that separating the summit of Mont Blanc
from sea level. The whole region was bristling with spikes
and circles. Philolaus, with its elliptical crater, stood
predominant at a height of 5,550 feet, and seen from this distance the disc showed a very fantastical appearance. Landscapes were presented to the eye under very different conditions from those on the earth.

The moon having no atmosphere, the consequences
arising from the absence of this gaseous envelope have already been shown. No twilight on its surface; night following day and day following night with the suddenness of a
lamp which is extinguished or lighted amid profound darkness—no transition from cold to heat, the temperature
falling in an instant from boiling point to the cold of space.

Another consequence of this want of air is that absolute
darkness reigns where the sun's rays do not penetrate. That
which on earth is called diffusion of light, that luminous
matter which the air holds in suspension, which creates the
twilight and the daybreak, which produces tints, shades,
penumbras, all the magic of chiaroscuro, does not exist on
the moon. Hence the harshness of contrasts, which only
admit of two colors, black and white. If a Selenite were to
shade his eyes from the sun's rays, the sky would seem absolutely black, and the stars would shine to him as on the
darkest night. Judge of the impression produced on Barbicane and his three friends by this strange scene! Their eyes

were confused. They could no longer grasp the respective distances of the different plains. A lunar landscape without the softening of the phenomena of chiaroscuro could not be rendered by an earthly landscape painter: it would be spots of ink on a white page—nothing more.

This aspect was not altered even when the projectile, above the 80th degree, was separated from the moon only by a distance of 50 miles, nor even when, at five in the morning, it passed at less than 25 miles from the mountain of Gioja, a distance reduced by the glasses to a quarter of a mile. It seemed as if the moon might be touched by the hand! It seemed impossible that, before long, the projectile would not strike it, if only at the North Pole, the brilliant arch of which was so distinctly visible on the black sky.

Michel Ardan wanted to open one of the windows and throw himself on to the moon's surface! A very useless attempt, for if the projectile could not attain any point whatever of the satellite, Michel, carried along by its motion, could not attain it either.

At that moment, at six o'clock, the lunar pole appeared. The moon presented itself to the travelers' gaze one half brilliantly lit up, while the other disappeared in the darkness. Suddenly the projectile passed the line of demarcation between intense light and absolute darkness, and was plunged in profound night!

14. A Night of Fifteen Days

AT THE moment when this phenomenon so rapidly took place, the projectile was skirting the moon's north pole at less than 25 miles' distance. Some seconds had sufficed to plunge it into the absolute darkness of space. The transition was so sudden, without shade, without gradation of light, without attenuation of the luminous waves, that the orb seemed to have been extinguished by a powerful blow.

"Melted, disappeared!" Michel Ardan exclaimed, aghast.

Indeed, there was neither reflection nor shadow. Nothing more was to be seen of that disc, formerly so dazzling. The darkness was complete, and rendered even more so by the rays from the stars. It was the blackness in which the lunar nights are steeped, nights which last 354½ hours and result from the equality of the lateral and rotatory movements of the moon.

In the interior of the projectile the obscurity was complete. The travelers could not see each other. However desirous Barbicane might be to husband the gas, the reserve of which was small, he was obliged to use it in order to provide them with light.

"Devil take the sun," exclaimed Michel Ardan, "which forces us to expend gas, instead of giving us his rays gratuitously."

"Don't accuse the sun," said Nicholl. "It is not at fault. It is the moon which has placed itself like a screen between us and the sun."

"It is the sun!" continued Michel.

"It is the moon!" retorted Nicholl.

An idle dispute, which Barbicane put an end to by saying: "My friends, it is neither the fault of the sun nor of the moon. It is the fault of the *projectile*, which, instead of rigidly following its course, has awkwardly missed it. To be more just, it is the fault of that unfortunate meteor which has so deplorably altered our first direction."

"Well," replied Michel Ardan, "as the matter is settled, let us have breakfast. After a whole night of watching we need to build ourselves up a little."

This proposal meeting with no contradiction, Michel prepared the repast in a few minutes. But they ate for eating's sake, they drank without toasts, without hurrahs. The bold travelers, borne away into gloomy space without their accustomed sun's rays, felt a vague uneasiness. Darkness bound them on all sides. But they discussed the interminable night of 354½ hours, or, nearly 15 days, which the law of physics has imposed on the inhabitants of the moon.

Barbicane gave his friends some explanation of the causes and the consequences of this curious phenomenon.

"Curious indeed," said they, "for, if each hemisphere of the moon is deprived of solar light for 15 days, the area above which we now float does not even enjoy during its long night any view of the earth so beautifully lit up. In a word the moon has no "moon" visible on one side. Now if this were the case with the earth—if for example, Europe never saw the moon, and it was only visible at the poles —imagine to yourself the astonishment of a European on arriving in Australia."

"They would make the voyage just to see the moon!" replied Michel.

"Well," continued Barbicane, "such must be the astonishment of the Selenites who inhabit the face of the moon opposite to the earth, a face which is ever invisible to our fellow earth men."

"And which we should have seen," added Nicholl, "if we had arrived here when the moon was new, that is to say fifteen days later."

"I will add, to make amends," continued Barbicane, "that the inhabitants of the visible face are singularly favored by nature, to the detriment of their brethren on the invisible face. The inhabitants of the dark side have dark nights of 354 hours without one single ray to break the darkness. Those on the light side, on the contrary, when the sun which has given its light for fifteen days sinks below the horizon, see a splendid orb rise on the opposite horizon. It is the earth, which is thirteen times greater than that diminutive moon that we know—the earth which appears thirteen times greater in size than the full moon—the earth which only disappears at the moment when the sun reappears in its turn!"

"Nicely worded," said Michel. "Slightly academic, perhaps."

"It follows, then," continued Barbicane, "that the visible face of the disc must be very agreeable to inhabit, since it always looks on either the sun when the moon is full, or on the earth when the moon is new."

"But," said Nicholl, "that advantage must be overcompensated by the insupportable heat which the light brings with it."

"The inconvenience, in that respect, is the same for the two faces, for the earth's light is evidently deprived of heat. But the invisible face gets far more heat than the visible face. I say that for *you*, Nicholl, because Michel will probably not understand."

"Thank you," said Michel.

"Indeed," continued Barbicane, "when the invisible face receives at the same time light and heat from the sun, it is because the moon is new, that is to say, it is situated between the sun and the earth. It follows, then, considering the position which the invisible face occupies in opposition when the moon is full, that it is nearer to the sun by twice its distance from the earth; and that distance may be estimated at 400,000 miles. So the invisible face is that much nearer to the sun when it receives its rays."

"Quite right," replied Nicholl.

"On the contrary," continued Barbicane.

"One moment," said Michel, interrupting his grave companion.

"What do you want?"

"I ask to be allowed to continue the explanation."

"And why?"

"To prove that I understand."

"Get along with you," said Barbicane, smiling.

"On the contrary," said Michel, imitating the tone and gestures of the president, "on the contrary, when the visible face of the moon is lit by the sun, it is because the moon is full, that is to say, opposite the sun with regard to the earth. The distance separating it from the sun is then increased in round numbers to 400,000 miles, and the heat which it receives must be a little less."

"Very well said!" exclaimed Barbicane. "Do you know, Michel, that for an amateur you are intelligent."

"Yes," replied Michel coolly, "we are all so in my country."

Barbicane gravely clasped the hand of his amiable companion, and continued to enumerate the advantages reserved for the inhabitants of the visible face.

Among others, he mentioned eclipses of the sun, which take place only on this side of the lunar disc, since, in order that they may take place, it is necessary for the moon to be *in opposition*. These eclipses, caused by the interposition of the earth between the moon and the sun, can last *two hours;* during which time, by reason of the rays refracted by its atmosphere, the terrestrial globe can appear as nothing but a black point upon the sun.

"So," said Nicholl, "the invisible hemisphere is very ill supplied, very ill treated, by nature."

"Never mind," replied Michel; "if we ever become Selenites, we will inhabit the visible face. I like the light."

"Unless, by any chance," answered Nicholl, "the atmosphere should be condensed on the other side, as certain astronomers pretend."

"That would be a consideration," said Michel.

Breakfast over, the observers returned to their post. They tried to see through the darkened windows by extinguishing all light in the projectile. But not a luminous spark made its way through the darkness.

One inexplicable fact preoccupied Barbicane. Why, having passed within such a short distance of the moon—about 25 miles only—why had the projectile not fallen? If its speed had been enormous, he could have understood that the fall would not have taken place. But with a relatively moderate speed, the projectile's resistance to the moon's attraction could not be explained. Was the projectile under some foreign influence? Did some kind of body retain it in the ether? It was quite evident that it could never reach any point of the moon. Where was it going? Was it going farther from, or nearing, the disc? Was it being borne in that profound darkness through the infinity of space? How could they learn, how calculate, in the midst of this night? All these questions made Barbicane uneasy, but he could not solve them.

Certainly, the invisible moon was *there,* perhaps only some few miles off. But neither he nor his companions could see it. If there was any noise on its surface, they could not hear it. Air, that medium of sound, was wanting to transmit the groanings of that moon which the Arabic legends call "a man already half granite, and still breathing."

One must allow that that was enough to aggravate the most patient observers. It was the unknown dark side of the moon which was stealing from their sight. The very side about which they knew the least. The side which 15 days sooner, or 15 days later, had been, or would be, splendidly illuminated by the solar rays, was then being lost in utter darkness. In 15 days where would the projectile be? Who could say? Where would it be drawn by the powers of the conflicting attractions that are present in space? The disappointment of the travelers in the midst of this utter darkness may be imagined. All observation of the lunar disc was impossible. The constellations alone claimed all their attention; and we must allow that astronomers such as Faye, Charconac, and Secchi never found themselves in circumstances so favorable for the observation of these stars.

Indeed, nothing could equal the splendor of this starry world, bathed in limpid ether. Its diamonds set in the heavenly vault sparkled magnificently. The eye took in the firmament from the Southern Cross to the North Star, those two constellations which in 12,000 years, by reason of the succession of equinoxes, will become the earth's polar stars. Imagination loses itself in this sublime infinity, amid which the projectile was gravitating, like a new star created by the hand of man. From a natural cause, these constellations shone with a soft luster. They did not twinkle, for there was no atmosphere which, by the intervention of its layers unequally dense and of different degrees of humidity, produces this scintillation. These stars were soft eyes, looking out into the dark night, amid the silence of absolute space.

Long did the travelers stand mute, watching the constellated firmament, upon which the moon, like a vast screen, made an enormous black hole. But at length a painful sensation drew them from their watchings. This was an intense cold, which soon covered the inside of the window glass with a thick coating of ice. The sun was no longer warming the projectile with its direct rays, and thus it was losing the heat stored up in its walls by degrees. This heat was rapidly evaporating into space by radiation, and a considerably lower temperature was the result. The humidity of the interior was changed into ice upon contact with the glass, preventing all observation.

Nicholl consulted the thermometer, and saw that it had fallen to zero. So that, in spite of the many reasons for economizing, Barbicane, after having begged light from the gas, was also obliged to beg for heat. The projectile's low temperature was no longer endurable. Its tenants would have frozen to death.

"Well," observed Michel, "we cannot reasonably complain of the monotony of our journey! What variety we have had, at least in temperature. Now we are blinded with light and saturated with heat, like the Indians of the pampas, now plunged into profound darkness, amid the cold, like the Eskimos of the North Pole. No, indeed, we can't complain. Nature does wonders in our honor."

"But," asked Nicholl, "what is the temperature outside?"

"Exactly that of the planetary space," replied Barbicane.

"Then," continued Michel Ardan, "would not this be the time to make the experiment which we dared not attempt when we were drowned in the sun's rays?"

"It is now or never," replied Barbicane, "for we are in a good position to verify the temperature of space, and see if Fourier or Pouillet's calculations are exact."

"In any case it is cold," said Michel. "See, the steam of the interior is condensing on the glasses of the windows. If the fall continues, the vapor of our breath will fall in snow."

"Let us prepare a thermometer," said Barbicane.

We may imagine that an ordinary thermometer would afford no result under the circumstances in which this instrument was to be exposed. The mercury would have been frozen in its ball, as below 42° Fahrenheit below zero it is no longer liquid. But Barbicane had furnished himself with a spirit thermometer on Wafferdin's system, which gives the minima of excessively low temperatures.

Before beginning the experiment, this instrument was compared with an ordinary one, and then Barbicane prepared to use it.

"How shall we set about it?" asked Nicholl.

"Nothing is easier," replied Michel Ardan, who was never at a loss. "We open the window and throw out the instrument. It follows the projectile with exemplary docility, and a quarter of an hour after, we draw it in."

"With the hand?" asked Barbicane.

"With the hand," replied Michel.

"Well, then, my friend, do not expose yourself," answered Barbicane, "for the hand that you draw in again will

be nothing but a stump frozen and deformed by the frightful cold."

"Really!"

"You will feel as if you had had a terrible burn, like that
of iron at a white heat. Whether the heat leaves our bodies
briskly or enters briskly, it is exactly the same thing. Besides, I am not at all certain that the objects we have thrown
out are still following us."

"Why not?" asked Nicholl.

"Because, if we are passing through an atmosphere of the
slightest density, these objects will be retarded. Again, the
darkness prevents our seeing if they still float around us.
But in order not to expose ourselves to the loss of our
thermometer, we will fasten it, and we can then more easily
pull it back again."

Barbicane's advice was followed. Through the window
rapidly opened Nicholl threw out the instrument, which was
held by a short cord, so that it might be more easily drawn
up. The window had not been opened more than a second,
but that second had sufficed to let in a most intense cold.

"The devil!" exclaimed Michel Ardan. "It is cold enough
to freeze a white bear."

Barbicane waited until half an hour had elapsed, which
was more than time enough to allow the instrument to fall
to the level of the surrounding temperature. Then it was
rapidly pulled in.

Barbicane calculated the quantity of spirits of wine over-
flowed into the little vial soldered to the lower part of the
instrument, and said: "218° Fahrenheit below zero!"

Pouillet was right and Fourier wrong. That was the undoubted temperature of the starry space. Such is, perhaps, also the temperature of the lunar continents when the orb of night has lost by radiation all the heat which fifteen days of sun have poured into it.

15. Hyperbola or Parabola

We may, perhaps, be astonished to find Barbicane and his companions so little occupied with the future reserved for them in the metal prison which was bearing them through the infinity of space. Instead of asking where they were going, they passed their time making experiments, as if they had been quietly installed in their own study.

We might answer that men so strong minded were above such anxieties—that they did not trouble themselves about such trifles—and that they had something else to do than to occupy their minds with the future.

The truth was that they were not masters of their projectile; they could neither check its course nor alter its direction.

A sailor can change the head of his ship as he pleases; a balloonist can give a vertical motion to his balloon. These space travelers on the contrary, had no power over their vehicle. Every maneuver was forbidden. Hence the inclination to let things alone, or, as the sailors say, "let her run."

Where did they find themselves at this moment, at eight o'clock in the morning of the day called upon the earth the 6th of December? Very certainly in the neighborhood of the moon, and even near enough for it to look to them like an enormous black screen upon the firmament. As to the distance which separated them, it was impossible to estimate it. The projectile, held by some unaccountable force, had been within four miles of grazing the satellite's north pole.

But since entering the cone of the moon's shadow these last two hours, had the distance increased or diminished? Every point of mark was wanting by which to estimate both the direction and the speed of the projectile.

Perhaps it was rapidly leaving the moon, so that it would soon quit the pure shadow. Perhaps, again, on the other hand, it might be nearing it so much that in a short time it might strike some high point on the invisible hemisphere, which would doubtlessly have ended the journey much to the detriment of the travelers.

A discussion arose on this subject, and Michel Ardan, always ready with an explanation, gave it as his opinion that the projectile, held by the lunar attraction, would end by falling on the surface of the moon like a meteorite falling on earth.

"First of all, my friend," answered Barbicane, "every meteorite does not fall to the earth. Only a small proportion do so. If we had been turned into a meteorite, it does not necessarily follow that we should ever reach the surface of the moon."

"But if only we approach near enough, I don't see how—" replied Michel.

"Pure mistake," interrupted Barbicane. "Have you not seen shooting stars rush through the sky by thousands at certain seasons?"

"Yes."

"Well, these stars only shine when they are heated by

gliding over the atmospheric layers. Now, if they enter the atmosphere, they pass at least within forty miles of the earth, but they seldom fall upon it. The same with our projectile. It may approach very near to the moon, and yet not fall upon it."

"But then," asked Michel, "I shall be curious to know how our erring vehicle will act in space."

"I see but two hypotheses," replied Barbicane, after some moments' reflection.

"What are they?"

"The projectile has the choice between two mathematical curves, and it will follow one or the other according to the speed with which it is animated, and which at this moment I cannot estimate."

"Yes," said Nicholl, "it will follow either a parabola or a hyperbola."

"Just so," replied Barbicane. "With a certain speed it will assume the parabola, and with a greater the hyperbola."

"I like those grand words," exclaimed Michel Ardan. "One knows directly what they mean. And pray what is your parabola, if you please?"

"My friend," answered the captain, "the parabola is a curve of the second order, the result of the section of a cone intersected by a plane parallel to one of its sides."

"Ah! Ah!" said Michel, in a satisfied tone.

"It is very nearly," continued Nicholl, "the course described by a bomb launched from a mortar."

"Perfect! And the hyperbola?"

"The hyperbola, Michel, is a curve of the second order, produced by the intersection of a conic surface and a plane parallel to its axis, and constitutes two branches separated one from the other, both tending indefinitely in the two directions."

"It is possible!" exclaimed Michel Ardan in a serious tone, as if they had told him of some serious event. "What I particularly like in your definition of the hyperbola is that it is still more obscure than the word you pretend to define."

Nicholl and Barbicane cared little for Michel Ardan's fun. They were deep in a scientific discussion. What curve the projectile would follow was their hobby. One maintained the hyperbola, the other the parabola. They gave each other reasons bristling with x. Their arguments were couched in language which made Michel jump. The discussion was hot, and neither would give up his chosen curve to his adversary.

This scientific dispute lasted so long that it made Michel very impatient.

"Now, gentlemen cosines, will you cease to throw parabolas and hyperbolas at each other's heads? I want to understand the only interesting question in the whole affair. We shall follow one or other of these curves? Good. But where will they lead us?"

"Nowhere," replied Nicholl.

"How, nowhere?"

"Evidently," said Barbicane, "they are open curves, which may be prolonged indefinitely."

"Ah, savants!" cried Michel. "And what are either the one or the other to us from the moment we know that they equally lead us into infinite space?"

Barbicane and Nicholl could not forbear smiling. They had just been creating "art for art's sake." Never had so idle a question been raised at such an inopportune moment. The sinister truth remained that, whether hyperbolically or parabolically borne away, the projectile would never again meet either the earth or the moon.

What would become of these bold travelers in the immediate future? If they did not die of hunger, if they did not die of thirst, then in a few days, when the gas failed, they would die from want of air, unless the cold had killed them first. Still, important as it was to economize the gas, the excessive lowness of the surrounding temperature obliged them to consume a certain quantity. Strictly speaking, they could do without its *light*, but not without its *heat*. Fortunately the heat generated by Reiset's and Regnaut's apparatus raised the temperature of the interior of the projectile a little, and without much expenditure they were able to keep it bearable.

But observations had now become very difficult. The dampness of the projectile was condensed on the windows and congealed immediately. This cloudiness had to be dispersed continually in the hope that they would see some phenomena of the highest interest.

But up to this time the moon remained dumb and dark. It did not answer the multiplicity of questions put by these ardent minds. This situation drew a reflection from Michel, apparently a just one:

"If ever we begin this journey over again, we shall do well to choose the time when the moon is at the full."

"Certainly," said Nicholl, "that circumstance will be more favorable. I allow that the moon, immersed in the sun's rays, will not be visible during the transit, but instead we should see the earth, which would be full. And what is more, if we were drawn around the moon at this moment, we should at least have the advantage of seeing the invisible part of its disc magnificently lit."

"Well said, Nicholl," replied Michel Ardan. "What do you think, Barbicane?"

"I think this," answered the grave president: "If ever we begin this journey again, we shall start at the same time and under the same conditions. Suppose we had attained our end, would it not have been better to have found continents in broad daylight than a country plunged in utter darkness? Would not our first installation have been made under better circumstances? Yes, evidently. As to the invisible side, we could have visited it in our exploring expeditions on the lunar globe. So that the time of the full moon was well chosen. But we ought to have arrived at the end; and in order to have so arrived, we ought to have suffered no deviation on the road."

"I have nothing to say to that," answered Michel Ardan. "Here is, however, a good opportunity lost of observing the other side of the moon."

But the projectile was now describing in the shadow an incalculable course which no sight mark would allow them to ascertain. Had its direction been altered, either by the influence of the lunar attraction, or by the action of some unknown star? Barbicane could not say. But a change had taken place in the relative position of the vehicle, and Barbicane verified it about four in the morning.

The change consisted in this, that the base of the projectile had turned toward the moon's surface, and was so held by a perpendicular passing through its axis. The attraction, that is to say the weight, had brought about this alteration. The heaviest part of the projectile inclined toward the invisible disc as if it would fall upon it.

Was it falling? Were the travelers attaining that much-desired end? No. And the observation of a sign point, quite inexplicable in itself, showed Barbicane that his projectile was not nearing the moon, and that it had shifted by following an almost concentric curve.

This point of mark was a luminous brightness which Nicholl sighted suddenly on the limit of the horizon formed by the black disc. This point could not be confounded with a star. It was a reddish incandescence which increased by degrees, a decided proof that the projectile was shifting toward it and not falling normally on the surface of the moon.

"A volcano! It is a volcano in action!" cried Nicholl. "A disemboweling of the interior fires of the moon! That world is not quite extinguished."

"Yes, an eruption," replied Barbicane, who was carefully studying the phenomenon through his night glass. "What should it be, if not a volcano?"

"But, then," said Michel Ardan, "in order to maintain that combustion, there must be air. So the atmosphere does surround that part of the moon."

"Perhaps so," replied Barbicane, "but not necessarily. The volcano, by the decomposition of certain substances, can provide its own oxygen, and thus throw flames into space. It seems to me that the deflagration, by the intense brilliancy of the substances in combustion, is produced in pure oxygen. We must not be in a hurry to proclaim the existence of a lunar atmosphere."

The fiery mountain must have been situated about 45° S. lat. on the invisible part of the disc. But, to Barbicane's great displeasure, the curve which the projectile was describing was taking it far from the point indicated by the eruption. Thus he could not determine its nature exactly. Half an hour after being sighted, this luminous point had disappeared behind the dark horizon. But the verification of this phenomenon was of considerable consequence in their selenographic studies. It proved that all heat had not yet disappeared from the bowels of this globe, and where heat exists, who can affirm that the vegetable kingdom, nay, even the animal kingdom itself, has not up to this time resisted all destructive influences? The existence of this volcano in eruption, unmistakably seen by these earthly savants, would doubtless give rise to many theories favorable to the grave question of the habitability of the moon.

Barbicane allowed himself to be carried away by these reflections. He forgot himself in a deep reverie in which the mysterious destiny of the lunar world was uppermost. He was seeking to combine together the facts observed up to that time when a new incident recalled him briskly to reality. This incident was more than a cosmical phenomenon, it was a threatened danger, the consequences of which might be disastrous in the extreme.

Suddenly, in the midst of the ether, in the profound darkness, an enormous mass appeared. It was like a moon, but an incandescent moon whose brilliancy was all the more intolerable as it cut sharply on the frightful darkness of space. This mass, of a circular form, threw a light which filled the projectile. The forms of Barbicane, Nicholl, and Michel Ardan, bathed in its white sheets, assumed that livid spectral appearance, bathed in blue and yellow light, colors which magicians produce by burning table salt in alcohol.

"By Jove," cried Michel Ardan, "we are hideous! What is that ill-conditioned moon?"

"That is a flaming meteor," replied Barbicane.

"A meteor burning in space?"

"Yes."

This shooting globe, suddenly appearing in shadow at a distance of about 200 miles was probably 6,000 feet in diameter. It was traveling at a speed of about 15 miles per second, right in the projectile's path and must reach it in minutes. As it approached it grew to enormous proportions.

Imagine, if possible, the situation of the travelers! It is impossible to describe it. In spite of their courage, their cool composure, their carelessness of danger, they were mute, motionless with stiffened limbs, a prey to frightful terror. Their projectile, the course of which they could not alter, was rushing straight at this ignited mass, more intense than the open mouth of an oven. It seemed as though they were being precipitated toward an abyss of fire.

Barbicane had seized the hands of his two companions, and all three looked through their half-open eyelids upon that asteroid heated to a white heat. If thought was not destroyed within them, if their brains still functioned, they must have given themselves up for lost.

Two minutes after the sudden appearance of the meteor —to them two centuries of anguish—the projectile seemed almost about to strike it, when the globe of fire burst like a bomb, but without making any noise in that void where sound, which is but the agitation of the layers of air, could not be generated.

Nicholl uttered a cry, and he and his companions rushed to the window. What a sight! What pen can describe it? What palette is rich enough in colors to reproduce so magnificent a spectacle?

It was like the opening of a crater, like the scattering of an immense conflagration. Thousands of luminous fragments lit up and irradiated space with their fires. Every size, every color, was there intermingled. There were rays of yellow and pale yellow, red, green, gray—a crown of fireworks of all colors. Of the enormous and much-dreaded globe there remained nothing but these fragments carried in all directions, now asteroids in their turn, some flaming like a sword, some surrounded by a whitish cloud, and others leaving behind them trains of brilliant cosmical dust.

These incandescent blocks crossed and struck one another, scattering still smaller fragments, some of which struck the projectile. The left window was cracked by a violent shock. It seemed to be floating amid a hail of howitzer shells, the smallest of which might destroy it instantly.

The light which saturated the ether was so wonderfully intense that Michel, drawing Barbicane and Nicholl to his window, exclaimed, "The invisible moon is visible at last!"

And through a luminous emanation, which lasted some seconds, the whole three caught a glimpse of that mysterious disc which the eye of man now saw for the first time. What could they distinguish at a distance which they could not estimate? Some lengthened bands along the disc, real clouds formed in the midst of a very confined atmosphere, from which emerged not only all the mountains, but also projections of less importance; its circles, its yawning craters, as capriciously placed as on the visible surface. Then immense spaces, no longer arid plains, but real seas, oceans, widely distributed, reflecting on their liquid surface all the dazzling magic of the fires of space; and, lastly, on the surface of the continents, large dark masses, looking

like immense forests under the rapid illumination of
liance.

Was it an illusion, a mistake, an optical illusion? Could
they give a scientific assent to an observation so superfi-
cially obtained? Dared they pronounce upon the question
of its habitability after so slight a glimpse of the invisible
disc?

But the lightnings in space subsided by degrees. The
asteroids dispersed in different directions and were extinguished in the distance. The ether returned to its accustomed darkness. The stars, eclipsed for a moment, again
twinkled in the firmament, and the disc, so hastily discerned, was again buried in impenetrable night.

16. The Southern Hemisphere

THE PROJECTILE had just escaped a terrible danger, and a
very unforeseen one. Who would have thought of such an
encounter with meteors? These erring bodies might create
serious perils for the travelers. They were to them so many
sandbanks upon that sea of ether which, less fortunate than
sailors, they could not escape. But did these adventurers
complain of space? No, not since nature had given them the
splendid sight of a cosmical meteor bursting from expansion, since this inimitable firework, which no mortal could
imitate, had lit up for some seconds the invisible glory of
the moon. In that flash continents, seas, and forests had
become visible to them. Did an atmosphere, then, bring to
this unknown face its life-giving atoms? Questions still insoluble, and forever closed against human curiosity!

It was then half-past three in the afternoon. The projectile was following its curvilinear direction around the moon. Had its course been again altered by the meteor? It was to be feared so. But the projectile must describe a curve unalterably determined by the laws of mechanical reasoning. Barbicane was inclined to believe that this curve would be a parabola rather than a hyperbola. But admitting the parabola, the projectile must quickly have passed through the cone of shadow projected into space opposite the sun. This cone, indeed, is very narrow, the angular diameter of the moon being so little when compared with the diameter of the sun. It would seem that by now they should have left this shadow. Yet, whatever had been the speed of the projectile—and it could not have been insignificant—its period of darkness continued. That was evident, but perhaps that would not have been the case in a supposed rigidly parabolical trajectory—a new problem which tormented Barbicane's brain, imprisoned as he was in a circle of unknowns which he could not solve.

None of the travelers thought of taking an instant's repose. Each one watched for an unexpected fact which might throw some new light on their astronomical studies. About five o'clock Michel Ardan distributed, under the name of dinner, some pieces of bread and cold meat, which were quickly swallowed without the other two abandoning their window, the glass of which was incessantly encrusted by the condensation of vapor.

About 5:45 P.M. Nicholl, armed with his telescope, sighted toward the southern border of the moon, and in the direction followed by the projectile, some bright points cut upon the dark shield of the sky. They looked like a succes-

sion of sharp points lengthened into a tremulous line. .
were very bright and had the appearance of the new moon's
crescent.

They could not be mistaken. It was no longer a simple
meteor. This luminous ridge had neither color nor motion.
Nor was it a volcano in eruption. And Barbicane did not
hesitate to pronounce upon it.

"The sun!" he exclaimed.

"What! The sun?" answered Nicholl and Michel Ardan.

"Yes, my friends, it is the sun itself lighting up the summit of the mountains situated on the southern borders of the
moon. We are evidently nearing the South Pole."

"After having passed the North Pole," replied Michel.
"We have made the circuit of our satellite, then?"

"Yes, my good Michel."

"Then, no more hyperbolas, no more parabolas, no more
open curves to fear?"

"No, but a closed curve."

"Which is called——"

"An ellipse. Instead of losing itself in interplanetary
space, it is probable that the projectile will describe an elliptical orbit around the moon."

"Indeed!"

"And that it will become its satellite."

"Moon of the moon!" cried Michel Ardan.

"Only, I would have you observe, my worthy friend,"
replied Barbicane, "that we are none the less lost for that."

"Yes, in another manner, and much more pleasantly,"
answered the Frenchman with his most amiable smile.

17. Tycho

AT SIX in the evening the projectile passed the South Pole at less than 40 miles off, a distance equal to that already reached at the North Pole. The elliptical curve was being rigidly carried out.

At this moment the travelers once more entered the blessed rays of the sun. They saw once more those stars which move slowly from east to west. The sun was saluted by a triple hurrah. With its light it also sent heat, which soon pierced the metal walls. The glass resumed its accustomed appearance. The layers of ice melted as if by enchantment; and immediately, for economy's sake, the gas was put out, the air apparatus alone consuming its usual quantity.

"Ah," said Nicholl, "these rays of heat are good. With what impatience must the Selenites wait the reappearance of the orb of day."

"Yes," replied Michel Ardan, "imbibing at it were the brilliant ether, light and heat—all life is contained in them."

At this moment the bottom of the projectile deviated somewhat from the lunar surface, in order to follow the slightly lengthened elliptical orbit. From this point, had the earth been at the full, Barbicane and his companions could have seen it, but immersed in the sun's irradiation it was quite invisible. Another spectacle attracted their attention, that of the southern part of the moon, brought by the telescopes to within 450 yards. They did not again leave the windows, and noted every detail of this fantastical continent.

Mounts Doerfel and Leibnitz formed two separate

groups very near the South Pole. The first group extended from the pole to the 84th parallel, on the eastern part of the orb; the second occupied the eastern border, extending from 65° lat. to the pole.

On their capriciously formed ridge appeared dazzling sheets, as mentioned by the astronomer Père Secchi. With more certainty than the illustrious Roman Barbicane was able to recognize their nature.

"They are snow-covered slopes," he exclaimed.

"Snow?" repeated Nicholl.

"Yes, Nicholl, snow, the surface of which is deeply frozen. See how they reflect the luminous rays. Cooled lava would never give out such intense reflection. There must then be water, there must be air on the moon. As little as you please, but the fact can no longer be contested." No, it could not be. And if ever Barbicane should see the earth again, his notes will bear witness to this great fact in his selenographic observations.

These mountains of Doerfel and Leibnitz rose in the midst of plains which were bounded by an indefinite succession of circles and ramparts. These two chains are the only ones met with in this region of circles. Comparatively but slightly marked, they throw up here and there some sharp points, the highest summit of which attains an altitude of 24,600 feet.

But the projectile was high above all this landscape, and the mountain tops disappeared in the intense brilliancy of the disc. To the eyes of the travelers there reappeared that original aspect of the lunar landscapes, raw in tone, without gradation of colors, and without degrees of shadow, roughly black and white, from the want of diffusion of light.

But the sight of this desolate world did not fail to captivate them by its very strangeness. They were moving over this region as if they had been borne on the breath of some storm, watching heights emerge under their feet, piercing the cavities with their eyes, going down into the rifts, climbing the ramparts, sounding these mysterious holes, and leveling all cracks. But they saw no trace of vegetation, no appearance of cities, nothing but stratification, beds of lava, overflowings polished like immense mirrors, reflecting the sun's rays with overpowering brilliancy. Nothing belonging to a *living* world—everything to a dead world, where avalanches, rolling from the summits of the mountains, would disperse noiselessly at the bottom of the abyss, retaining the motion but wanting the sound. In any case it was the image of death, without its being possible even to say that life had ever existed there.

Michel Ardan, however, thought he recognized a heap of ruins, to which he drew Barbicane's attention. It was about the 80th parallel, in 30° long. This heap of stones, rather regularly placed, represented a vast fortress, overlooking a long rift, which in former days had served as a bed to the rivers of prehistorical times. Not far from that Short Mountain rose to a height of 17,400 feet, equal to the Asiatic Caucasus. Michel Ardan, with his accustomed ardor, maintained the "evidences" of his fortress. Beneath the mountain he discerned the dismantled ramparts of a town: here the still-intact arch of a portico, there two or three columns lying under their base; farther on, a succession of arches which must have supported the conduit of an aqueduct; in another part the sunken pillars of a gigantic bridge, run into the thickest parts of the rift. He distinguished all this, but with so much imagination in his glance, and through a telescope so fantastical, that we could hardly believe his observation. But who could affirm, who would dare to say, that the amiable fellow did not really see that which his two companions would not see?

Moments were too precious to be sacrificed in idle discussion. The Selenite city, whether imaginary or not, had already disappeared afar off. The distance of the projectile from the moon was on the increase and the details of the soil were being lost in a confused jumble. The reliefs, the circles, the craters, and plains alone remained, and still showed their boundary lines distinctly. At this moment, to the left, lay extended one of the finest circles of lunar topography, one of the curiosities of this continent. It was Newton, which Barbicane recognized without trouble by referring to the *Mappa Selenographica.*

Newton is situated in exactly 77° S. lat., and 16° E. long. It forms a ringed crater the ramparts of which, rising to a height of 21,300 feet, seemed impassable.

Barbicane made his companions observe that the height of this mountain above the surrounding plain was far from equaling the depth of its crater. This enormous hole was beyond all measurement, and formed a gloomy abyss, the bottom of which the sun's rays could never reach. There, according to Humboldt, reigns utter darkness, which the light of the sun and the earth cannot break. Mythologists could well have made it the mouth of hell.

"Newton," said Barbicane, "is the most perfect type of these ringed mountains, of which the earth possesses no sample. They prove that the moon's formation, by means of cooling, is due to violent causes; for while, under the pressure of internal fires the reliefs rise to considerable height, the depths withdraw far below the lunar level."

"I do not dispute the fact," replied Michel Ardan.

Some minutes after passing Newton, the projectile was directly over Mount Moret. It skirted the summits of Blancanus at a distance, and at about 7:30 P.M. reached the circle of Clavius.

This circle, one of the most remarkable on the moon, is situated in 58° S. lat. and 15° E. long. Its height is estimated at 22,950 feet. The travelers, at a distance of 24 miles (reduced to four by their glasses) could admire this vast crater in its entirety.

"Terrestrial volcanoes," said Barbicane, "are but molehills compared with those of the moon. Measuring the old craters formed by the first eruptions of Vesuvius and Etna we find them little more than three miles in breadth. In France the circle of Cantal measures six miles across; at Ceyland the circle of the island is forty miles, which is considered the largest on the globe. What are these diameters against that of Clavius, which we overlook at this moment?"

"What is its breadth?" asked Nicholl.

"It is 150 miles," replied Barbicane. "This circle is certainly the most important on the moon, but many others measure 150, 100, or 75 miles."

"Ah, my friends," exclaimed Michel, "can you picture to yourselves what this now peaceful orb of night must have been when its craters, filled with thunderings, vomited at the same time smoke and tongues of flame. What a wonderful spectacle then, and now what decay! This moon is nothing more than a thin carcase of fireworks whose squibs, rockets, serpents, and suns, after a superb brilliancy, have left but sadly broken cases. Who can say the cause, the reason, the motive force of these cataclysms?"

Barbicane was not listening to Michel Ardan; he was contemplating these ramparts of Clavius, formed by large mountains spread over several miles. At the bottom of the immense cavity burrowed hundreds of small extinguished craters, riddling the soil like a colander, and overlooked by a peak 15,000 feet high.

Around the plain appeared desolation. Nothing so arid as these reliefs, nothing so sad as these ruins of mountains, and, if we may so express ourselves, these fragments of peaks and mountains which strewed the soil. The satellite seemed to have burst at this spot.

The projectile was still advancing, and this movement did not subside. Circles, craters, and uprooted mountains succeeded each other incessantly. No more plains; no more seas. A never-ending Switzerland and Norway. And lastly, in the center of this region of crevasses, the most splendid mountain on the lunar disc, the dazzling Tycho, by which posterity will ever preserve the name of the illustrious Danish astronomer.

In observing the full moon in a cloudless sky no one has failed to remark this brilliant point of the southern hemisphere. Michel Ardan used every metaphor that his imagination could supply to designate it by. To him this Tycho was a focus of light, a center of irradiation, a crater vomiting rays. It was the tire of a brilliant wheel, an *asteria* enclosing the disc with its silver tentacles, an enormous eye filled with flames, a glory carved for Plato's head, a star launched by the Creator's hand, and crushed against the face of the moon!

Tycho forms such a concentration of light that the inhabitants of the earth can see it without glasses, though at a

distance of 240,000 miles! Imagine, then, its intensity to the
eye of observers placed at a distance of only 50 miles! Seen
through this pure ether, its brilliancy was so intolerable that
Barbicane and his friends were obliged to blacken their
glasses with the gas smoke before they could bear the splendor. Then silent, scarcely uttering an interjection of admiration, they gazed, they contemplated. All their feelings,
all their impressions, were concentrated in that look, as
under any violent emotion all life is concentrated at the
heart.

Tycho belongs to the system of radiating mountains, like
Aristarchus and Copernicus; but it is of all the most complete and decided, showing unquestionably the frightful
volcanic action to which the formation of the moon is due.
Tycho is situated in 43° S. lat. and 12° E. long. Its center is
a crater 50 miles wide. It assumes a slightly elliptical form,
and is surrounded by an enclosure of ringed ramparts
which on the east and west overlook the outer plain from a
height of 15,000 feet. It is a group of Mont Blancs, placed
around one common center and crowned by radiating
beams.

What this incomparable mountain really is, with all the
projections converging toward it, and the interior excrescences of its crater, photography itself could never represent. Indeed, it is during the full moon that Tycho is seen in
all its splendor. Then all shadows disappear, the foreshort-
ening of perspective disappears, and all proofs become
white—a disagreeable fact, for this strange region would
have been marvelous if reproduced with photographic exactness. It is but a group of hollows, craters, circles, a
network of crests; then, as far as the eye could see, a whole

volcanic network cast upon this encrusted soil. One can then understand that the bubbles of this central eruption have kept their first form. Crystallized by cooling, they have stereotyped that aspect which the moon formerly presented when under the Plutonian forces.

The distance which separated the travelers from the annular summits of Tycho was not so great but that they could catch the principal details. Even on the causeway forming the fortifications of Tycho, the mountains hanging onto the interior and exterior sloping flanks rose in stories like gigantic terraces. They appeared to be higher by 300 or 400 feet to the west than to the east. No system of terrestrial encampment could equal these natural fortifications. A town built at the bottom of this circular cavity would have been utterly inaccessible.

Inaccessible and wonderfully extended over this soil covered with picturesque projections! Indeed, nature had not left the bottom of this crater flat and empty. It possessed its own peculiar orography, a mountainous system, making it a world in itself. The travelers could distinguish clearly cones, central hills, remarkable positions of the soil, naturally placed to receive the chefs d'œuvre of Selenite architecture. There was marked out the place for a temple, here the ground of a forum, on this spot the plan of a palace, in another the plateau for a citadel; the whole overlooked by a central mountain of 1,500 feet. A vast circle, in which ancient Rome could have been held in its entirety ten times over.

"Ah," exclaimed Michel Ardan, enthusiastic at the sight, "what a grand town might be constructed within that ring of mountains! A quiet city, a peaceful refuge, beyond all human misery. How calm and isolated those misanthropes, those haters of humanity might live there, and all who have a distaste for social life!"

"All! It would be too small for them," replied Barbicane simply.

18. Grave Questions

THE PROJECTILE had passed the immense concavity of Tycho, as Barbicane and his two companions stared at the brilliant rays which the celebrated mountain shed so curiously all over the horizon.

What was this radiant glory? What geological phenomenon had created these ardent beams? This question occupied Barbicane's mind.

Under his eyes ran in all directions luminous furrows, raised at the edges and concave in the center, some were 12 miles, others 30 miles broad. These brilliant trains extended in some places to within 600 miles of Tycho, and seemed to cover half of the Southern Hemisphere. One of these jets extended as far as the circle of Neander, situated on the 40th meridian. Another, by a slight curve, furrowed the "Sea of Nectar," breaking against the chain of Pyrenees, after a circuit of 800 miles. Others, toward the west, covered the "Sea of Clouds" and the "Sea of Humors" with a luminous network. What was the origin of these sparkling rays, which shone on the plains as well as on the reliefs, at whatever height they might be? All sprang from a common center, the crater of Tycho. Herschel attributed their brilliancy to currents of lava congealed by the cold, an opinion, however, which has not been generally adopted. Other astronomers have seen in these inexplicable rays a kind of moraines, rows of erratic blocks, which had been thrown up at the period of Tycho's formation.

"And why not?" asked Nicholl of Barbicane, who was relating and rejecting these different opinions.

"Because the regularity of these luminous lines and the violence necessary to carry volcanic matter to such distances are inexplicable."

"Eh! By Jove!" replied Michel Ardan, "it seems easy enough to me to explain the origin of these rays."

"Indeed?" said Barbicane.

"Indeed," continued Michel. "It is enough to say that it is a vast star, similar to that produced by a ball or a stone thrown at a square of glass!"

"Well!" replied Barbicane, smiling. "And what hand would be powerful enough to throw a ball to give such a shock as that?"

"The hand is not necessary," answered Nicholl, not at all confounded; "and as to the stone, let us suppose it to be a comet."

"Ah, those much-abused comets!" exclaimed Barbicane. "My brave Michel, your explanation is not bad; but your comet is useless. The shock which produced that rent must have come from the inside of the star. A violent contraction of the lunar crust, while cooling, might suffice to imprint this gigantic star."

"A contraction! Something like a lunar stomach ache," said Michel Ardan.

"Besides," added Barbicane, "this opinion is that of an English savant, Nasmyth, and it seems to me sufficiently to explain the radiation of these mountains."

"That Nasmyth was no fool!" replied Michel.

Long did the travelers, whom such a sight could never weary, admire the splendors of Tycho. Their projectile, saturated with luminous gleams in the double irradiation of sun and moon, must have appeared like an incandescent globe. They had passed suddenly from excessive cold to intense heat. Nature was thus preparing them to become Selenites. Become Selenites! That idea brought up once more the question of the habitability of the moon. After what they had seen, could the travelers solve it? Would they decide for or against it? Michel Ardan persuaded his two friends to form an opinion, and asked them directly if they thought that men and animals were represented in the lunar world.

"I think that we can answer," said Barbicane; "but according to my idea the question ought not to be put in that form. I ask it to be put differently."

"Put it your own way," replied Michel.

"Here it is," continued Barbicane. "The problem is a double one, and requires a double solution. Is the moon *habitable?* Has the moon ever been *inhabitable?*"

"Good!" replied Nicholl. "First let us see whether the moon is habitable."

"To tell the truth, I know nothing about it," answered Michel.

"And I answer in the negative," continued Barbicane. "In its actual state, with its surrounding atmosphere certainly very much reduced, its seas for the most part dried up, its insufficient supply of water restricted, vegetation, sudden alterations of cold and heat, its days and nights of 354 hours—the moon does not seem habitable to me, nor does it seem propitious to animal development, nor sufficient for the wants of existence as we understand it."

"Agreed," replied Nicholl. "But is not the moon habitable for creatures differently organized from ourselves?"

"That question is more difficult to answer, but I will try; and I ask Nicholl if *motion* appears to him to be a necessary result of *life,* whatever be its organization?"

"Without a doubt!" answered Nicholl.

"Then, my worthy companion, I would answer that we have observed the lunar continent at a distance of 500 yards at most, and that nothing seemed to us to move on the moon's surface. The presence of any kind of life would have been betrayed by its attendant marks, such as divers buildings, and even by ruins. And what have we seen? Everywhere and always the geological works of nature, never the work of man. If, then, there exist representatives of the animal kingdom on the moon, they must have fled to those unfathomable cavities which the eye cannot reach; which I cannot admit, for they must have left traces of their passage on those plains which the atmosphere must cover, however slightly raised it may be. These traces are nowhere visible. There remains but one hypothesis, that of a living race to which motion, which is life, is foreign."

"One might as well say, living creatures which do not live," replied Michel.

"Just so," said Barbicane, "which for us has no meaning."

"Then we may form our opinion?" said Michel.

"Yes," replied Nicholl.

"Very well," continued Michel Ardan, "the Scientific Commission assembled in the projectile of the Gun Club, after having founded their argument on facts recently observed, decide unanimously upon the question of the habitability of the moon—'*No!* The moon is not habitable.' "

This decision was consigned by President Barbicane to his notebook, where the minutes of the sitting of the 6th of December may be seen.

"Now, said Nicholl, "let us attack the second question, an indispensable complement of the first. I ask the honorable commission, if the moon is not habitable, has it ever been inhabited, Citizen Barbicane?"

"My friends," replied Barbicane, "I did not undertake this journey in order to form an opinion on the past habitability of our satellite; but I will add that our personal observations only confirm me in this opinion. I believe, indeed I affirm, that the moon has been inhabited by a human race organized like our own; that it has produced animals anatomically formed like the terrestrial animals: but I add that these races, human and animal, have had their day, and are now forever extinct!"

"Then," asked Michel, "the moon must be older than the earth?"

"No," said Barbicane decidedly, "but a world which has grown old quicker, and whose formation and deformation have been more rapid. Relatively, the organizing force of matter has been much more violent in the interior of the moon than in the interior of the terrestrial globe. The actual state of this cracked, twisted, and burst disc abundantly proves this. The moon and the earth were nothing but gaseous masses originally. These gases have passed into a liquid state under different influences, and the solid masses have been formed later. But most certainly our sphere was still gaseous or liquid, when the moon was solidified by cooling, and had become habitable."

"I believe it," said Nicholl.

"Then," continued Barbicane, "an atmosphere surrounded it, the waters contained within this gaseous envelope could not evaporate. Under the influence of air, water, light, solar heat, and central heat, vegetation took possession of the continents prepared to receive it, and certainly life showed itself about this period, for nature does not expend itself in vain; and a world so wonderfully formed for habitation must necessarily be inhabited."

"But," said Nicholl, "many phenomena inherent in our satellite might cramp the expansion of the animal and vegetable kingdom. For example, its days and nights of 354 hours?"

"At the terrestrial poles they last six months," said Michel.

"An argument of little value, since the poles are not inhabited."

"Let us observe, my friends," continued Barbicane, "that if in the actual state of the moon its long nights and long days created differences of temperature insupportable to organization, it was not so at the historical period of time. The atmosphere enveloped the disc with a fluid mantle; vapor deposited itself in the shape of clouds; this natural screen tempered the ardor of the solar rays, and retained the nocturnal radiation. Light, like heat, can diffuse itself in the air; hence an equality between the influences which no longer exists, now that that atmosphere has almost entirely disappeared. And now I am going to astonish you."

"Astonish us?" said Michel Ardan.

"I firmly believe that at the period when the moon was inhabited, the nights and days did not last 354 hours!"

"And why?" asked Nicholl quickly.

"Because most probably then the rotary motion of the moon upon its axis was not equal to its revolution, an equality which presents each part of its disc during fifteen days to the action of the solar rays."

"Granted," replied Nicholl, "but why should not these two motions have been equal, as they are really so?"

"Because that equality has only been determined by terrestrial attraction. And who can say that this attraction was powerful enough to alter the motion of the moon at that period when the earth was still fluid?"

"Just so," replied Nicholl; "and who can say that the moon has always been a satellite of the earth?"

"And who can say," exclaimed Michel Ardan, "that the moon did not exist before the earth?"

Their imaginations carried them away into an indefinite field of hypothesis. Barbicane sought to restrain them.

"Those speculations are too high," he said, "problems utterly insoluble. Do not let us enter upon them. Let us only admit the insufficiency of the primordial attraction, and then by the inequality of the two motions of rotation and revolution, the days and nights could have succeeded each other on the moon as they succeed each other on the earth. Besides, even without these conditions, life was possible."

"And so," asked Michel Ardan, "humanity has disappeared from the moon?"

"Yes," replied Barbicane, "after having doubtless remained persistently for millions of centuries; by degrees the atmosphere becoming rarefied, the disc became uninhabitable, as the terrestrial globe will one day become by cooling."

"By cooling?"

"Certainly," replied Barbicane; "as the internal fires became extinguished, and the incandescent matter concentrated itself, the lunar crust cooled. By degrees the consequences of these phenomena showed themselves in the disappearance of organized beings, and by the disappearance of vegetation. Soon the atmosphere was rarefied, probably withdrawn by terrestrial attraction; then aerial departure of respirable air, and disappearance of water by means of evaporation. At this period the moon, becoming uninhabitable, was no longer inhabited. It was a dead world, such as we see it today."

"And you say that the same fate is in store for the earth?"

"Most probably."

"But when?"

"When the cooling of its crust shall have made it uninhabitable."

"And have they calculated the time which our unfortunate sphere will take to cool?"

"Certainly."

"And you know these calculations?"

"Perfectly."

"But speak, then, my clumsy savant," exclaimed Michel Ardan, "for you make me boil with impatience!"

"Very well, my good Michel," replied Barbicane quietly; "we know what diminution of temperature the earth undergoes in the lapse of a century. And according to certain calculations, this mean temperature will, after a period of 400,000 years, be brought down to zero!"

"Four hundred thousand years!" exclaimed Michel. "Ah! I breathe again. Really I was frightened to hear you; I imagined that we had not more than 50,000 years to live."

Barbicane and Nicholl could not help laughing at their

companion's uneasiness. Then Nicholl, who wished to end the discussion, put the second question, which had just been considered again.

"Has the moon been inhabited?" he asked.

The answer was unanimously in the affirmative. But during this discussion, fruitful in somewhat hazardous theories, the projectile was rapidly leaving the moon: the lineaments faded away from the travelers' eyes, mountains were confused in the distance; and of all the wonderful, strange, and fantastical forms of the earth's satellite there soon remained nothing but the imperishable remembrance.

19. A Struggle Against the Impossible

For a long time Barbicane and his companions looked silently and sadly upon that world which they had seen only from a distance, as Moses saw the land of Canaan, and which they were leaving without a possibility of ever returning to it. The projectile's position with regard to the moon had altered, and the base was not turned to the earth.

This change, which Barbicane verified, did not fail to surprise them. If the projectile was to gravitate around the satellite in an elliptical orbit, why was not its heaviest part turned toward it, as the moon turns its to the earth? That was a difficult point.

In watching the course of the projectile they could see that on leaving the moon it followed a course analogous to that traced in approaching it. It was describing a very long ellipse, which would most likely extend to the point of equal attraction, where the influences of the earth and its satellite are neutralized.

Such was the conclusion which Barbicane very justly drew from facts already observed, a conviction which his two friends shared with him.

"And when arrived at this dead point, what will become of us?" asked Michel Ardan.

"We don't know," replied Barbicane.

"But one can draw some hypotheses, I suppose?"

"Two," answered Barbicane; "either the projectile's speed will be insufficient, and it will remain forever immovable on this line of double attraction——"

"I prefer the other hypothesis, whatever it may be," interrupted Michel.

"Or," continued Barbicane, "its speed will be sufficient, and it will continue its elliptical course, to gravitate forever around the orb of night."

"A revolution not at all consoling," said Michel, "to pass to the state of humble servants to a moon whom we are accustomed to look upon as our own handmaid. So that is the fate in store for us?"

Neither Barbicane nor Nicholl answered.

"You do not answer," continued Michel impatiently.

"There is nothing to answer," said Nicholl.

"Is there nothing to try?"

"No," answered Barbicane. "Do you pretend to fight against the impossible?"

"Why not? Do one Frenchman and two Americans shrink from such a word?"

"But what would you do?"

"Subdue this motion which is bearing us away."

"Subdue it?"

"Yes," continued Michel, getting animated, "or else alter it, and employ it to the accomplishment of our own ends."

"And how?"

"That is your affair. If artillerymen are not masters of their projectile they are not artillerymen. If the projectile is to command the gunner, we had better ram the gunner into the gun. My faith, fine savants, who do not know what is to become of us after inducing me——"

"Inducing you!" cried Barbicane and Nicholl. "Inducing you! What do you mean by that?"

"No recrimination," said Michel. "I do not complain, the trip has pleased me, the projectile agrees with me; but let us do all that is humanly possible to do—fall somewhere, even if only on the moon."

"We ask no better, my worthy Michel," replied Barbicane, "but means fail us."

"We cannot alter the motion of the projectile?"

"No."

"Nor diminish its speed?"

"No."

"Not even by lightening it?"

"What would you throw out?" said Nicholl. "We have no ballast on board; and indeed it seems to me that if lightened it would go much quicker."

"Slower."

"Quicker."

"Neither slower nor quicker," said Barbicane, wishing to make his two friends agree; "for we float in space, and must no longer consider specific weight."

"Very well," cried Michel Ardan in a decided voice; "then there remains but one thing to do."

"What is it?" said Nicholl.

"Breakfast," answered the cool, audacious Frenchman, who always brought up this solution at the most difficult juncture.

In any case, if this operation had no influence on the projectile's course, it could at least be tried without inconvenience, and even with success, from a stomachic point of view. Certainly Michel had none but good ideas.

They breakfasted then at two in the morning; the hour mattered little. Michel served his usual repast, crowned by a glorious bottle drawn from his private cellar. If ideas did not then crowd into their brains, we must despair of Chambertin, 1853. The repast finished, observation began again. Around the projectile, at an invariable distance, were the objects which had been thrown out. Evidently, in its translatory motion around the moon, it had not passed through any atmosphere, for the specific weight of these different objects would have checked their relative speed.

On the side of the terrestrial sphere nothing was to be seen. The earth was but a day old, having been new the night before at twelve; and two days must elapse before its crescent, freed from the solar rays, would serve as a clock to the Selenites, as in its rotary movement each of its points after 24 hours repasses the same lunar meridian.

On the moon's side the sight was different; the orb shone in all its splendor amid innumerable constellations whose purity could not be troubled by its rays. On the disc, the plains were already returning to the dark tint which is seen from the earth. The other part of the nimbus remained bril-

liant, and in the midst of this general brilliancy Tycho
shone prominently like a sun.

Barbicane had no means of estimating the projectile's
speed, but reasoning showed that it must uniformly decrease, according to the laws of mechanical reasoning. Having admitted that the projectile was describing an orbit
around the moon, this orbit must necessarily be elliptical;
science proves that it must be so. No motive body circulating around an attracting body fails in this law. Every orbit
described in space is elliptical. And why should the projectile of the Gun Club escape this natural arrangement? In
elliptical orbits, the attracting body always occupies one of
the foci; so that at one moment the satellite is nearer and at
another farther from the orb around which it gravitates.
When the earth is nearest the sun it is in its perihelion; and
in its aphelion at the farthest point. Speaking of the moon,
it is nearest to the earth in its perigee, and farthest from it in
its apogee. To use analogous expressions, with which the
astronomers' language is enriched, if the projectile remains
as a satellite of the moon, we must say that it is in its
"aposelene" at its farthest point and in its "periselene" at its
nearest. In the latter case, the projectile would attain its
maximum of speed; and in the former its minimum. It was
evidently moving toward its aposelenitical point, and Barbicane had reason to think that its speed would decrease up
to this point, and then increase by degrees as it neared the
moon. This speed would even become nil if this point joined
that of equal attraction. Barbicane studied the consequences of these different situations, and was thinking what
inference he could draw from them, when he was roughly
disturbed by a cry from Michel Ardan.

"By Jove!" he exclaimed. "I must admit we are down-right simpletons!"

"I do not say we are not," replied Barbicane; "but why?"

"Because we have a very simple means of checking this speed which is bearing us from the moon, and we do not use it!"

"And what is the means?"

"To use the recoil contained in our rockets."

"Done!" said Nicholl.

"We have not used this force yet," said Barbicane, "it is true, but we will do so."

"When?" asked Michel.

"When the time comes. Observe, my friends, that in the position occupied by the projectile, an oblique position with regard to the lunar disc, our rockets, in slightly altering its direction, might turn it from the moon instead of drawing it nearer?"

"Just so," replied Michel.

"Let us wait, then. By some inexplicable influence the projectile is turning its base toward the earth. It is probable that at the point of equal attraction its conical cap will be directed rigidly toward the moon; at that moment we may hope that its speed will be nil; then will be the moment to act, and with the influence of our rockets we may perhaps provoke a fall directly on the surface of the lunar disc."

"Bravo!" said Michel. "What we did not do, what we could not do on our first passage at the dead point, because the projectile was then endowed with too great a speed."

"Very well reasoned," said Nicholl.

"Let us wait patiently," continued Barbicane. "Putting

every chance on our side, and after having so much de-spaired, I may say I think that we shall gain our end."

This conclusion was a signal for Michel Ardan's hips and hurrahs. And none of the audacious boobies remembered the question that they themselves had solved in the nega-tive. No, the moon is not inhabited; no, the moon is prob-ably not habitable. And yet they were going to try every-thing to reach it.

One single question remained to be solved. At what pre-cise moment the projectile would reach the point of equal attraction, on which the travelers must play their last card. In order to calculate this to within a few seconds, Barbicane had only to refer to his notes, and to reckon the different heights taken on the lunar parallels. Thus the time neces-sary to travel over the distance between the dead point and the South Pole would be equal to the distance separating the North Pole from the dead point. The hours representing the time traveled over were carefully noted, and the calcu-lation was easy. Barbicane found that this point would be reached at one in the morning on the night of the 7th–8th of December. So, that, if nothing interfered with its course, it would reach the given point in twenty-two hours.

The rockets had primarily been placed to check the fall of the projectile upon the moon, and now they were going to employ them for a directly contrary purpose. In any case they were ready, and they had only to wait for the moment to set fire to them.

"Since there is nothing else to be done," said Nicholl, "I make a proposition."

"What is it?" asked Barbicane.

"I propose to go to sleep."

"What a motion!" exclaimed Michel Ardan.

"It is 40 hours since we closed our eyes," said Nicholl. "Some hours of sleep will restore our strength."

"Never," interrupted Michel.

"Well," continued Nicholl, "everyone to his taste; I shall go to sleep." And stretching himself on the divan, he soon snored like a 48-pounder.

"That Nicholl has a good deal of sense," said Barbicane; "presently I shall follow his example." Some moments after his continued bass supported the captain's baritone.

"Certainly," said Michel Ardan, finding himself alone, "these practical people have sometimes most opportune ideas."

And with his long legs stretched out, and his great arms folded under his head, Michel slept in his turn.

But this sleep could be neither peaceful nor lasting, the minds of these three men were too much occupied, and at about seven in the morning, all three got up at the same instant.

The projectile was still leaving the moon, and turning its conical part more and more toward it.

An explicable phenomenon, but one which happily served Barbicane's ends.

Seventeen hours more, and the moment for action would have arrived.

The day seemed long. However bold the travelers might be, they were greatly impressed by the approach of that moment which would decide all—either precipitate their fall onto the moon, or forever chain them in an immutable orbit. They counted the hours as they passed too slow for their wish; Barbicane and Nicholl were obstinately plunged in their calculations, Michel going and coming between the narrow walls, and watching that impassive moon with a longing eye.

At times recollections of the earth crossed their minds. They saw once more their friends of the Gun Club, and the dearest of all, J. T. Maston. At that moment the honorable secretary must be filling his post on the Rocky Mountains. If he could see the projectile through the glass of his gigantic telescope, what would he think? After seeing it disappear behind the moon's South Pole, he would see them reappear by the North Pole! They must therefore be a satellite of a satellite! Had J. T. Maston given this unexpected news to the world? Was this the dénouement of this great enterprise?

But the day passed without incident. The terrestrial midnight arrived. The 8th of December was beginning. One hour more, and the point of equal attraction would be reached. What speed would then animate the projectile? They could not estimate it. But no error could vitiate Barbicane's calculations. At one in the morning this speed ought to be and would be nil.

Besides, another phenomenon would mark the projectile's stopping point on the neutral line. At that spot the two attractions, lunar and terrestrial, would be annulled. Objects would "weigh" no more. This singular fact, which had surprised Barbicane and his companions so much in going, would be repeated on their return under the very same conditions. At this precise moment they must act.

Already the projectile's conical top was sensibly turned toward the lunar disc, presented in such a way as to utilize the whole of the recoil produced by the pressure of the rocket apparatus. The chances were in favor of the travelers. If its speed was utterly neutralized on this dead point, a decided movement toward the moon would suffice, however slight, to determine its fall.

"Five minutes to one," said Nicholl.

"All is ready," replied Michel Ardan, directing a lighted match to the flame of the gas.

"Wait!" said Barbicane, holding his chronometer in his hand.

At that moment weight had no effect. The travelers felt in themselves the entire disappearance of it. They were very near the neutral point, if they did not touch it.

"One o'clock," said Barbicane.

Michel Ardan applied the lighted match to a train in communication with the rockets. No detonation was heard in the inside, for there was no air. But, through the windows Barbicane saw trailing smoke but no flames.

The projectile sustained a certain shock, which was sensibly felt in the interior.

The three friends looked and listened without speaking, and scarcely breathing. One might have heard the beating of their hearts amid this perfect silence.

"Are we falling?" asked Michel Ardan, at length.

"No," said Nicholl, "since the bottom of the projectile is not turning to the lunar disc!"

At this moment Barbicane, quitting the window, turned to his two companions. He was frightfully pale, his forehead wrinkled, and his lips contracted.

"We are falling!" he said.

"Ah!" cried Michel Arden, "onto the moon?"

"Onto the earth!"

"The devil!" exclaimed Michel Ardan, adding philosophically, "Well, when we came into this projectile we were
very doubtful as to the ease with which we should get out of
it!"

And now this fearful fall had begun. The speed retained
had borne the projectile beyond the dead point. The explosion of the rockets could not divert its course. This speed in
going had carried it over the neutral line, and in returning
had done the same thing. The laws of physics condemned it
*to pass through every point which it had already gone
through.* It was a terrible fall, from a height of 160,000
miles, and no springs to break it. According to the laws of
gunnery, the projectile must strike the earth with a speed
equal to that with which it left the mouth of the columbiad,
a speed of 48,000 feet in the last second.

But to give some figures of comparison, it has been reckoned that an object thrown from the top of the towers of
Notre Dame, the height of which is only 200 feet, will arrive on the pavement at a speed of 240 miles per hour. Here
the projectile must strike the earth with a speed of 115,200
miles per hour.

"We are lost!" said Michel coolly.

"Very well, if we die," answered Barbicane, with a sort
of religious enthusiasm, "the result of our travels will be
magnificently spread. It is His own secret that God will tell
us! In the other life the soul will want to know nothing,
either of machines or engines! It will be identified with
eternal wisdom!"

"In fact," interrupted Michel Ardan, "the whole of the
other world may well console us for the loss of that inferior
orb called the moon!"

Barbicane crossed his arms on his breast, with a motion of sublime resignation, saying at the same time:

"The will of heaven be done!"

20. The Soundings of the *Susquehanna*

WELL, LIEUTENANT, and our soundings?"

"I think, sir, that the operation is nearing its completion," replied Lieutenant Bronsfield. "But who would have thought of finding such a depth so near inshore, and only 200 miles from the American coast?"

"Certainly, Bronsfield, there is a great depression," said Captain Blomsberry. "In this spot there is a submarine valley worn by Humboldt Current, which skirts the coast of America as far as the Strait of Magellan."

"These great depths," continued the lieutenant, "are not favorable for laying telegraphic cables. A level bottom like that supporting the American cable between Valentia and Newfoundland is much better."

"I agree with you, Bronsfield. With your permission, Lieutenant, where are we now?"

"Sir, at this moment we have 3,508 fathoms of line out, and the ball which draws the sounding lead has not yet touched the bottom; for if so, it would have come up of itself."

"Brook's apparatus is very ingenious," said Captain Blomsberry; "it gives us very exact soundings."

"Touch!" cried at this moment one of the men at the forewheel, who was superintending the operation.

The captain and the lieutenant mounted the quarterdeck.

"What depth have we?" asked the captain.

"It is 3,627 fathoms," replied the lieutenant, entering it in his notebook.

"Well, Bronsfield," said the captain, "I will take down the result. Now haul in the sounding line. It will be the work of some hours. In that time the engineer can light the furnaces, and we shall be ready to start as soon as you have finished. It is ten o'clock, and with your permission, Lieutenant, I will turn in."

"Do so, sir; do so!" replied the lieutenant obligingly.

The captain of the *Susquehanna,* as brave a man as need be, and the humble servant of his officers, returned to his cabin and slept a peaceful sleep.

The eleventh day of December was drawing to a close in a magnificent night.

The *Susquehanna,* a Navy corvette of 500 horsepower, was taking soundings in the Pacific Ocean about 200 miles off the American coast, following that long peninsula which stretches down the coast of Mexico.

The wind had dropped by degrees. There was no disturbance in the air. The pennant hung motionless from the main top gallant mast-truck.

Captain Jonathan Blomsberry was cousin of Colonel Blomsberry, one of the most ardent supporters of the Gun Club. He could not have wished for finer weather in which to bring to a close his delicate operations of sounding. His corvette had not even felt the great tempest, which had swept away the clouds over the Rocky Mountains and allowed the spectators to observe the course of the famous projectile.

Everything went well. The series of soundings taken by

the *Susquehanna* had for its aim the finding of a favorable spot for laying a submarine cable to connect the Hawaiian Islands with the coast of America.

It was a great undertaking, instigated by a powerful company. Its managing director, the farseeing Cyrus Field, purposed covering all the islands of Oceanica with a vast electrical network. It was an immense enterprise and one worthy of American genius.

To the corvette *Susquehanna* had been given the first sounding operations. It was on the night of the 11th–12th of December. She was in exactly 27° 7′ N. lat., and 41° 37′ W. long., on the meridian of Washington.

The moon, then in its last quarter, was beginning to rise above the horizon.

After the departure of Captain Blomsberry, the lieutenant and some officers were standing together on the poop. At the appearance of the moon, their thoughts turned to that orb which the eyes of a whole hemisphere were contemplating. The best naval telescopes could not have discerned the projectile traveling above this hemisphere, and yet all were focused on that brilliant disc.

"They have been gone ten days," said Lieutenant Bronsfield at last. "What has become of them?"

"They have arrived, Lieutenant," exclaimed a young midshipman, "and they are doing what all travelers do when they arrive in a new country, taking a walk!"

"Oh, I am sure of that, if you tell me so, my young friend," said Lieutenant Bronsfield, smiling.

"But," continued another officer, "their arrival cannot be doubted. The projectile was to reach the moon when full on the 5th at midnight. It is now the 11th of December, which makes six days. And in six times 24 hours, without darkness, one would have time to settle comfortably. I fancy I see my brave countrymen encamped at the bottom of some valley, on the borders of a Selenite stream, near a projectile half buried by its fall amid volcanic rubbish, Captain Nicholl beginning his leveling operations, President Barbicane writing out his notes, and Michel Ardan embalming the lunar solitudes with the perfume of his——"

"Yes, it must be so, it is so!" exclaimed the young midshipman, worked up to a pitch of enthusiasm by this ideal description from his superior officer.

"I should like to believe it," replied the lieutenant, who was quite unmoved. "Unfortunately direct news from the lunar world is still wanting."

"Beg pardon, Lieutenant," said the midshipman, "but can't President Barbicane write?"

A burst of laughter greeted this answer.

"No letters!" continued the young man quickly. "The postal administration has something to see to there."

"Might it not be the telegraphic service that is at fault?" asked one of the officers ironically.

"Not necessarily," replied the midshipman, not at all confused. "But it is very easy to set up a graphic communication with the earth."

"And how?"

"By means of the telescope at Longs Peak. You know it brings the moon to within four miles of the Rocky Mountains, and that it shows objects on its surface of only nine feet in diameter. Very well; let our industrious friends construct a gigantic alphabet; let them write words three fathoms long, and sentences three miles long, and then they can send us news of themselves."

The young midshipman, who had a certain amount of imagination, was loudly applauded; Lieutenant Bronsfield allowing that the idea was possible, but observing that if by these means they could receive news from the lunar world they could not send any from the terrestrial, unless the Selenites had instruments fit for taking distant observations at their disposal.

"Evidently," said one of the officers; "but what has become of the travelers? What they have done, what they have seen that must interest us. Besides, if the experiment has succeeded—which I do not doubt—they will try it again. The columbiad is still sunk in the soil of Florida. It is now only a question of powder and shot; and every time the moon is at its zenith a cargo of visitors may be sent to visit."

"It is clear," replied Lieutenant Bronsfield, "that J. T. Maston will one day join his friends."

"If he will have me," cried the midshipman, "I am ready!"

"Oh, volunteers will not be wanting," answered Bronsfield; "and if it were allowed, half of the earth's inhabitants would migrate to the moon!"

This conversation between the officers of the *Susquehanna* was kept up until nearly one in the morning. We cannot say what blundering systems were broached, what inconsistent theories advanced by these bold spirits. Since Barbicane's attempt, nothing seemed impossible to the Americans. They had already designed an expedition, not only of savants, but of a whole colony toward the Selenite borders, and a complete army, consisting of infantry, artillery, and cavalry, to conquer the lunar world.

At one in the morning the hauling in of the sounding line was not yet completed; 1,670 fathoms were still out, which would entail some hours' work. According to the commander's orders the fires had been lighted to get up a full head of steam. The *Susquehanna* could have started that very instant.

At that moment, at 1:17 A.M., Lieutenant Bronsfield was preparing to leave the watch and return to his cabin, when his attention was attracted by a distant hissing noise. His comrades and himself first thought that this hissing was caused by the letting off of steam; but lifting their heads, they found that the noise was produced in the highest regions of the air. They had no time to question each other before the hissing became frightfully intense, and suddenly there appeared to their dazzled eyes an enormous meteor, ignited by the rapidity of its course and its friction through the atmospheric strata.

This fiery mass grew larger to their eyes, and fell, with the noise of thunder, upon the bowsprit, which it smashed close to the stem, and buried itself in the waves with a deafening roar!

A few feet nearer, and the *Susquehanna* would have foundered with all on board!

At this instant Captain Blomsberry appeared, half dressed, and rushing on to the forecastle deck, whither all the officers had hurried, exclaimed, "With your permission, gentlemen, what has happened?"

And the midshipman, making himself as it were the echo of the body, cried, "Commander, it is 'they' come back!"

21. J. T. Maston Recalled

"I𝐓 𝐈𝐒 'they' come back again!" the young midshipman had said, and everyone had understood him. No one doubted but that the meteor was the projectile of the Gun Club. As to the travelers which it enclosed, opinions were divided regarding their fate.

"They are dead!" said one.

"They are alive," said another; "the crater is deep, and the shock was deadened."

"But they must have lacked for air," continued a third speaker; "they must have died of suffocation."

"Burned!" replied a fourth. "The projectile was nothing but an incandescent mass as it crossed the atmosphere."

"What does it matter!" they exclaimed unanimously. "Living or dead, we must pull them out!"

But Captain Blomsberry had assembled his officers, and "with their permission," was holding a council. They must decide upon something to be done immediately. The more hasty ones were for fishing up the projectile. A difficult operation, though not an impossible one. But the corvette had no proper machinery, which must be both fixed and powerful; so it was resolved that they should put in at the nearest port, and give information to the Gun Club of the projectile's fall.

This determination was unanimous. The choice of the port had to be discussed. The neighboring coast had no anchorage on 27° lat. Higher up, above the peninsula of Monterey, stands the important town from which it takes its name; but seated on the borders of a perfect desert it was not connected with the interior by a network of telegraphic wires, and electricity alone could spread these important news fast enough.

Some distance above Monterey lay San Francisco Bay. Through the capital of the gold country communication would be easy with the heart of the Union. And in less than two days the *Susquehanna*, by putting on high pressure, could arrive in that port. She must therefore start at once.

The pressure was up; they could set off immediately. Two thousand fathoms of line were still out, which Captain Blomsberry, not wishing to lose precious time in hauling in, resolved to cut.

"We will fasten the end to a buoy," said he, "and that buoy will show us the exact spot where the projectile fell."

"Besides," replied Lieutenant Bronsfield, "we have our situation exact—27° 7′ N. lat. and 41° 37′ W. long."

"Well, Mr. Bronsfield," replied the captain, "now, with your permission, we will have the line cut."

A strong buoy, strengthened by a couple of spars, was thrown into the ocean. The end of the rope was carefully lashed to it; and left to the rise and fall of the billows, the buoy would not sensibly deviate from the spot.

The course was set north-northeast, and the corvette steamed direct for San Francisco. It was three in the morning.

There were 450 miles to cross; it was nothing for a good vessel like the *Susquehanna*. In 36 hours she had covered that distance; and on the 14th of December, at 1:27 A.M., she entered San Francisco Bay.

At the sight of a Navy ship arriving at full speed, with her bowsprit broken, public curiosity was greatly roused. A dense crowd soon assembled on the wharf waiting for them to disembark.

After casting anchor, Captain Blomsberry and Lieutenant Bronsfield soon came ashore.

"The telegraph?" they asked, without answering one of the thousand questions addressed to them.

The officer of the port conducted them to the telegraph office through a crowd of spectators.

Some minutes later four telegrams went out—the first to the Secretary of the Navy at Washington, D.C., the second to the vice president of the Gun Club, Baltimore; the third to the Hon. J. T. Maston, Longs Peak, Rocky Mountains; the fourth to the subdirector of the Cambridge Observatory, Massachusetts.

It was worded as follows:

> In 20° 7′ N. lat., and 41° 37′ W. long., on the 12th of December, at seventeen minutes past one in the morning, the projectile of the columbiad fell into the Pacific. Send instructions.—BLOMSBERRY, Commander *Susquehanna.*

Five minutes afterward the whole of San Francisco learned the news. Before six in the evening every state of the Union had heard of the great catastrophe; and after midnight the whole of Europe knew by cable the result of the great American experiment. We will not attempt to picture the effect produced on the entire world by that unexpected dénouement.

On receipt of the telegram the Secretary of the Navy telegraphed to the *Susquehanna* to wait in San Francisco Bay without extinguishing her fires. Day and night she must be ready to put to sea.

The Cambridge Observatory called a special meeting; and, with that composure which distinguishes learned bod-

ies in general, peacefully discussed the scientific bearings of
the question. At the Gun Club there was an "explosion."
All the gunners were assembled. Vice President the Hon.
Wilcome was in the act of reading the premature dispatch,
in which J. T. Maston and Belfast announced that the
projectile had just been seen in the gigantic reflector of
Longs Peak, and also that it was held by lunar attraction,
and was playing the part of under-satellite to the lunar
world.

We know the truth on that point.

But on the arrival of Blomsberry's dispatch, so decidedly
contradicting J. T. Maston's telegram, two parties were
formed in the bosom of the Gun Club. On one side were
those who admitted the fall of the projectile, and consequently the return of the travelers; on the other, those who
believed in the observations of Longs Peak concluded that
the commander of the *Susquehanna* had made a mistake.
To the latter the pretended projectile was nothing but a
meteor! Nothing but a meteor, a shooting globe, which in
its fall had smashed the bows of the corvette. It was difficult
to answer this argument, for the speed with which it was
animated must have made observation very difficult. The
commander of the *Susquehanna* and her officers might have
made a mistake in all good faith; one argument, however,
was in their favor, namely: that if the projectile had fallen
on the earth, its place of meeting with the terrestrial globe
could only take place on this 27° N. lat., and (taking into
consideration the time that had elapsed, and the rotary motion of the earth) between 41° and 42° W. long. In any
case, it was decided in the Gun Club that the Blomsberry
brothers, Bilsby, and Major Elphinstone should go straight

to San Francisco, and consult as to the means of raising the projectile from the depths of the ocean.

These devoted men set off at once; and the railroad, which would soon cross the entire American continent, took them as far as St. Louis, where the swift stage awaited them. Almost at the same moment in which the Secretary of the Navy, the vice president of the Gun Club, and the Sub-director of the observatory received the dispatch from San Francisco, the Honorable J. T. Maston was experiencing the greatest excitement of his life, an excitement which even the bursting of his pet gun, which had more than once nearly cost him his life, had not roused. We may remember that the secretary of the Gun Club had started soon after the projectile (and almost as quickly) for the station on Longs Peak, in the Rocky Mountains, J. Belfast, director of the Cambridge Observatory, accompanying him. Arrived there, the two friends had installed themselves at once, never quitting the summit of their enormous telescope. We know that this gigantic instrument had been set up according to the reflecting system, called by the English "front view." This arrangement subjected all objects to but one reflection, making the view consequently much clearer; the result was that, when they were taking observation, J. T. Maston and Belfast were located in the *upper* part of the instrument and not in the lower, which they reached by a circular staircase, a masterpiece of lightness, while below them opened a metal well terminated by the metallic mirror, which measured 280 feet in depth.

It was on a narrow platform placed above the telescope that the two savants passed their existence, execrating the day which hid the moon from their eyes, and the clouds which obstinately veiled it during the night.

What, then, was their delight when, after some days of waiting, on the night of the 5th of December, they saw the vehicle which was bearing their friends into space! To this delight succeeded a great deception, when, trusting to a cursory observation, they launched their first telegram to the world, erroneously affirming that the projectile had become a satellite of the moon, gravitating in an immutable orbit.

From that moment it had never shown itself to their eyes —a disappearance all the more easily explained, as it was then passing behind the moon's invisible disc; but when it was time for it to reappear on the visible disc, one may imagine the impatience of the fuming J. T. Maston and his not less impatient companion. Each minute of the night they thought they saw the projectile once more, and they did not see it. Hence constant discussions and violent disputes between them, Belfast affirming that the projectile could not be seen, J. T. Maston maintaining that "it had put his eyes out."

"It is the projectile!" repeated J. T. Maston.

"No," answered Belfast; "it is lunar dust."

"Well, we shall see it tomorrow."

"No, we shall not see it any more. It is carried into space."

"Yes!"

"No!"

And at these moments, when contradictions rained like hail, the well-known irritability of the secretary of the Gun Club constituted a permanent danger for the Honorable

Belfast. The existence together for these two would soon have become impossible; but an unforeseen event cut short their everlasting discussions.

During the night, from the 14th to the 15th of December, the two irreconcilable friends were busy observing the lunar disc, J. T. Maston abusing the learned Belfast, by his side, as usual; the secretary of the Gun Club maintaining for the thousandth time that he had just seen the projectile, and adding that he could see Michel Ardan's face looking through one of the windows, at the same time enforcing his argument by a series of gestures which his formidable hook rendered very unpleasant.

At this moment Belfast's servant appeared on the platform (it was ten at night) and gave him a dispatch. It was the commander of the *Susquhanna's* telegram.

Belfast tore the envelope and read, and uttered a cry.

"What!" said J. T. Maston.

"The projectile!"

"Well!"

"Has fallen to the earth!"

Another cry, this time a perfect howl, answered him. He turned toward J. T. Maston. The unfortunate man, imprudently leaning over the metal tube, had disappeared into the immense telescope. A fall of 280 feet! Belfast, dismayed, rushed to the orifice of the reflector.

He breathed. J. T. Maston, caught by his metal hook, was holding on by one of the rings which bound the telescope together, uttering fearful cries.

Belfast called. Help was brought, tackle was let down, and they hoisted up, not without some trouble, the imprudent secretary of the Gun Club.

He reappeared at the upper orifice unhurt.

"Ah," said he, "if I had broken the mirror!"

"You would have paid for it," replied Belfast severely.

"And that cursed projectile has fallen?" asked J. T. Maston.

"Into the Pacific!"

"Let us go!"

A quarter of an hour after, the two savants were rapidly descending the Rocky Mountains; two days later, at the same time as their friends of the Gun Club, they arrived at San Francisco, having exhausted five horses on the road.

Elphinstone, the brothers Blomsberry, and Bilsby rushed toward them on their arrival.

"What shall we do?" they exclaimed.

"Fish up the projectile," replied J. T. Maston, "and the sooner the better."

22. Recovered from the Sea

THE SPOT where the projectile sank under the waves was exactly known; but machinery to grasp it and bring it to the surface of the ocean was still wanting. It must first be invented, then made. American engineers could not be troubled with such trifles. The grappling irons once fixed, by their help they were sure to raise it in spite of its weight, which was lessened by the density of the liquid in which it was plunged.

But fishing up the projectile was not the only thing to be thought of. They must act promptly in the interest of the travelers. No one doubted that they were still living.

"Yes," repeated J. T. Maston incessantly, whose confidence gained over everybody, "our friends are clever people, and they cannot have fallen like simpletons. They are alive, quite alive; but we must make haste if we wish to find them so. Food and water do not trouble me; they have enough for a long while. But air, air, that is what they will soon want; so quick, quick!"

And they did go quick. They fitted up the *Susquehanna* for her new destination. Her powerful machinery was brought to bear upon the hauling chains. The aluminum projectile weighed only 19,250 pounds, a weight much less than that of the transatlantic cable which had been drawn up under similar conditions. The only difficulty was in fishing up a cylindro-conical projectile the walls of which were so smooth as to offer no hold for the hooks. On that account Engineer Murchison hastened to San Francisco, and had some enormous grappling irons fixed on an automatic system, which would never let the projectile go if it once succeeded in seizing it in its powerful claws. Diving suits were also prepared, which through this impervious covering allowed the divers to observe the bottom of the sea. He also had put on board an apparatus of compressed air very cleverly designed. There were perfect chambers pierced with scuttles, which, with water let into certain compartments, could draw it down into great depths. These apparatuses were at San Francisco, where they had been used in the construction of a submarine breakwater; and very fortunately it was so, for there was no time to construct any. But in spite of the perfection of the machinery, in spite of the ingenuity of the savants entrusted with the use of them, the success of the operation was far from being certain. How great were the chances against them, the projectile being 20,000 feet under the water! And if even it was brought to the surface, how would the travelers have borne the terrible shock which 20,000 feet of water had perhaps not sufficiently broken? At any rate they must act quickly. J. T. Maston hurried the workmen day and night. He was ready to don the diving suit himself, or try the air apparatus, in order to reconnoiter the situation of his courageous friends.

But in spite of all diligence displayed in preparing the different engines, in spite of the considerable sum placed at the disposal of the Gun Club by the Government, five long days that seemed like centuries elapsed before the preparations were complete. During this time public opinion was excited to the highest pitch. Telegrams were exchanged incessantly throughout the entire world by means of wires and electric cables. The saving of Barbicane, Nicholl, and Michel Ardan was an international affair. Everyone who had subscribed to the Gun Club was directly interested in the welfare of the travelers.

At length the hauling chairs, the air chambers, and the automatic grappling irons were put on board. J. T. Maston, Engineer Murchison, and the delegates of the Gun Club were already in their cabins. They started at 8:00 P.M. on the 21st of December, in a beautiful sea, with a northeasterly wind, and rather sharp cold. The whole of San Francisco was gathered on the wharf, greatly excited but silent, reserving their hurrahs for the return. Steam was fully up, and the propeller of the *Susquehanna* carried them briskly out of the bay.

It is needless to relate the conversations on board between the officers, sailors, and passengers. All these men

had but one thought. All these hearts beat under the same
emotion. While they were hastening to help them, what
were Barbicane and his companions doing? What had become of them? Were they able to attempt any bold maneuver to regain their liberty? None could say. The truth is that
every attempt must have failed! Immersed nearly four miles
under the ocean, this metal prison defied every effort of its
prisoners.

On the 23rd at eight in the morning, the *Susquehanna*
was due at the fatal spot. They must wait till twelve to take
the reckoning exactly. The buoy to which the sounding line
had been lashed had not yet been recognized.

At twelve Captain Blomsberry, assisted by his officers
who superintended the observations, took the reckoning in
the presence of the delegates of the Gun Club. Then there
was a moment of anxiety. Her position decided, the *Susquehanna* was found to be some minutes to westward of the
spot where the projectile had disappeared beneath the
waves.

The ship's course was then changed so as to reach this
exact point.

At 12:47 P.M. they reached the buoy; it was in perfect
condition, and must have shifted but little.

"At last!" exclaimed J. T. Maston.

"Shall we begin?" asked Captain Blomsberry.

"Without losing a second."

Every precaution was taken to keep the corvette almost
completely motionless. Before trying to seize the projectile,
Engineer Murchison wanted to find its exact position at the
bottom of the ocean. The submarine apparatus destined for
this expedition was supplied with air. The working of these

engines was not without danger, for at 20,000 feet below the surface of the water, and under such great pressure, they were exposed to fracture, the consequences of which would be dreadful.

J. T. Maston, the brothers Blomsberry, and Engineer Murchison, without heeding these dangers, took their places in the air chamber. The commander, posted on his bridge, superintended the operation, ready to stop or haul in the chains on the slightest signal. The propeller had been shipped, and the whole power of the machinery collected on the capstan would have quickly drawn the apparatus on board. The descent began at 1:25 A.M., and the chamber, drawn under by the reservoirs full of water, disappeared.

The emotion of the officers and sailors on board was now divided between the prisoners in the projectile and the prisoners in the submarine apparatus. As to the latter, they forgot themselves and, glued to the windows, studied the depths through which they were passing.

The descent was rapid. At 2:17 A.M. J. T. Maston and his companions had reached the bottom of the Pacific; but they saw nothing but a sandy bottom no longer animated by either fauna or flora. By the light of their lamps, furnished with powerful reflectors, they could see the dark beds of the ocean for a considerable extent of view, but the projectile was nowhere to be seen.

The impatience of these bold divers cannot be described, and having an electrical communication with the corvette, they made a signal already agreed upon, and for the space of a mile the *Susquehanna* moved their chamber along some yards above the bottom.

Thus they explored the whole submarine plain, deceived

at every turn by optical illusions which almost broke their hearts. Here a rock, there a projection from the ground, seemed to be the much-sought-for projectile; but their mistake was soon discovered, and then they were in despair.

"But where are they? Where are they?" cried J. T. Maston. And the poor man called loudly upon Nicholl, Barbicane, and Michel Ardan, as if his unfortunate friends could either hear or answer him through such an impenetrable medium. The search continued under these conditions until the vitiated air compelled the divers to ascend.

The hauling in began about six in the evening, and was not ended before midnight.

"Tomorrow," said J. T. Maston, as he set foot on the bridge of the corvette.

"Yes," answered Captain Blomsberry.

"And on another spot?"

"Yes."

J. T. Maston did not doubt of their final success, but his companions, no longer upheld by the excitement of the first hours, understood all the difficulty of the enterprise. What seemed easy at San Francisco seemed here in the wide ocean almost impossible. The chances of success diminished in rapid proportion; and it was from chance alone that the meeting with the projectile might be expected.

The next day, the 24th, in spite of the fatigue of the previous day, the operation was renewed. The corvette advanced some minutes to westward, and the apparatus, provided with air, bore the same explorers to the depths of the ocean.

The whole day passed in fruitless research; the bed of the

sea was a desert. The 25th brought no other result, nor the 26th.

It was disheartening. They thought of those unfortunates shut up in the projectile for 26 days. Perhaps at that moment they were experiencing the first approach of suffocation; that is, if they had escaped the dangers of their fall. The air was spent, and doubtless with the air all their morale.

"The air, possibly," answered J. T. Maston resolutely, "but their morale never!"

On the 28th, after two more days of search, all hope was gone. This projectile was but an atom in the immensity of the ocean. They must give up all idea of finding it.

But J. T. Maston would not hear of going away. He would not abandon the place without at least discovering the tomb of his friends. But Commander Blomsberry could no longer persist, and in spite of the exclamations of the worthy secretary, was obliged to give the order to sail.

On the 29th of December, at 9 A.M., the *Susquehanna,* heading northeast, resumed her course toward San Francisco Bay.

It was ten in the morning; the corvette was under half steam, as if regretting to leave the spot where the catastrophe had taken place, when a sailor, perched on the main topgallant crosstrees, watching the sea, cried suddenly:

"A buoy on the lee bow!"

The officers looked in the direction indicated, and by the help of their glasses saw that the object signaled had the appearance of one of those buoys which are used to mark the passages of bays or rivers. But, singular to say, a flag floating on the wind surmounted its cone, which emerged five or six feet out of water. This buoy shone under the rays of the sun as if it had been made of plates of silver. Commander Blomsberry, J. T. Maston, and the delegates of the Gun Club were mounted on the bridge, examining this object straying at random on the waves.

All looked with feverish anxiety, but in silence. None dared give expression to the thoughts which came to the minds of all.

The corvette approached to within two cables' length of the object.

A shudder ran through the whole crew. That flag was the American flag!

At this moment a perfect howling was heard; it was the brave J. T. Maston, who had just fallen all in a heap. Forgetting on the one hand that his right arm had been replaced by an iron hook, and the other that a simple gutta-percha cap covered his cranium, he had given himself a formidable blow.

They hurried toward him, picked him up, restored him to life. And what were his first words?

"Ah, trebly brutes! Quadruply idiots! Quintuply boobies that we are!"

"What is it?" exclaimed everyone around him.

"What is it?"

"Come, speak!"

"It is, simpletons," howled the terrible secretary, "it is that the projectile only weighs 19,250 pounds!"

"Well?"

"And that it displaces twenty-eight tons, or in other words 56,000 pounds, and that consequently it *floats!*"

Ah, what stress the worthy man laid on the verb "float!"

And it was true! All, yes! All these savants had forgotten this fundamental law, namely, that on account of its specific lightness, the projectile, after having been drawn by its fall to the greatest depths of the ocean, must naturally return to the surface. And now it was floating quietly at the mercy of the waves.

The boats were put to sea. J. T. Maston and his friends had rushed into them! Excitement was at its height! Every heart beat loudly while they rushed toward the projectile. What did it contain? Living or dead?

Living, yes! Living, at least unless death had struck Barbicane and his two friends since they had hoisted the flag. Profound silence reigned on the boats. All were breathless. Eyes no longer saw. One of the windows of the projectile was open. Some pieces of glass remained in the frame, showing that it had been broken. This window was actually five feet above the water.

A boat came alongside, that of J. T. Maston, and J. T. Maston rushed to the broken window.

At that moment they heard a clear and merry voice, the voice of Michel Ardan, exclaiming in an accent of triumph:

"White all, Barbicane, white all!"

Barbicane, Michel Ardan, and Nicholl were playing at dominoes!

23. The End

WE MAY remember the intense sympathy which had accompanied the travelers on their departure. If at the beginning of the enterprise they had excited such emotion both in the old and the new world, with what enthusiasm would they be received on their return! The thousands of spectators who had beset the peninsula of Florida, would they not rush to meet these sublime adventurers? Those legions of strangers, hurrying from all parts of the globe toward the American shores, would they leave the Union without having seen Barbicane, Nicholl, and Michel Ardan? No! And the ardent passion of the public was bound to respond worthily to the greatness of the enterprise. Human creatures who had left the terrestrial sphere, and returned after this strange voyage into celestial space, could not fail to be received as the prophet Elias would be if he came back to earth. To see them first, and then to hear them, such was the universal longing.

Barbicane, Michel Ardan, Nicholl, and the delegates of the Gun Club, returning without delay to Baltimore, were received with indescribable enthusiasm, The notes of President Barbicane's voyage were ready to be given to the public. The New York *Herald* bought the manuscript at a price not yet known, but which must have been very high. Indeed, during the publication of "A Journey to the Moon," the sale of this paper amounted to 5,000,000 copies. Three days after the return of the travelers to the earth, the slightest detail of their expedition was known. There remained nothing more but to see the heroes of this superhuman enterprise.

The expedition of Barbicane and his friends around the moon had enabled them to correct the many admitted theories regarding the terrestrial satellite. These savants had observed *de visu*, and under particular circumstances. They knew what systems should be rejected, what retained with regard to the formation of that orb, its origin, its habitability. Its past, present, and future had even given up their last secrets. Who could advance objections against conscientious observers, who at less than 24 miles' distance had marked that curious mountain of Tycho, the strangest system of lunar orography? How answer those savants whose sight had penetrated the abyss of the Plato crater? How contradict those bold ones whom the chances of their enterprise had borne over that invisible face of the disc, which no human eye until then had ever seen? It was now their turn to impose some limit on that selenographic science, which had reconstructed the lunar world as Cuvier did the skeleton of a fossil, and say, "The moon *was* this, a habitable world, inhabited before the earth! The moon *is* that, a world uninhabitable, and now uninhabited."

To celebrate the return of its most illustrious member and his two companions, the Gun Club decided upon giving a banquet, but a banquet worthy of the conquerors, worthy of the American people, and under such conditions that all the inhabitants of the Union could directly take part in it.

All the main lines of the country's railroads were joined by temporary rails, and on all the platforms, lined with the same flags, and decorated with the same ornaments, were tables laid and all served alike. At certain hours, successively calculated, timed by electric clocks, the population were invited to take their place at the banquet tables. For four days, from the 5th to the 9th of January, the trains were stopped. Only one engine at full speed, drawing a triumphal carriage had the right of traveling for those four days on the railroads of the United States.

The engine was manned by a driver and a stoker, and bore, by special favor, the Hon. J. T. Maston, secretary of the Gun Club. The carriage was reserved for President Barbicane, Colonel Nicholl, and Michel Ardan. At the whistle of the driver, amid the hurrahs, and all the admiring vociferations of the American language, the train left the platform of Baltimore. It traveled at a speed of 160 miles an hour. But what was this speed compared with that which had carried the three heroes from the mouth of the columbiad?

And now will this attempt, unprecedented in the annals of travels, lead to any practical result? Will direct communication with the moon ever be established? Will they ever lay the foundation of a traveling service through the solar world? Will they go from one planet to another, from Jupiter to Mercury, and after a while from one star to another, from the Polar to Sirius? Will this means of locomotion allow us to visit those suns which swarm in the firmament?

To such questions no answer can be given. But knowing the bold ingenuity of the race, no one would be astonished if the Americans seek to make some use of President Barbicane's attempt.

Thus, some time after the return of the travelers, the public received with marked favor the announcement of a company, with a capital of $100,000,000, divided into 100,000,000 shares of $1,000 each, under the name of the "National Company of Interstellar Communication." President, Barbicane; vice president, Captain Nicholl; secretary, J. T. Maston; director of movements, Michel Ardan.

And as it is part of the American temperament to foresee everything in business, even failure, the Honorable Harry Trolloppe, judge commissioner, and Francis Drayton, magistrate, were nominated beforehand!

ABOUT JULES VERNE

About Jules Verne

JULES VERNE lived through an age of dazzling scientific discoveries, and no man did more to dramatize their meaning to the world than this brilliantly imaginative French writer. In his books he took his readers on marvelous journeys into new worlds where science could do things previously thought impossible. Not only did he describe existing marvels like balloon flight, but with amazing prophetic power he conceived and wrote about things not yet invented, such as the submarine and the space rocket.

The man who was to illuminate this new age of science was born in 1828 at Nantes, France, in a world strongly influenced by the past. The famous old sailing port on the Loire River had once been a world trading center, and the dipping sails of fishing boats and schooners were still a familiar sight around the harbor.

Sandy-haired, ruddy-faced and active, the boy resembled the Breton sea merchants of his mother's family, the de la Feyes. He loved to listen to sailors' stories along the waterfront, and with his younger brother Paul he spent hours exploring the river in a leaky old sailboat.

His soaring imagination transformed these expeditions into adventures involving mysterious islands, sea battles and pirates' derring-do. At one point, he even slipped away from home to ship as a cabin boy on a small schooner. He was brought back at the next port by his father, who did not intend Jules to pursue adventure on the high seas, but to study law, as the Vernes had for generations.

The intellectual and the adventurous—both these strains were strong in the boy's nature and both were to be reflected in the books he wrote. Verne shared his father's passion for reading and literature. He worshiped the great French writers and began to write poetry at an early age. A good scholar, his dedication to study at the lycée and at the University of Nantes later gave him the ability to digest the vast amounts of scientific fact that would make his books unique in fiction.

Verne did not protest against studying law, for this meant going to Paris, where he would be close to his literary idols, Victor Hugo and Alexander Dumas. Through a former schoolmate he met Hugo, and later the Dumas, *pere* and *fils,* with whom he collaborated in writing for the theater.

In 1851 Verne finally wrote his father that he was giving up law for literature. By this decision he cut off his allowance from home, as well as the prospect of a comfortable law practice in Nantes, but his mind was made up. Even when cholera spread to Paris from the Crimean War Verne stayed on, working hard at his writing.

All Paris was fascinated by balloon travel at this period. An article which Verne wrote led to a meeting with the famous aerial photographer, Felix Nadar, who encouraged him to write a book-length story of a balloon voyage and submit it to the publisher Hetzel. Hetzel was impressed, but handed back the manuscript, advising Verne to rewrite it as fiction. "People want to be amused, not educated," he said.

Verne rewrote, but wisely kept enough factual material to give the story a scientific reality. The book, *Five Weeks in a Balloon,* which appeared in 1863, was such a success that Hetzel immediately offered Verne a contract to write two such books a year for the next twenty years at an annual salary of 20,000 francs.

What Jules Verne had done was to invent an entirely new and compelling type of story—the *voyage extraordinaire,* an adventure soundly based in scientific theory.

Verne was now financially set. He married a widow with two daughters, and the family settled down to a quiet, well-regulated existence in Paris. Verne rose at five every morning and wrote until noon. In the afternoons he would read scientific literature at various libraries, carefully checking his figures, calculations and facts. Even then, he turned over his completed manuscripts to a professor of mathematics for further checking.

Five Weeks in a Balloon had taken Europe by storm. Every balloon sighted over Paris or London was identified as the *Victoria,* the name of the balloon in this story. After its success, Verne and his publisher, Hetzel, searched for other subjects that would have the same universal appeal. Verne found one when he talked with men who had explored the crater of the Italian volcano Stromboli. The result was *Voyage to the Center of the Earth.*

His next books, *A Trip to the Moon* and *Around the Moon* grew out of his concern with the American Civil War and the consequent developments in ordnance. One of the moon-bound travelers, Michel Ardan, is a portrait of Felix Nadar, and the name Ardan is a scrambling of Nadar.

About this time, Verne acquired a yacht, and took great pleasure in sailing it along the coasts of France and England. The longest actual voyage Verne ever took was in 1867, when he went from England to America on the steamer *Great Eastern,* which had helped to lay the Atlantic cable. During the trip Verne spent hours talking with members of the crew and with Cyrus Field, the cable's inventor, about the cable-laying and the mysteries of the ocean's depths. By the time he had returned to France his new book, *20,000 Leagues Under the Sea* was well under way.

Written when Verne was at the top of his creative powers and dealing with his favorite subject, the sea, *20,000 Leagues* is generally considered Verne's best book. It was undoubtedly his favorite, and it expressed his own passion for individual freedom in the person of its main character, the autocratic and fiercely independent Captain Nemo. There was so much popular conjecture about Captain Nemo that Verne finally revealed the captain's past and his ultimate fate in his next book, *Mysterious Island.*

The other "hero" of *20,000 Leagues* was the underwater vessel Captain Nemo commanded. The *Nautilus* was named after Robert Fulton's experimental undersea craft, but it preceded Simon Lake's sea-going *Argonaut* by over 20 years, and it was, in fact, the first successful submarine.

20,000 Leagues was rivaled in popularity only by *Around the World in Eighty Days,* which Verne wrote and researched during the tumultuous days of the Franco-Prussian War. Paris was under siege, and Verne went back and forth from his home in Amiens to the Paris libraries with a military pass. At home, Verne would retire to his quiet study at the top of his house. Here he would carefully trace Phineas Fogg's astonishing itinerary on a great map of the world that showed, also, the routes taken by the *Victoria* and the *Nautilus.*

When *Around the World* appeared in 1872 it was an overwhelming success in England and America as well as in France, where people were sick of war and conflict and found hope and escape in the ingenious travels of Phineas Fogg. A dramatization was equally successful, and Verne was made a Chevalier of the Legion of Honor and acclaimed by the French Academy.

When he sailed that summer on his new, 100-foot steam yacht, *Saint-Michel III,* down the coast to Algiers, his progress made headlines and he was greeted like visiting royalty.

Verne was now in his fifties, but he was young in spirit and enjoyed the companionship of his son Michel and favorite nephew Gaston, who accompanied him on his trips.

Then came a series of misfortunes. In a sudden fit of madness, with the confused idea of making his uncle a hero, Verne's nephew shot him in the leg, and the painful wound crippled Verne for life.

As soon as he had recovered somewhat, Verne went sailing on his beloved yacht, but he couldn't keep his balance in the pitching sea. Rather than be an inactive passenger on his own ship, he sold the *Saint-Michel III.*

Not long afterward came the death of his father, whom Verne had called "his captain and his conscience." This blow was followed by his mother's death and then that of his brother Paul.

Verne retreated into his writing, still concerned with scientific invention but more and more obsessed with the tyranny he saw in the world. In subsequent books he foretold the advent of poison gas, atomic energy, and the rocket-propelled guided missile.

When he died in 1905, Verne had written nearly a hundred books. Most of the advances he dreamed of have since been realized. Yet his stories continue to influence writers and to entertain new generations of readers, who marvel at their fascinating scientific detail and are entranced by the exciting world of adventure they create.